PERM

**PERMUTED PRESS**

NEEDS **YOU** TO HELP

SPREAD THE INFECTION

FOLLOW US!

 FACEBOOK.COM/PERMUTEDPRESS

 TWITTER.COM/PERMUTEDPRESS

REVIEW US!

WHEREVER YOU BUY OUR BOOKS, THEY CAN BE REVIEWED! **WE WANT TO KNOW WHAT YOU LIKE!**

GET INFECTED!

SIGN UP FOR OUR MAILING LIST AT **PERMUTEDPRESS.COM**

PERMUTED PRESS

MW01028231

CONTAGIOUS CHAOS

BOOK III IN THE CONTAGIUM SERIES

EMILY GOODWIN

A PERMUTED PRESS book

ISBN (trade paperback): 978-1-61868-365-6
ISBN (eBook): 978-1-61868-364-9

Contagious Chaos (Contagium Book 3) copyright © 2014
by Emily Goodwin
All Rights Reserved.
Cover art by Dean Samed, Conzpiracy Digital Arts

This book is a work of fiction. People, places, events, and situations are
the product of the author's imagination. Any resemblance to actual
persons, living or dead, or historical events, is purely coincidental.

No part of this book may be reproduced, stored in a retrieval system, or
transmitted by any means without the written permission of the author
and publisher.

PERMUTED
PRESS

ACKNOWLEDGMENTS

I would like to thank my family, friends, and fans for encouraging me to write and for believing in this series from the start. Thank you Megan, Stephanie, Lori, and Lindsay for all of your help, feedback, and excitement about this series and especially this book. Thank you Jarred Johnson for helping me come up with this book's title. And I would like to thank Jacob from Permuted Press for having faith in me as well as this series.

To Amelia,
You're not even born yet and
you already have a book dedicated to you.
I love you.

Monsters are real…they live inside us. And sometimes they win.
- Stephen King

PART ONE

CHAPTER ONE

It never occurred to me to look up until it was too late. Someone jumped down, landing hard on my back. I fell forward and the wind was knocked out of me. Another launched himself down at Rider. Rider dodged out of the way and rolled to my side. He kicked the guy on top of me hard in the ribs. The guy cried out and pulled a gun from his side holster.

"No!" I shouted. I struggled to get my own weapon. The other guy was faster. My fingers closed on my knife right as the shot rang out. Birds took flight, the flapping of their wings echoing off the trees. Rider fell to his knees, his hands on his stomach. Blood pooled around his fingers.

"No!" I screamed again. I closed my hand around the knife and sprang up. "Rider!" I cried, rushing over to him. Tears blurred my vision.

"Riss," he muttered and started coughing. Blood bubbled from his lips.

I crawled to him, crying. He reached out for me and just as our fingers touched, I was jerked away. I swung my hand around and made contact with whoever had a handful of my hair. He yelled and kicked me in the back, his foot hitting my kidney.

I thrashed forward, desperately wanting to get away and get to Rider. I raised my hand again and brought the point of the knife down on the guy's foot.

"Dumb bitch," he said and grabbed my wrist. The guy who shot Rider walked over. He laughed when he saw me struggling.

"This one seems like fun," he said and kicked the knife from my hand.

"I will kill you both!" I threatened. I elbowed the guy who was holding me in the ribs and brought my foot up to smash his balls. His grip on my hair loosened and I was able to pull away. The other guy leaned in to grab me. I reached behind me to get the M9 but it wasn't there. It must have fallen out when the bastard landed on me.

I didn't have time to get the M16 from around my neck. Something stuck me in the back of the head. Stunned, I wavered. Then I felt a heavy blow to my knees, causing me to fall. I made one last attempt to get to Rider, who was coughing and gurgling up blood.

"I'm sorry," I cried. My fingers closed around his. He gave them one last squeeze. I made a mad grab for his pistol. I grabbed it, aimed at my attacker and pulled the trigger.

Nothing happened. Unlike me, Rider was smart and kept his safety on. From behind, someone kicked me in the side and then kicked the pistol out of my hands. He raised his foot and it came crashing down on my ribs. A horrible, biting, sharp pain flooded my body. It hurt so bad I could barely breathe.

Hands harshly grabbed a handful of my hair and pulled me back, dragging me over the rough ground. I cried out in protest and in pain when another blow came to my ribcage. Heavy, rough hands gripped my arms.

The guy who attacked Rider picked up my pistol and hit me in the temple. My vision was fuzzy and blood dripped in my face. I struggled to get away, trying to twist and sink my fingernails into my attacker's skin.

I couldn't get my feet to work properly. I was a couple yards away from Rider now. I reached up and dug my nails into the guys arm.

"Ah!" he yelled. I heard the familiar sound of a magazine sliding into a gun. The guy stopped dragging me. I felt a bone shattering pain in the back of my head.

And then everything went black.

CHAPTER TWO

Radiating, heart stopping pain woke me up. I was sprawled out on a clammy cement floor. The air was rancid and something dripped, splashing into a shallow puddle. Little droplets of liquid splashed onto my face. My vision was too fuzzy to tell if it was blood or water.

I took a deep breath and was hit with a dizzying round of pain again. It took all the strength I had to move my hand to my tender torso. I flinched when my hand touched my ribs. I took a shallow breath and slowly sat up.

I couldn't do it. I collapsed back down, sending red hot hurt across my entire rib cage. I closed my eyes and carefully touched each rib, certain that no less than two on the right side were cracked if not completely broken. I could barely breathe the pain was so intense.

I was shivering uncontrollably, which wasn't helping the situation at all. With my cheek pressed to the cold, dirty floor, I concentrated on getting enough oxygen. After a minute, I pushed myself up again. Every part of me screamed in protest. What the hell had been done to me? I felt as if I had been hit by a truck, thrown down a flight of stairs…or dragged through a field and then into a mental hospital.

I opened my eyes. Yes, the latter was what had happened. Vomit threatened to come up but was choked down by a sob.

Rider.

I crawled to the front of the room, which felt more like a cell. I assumed I was in some sort of solitary confinement or holding area for psychotic and violent patients. I heard the distant shuffle of feet and the murmur of hushed voices. A rolling office chair and a stained coffee cup sat a few feet to the right of the door, which was a combination see-through plastic and metal. Candy wrappers littered the space around it.

A hand gun rested on the faded blue cushion of the chair.

I desperately looked around for Rider. Suddenly remembering that I might not be alone, I turned—a bad move on my part. Pain hit me like a fist in the face. I doubled over, feeling like I might really puke.

The shuffling of feet turned into footfalls and the voices grew louder. I scuttled back to my spot on the floor and lay down again.

"...took his weapons. He was still breathing when we brought the bitch inside," a gruff voice spoke.

"She put up a good fight, 'eh? Heard she got Pauly pretty good."

"Hells yeah. Adrian—I mean Dre—will get a kick outta her. What do we do with her until he gets back?"

"Kisha says to leave her be. And don't mess up her face. You know Dre likes 'em pretty."

The two men came to a stop in front of the room, peering in through the door. I didn't move a muscle. One of them picked up the gun and pulled back the hammer, a sound I was familiar with. He plopped heavily in the chair and the wheels skidded back under his weight.

"Get off your ass, Joe!" the gruffer of the two voices shouted. "You're such a lazy piece of shit," he huffed.

"Get off it, Cutter!" Joe shifted his weight, causing the chair to creak. "What's she gonna do? She's still knocked out cold."

Cutter laughed—it was deep and husky and vile. "Yeah, I clocked her good."

I made a mental note of that. I had no idea how I'd do it, but I was going to crack Cutter's skull until his brain oozed out.

"Can we play with her?" Joe asked.

"I told you—leave her be! Dre should be back in a few. Then we'll decide."

"Yeah," Joe agreed.

"Don't. Touch. Her," Cutter reiterated.

"Fuck you, Cutter," Joe jeered. "I can handle my own shit."

"We'll see about that," Cutter mumbled and walked away. "Come on, we have to get that ginger prick's body before it attracts the biters."

Thinking they had both left, I was just about to look up when I heard the chair creak again. I didn't want to move until he was gone. But then what? I was locked in a maximum security mental hospital. There was no way I could get myself out of this.

Deciding it was now or never, I took a sharp intake of breath as if I was just waking up. That, of course, hurt like a motherfucker.

"Hey!" Joe dumbly yelled.

I slowly pushed myself up.

"Hey! Hey girl!" he shouted. "Are you awake?"

I groaned and pushed myself up farther and momentarily considered acting like I was waking up dead—as in zombie dead. But that might have gotten me shot. I pulled myself to my knees, the pain in my rib cage blinding. "No, I'm still asleep, dipshit," I sneered.

"About time you woke up. Lucky you got a nap," he told me, his voice muffled behind the closed door; the sliding window in the center of the door was open. I wasn't sure if he was trying to be nice.

"Yeah, so *lucky*."

I looked into the hall. Joe was no taller than me, incredibly pale, very thin, and had a wispy blonde chin strip of a beard that was grown out and banded together. His gray eyes widened and his nostrils flared. He jumped up from the chair.

"Calm your shit," I spat, just to piss him off. I had a nagging feeling he didn't like being told what to do.

"Watch your mouth," he warned me.

"Or what, you'll beat me up?" I glared at him, swallowing the lump of fear in my throat.

"Just you wait. Wait till Dre gets back. You'll wish *beat* is all he does."

"Yup. I'll wait. I'm not going anywhere, dumbass." Insulting him made me feel less afraid. Really, it should have been packing the fear into me. I had no idea what Joe was capable of or if he was even sane. I wondered if I should reason with him, let him know we are on the same side: living in this dead world.

No. They shot Hayden that time we were sitting on the tailgate—not far from the compound—and now Rider. Tears pricked the corners of my eyes when I thought of them. I knew Hayden heard the shot. He would come for me; I didn't want him to, but I knew he would. If he was lucky, Ivan held him back until they came up with a plan. I hoped to God they had gotten to Rider in time.

It was absolutely ridiculous to hold onto that shred of hope. I wanted so desperately to believe that Rider was going to pull through. I wanted to see his big smile, blue eyes, and messy red hair again.

"Listen here," Joe sneered and bent close to the door. Before he could put the fear of God in me, he straightened up and looked down the hall. "Anything?" he shouted.

"No," a female voice answered. "Just the red head and the bitch. Fucking stupid, if you ask me. I don't know what the hell they were trying to accomplish. Doesn't matter now, I suppose."

My heart skipped a beat and I had to remind myself not to look up with a doe-eyed look. They hadn't found Hayden. He was still alive. And if he was still alive, then Rider had a chance.

"This is her?" the woman asked. "I thought she'd be bigger from how Cutter described her." She leaned close to the door and inspected me as if I was a zoo animal. I wished I was able to run to the window with my teeth bared.

She smacked gum, chewing with her lips apart. As she continued to look me over, I glanced at her as well. She had on dark jeans that were a size too small; they squeezed her narrow waist so much that skin spilled over the waistband. Her t-shirt was cut so that it fell off her shoulder, and the ends were gathered and balled up, held together with a scrunchy. Her hair baffled me; half was in braids that ended in perfect spiral curls. Who the fuck curled their hair when freaking zombies ran amuck?

Rainbow laces were loosely tied in her high-top Converse shoes and gold bangle bracelets rattled from each arm. She stood up and flicked her hair back, revealing large hoop earrings as well. She couldn't be older than twenty-one.

Her brown eyes lingered on me for a few more seconds. Then she waved her hands and spun around. "Leave her be. Once my Dre-Dre gets back, we'll figure somethin' out."

"You're the boss, Kisha."

"Uh-huh," Kisha replied, her words high pitched at the ends like she was just so innocent. Without so much as one look back, she walked down the hall. A moment later, Joe followed.

I was alone as far as I could tell. I could hear voices echoing through the hall, but I couldn't make out a word of what was being said. They steadily grew louder. I moved to the front of the room and turned my head, only able to see their shadows.

"You fucking retard!" someone yelled.

"It's not my fault!" Cutter yelled back. "You saw the way that bitch cut up Pauly. What was I supposed to do? She's the one we wanted, anyway."

"You left someone behind!" the other guy spat. "Dre's not gonna be happy about this."

"Dre won't fucking know if you keep your goddamn mouth shut!"

The other guy laughed. "You want to lie to Dre?"

"That kid was shot! In the stomach. No way's he's gonna recover from that!" I put my hands on the plastic door. My heart sped up. They were talking about Rider. "He's not a threat!"

"Bullshit!" the other guy screamed. "How do we know he didn't run off to his buddies, huh? Tell them we took their bitch? They'll come after her, come after us! You fucked up, Cutter. You and Pauly both. And I'm telling Dre."

"No, you're not," Cutter threatened. I heard the sound of a fist smacking into someone's flesh. I pressed my face against the window. Cutter leaned back and threw his arm forward again. Whoever he hit fell. "It's a shame," he said as he bent over and grabbed the guy by the ankles, "that the bitch shot you before we could stop her." He laughed and dragged the guy away. A few seconds later, a gun fired, causing me to jump.

I pushed away from the bars. Holy shit. Cutter just killed one of his own to save his ass. He terrified me more than any zombie. My breath came out in ragged huffs. Trembling, I put my hand over my mouth. Rider was alive. He had gotten away. He had a chance!

I moved my hand from my mouth to my chest; my heart was beating so fast it hurt. I forced myself to take a slow, deep breath and winced from the pain. I closed my eyes and took another. I moved away from the front of the room and began to feel the panic of being trapped. I looked around for anything useful. An uncomfortable bed was bolted to the floor. My eyes traced over the four-point leather restraints. I clenched my teeth and whimpered in defeat. There was nothing in here that could help at all.

I had been in jail once before and in juvie twice. Though, I had never come close to a maximum security hospital for the criminally insane. The chance for escape was low for me with this one. I closed my eyes and thought about how bad my ribs hurt. I was terrified and thinking about the pain distracted me from my fear.

It didn't last long, however. The image of Hayden's face lingered in my memory. I hated that he was worrying about me. I hated what he had to be going through.

"...no, I'll be fine. She's locked up, you dumb-bo," Kisha told someone, her voice gradually growing loud enough for me to hear. I took a shaky breath and waited.

"Hi *Hayden*," she said in a girly voice and sat in the rolling chair. My heart skipped a beat at the sound of his name. Hayden? How did she know about Hayden? Oh my God—they must have gotten him too! My hand flew to the dog tags that hung around my neck. Oh, right. *Idiot*, I thought, *she thinks I'm Hayden*.

"I'm Kisha. So, you stumbled upon our hide out. How did you get here?"

"I walked," I said simply.

She laughed and the sound was like wind chimes. "Duh! Where did you come from?"

"Kentucky."

"Wow! You walked all the way from *Kentucky*?" she asked, trying to pronounce the state's name in a southern accent.

"Yup."

"Where are your friends?" she asked and dropped some of her charm.

"Dead," I said bitterly.

She laughed again. "Come on, Hayden, we don't have to be like this. We're just talkin', ya know, like girls do."

I glared at her.

"So," she pressed. "Tell me straight. Where are your friends? Do they know you're here?"

"They did. But they're dead now." My heart beat in my throat. I looked up, refusing to cry. I needed to hold it together.

"Where did you two get your guns? You both had big machine guns, right?"

"We found them."

"Mh-hm," she muttered. "You're in the army," she began, and I resisted the urge to roll my eyes and correct her. "So are you *sure* you just found them? The government didn't supply you with guns?"

"Yes, the government gave us each a single machine gun and sent us on our merry way," I spat dryly.

She narrowed her eyes, glared and me, and sighed. "You're gonna be a fun one, aren't ya?"

When I didn't say anything in response, she continued drilling me. "Come on now and just tell the truth. It will make it easier on you." She flashed a sickening smile. Though her lips curved up, her eyes remained dark and void of emotion. "Who are you?"

"Just a small town girl," I calmly stated.

One of her eyebrows shot up and she leaned back. "Uh, ok. And how did you get here?" she asked again, as if asking me the second time would make me suddenly tell the truth.

I tipped my head up and looked into her eyes, keeping my face neutral.

"How did you get here?" she repeated, her tone darker.

"We wandered," I sighed. "We went anywhere just trying to escape the zombies."

She leaned back in the chair. "I see. And you just thought you could move in on our set up?"

"Of course not; there were only two of us." I took a jagged breath. "Listen, Kisha. I think this is a misunderstanding. We had no intentions on moving in or whatever. As far as I'm concerned, there are only two teams right now: dead and alive. Seeing that we are both alive, I think something can be worked out, don't you?" I reasoned.

She huffed, flipped her hair, and crossed her arms. "Outsiders are threats. We're fine without you."

"Then let me go. I'm just one girl; I can't do any damage," I pleaded.

"We're not done with you...yet," she threatened. She cast me one more telling glance before getting up and striding down the hall. I got up and thoroughly searched the seclusion cell, knowing it was a moot point since it was a *cell* after all. I walked back and forth, trying to will the stiffness out of my body.

It was my damn injured ribs that hindered me. I couldn't take a deep breath, straighten up, or twist my torso without pain crippling me. And I was so incredibly thirsty to the point of feeling sick.

Feeling hopeless, I sat on the hard bed and tried to come up with a plan. Maybe I could fake the extent of my injuries to get some sort of medical attention. I planned to punch whoever came in to look at me hard in the throat so he couldn't call for help and slam his head into the cement walls at least twice before making a break for it.

Then I'd no doubt run into a closed door or a locked hall...or get shot.

Dammit.

I just didn't see a way out for me unless I reasoned and bartered...and that plan didn't seem too promising considering I had just witnessed Cutter plunge a knife into someone he knew with no hesitation. Slowly, I rose from the bed and walked to the front of the room. My fingers wrapped around the cool, sticky metal that lined the small window. For good measure, I gave it a shake. As expected, the door didn't so much as budge.

I looked for the lock and was confused for a few seconds when I didn't find it. Then I remembered Brock saying that this facility was rather new; everything was no doubt controlled electronically now, as was almost everything before the outbreak. The only 'key' was inside some sort of electrical device. Hell, maybe there was even an app for it.

I ran my hands through my hair and took careful deep breaths, unable to keep Hayden off my mind. I wanted to look into his hazel eyes, to hear him laugh, to feel his touch on my skin. I wanted to hold him and tell him I loved him.

Hours passed and I couldn't sit any longer. I got up and paced around the cell, ignoring the pain every breath caused. My throat was beginning to burn from being so dry. My stomach grumbled with hunger, though I didn't think I'd be able to eat if a feast was laid out in front of me.

Voices floated down the hall. Angry voices; it sounded like two men arguing. The identifiable sound of someone getting a fist to the face made me jump. Someone whistled and the sound of pounding feet echoed through the dark hall. I moved to the front and pressed my cheek against the door.

The fuzzy outlines of three men became visible. Only two were walking, the third was being dragged. Ignoring my stares, the guys pulled the body in front of the room across from mine. One of the men let go of the unconscious man's hand, which smacked against the concrete floor with a thud. He hurried off down the hall to press the button on whatever controlled the locks.

The door clicked open, and the body was deposited inside.

"Let him rot," one of the men grumbled.

"Traitor," the other spat. They cast curious looks at me but walked away. I put a hand on the door frame and peered across the way. His back was to me, so I couldn't see his face.

"Hey," I said quietly. "Knocked out cold," I speculated when the man didn't respond. I shook my head and plodded back to the metal bed. I stared straight ahead and tried not to panic. Forcing myself to remain calm, I counted to one hundred. As soon as I began to count backwards, the guy groaned. I watched, waiting for him to come to.

Slowly, he sat up, rubbed his head, and looked around. He let out a heavy sigh of annoyance, as if waking up in a seclusion room was something he'd done before. He stood and stepped close to the see through bars. The dim hallway light illuminated his face. Dark brown eyes peered at me curiously. He had a mess of black hair and tan skin. I wasn't expecting him to be so young—or so attractive.

"Hey," he finally responded. "You're the girl they found?"

"Define found," I said back cattily.

He laughed and flashed a white smile. "Yeah, the boys are a little, uh, unorthodox, I suppose."

"Yeah," I agreed.

"I'm Carlos," he introduced.

"Hayden," I said, sticking with the lie. "Why are you in here?" I blurted.

"Long story," he chuckled.

"I'm not going anywhere. And neither are you," I pointed out.

"Right, right. Why am I here? Originally it was for depression. I overdosed twice but passed out before I took enough to kill myself. But I'm *here* because I want out."

"Out?" I asked, swallowing my pounding heart.

"Yeah, out."

"Why can't you leave?"

"Oh, I can leave," he told me. Seeing my confusion, he continued. "Leaving is suicide," he laughed. "But I don't want to die anymore. I got no support out there. There's no way I'll make it. I want to leave the gang; I wanted to before all hell broke loose." He leaned on the bars and laughed. "I was supposed to get out a month after the first guy went crazy."

"Get out?" I asked, and then suddenly realized that Carlos had never left in the first place. He had been a patient. And if he was admitted, then the others probably had been too. It made sense, now that I thought about it. And most likely they were insane and dangerous and had been locked up for a reason...

The maximum security factor suddenly seemed favorable. It kept dangerous people in, and it would keep dangerous people out, but what had happened to the guards, doctors, and nurses? How did Dre come into power?

"Yeah," Carlos answered. "I started new meds that really helped with the depression. I was gonna get my GED, go to college, and make a life for myself. My uncle was gonna let me move in with him up in Jersey. A fresh start, ya know?"

"I do," I told him.

"I thought I was lucky," he said with a laugh. "When we figured out what happened, we thought we were safe in here. And I already had a spot in his gang." He shook his head. "I should have known better." He sighed and looked across the hall. "What's your story?" he asked, tipping his head back a bit.

My story? My story was that I had left the safety of our compound with four of my friends in search of supplies and survivors. We were in a ransacked house when a vintage black Mustang drove past, one we recognized as belonging to the people who shot Hayden a few months ago. We followed it here; Rider and I spilt from the group to get a closer look. Then we were ambushed, attacked, and I woke up in here. My heart broke thinking of Hayden. I hated being separated from him. "My friend and I were looking for survivors. We saw tire tracks and followed them."

"You have a camp?" he inquired.

I shook my head. "No. We're always on the move."

He narrowed his eyes. "You look too well fed to be on the move. I've seen my fair share of drifters, even before shit hit the fan. You're from a camp."

"Why do you care?" I spat.

"Oh, I don't. *They* do," he whispered. "Listen," he said with urgency. "Whatever you do, don't—"

He cut off when someone came down the hall. The man who called himself Cutter stopped in front of my door.

"The girl doesn't know anything," Carlos said quickly. "I already questioned her."

"Fuck off," Cutter said over his shoulder. "Why would I trust her, and why would I trust *you*, traitor?" he jeered. I caught a glimpse of Carlos's face; his dark eyes were full of pity.

Oh shit.

* * *

"Unlock it!" Cutter yelled. The door clicked open. He held up a knife, weak light shining off the silver blade. "Don't even think about it," he taunted. "Get up."

I stood quickly, grimacing in pain. Knowing this was going to hurt, I took a breath and braced myself. The moment Cutter stepped into my cell, I dropped and spun, kicking my leg out and knocking him off his feet. I scrambled up, moving slower than I wanted to. I kicked his right hand, sending the knife skidding out of the room and across the hall, sliding under the door to Carlos' room. He grabbed it before Cutter even noticed what had happened.

My body doubled over in pain. Cutter sprang to his feet, grabbed a fistful of my hair, and yanked me up. With his other hand, he hit the side of my head. I sank to the ground, my vision fuzzy. Heavy hands grabbed my shoulders and flipped me over. He pinned me down, straddling me.

"Keep struggling, hot stuff. It feels good when you squirm." His fist hit my face once more before he took a handful of my hair. "You like that, bitch?" he jeered. He yanked my head up, and I cried out. I planted my hands on the ground and raised my right leg, kneeing him in the back. He fell across me. Searing pain webbed across my rib cage. I clasped my hands around his face and dug my fingernails into his skin. Cutter rolled off of me.

"Cutter!" someone shouted. "What's going on in there?"

Cutter froze, knowing he wasn't supposed to hurt me. His eyes met mine for a millisecond before he backed off.

"Nothing!" he yelled. "Bitch took a swing at me, that's all."

"Cutter!" a high pitched voice screamed. "What the hell are you doing in there?" Kisha's voice grew louder as she moved down the hall. "Bring her here!" she ordered. "Now!"

"Yes, ma'am," Cutter replied. He moved to grab me; I shied away. "You'll pay for this," he threatened and hit me once more, knocking me out.

When I came to, I was sitting in a chair. My arms and legs were strapped down. I had a horrible ringing in my ears and a pounding headache.

"Hi, Hayden," Kisha said with fake charm, her voice as irritating as nails on a chalk board. I blinked and looked around the room; it was dimly lit and empty except for the chair I was sitting in, a table, and two chairs on its other side. Through a window, I saw that daylight had vanished. Knowing that hours had passed since I had last seen my friends made my stomach flip-flop with nerves. I wanted out. I needed out.

"Glad you finally woke up," she sneered, crossing her arms to show off the gun she had tucked into an ugly, overly-bedazzled jacket. "I have a few questions for you. If you answer like a good girl, everything will be fine."

I didn't open my mouth to spit back a sarcastic remark.

Instead, I tried to keep breathing. Cutter leaned over me, grinning. He placed his hand on my cheek and exhaled. His breath smelled like stale cigarettes. He let his hand fall, his fingers trailing down my neck and caressing my collar bone. I shivered in disgust.

He laughed and leaned in closer. With his face inches from mine, he parted his lips. And I head butted him. He recoiled; one hand flew to his nose and the other landed hard on my face.

"Bitch!" he yelled and raised his fist.

"Cutter!" Kisha yelled. "What are you doing?"

Cutter snarled at me, exhaled, and lowered his hand.

"Save it," Kisha said in a level tone. Her dark eyes met mine and her mouth curved into a wicked smile. "Come," she ordered Cutter, who took a step back. He looked away and then jumped at me again, trying to scare me. I set my face and glowered at him.

He flicked off the lights when he left the room. Totally in the dark, I couldn't see anything. I kept my eyes focused on what I thought was the doorway, but I was soon seeing gray shapes moving around the room that I knew only existed in my head.

I jerked my arms, causing the leather straps to cut into my skin. The arms of the chair weren't going to break easily. I planted my feet on the ground, grabbed the arms of the chair, and tried to stand. The legs wiggled slightly, but were bolted to the floor. I repeated the effort again and again, until I was out of breath. I exhaled and was reminded of my broken ribs. The chair had loosened; I could probably break it free with one more tug...once I could breathe again.

I shook my head. How was I going to get out of this one? If every breath hurt, could I really run to safety?

"Maybe," I said aloud. My sophomore year of high school I dated Cory Thomas, the starting quarterback for our school's football team. He was tall, blonde, and two years older than me. My stepdad Ted did not approve. Three days before the homecoming game, Cory broke several ribs during practice. But he played, and played well. He ended up in the hospital after the game, though.

If he could push past the pain for the sake of a stupid football game, then I could do it for my life. I nodded in the dark. I had to do it.

Rider's face flashed across my mind; I had more than just my life to fight for. I wanted revenge.

Footfalls echoed through the empty hall. I swallowed any

EMILYGOODWIN

doubt and straightened up. Rage fueled my weak body. A cone of light from a flashlight illuminated the door. The person carrying it stopped and shut it off. A second later, the lights flicked on. I blinked and my eyes tried to adjust.

"Wakey-wakey!" Kisha cooed. A man I assumed to be Dre followed her in. He was my height, but muscular. Tattoos and scars covered his tan arms. His head was shaved clean and a thin beard covered the bottom half of his face.

"Hi, Hayden," he said to me, his eyes glinting with pleasure when he spoke my name, as if he expected me to be surprised.

I raised an eyebrow and leaned back in the chair.

"I'm Dre. I run this place. I got people to take care of. Ya understand, right?"

I pressed my lips together and didn't respond.

Dre sighed dramatically and cracked his knuckles. "We can't risk strangers walking into our camp, ya know?"

Yes, I did know. And I agreed. But I'd be damned to tell him that.

"So," he continued. "I've got some questions for you." He walked behind my chair; my nerves tingled because I could no longer see him. "Where did you come from?"

"Kentucky," I said shortly.

"Is your camp there?"

"I don't have a camp," I told him.

Dre put a hand on my shoulder. "Yes, you do. Where is it?"

"I don't have a camp," I repeated.

Kisha's eyes widened and she smiled, watching Dre. My heart beat faster.

"Where is your camp?" he asked again, saying each word slowly.

"I don't have a camp," I said for the third time. Dre walked around me, his fingers sliding down my arm. He held something in his other hand and a flicker of fear ran through me when I recognized the taser. Dre turned it on and pressed a little black button. A blue line of electricity zapped from the prongs.

"Tell me where your camp is," he said through clenched teeth and let go of the button.

"I don't have a camp," I said flatly, feeling like a broken record.

He pressed the taser to my abdomen.

"Yes you do."

The jolt of electricity shocked through my body and continued

- 26 -

to tingle after Dre released the taser.

"Thing is, *Hayden*, my boys have now shot two of your friends."

My blood ran cold. I struggled to keep my face neutral. "I don't know what you're talking about," I said.

He pressed the taser to my skin again, his finger hovering over the button. My body tensed as I waited for the shock. "Yes you do. You think we'd forget a pretty face like this? You have a camp." He took a step back and crossed his arms. "You have food. You have weapons. You have that truck with the gun mounted in the back."

I shook my head, feeling like I was sinking in frigid water. "No, I don't. You're thinking of someone else."

Dre laughed, put the taser in a pocket of his baggy jeans, and hit me—his fist smacking into the same spot where Cutter had hit me. The pain made me nauseous.

"Tell me where the camp is. I know you have one. Some of your other friends went after my boys."

Fuck. They did. And they killed two and injured another. "No," I told him defiantly.

He hit me again. "Listen, bitch, you tell me where the camp is or—"

"Or what?" I interrupted. "You'll kill me?"

"You'll be begging for death."

I rolled my eyes. "Oh, please. Seen enough cheesy mob movies? If you're gonna threaten me, at least make them original. I bet Bubba the executioner is on his way with a big bag of knives, am I right?"

The only answer I got was Dre's fist landing on my forearm and the taser pressing into my right shoulder.

"Last chance—tell me where the camp is!" Dre demanded.

I forced myself to keep from screaming. "No. Kill me...and then you'll never know."

Dre let out a breath and stared at me. Waiting for his next move was almost as bad as being beaten. Finally, he stood, walked over to Kisha, and took something from her. A wicked smile revealed Dre's yellowed teeth. He turned around, holding up a large knife. Fear swelled in my heart.

"Time for some fun," he leered. Part of my brain screamed to just make up some lie to halt the torture. I was positive this wasn't going to end well no matter what I told them. I had to hold out as long as I could. I had something they needed; I hoped they

EMILYGOODWIN

wouldn't kill me just yet. Hayden would do something; that I was sure of.

Dre rested the tip of the knife on my arm. "Let's make this simple," he began. "Do you have a camp?"

"You already said you knew the answer to that one, asshole," I retorted.

Dre added pressure to the knife. I watched the blade push down my skin. "Where is your camp?"

"I never was good with directions," I told him innocently. The blade punctured my skin. A cry escaped my lips and a tiny bead of blood surfaced.

"Where is it?"

"I'm drawing a blank. All those blows to the head must have messed with my memory."

Dre dragged the knife down my arm, slowly tearing my skin. I couldn't help but cry out again. Blood dripped to the floor.

"Tell me," he demanded. I curled my lips over my teeth and kept my mouth shut. Dre put the tip of the knife into the cut and pushed down. I screamed when he dragged it through my broken skin. He asked me where the camp was again and repeated the horrible process of deepening the wound. He moved behind me and put a hand on my shoulder.

"I'm not playing around," he warned. He raised the knife to my throat. "Tell me where the camp is or I'll slit your throat."

"Go ahead and do it," I tried to snarl, but my voice faltered. My body hurt and tears blurred my vision.

"Just do it!" Kisha encouraged.

"Not yet," Dre scolded.

I closed my eyes, tears rolled down my cheeks, and I let out a breath. My hands were shaking uncontrollably. I pressed them on the arms of the chair. Blood spilled from the gash in my left arm.

Dre let the knife clatter to the floor, splattering my blood on the white tile and knelt down in front of me. "You're gonna wish I had killed you, you stupid cunt."

"I'll kill myself," I threatened. "With the blood loss it won't be hard." I looked at my bleeding arm and then back at Dre.

Angered, he grabbed the taser and pressed it against my neck. My hair blocked some of the shock. Still, the electricity shot through my body and I thought I was going to have a heart attack. I let my eyes roll back and my head drop.

Dre pulled the taser back and stood.

"Did you kill her?" Kisha asked, her voice shrill.

Dre's fingers pressed against my neck. "No. She's alive. Just knocked out." I heard feet scuffle away. I opened one eye and saw that Dre was a few feet in front of me with his back turned. Heart racing, I wrapped my hands around the arms of the chair. I pressed my feet on the ground and sprang up.

The bolts didn't snap like I had hoped. Kisha screamed and Dre whirled around. He advanced on me fast and his eyes brimmed with insanity.

CHAPTERTHREE

"Shouldn't I stop the bleeding?"

"What are you going to stop it with, your hands?"

"Oh, right."

"Hayden?" a man asked. "Can you hear me?"

Carlos. I remembered his boyish face.

"Mmmhh," I moaned. My vision began to focus. A young woman leaned over me. Dark roots had grown out from bleach-blonde, shoulder-length hair. Her skin was weathered around the mouth and little scabs covered her chin and nose. Deep bags hung under her eyes and her hair was thinning at her forehead. She would be the perfect model for a Many Faces of Meth poster.

It felt as if my head was stuck in a vice that was continually cracking and twisting around my skull. I tried to push myself up; excruciating pain stung my left arm. My mind flashed back to Dre and the interrogation. I groaned again.

"Need a hand?" the woman asked. I nodded and allowed her to help me up. I leaned against the wall.

"Thanks," I panted.

"You're welcome," she said. Her voice was honey smooth, which didn't match her worn appearance. "You look terrible."

I tried to smile and realized my lip was swollen. "I feel terrible."

She untwisted the cap off a bottle of water. "Here," she offered and held the bottle out to me. I took it and sipped slowly.

"What are you doing in here?" I asked, not worried about sounding ungrateful.

"Making sure you don't kill yourself," she told me.

"Oh."

"She's being punished," Carlos piped up. "Piss off Queen Kisha you get locked up for the night."

The woman wrinkled her nose and shook her head. "That fucking bitch," she muttered. "I swear, I'd kill her if I could."

"Don't talk like that," Carlos warned. "If the wrong person hears you, you're dead."

"Everyone's the wrong person," she huffed. "Except you, Spider."

"I don't go by that anymore," he reminded her. "And thanks."

"Seriously," the woman huffed again. "I hate her. I don't know why Dre is with her. He can do so much better," she spat bitterly.

I took another drink of water before I carefully poured some over the cut on my arm. "You guys don't like it here?" I asked feebly.

"Hell no," Carlos said at the same time the woman said, "It's safe."

"There are other safe places," I said softly.

"You really do have a camp somewhere, don't you?" she asked.

I did my best to glare at her. "I'm not stupid. Being nice to me isn't going to get you answers."

She held up her hands. "I'm not trying to get answers. I hate that nasty whore just as much as you do. If there really is somewhere safe..." she trailed off.

"It won't work," Carlos reminded her. "What do you think happened to me last time?"

"What happened?" I asked.

"I tried to leave. I got caught. Dre beat me an inch from my life. Said I was gonna tell people about our set up here. Said I was gonna come back and take all the supplies."

"He's running low on supplies," I mused.

"How did you know?" the woman asked, sounding shocked.

"Desperation," I answered. "Why else go through the trouble of torturing me if he wasn't desperate for supplies?"

"She's right," Carlos spoke. "The guys just take. When there's no one left to take from, they don't know what to do."

"Why don't you just tell them where your camp is?" the woman asked.

I shook my head. "My friends are good people. I'd rather go through seven floors of hell than give them up."

"They must be really important to you," she said quietly.

"They are my only reason for living in this dead world," I affirmed. The woman bit her lip and looked at the floor. There was something about her, something desperate that made me want to trust her, help her even. *Don't be stupid*, I told myself. "What's your name?" I asked.

"Treasure," she replied.

"Your real name?"

"Margret. Don't call me that," she requested after a moment.

"I won't. Why are you here, Treasure, if you hate it?"

"I've been here," she told me and picked at a scab on her nose. "I was visiting my cousin," she said quickly. Her eyes darted to the floor and she tapped her fingernails together. "She has hallucinations." Her voice dropped and I almost couldn't hear her. "She killed her daughter. But she was possessed." Treasure twitched. "Or at least that's what she thought. Then this place went on lock down; no one could leave. I thought one of the guys from maxi got out."

"How did it get like this?" I asked and grimaced when I moved my legs. My muscles were stiff and sore. Just how long was I out?

"It took a while," Treasure said, her voice low. "At first it seemed like we were all on a team, ya know, living verses the dead. It was just about making it to the next day alive. The food started to run out...there was panic and eventually a riot. And then Dre," she breathed, her voice almost dreamy, "took over. And it's been like this ever since."

"Was anyone on the inside infected?" I inquired.

She nodded. "We lost, what, a hundred people?" she asked Carlos.

"Give or take a few," he replied.

"What happened to your cousin?" I asked Treasure.

She shook her head. "She didn't make it."

"Sorry," I said. I forced myself up right and slowly stretched my arms forward.

"It's alright," she told me. "She was crazy."

I pushed myself up, wincing and crying out more than once. I looked down the dimly lit hall; it was empty. "What time is it?" I asked suddenly.

"Uh, prolly around four in the morning," Treasure answered.

I paced—very slowly—around the room. My legs loosened up after a few minutes. I took a deep breath and doubled over.

"What's wrong?" Treasure asked.

"I think a few ribs are broken," I answered shortly.

"Shit," she swore. "You really do look terrible."

"Thanks." I sank down on the bed. My eyelids were heavy and

my body begged me to go to sleep. There was no way my mind would allow me to drift off peacefully.

"Rest," Treasure suggested.

I shook my head. "I need to come up with a plan," I told her.

"Honey, you're locked up. Ain't no plan gonna get you out," she said pointedly.

"You're right. But I…I just can't give up."

"You remind me of my sister," she said softly. After several minutes she spoke again, so quiet I could barely hear her. "If there was a way out, I'd go with you."

I nodded and leaned against the wall. I closed my eyes and concentrated on taking slow breaths. I could only inhale halfway without feeling pain. I thought about Hayden, Ivan, Brock, and Wade. I wondered what they were doing. I felt guilty for causing them trouble; I knew they'd be worrying and I knew Hayden was probably freaking the fuck out.

"Hayden?" Treasure asked, pulling me from my dark reverie.

"Yeah?"

"You don't have to tell me where it is, but do you really have a camp?"

"No," I said and watched her shoulders sag. "It's better than a camp."

She smiled, making the skin on her face crinkle. "What's it like?"

"Safe. Organized. The people are happy, well as happy as they can be."

Carlos laughed. "There's no way a place like that can exist. What is it, run by super heroes?"

"Even better; US Marines."

Treasure's eyes flicked to the dog tags. "Are you one of them?"

I didn't want to lie. For some reason, lying about being a Marine felt wrong to me. I opened my mouth to tell her that I was part of something else when the lights turned off. I heard Treasure get up and move to the front of the room.

"Hello?" she called. "What's going on? What's happening?"

"Generator went out," Carlos speculated. "It's happened before."

"No," Treasure said, her voice trembling. "They just filled it up. I saw the guys come back with the gas."

We sat in silence for several minutes before the lights flickered back on.

"Thank God," Treasure breathed. "I hate the dark."

"Get used to it," Carlos told her. "The gas will run out someday. And then we will all be fucked. The internal locks are controlled electronically."

"Not anytime—" Treasure cut off abruptly with a scream when the lights went out again. Then they came back on. "Ok, what the hell is going on?" she asked and moved over to me, not wanting to be alone. "I don't like this!" she cried.

The light began to get brighter. I looked out into the hall, eyes glued to the fluorescent lights. The yellow glow increased, the fixture humming with electricity. I turned my head just in time. The bulbs exploded, raining glass down on the concrete floor.

Muffled shouts echoed above us. Treasure's hand found mine as if I could protect anyone in the state I was in. The shouts turned into screams and soon gunfire boomed in the distance. Treasure whimpered.

I was listening so intently to what was going on above us that I didn't notice the sound of feet crunching on the broken glass until they were in front of our room. I jumped when the door creaked open.

"It's me," Carlos whispered. "The locks must have shorted out. Come on, let's get out of here." He extended his hand, accidentally poking me in the face. My breathing quickened and my heart threatened to beat out of my chest. I didn't want to put my life in his hands, afraid he might take it away. Seeing that I didn't have another choice, I took his hand.

It was a battle just getting up the stairs. I was winded by the time we reached ground level. Flashlights bobbed in someone's hand. Treasure grabbed my arm and pulled me around a corner.

"Hey!" Carlos yelled. "What's going on?"

"Zombies!" the guy answered and pressed a flashlight into Carlos' hands. "They got through the fence. They're surrounding us!"

"What do we do?"

"Fight 'em off! Come on!"

"I gotta arm myself," Carlos replied. "I'll meet ya out there." The guy scurried past. Carlos waved to us. Treasure kept a death grip on my hand. "If I get us out of here," he whispered, "will you take us to your camp?"

"Yes," I promised. "If you get us out of here."

"I don't want to go out there with those monsters!" Treasured cried.

"Do you want to stay in here with these monsters?" Carlos asked. "The raids, the beatings, the rapes; are they any better in here?"

She shook her head. "Is the camp far?"

"Yes. We'll need a car," I told her.

"I can't get you a car," Carlos whispered and took a step forward. Apprehensively, I followed.

"That's fine. Just get us out of here and I'll find one I can hotwire."

"You can hotwire cars?" he asked, stopping to dubiously stare at me.

"You're not the only one who's been locked up," I admitted ruefully, though I was in jail, not a state hospital. "Let's go; we're wasting time."

We snaked down a hall, hid in a room to allow more thugs to run past us, and went through a set of double doors.

Adrenaline caused my pain to fade. I crouched down and looked outside. Headlights illuminated the hospital yard. I traced the fence with my eyes but was unable to see the break...or any zombies.

"Is there another way out?" I asked.

"Of course," Carlos said. "But no one is here. Let's go."

I shook my head. "Not without knowing what we're up against. There could be hundreds of zombies out there. We wouldn't stand a chance, even if we were armed."

Carlos smiled and extracted Cutter's knife. I shook my head and pressed a smile. "It'll help but it's not enough."

He nodded. "This way. There's a window that looks out over the east section of the yard."

"Take us there."

"Can't we just leave?" Treasure whimpered.

I desperately wanted to run out that door. "No," I said with a shake of my head. "We could get out there and be surrounded."

"Ok," she agreed. "Let's go—quick!"

The three of us scurried down the hall while all hell broke loose outside. I remembered the time when zombies had breached our fences at home base; I was terrified. Not only was facing a shit ton of zombies all at once something I never wanted to do, but facing them and fearing that they would break into the place we called home was even worse.

"There," Carlos whispered. "You can see outside through those windows."

I walked past him into a dark room and bumped into a table, sending red and black checkers rolling across the floor. A faint glow illuminated a large square window. I moved to it, apprehension building in my heart. Shouts echoed off the cool glass. Shots rang out chaotically. I squinted, trying to descry who was alive and who was undead.

"There's a herd," I whispered, not bothering to turn my head to look at the others. "They're surrounding something. I can't tell what, though." I shook my head and slowly exhaled, my breath clouding the glass. "Take a guess; it can only be one thing." I gazed into the hazy darkness. "I don't think they're going anywhere. Not until whatever — or whoever — is eaten."

"So let's go then!" Carlos urged. "Out the back."

I nodded. "Yeah, but I don't have a plan. Where are we going once we get out? And *how* are we getting out? Isn't the back all fenced in?"

"No, it's not," Carlos said.

"It's not?" Treasure echoed, her voice high and tight.

"Not anymore. When we dug the trench, we put in two emergency tunnels under the fence. They're covered up with branches and weeds. That way, if any undead followed us back, we could get through the fence without letting them in."

"That's actually really smart," I blurted.

Carlos smiled, casting dark, eerie shadows across his young face. "It was my idea. I used to run from my neighbor's dogs when I was a kid. I escaped many times by barely squeezing through a ditch under the fence. The dogs were too big to get through."

"Ok, great. Take us to the tunnels. Once we're out we need somewhere to go."

"Those old buildings," Treasure suggested.

"The greenhouses," I spoke, and fear fluttered through my heart. Hayden's truck was hidden in one of the old greenhouses. What if it wasn't there anymore? "Yes, that will work." I looked out the window not liking my plan. It sucked, I was aware, but it was the only one I could come up with. "Look!" I said suddenly. "The zombies are crowded around…what is that, a truck?"

I put a hand on the window and leaned forward, narrowing my eyes. It was a truck. An old white and red Ford. Zombies crowded around the bed, reaching and clawing. Something had to be in it…something alive and edible. My eyes flicked several yards behind it at the make-shift fence that the truck had driven through.

I looked at the truck again. Zombies shuffled through the hospital yard and crowded around the vehicle, blocking out the illuminated headlights. What the hell was in the bed? Had someone tried to reach the safety of the hospital walls? I shook my head; it didn't make sense to drive through the fence. It was crappily built to say the least, but it would have at least slowed down a herd.

Something flapped from the antenna of the truck. I rested my forehead against the window but was unable to tell exactly what it was, though it looked like some sort of homemade flag. What the hell was going on?

I tore my eyes away. "Ok," I breathed. "They seem distracted by whoever is in that truck. I think we can sneak out the back."

Carlos made a move to dart out the door.

"But first we need to arm ourselves." I looked into Carlos' eyes. "What can you get us?"

He held up the knife that I had taken from Cutter. "I can try and get more. Stay here; I can pass through the halls no questions asked; I was gonna get out in the morning anyway. You two...it'll raise a few questions."

Without so much as a look back, he darted away, flashlight bobbing as he ran.

"Hayden?" Treasure asked shakily. The lights from outside illuminated the room just enough to see her dark silhouette.

"Yeah?" I responded.

"What are they like?"

"They really are monsters," I answered automatically. "And just as bad as you'd think."

"I've been in here since it happened," she whimpered. "Are they like zombies in the movies?"

I shook my head. "It depends on what movies you've watched." I turned back to the window. Men ran around the truck, shooting at the zombies. Two zombies broke away from the struggle to get a piece of whatever was in the truck and advanced on a guy with a shotgun. He didn't have the chance to pull the trigger. A pit formed in my stomach. As much as I hated the guys who ran this place, seeing anyone get eaten by zombies made me sick.

I exhaled and whirled around; Treasure jumped. I moved to the center of the room and sat on the edge of a table. I slowly pushed my shoulders back and gently stretched. I pulled on my hair as I waited. Suddenly, the thought of Carlos leaving us dawned on me. I felt like an idiot for not considering it before. And why wouldn't he? I was injured and would only slow him down, not to mention the fact that he didn't know me at all. Would I come back for him if the roles were reversed? I wasn't sure I would.

I bit my lip. This was my chance to get out. I didn't know where the tunnels were, but I wasn't going to sit idly by. I told myself that I would give Carlos one more minute and then I was getting my ass out of here. I counted to sixty in my head. Then I counted back to zero.

Two minutes.

I counted once more and pushed myself off the desk. "Let's go," I said to Treasure.

"Carlos!" she stammered. "H-he's not back yet!"

"I don't think he is coming back," I said bitterly. I set my jaw and took a step toward the door. That was what I got for trusting someone who just admitted he was in a gang. Treasure took my hand and I yanked it away. Not only was it annoying, but it hindered my ability to fight.

"Treasure? Hayden?" a male voice called from down the hall.

"Carlos?" Treasure squealed.

"Yeah. You guys leaving without me?" he asked with a laugh.

"We thought you left us," I replied flatly. "Did you get weapons?"

Carlos tucked a flashlight under his arm and grinned. "Here," he said and handed me the knife. "You earned it." He handed a crowbar to Treasure and flashed a 9mm Glock. "I only got one loaded magazine," he said, shaking his head. "It'll do if we get in a tight spot; I'll use it as backup only," he said and held up the broken leg of a chair. A nail stuck out at the end.

"Great," I praised. "Let's go."

We hurried down the hall to get to the back doors. I held up my hand and edged forward to check out our surroundings once more before we burst into the night. "You have to get them in the head," I whispered. Treasure was shaking but managed to nod. "If any zombies spot us, turn off the flashlight, ok?"

"Ok," Carlos said, his voice weak.

"Take us right to the tunnels," I directed.

"I will," Carlos promised.

"Ok, on three," I whispered. "One, two—"

I opened the door. Wind blew loose strands of hair into my face. Ignoring them, my eyes darted around. Muted dawn light hid behind thick clouds. It was still too dark to see more than a few yards in front of us. Dry earth under my feet, I took a tentative step forward. I held the knife out in front of me, ready for an attack.

My heart was beating a million miles an hour. Carlos shined the flashlight around the yard.

"There," he whispered.

I nodded and took another step. Something scuttled to our left. I held up my hand and froze. Carlos covered the flashlight with his hand.

"What is it?" Treasured cried.

"Shh!" I demanded.

She whimpered and stumbled forward.

"Keep going," I said quietly. "Be ready."

Carlos uncovered the flashlight and angled the light down, casting a glow on the ground in front of us. Treasure grabbed the back of my shirt. Hoping it would calm her enough to keep her mouth shut, I didn't object and pressed on.

I smelled him before I heard the shuffling feet through the dry grass. Carlos spun around, lighting up the face of an S3. He raised his gun.

"No!" I loudly whispered. "Don't waste a bullet on him." I quickly moved forward, ripping my shirt from Treasure's grasp. I brought my arm up and shoved the knife into the gummy's open mouth. I yanked it out and shoved him back. "Keep going," I instructed.

Jogging, Carlos led the way. A few strides in and my ribs ached. I had to ignore it if I wanted to live. A strong gust stirred up dry dirt, blowing it into our faces. I closed my eyes and turned my head away from the wind. I blindly walked and tripped over a clump of weeds. Hitting the ground intensified the pain. I let out a grunt.

Carlos skidded to a stop and scooped me up. "Almost there, chica," he assured me. Keeping his arm linked under mine, he gently pulled me forward.

"I'm fine," I said and shrugged him off. I ran forward, not stopping until my hands closed around the chain-link fence. Arms extended, I leaned forward, panting.

"Help me find it!" Carlos called as he began searching along the fence line. Timidly, Treasure moved about a foot away from Carlos in the opposite direction. I needed to take a deep breath to rid myself of the winded feeling. Squeezing the fence in anticipation for the hurt I was sure to feel, I inhaled.

Something scratched at my hands. I yanked them back, almost dropping the knife. Fresh blood glistened on the mouth of a zombie. She turned her head, let out a harrowing yell, and thrashed against the fence.

Treasure screamed and fell to the ground, wrapping her arms around herself. Eyes wide with terror, I rushed forward and waited for the zombie to reach for me. Skin peeled off her arm as she forced it through the fence; I grabbed it, pulled her forward and jammed the knife into her eye socket. When I pulled it back, part of her rotten eyelid stuck to the blade. I wiped it off on the fence.

A gun firing made me jump. I whirled around to see Carlos aiming the gun at a fast moving S2 that had wandered away from the truck.

"Find the tunnel!" I yelled to Treasure. A hysterical sob escaped her lips. On her hands and knees, she madly felt around for the concealed escape route. The gun fired again and the zombie fell to the ground. Three more lumbered over in its place.

Oh shit.

Metal clanked behind me; I turned to see another zombie banging on the fence. I put my face close to the chain-link, baiting him. Half of his face was missing; maggots wriggled around in an empty eye socket. I stabbed the knife though his cheek and into his brain. He slumped to the ground, his skull cracking open on impact. The foul smell of rotten bodies hung in the air.

Carlos fired once more. Another S2 quickly staggered in our direction. I rushed forward, grabbed it by the hair, and yanked its head down, colliding it with my knee and breaking its nose. The bones pushed up into its already-mushy brain.

As soon as the body hit the ground, a half naked, fat zombie lunged at me. I leaned back and extended my foot, catching Fatty in the chest. I quickly shifted my weight and brought the knife into his ear. Pain drove me to the ground.

"Found it!" Treasure yelled. I could hear her throwing branches to the side. "Hurry!" she called to us.

"Go!" I told her. "There are too many on this side. Go!" I risked a glance behind me to see Treasure squirming through the tunnel. "Carlos, go!" I bellowed. "I'll distract them!" I pushed myself up, jumped over Fatty's body, pulling my shoulder back. In one swift movement, I jammed the knife into the cheek of another zombie.

Having missed his brain, the zombie roared and clawed at me. I put my hands on his shoulders and pushed. Bits of flesh were stuck in his teeth. His breath smelled like three day old road kill soaked in sewer water. I gagged.

The zombie opened its mouth and chomped the air. The knife was in my right hand. I intended to send the sharp metal deep into his moldy brain. But the fucker was strong. And I was weak. He pushed forward, knocking me backwards and off my feet. The knife slipped from my fingers.

Treasure screamed in the background. I thrust my left arm up, the palm of my hand hitting the zombie's chin. I pushed away as hard as I could. I turned my head to look for the knife. I couldn't see anything in the hazy dark; too much dust had been stirred up in our scuffle. Giving up, I put my free hand on the side of his head and snapped his neck.

It didn't kill him, but it moved his mouth a few more inches away from me. I placed my hands on the ground and pushed, pain shot through my chest and the cut on my left arm burned. The zombie thrashed his body around, trying to figure out how to bite me with his head permanently turned to the side. I dragged myself back and used the heel of my boot to shove his face away. Hands trembling, I slapped at the ground for the knife.

Hands landed on my shoulders. I jerked away.

"Whoa, it's just me," Carlos shouted over distant gunfire. He helped me to my feet.

"Thanks," I told him. He bent over and retrieved the knife. He wiped the bloody blade on his pants and extended it for me. I nodded another 'thank you' and turned.

"Hurry! Hurry!" Treasure screamed. She pressed her face against the fence. Tears streamed down her cheeks. Three zombies came out of the darkness, moving with alarming speed. One was missing an arm; a jagged shoulder bone and wispy muscle swung with each jarring step.

"I got this!" Carlos yelled and held up the gun. "Go!"

He fired once, the bullet landing in the middle of One Arm's forehead. I sprinted to the fence and dropped to my knees. The gun fired once more. With my elbows, I pulled myself forward, crying out from the pain it caused.

Treasure bent down and pulled me up. I jumped away from the tunnel. Nervous sweat dripped down my back. My heart felt like it was going to explode. I was all too aware that we had absolutely no idea what was behind us.

My breath came out in ragged panting. I wrapped trembling fingers around the wooden handle of the knife. A heavy rustling of leaves made my skin prickle with fear.

"Carlos!" Treasure screamed.

"Be quiet!" I ordered. "Unless you want to attract them to us!"

We should have heard another gunshot by now, taking out the third and final zombie. I joined Treasure at the fence, fear and adrenaline pumping through my veins like fire. I easily spotted the flashlight; it was tucked under Carlos' arm while he messed with the gun. He yelled in frustration and pulled the trigger.

Nothing happened. The gun was jammed. The flashlight fell from his grip as he pulled back the hammer.

"Forget it!" I yelled. "Just go!" Carlos didn't move. "Carlos! Run!" The gun landed on the ground with a thud. He scooped up the flashlight, whirled around, and dove into the tunnel. Another gust of wind blew just as I heard a branch snap.

Treasure screamed. "Carlos!" she dropped to the ground and reached under the fence for him.

The zombie he had been trying to shoot had both hands around his ankle. Carlos thrashed and kicked, doing his best to fight him off. In a mad dash, I landed too hard on the ground, causing a red flash of pain to sting my broken ribs. Not allowing it to stop me, I wrapped my hand around Carlos' wrist and pulled.

A yell of pain escaped his mouth. My eyes flitted to the zombie; it had sank its teeth into Carlos' leg. Another zombie hurried over. It fell to its knees and took a hold of Carlos' other leg. The other zombie snarled at it, like a jealous dog protecting its bone. I flattened my body to get a better reach under the fence.

"Pull!" I yelled to Treasure. On a count of three, we tugged on Carlos' body. His shoulders got caught on the sharp, jagged bottom of the fence. "Kick them!" I instructed Carlos. He madly moved his leg, blood soaking his jeans.

Twigs snapped behind us.

"Come on, come on," I muttered frantically. The zombies pulled back, not ready to give up their meal. Carlos screamed as another festering mouth clamped onto his leg. His nails dug into my hand.

Something fell on Treasure. She hysterically shouted and let go of Carlos' hand. I couldn't breathe while lying on my stomach. Gasping for air, I rolled to my back, twisting my arms over my head. I attempted to sit up and yank Carlos under the fence to safety.

A gummy, with the skin over his rib cage burned off, was fighting to sink its teeth into Treasure's jugular.

"Help me!" she begged. Abhorrence radiated through me. If I let go of Carlos, I could save Treasure. Not ready to give up yet, I kept my left hand locked around Carlos' wrist and twisted once more. I blindly swung my feet and kicked something; I wasn't sure if it was Treasure or the gummy.

Suddenly, my body jerked to the side, and I was painfully moving across the dry ground. Another zombie had joined the feast. This one had shiny blood and chunks of skin and clumps of what looked like fur over its arms. It grabbed Carlos by the middle and didn't waste any time pulling him back. With a death grip on my wrist, Carlos took me with him. If my arm went under the fence, I'd get bitten for sure. After one more kick at the gummy, I quickly rolled over so that I was lying on my extended arm.

Carlos squeezed my hand as a zombie ripped open his belly. They dragged him another few inches away. Still screaming, Carlos dug his fingers into my hand, causing little beads of blood to pool under his nails. Our eyes met for a fleeting moment.

I put my right hand on the fence and pushed off, Carlos' nails scraping and scratching long cuts as I ripped out of his grasp. I pulled myself to my feet and was overcome with dizziness. I stumbled forward and fell on top of the gummy, pushing him off of Treasure.

It was too dark to tell if my vision blacked out. Vomit burned in my throat and I rolled off the gummy, landing on the ground with a thud. Scrambling back, my hands pressed into sharp rocks. The gummy groaned; putrid liquid dripped from its open mouth. I had dropped the knife by the fence in my failed attempt to save Carlos. I felt around myself for anything I could use to kill the S3. I picked up a rock; it wasn't big enough to do any damage.

My hands closed around a stick. It wasn't strong enough to break though its skull, even though the bone had to be soggy and rotten. Nonetheless, I picked it up, pushed myself to my knees, and grabbed the gummy's head with one hand and pulled its face up. I shoved the stick upward through its chin. The stick popped through the soft flesh like butter. I felt it hit the roof of his mouth with slight resistance. I pressed his head down and jerked the stick up.

The gummy went limp.

Treasure had both hands on the fence crying uncontrollably. I staggered over to her, putting an arm on the metal for support. My body trembled and I felt like I was going to pass out. Dust floated through the stream of yellow from the flashlight, laying several feet away from us and on the other side of the fence. It would be almost pitch black without it.

The sounds of slurping and chewing filled the air. A shutter ran through my body. I closed my eyes for just a second and tried to get some composure. And then I realized that—other than the sounds of Carlos being eaten—the night was quiet.

Shit.

"We have to go," I panted. Either everyone was dead or the guys had taken care of the zombie situation inside the yard. And then they would be looking for us.

Treasure leaned against the fence, muttering incoherently.

"Now!" I said. I forced myself upright and put my hand on Treasure's. "They'll come for us," I warned and glanced nervously at the sky. It would be easy to spot us when the sun came up.

Trembling, she nodded and swallowed a sob. I retrieved the knife.

"Got your weapon?" I asked Treasure.

"I-I dropped it," she stuttered. I shook my head and stepped forward.

"I'll get you something. We have to go," I repeated. I grabbed Treasure's hand to pull her along. Her palm was slippery with warm blood. Wait, no it wasn't. Mine was. "Fuck," I cursed when I looked at my left arm. The fragile scab had been scraped off. Worried about getting infected, I used the knife to cut the hem off of my shirt. I wrapped it around the cut. It was a piss-poor bandage, but it would have to suffice for now.

"What do you think they'll do if they find us?" Treasure asked me, hiccupping.

"How the hell should I know?" I responded. "You're the one who lived with them." I shook my head. "From the little interaction I've had with your lovely roommates, I'm guessing whatever they do won't be fun. But they're *not* gonna find us."

"How can you be sure?"

"I'm not sure. Now be quiet," I snapped. "Please," I added.

Clouds rolled across the moon. I shivered, though the air was anything but cold. We walked for maybe thirty seconds before Treasure asked me another question.

"Where are we going?"

"I already told you," I whispered.

"Where?" she repeated.

"I'm trying to find the bridge."

"Bridge?"

"Yes. Bridge. Over the ditch."

"Where is the ditch?"

I was tempted to cut another strip off of my shirt and gag her with it. "I'm not sure," I said quietly. "Really, be quiet. I need to listen for zombies or...or others ok?"

"Mh-hm," she agreed.

I pressed my bleeding arm to my chest. It became harder to breathe with each step. I wasn't aware that my pace was slowing until Treasure was a good foot ahead of me. I shook myself and painfully took a deep breath. I was tired, hungry, and had to pee. We trudged onward.

Shuffling feet crashed through the dry underbrush. I heard the telltale death groan of a zombie several feet behind us. Treasure grabbed my hand and squealed.

"You're getting this one," I told her and turned around.

"No! Please, don't make me!"

I rolled my eyes. I was currently bleeding and hunched over in pain. Some comrade she was.

"I can't!"

"One isn't hard. You *can*."

She nodded. The zombie limped closer, stretching out its arms in our direction. I extended the knife and was able to focus on the zombie's face. The blood drained from my head and I felt like I was going to pass out. The knife slipped through my fingers. I looked into his faded eyes— eyes I knew well—and retched.

CHAPTERFOUR

"Rider," I said. Rider was part of my team, my friend. We had been through hell and back and we had been captured together. "Rider!"

He lumbered toward me, mouth open and arms outstretched.

No, no! This wasn't happening. "Rider, listen to me!" I shouted. "You have to be in there somewhere!" I cried hysterically. "Rider, stop!"

His cold, clammy hands closed on my arm and pulled it to his mouth.

"Rider, stop!" I repeated. "It's me, Orissa!" I sobbed. I twisted away; his left hand clamped down and his arm bent unnaturally. Anyone with the ability to feel pain would have let go, but Rider hung on and something snapped and popped. I screamed. "Rider!"

I ducked out of the way and behind him. I looped my arms through his and pulled him back and off his feet. He snarled, turning his head to try and rip a hunk of my skin off. I tripped over tangled grass growing over fallen branches. Rider crashed onto me and I couldn't breathe.

With my arms still around his, Rider was stuck. He thrashed, trying to get on his feet again. Keeping my hold, I scrambled up, faltered, and fell.

"Rider!" I yelled. "It's gonna be ok," I told him. And it was. I would take him back to the compound. Dr. Cara would think of something. She'd be able to reverse the virus. Rider would be ok; he had to be. He would be hooked up to IVs, given meds...he'd get better.

"Hayden!" Treasure screamed. "What are you doing?"

What was I doing? Rider wasn't going to be ok. He was dead. His brain was permanently damaged. He had been shot in the gut; his digestive juices had no doubt eaten away at his insides. There was no way he could survive that. Rider was a zombie.

"Should I kill him?" Treasure called. She stood a few feet from us, holding the knife and looking terrified.

"No!" I screamed. I squirmed out from underneath Rider and flipped on top of him, pinning him down with my weight. I put my hands on his shoulders, pressing his body into the ground. He turned his head, craning his neck to sink his teeth into my flesh. Tears streamed down my cheeks and splashed onto his face.

A chunk of skin was missing from Rider's neck. I stared at the bite mark as if I could will it away. A hysterical sob came from deep within; it shook my body and caused horrible pain. But the physical pain was nothing compared to how broken my heart was.

"Rider," I cried, barely able to speak. His teeth clicked as he tried to bite me again. "I'm sorry, I'm sorry," I sobbed.

"Hayden," Treasure said softly.

I whipped my head around. "Shut up!" I screamed. I turned back to Rider and completely broke down. He sat up and I struggled to keep him on the ground. Blood had soaked through the bandage on my left arm; Rider's dead eyes focused on it and he growled. "Please, Rider!" I begged. "You have to be in there somewhere. Please!"

"Hayden," Treasure said again, louder this time. "Look!"

I looked up to see an S2 stumbling toward us. Her hair hung in blood soaked clumps and strands of long human hair protruded from her mouth. Without thinking, I rolled off Rider and jumped up. I ran to the zombie, dropping to the ground, sticking my leg out, and spinning. She fell face first on the dirt. I tangled my fist in her hair and slammed her head into the hard ground until the bones cracked open on her forehead and her face was an unrecognizable pile of mush.

Rider had gotten to his feet again and limped over, attracted to the noise and blood. He dropped to his knees and grabbed my leg. His teeth clamped around my ankle but couldn't puncture the thick leather of my boots. I pulled my leg back and kicked him in the face.

"I'm sorry!" I called and scrambled to him. He had rocked back onto his butt. Using the palm of my hand, I shoved his head, disturbing his center of gravity. I pinned him down again, though harder this time. I was tiring; Rider never would. He would never feel anything again.

"Hayden," Treasure breathed. She stretched out her arm, extending the knife.

I shook my head, taking a sharp, jagged breath. "I can't. I-I..." I trailed off. Tears blurred my vision. I couldn't kill Rider. I didn't care that he was a zombie. He was still my friend. I was going to bring him with us. I nodded, wide eyed. Yes! He would stay in a stall. We could feed him and...and Dr. Cara could do research. It would make his existence worth something.

"Grab his feet," I ordered.

"What?" Treasure shook her head.

"Grab his fucking feet! We're going to carry him!"

Trembling, Treasure moved to Rider's feet. She wrapped her hands around his ankles. I pushed myself off of him, grabbing his wrists, and pulling his arms over his head.

"Lift him up," I instructed. When I pulled his arms off the ground, his right shoulder popped out of place. "Ah!" I cried. "Put him down!" I gently set Rider on the ground. "I'm so sorry. I'm sorry, Rider." Quickly, he sat up, thick saliva dripping from his open mouth. He advanced on me before I had a chance to move out of the way.

Rider knocked me over, his body pressing against mine. Searing hurt paralyzed me. He let out a throaty growl and dove down, ready to sink his teeth into me. Treasure grabbed the hem of his shirt and yanked. Rider jerked back but not off of me.

"Hey!" she shouted. "Hey, zombie!"

Her voice did nothing to get Rider's attention. I put my hands on his face and pushed. I curled my legs up to my breasts and, crying out in pain, was able to push off of Rider's chest. I spun around and grabbed at the dead, dry weeds, pulling myself to safety. My lungs begged for air but every breath was excruciating.

Treasure jumped over Rider and took a hold of my hand. She yanked me back and out of Rider's grasp.

"What are you doing?" she asked.

"He...I..." I couldn't form a rational sentence. What was I doing? Rider...Rider was gone. He was already dead. But I couldn't pick up the knife and plunge the pointy end into Rider's brain. Treasure took my hand and gave it a gently tug. I let my body move with her. Yes...I could leave him. That way I wouldn't have to kill him.

"No," I said aloud. I took the knife from Treasure. My hand trembled and I took a step forward. Rider was struggling to upright himself. I couldn't think about it. I just had to do it. As if my body was on autopilot, my feet moved of their own accord. I sank to my knees a foot from Rider. "I'm sorry," I whispered and drove the knife into his ear.

I wrapped my arms around his body right as it went limp. We fell to the ground together. I lay there, clutching him, crying. I heard Treasure's loud breathing and felt her presence as she knelt down next to me. Her hand gently landed on my back.

"I'm sorry," she said softly. Another sob desperately escaped my lips. My body shook and I thought I was going to puke. I pushed myself up and straightened Rider's torso. His blue eyes were frosted with death. His pale skin was gray and his lips were tinted blue. I smoothed out his shaggy red hair. Pain clutched my heart, causing me to fall over. I buried my head in his shirt, the smell of death choking me.

A shot rang out from behind us, causing Treasure to jump. I knew I should have been scared. But I was too numb. I put my hand on Rider's cold cheek.

"You were so brave," I told him. "I'll miss you," I whispered. Another shot echoed, even closer this time.

"Hayden," Treasure said and stood. The image of my Marine flashed through my mind. "Can we go?" she asked.

I turned back to Rider. I removed his dog tags, wrapped them around my wrist like a bracelet, and tried to close his eyes. His eyeballs were mushy and rotten; they pushed back into his skull when I touched them.

Treasure grabbed my arm and pulled me up. I didn't resist; I just stared at Rider, wide eyed until he disappeared from view.

* * *

"Is that it?" Treasure asked, after we had walked some distance. I squinted and was able to make out the black outline of the ditch. I nodded and slowed, searching for the bridge. We had traveled farther away from the hospital than I had planned and wasted precious minutes doubling back.

"It's weak," I warned. "One at a time. I'll go first." I took a step on the shaky wooden planks held up only by rope, suspended above the dark ditch. A strong gust swung the bridge almost as soon as I stepped onto it. I held onto the rope handles and prepared for it to collapse. My legs were weak by the time I reached the other side. "Ok, your turn," I said.

The bridge creaked under Treasure's weight, though she probably weighed less than I did. When she joined me, I debated on cutting the ropes. Deciding it would take up too much time and energy, we moved on. The wind became a continuous strong breeze, making it hard to hear what was lurking around us. If it wasn't for the telltale death moan and pungent smell of rotting, I wouldn't have noticed her until it was too late.

I held the knife up and waited for her to come to us. Her throat had been slit; a flap of flesh hung down onto her chest. I was too busy thinking that only a complete dumbass would try to kill a zombie by slitting its throat to notice the arrow. I didn't see it sticking out of her shoulder until after I sank the knife into her ear.

I put my foot on her chest and yanked it out. Holding it up to the moonlight, I carefully turned it. Maybe it was a stretch, but seeing the arrow gave me hope. I knew I wasn't the only person left in the world who hunted down zombies with a bow and arrows, but I was confident that I was the only person in a five mile radius who had diamond weaved, carbon arrows with expandable broadhead points. Plus, I recognized the dark colored fletching at the back.

"Why are you smiling like that?" Treasure asked. "It's creepy!"

I showed her the arrow. "This is mine!"

She shook her head, not following.

"I didn't shoot it, obviously. So that means my friends are close."

"Should we call for them?" she asked hopefully.

"Yes! Let's scream into the dark and hope only my friends hear us." I started walking, squinting in the darkness. "We need to go back this way," I said, pointing to my left. "And then over there." I held out the arrow. "Here," I told Treasure. "Hold it in the middle. If a zombie comes, aim for the eyes. It's the easiest way to get to their brain; you don't have to break through the skull."

Treasure swallowed, took the arrow, and nodded. "Is the whole world like this?"

"I think so," I said softly. "The whole US is at least; we've been all over. Big cities are way worse though; it's logical if you think about it."

"More people?"

"Yep."

We climbed up a hill. I paused, looking at our surroundings. We were in the open, away from the big trees that offered protection. Our silhouettes were too obvious against the lightening dawn sky. If my captors realized I was gone, they'd be pissed. I doubted they'd miss the opportunity to shoot me. Thinking about Dre, Cutter, and Kisha helped me keep my composure. I was going to make them bleed; make *them* beg for death if it was the last thing I did.

I pushed into a jog, which was made easy by going downhill. I tripped when I reached the bottom and tumbled down into the ditch.

"Hayden!" Treasure cried out.

I cringed at the volume of her voice.

"You ok?"

"Yeah," I tried to say. My voice died in my throat. I tried to take a breath and was hit with crippling pain and fell forward. Treasure picked her way to the bottom of the ditch and knelt down next to me.

"Maybe we should take a little break?" she suggested, looking rather worn herself. "You're hurt," she reminded me like I wasn't aware.

I held up a hand in protest. We couldn't stop; it would be the death of us. Literally. I put both hands on the ground and waited for the pain to subside. It didn't go away completely, but became manageable in a few seconds. I climbed to my feet; I wasn't able to straighten my shoulders without excruciating hurt. The unwelcome thought of a broken rib puncturing my lung forced its way into my already-terrified mind.

I counted ten steps before looking up. The greenhouses were nowhere in sight. Though, in the darkness, that didn't mean they were far. I hunched my shoulders again and took ten more steps. I slowed, ignoring my body's pleas to sit down.

"There it is," I exhaled. I winced when I lifted my arm to point to the dark shadow of the greenhouse. Treasure took my hand to help me up the side of the drainage ditch. I stumbled over a patch of thistles, and allowed her to link her arm through mine. Dead, dry grass crunched under our feet. I kept my eyes focused on the greenhouse. *Almost there*, I repeated in my head.

Treasure gasped. My heart skipped a beat. I snapped my attention to what she was looking at. A zombie lay a few feet to our left with an arrow buried in its head. I smiled and yanked it out. A metallic scrape echoed against the building.

"Did you hear that?" Treasure asked.

"Shh!" I pulled her down. "Don't move. It sounds like a human."

EMILYGOODWIN

"How can you tell?"

I shook my head and put my finger to my lips. I knew the sound of a magazine sliding out of a gun. I gripped the knife and the arrow. My plan was to play dead until they came closer. Then I'd spring up.

Gravel crunched under someone's feet. My hands trembled. Treasure's eyes were squeezed shut; she had let go of her arrow and had both hands over her mouth. I pressed myself against the ground. If I didn't move, I might be mistaken for a dead zombie...

"Play dead," I whispered to Treasure. "Quietly."

Slowly, she layed down. The crunching stopped and the snapping of dead weeds and sticks took its place. Whoever was out here was coming close. I began counting, imagining their footsteps. I felt their presence and knew they were just a few feet from us. My heart hammered in my chest. I tightened my fingers. *Five, four*...the pursuer took another step. *Three, two*...the person stopped next to me and knelt down, exhaling loudly. *One*.

CHAPTER FIVE

"Orissa?"

My eyes flew open.

"Oh my God, Riss!"

Hands landed on my arms. Tears pricked the corners of my eyes. Overwhelming joy and relief rendered me nonfunctional. I smiled, dropped my weapons, and reached for him. Brock took my outstretched hand. I drew in a breath. Treasure shot up, eyes darting from Brock to me.

"Is this one of your friends?" she asked.

I nodded.

Brock looked around nervously. "Riss, what's wrong?"

"She has broken ribs," Treasure answered robotically.

"I'm ok," I assured Brock.

"Yeah, sure you are," he replied sarcastically. He scooped me up.

I weakly protested.

"Follow me," he told Treasure. He ran to the green house, sat me down, and unlocked the door. Once inside, he relocked it and pulled his walkie-talkie from his belt and said, "I got her."

It was pitch black inside the green house. I felt myself swaying as I stood. Treasure shuffled forward and slipped her hand into mine. Ivan's hushed voice came over the walkie. How much I had missed the guys, hit me, and I felt emotional.

"They're on their way," Brock told me.

"Where are they?"

"They went in for you."

My heart skipped a beat and ice water pumped through my veins. They had gone in for me...and I wasn't there. I closed my eyes and planned on yelling at Hayden later, assuming there was a later. There *had* to be a later. If he got in, he could get out.

Brock clipped the walkie back onto his belt and clicked on a flashlight. "Holy shit," he exclaimed when he looked me over. "You're always covered in blood," he said with a slight smile. "You need to sit," he instructed and led me over to a pile of large bags filled with seeds. I sank down. "I'm Brock," he said quickly to Treasure.

"Hi," she replied with her eyes cast down. She crossed her arms and stepped closer to the light.

Brock untied my pathetic bandage and frowned at the wound. He pulled something from a vest pocket and ripped open an alcohol swab. "This is gonna sting," he warned.

I turned my head, closed my eyes, winced, and made a squeaking noise of pain.

"Sorry," he told me.

"No, thanks," I grimaced. "Why are you in here?"

He swiped the cut with another swab. "One of us had to live, ya know in case..." he trailed off and shook his head. "To report back."

"Good idea."

"Yeah," he agreed. "Though I never anticipated you getting out. You have no idea how glad I am I decided to stay."

"I bet I'm happier about it," I tried to say with a smile.

"Did the distraction work?"

"Distraction?"

Brock smiled. "The zombies."

"That was you guys?" I asked.

Brock nodded.

"Yes! That's how we got out."

Brock placed a piece of gauze over the cut and taped it to my dirty skin. He put his supplies back and hugged me.

I flinched.

"Shit, sorry. How bad is it?" he asked, eyes flicking to my middle.

"Pretty bad," I admitted.

He turned around. "Are you injured?" he asked Treasure.

"Not really," she answered. "Just a few scrapes."

"Sit," he instructed and stood up. He strode to the door.

"Where are you going?" Treasure asked.

"Keep watch," he replied. "Stay in here; you'll be fine."

She nodded and sat next to me, breathing heavily. Brock turned off the flashlight and slipped out the door. I closed my eyes and leaned back, loose strands of my hair catching in dusty cobwebs.

"Are we safe?" she asked.

Talking was the last thing I wanted to do. "Yes," I replied shortly.

"How will your friends find us?"

"They just will."

"Are you sure?" she whimpered.

"We need to be quiet," I urged. "If you want to stay safe."

"Oh, ok."

Obscure thoughts floated through my head as I tried to remain conscious.

* * *

Light from a flashlight blinded me. I must have passed out. I sat up, turning my head away from the light. Hayden rushed to me, dropping to his knees. I pushed myself forward and into his arms. His embrace killed, but it was so reassuring that I didn't object.

"Orissa," Hayden murmured. His hands moved from my waist to my face, gently cupping my cheeks. He tipped my head up and kissed me. The tears I had been holding back rolled down my face. Hayden broke away, using his fingers to brush the tears away. His hazel eyes were filled with worry; he held my gaze for a few seconds before looking me up and down.

"You're a mess...again," he said softly.

"That keeps happening," I replied, my voice choked with emotion. "You too," I said and gently put a finger over a bleeding gash on his forehead.

"It's not that bad," he said, brushing off my worry. "It doesn't even hurt." He ran a hand over my head, over my messy hair, and down my back. The other settled on my waist and he pulled me to him. I winced and whimpered. Hayden jerked back.

"She has broken ribs," Treasure told him.

Hayden stared at her, just now realizing that she was in here with us. I took the moment to look past him. Ivan and Wade's familiar faces were wonderful to see as well. Then it hit me and I felt like my ribs were being broken all over again.

"Rider?" Wade whispered.

"No," I whispered back and shook my head. I remembered the smell of his dead breath in my face, the way spit dripped in thick strings from his open mouth. I had pushed the knife into his skull. My stomach pulled in, causing my body to shudder. I retched but nothing but bile came up. I closed my eyes. "No," I repeated. It felt like I had been pushed backwards off a cliff, plummeting through ice cold, misty air. When I hit the bottom, a sob escaped my mouth. Hayden gently put his arms around me. "No...no," I dumbly stammered as I cried. I rested my head on Hayden's chest.

"It's ok," he soothed and ran his hand over my hair. Suddenly a sob twisted into a cough. My body shuddered from the pain. Hayden gently rubbed my back.

"We have to go," Brock stated hollowly.

Hayden nodded and stood.

Using him for leverage, I pulled myself to my feet.

"Hi," Treasure nervously spoke.

"We'll do introductions later," Hayden told her. "We do have to go," he echoed Brock's words and helped me along.

They guys had moved our vehicles away from the greenhouses to stay inconspicuous. Hayden said we had to run through a field, across a street, and into a parking lot where the truck would be overlooked among the dozen other cars. I was winded after only a minute of jogging. I focused on taking slow, steady breaths. I was in good shape. I could do this.

"*Orissa!*"

I whirled around. There was no one behind us. I pushed forward and heard my name called again. I stopped dead in my tracks. I knew that voice.

"Rider?" I panted. My eyes desperately scanned the horizon. The sun had crept up a little bit more, illuminating the vast field.

"Riss!" Hayden called and doubled back. "What's wrong?"

I looked across the field once more. "Nothing," I wheezed, looking into his worried eyes. "I thought I heard something."

"I didn't," he said quickly and took my hand. "Let's go."

I nodded and took off, struggling to keep up with Hayden. Only a few seconds later I was hit with a wave of dizziness. My vision blurred and my ears rang. Oh shit. I knew that feeling. It was only a matter of time before—

I didn't remember falling. The next thing I knew, Hayden had me wrapped in his arms. He was running across a street. My head bobbed with each jarring step. I felt like I was going to be sick again. Since I had nothing left to come up, I didn't worry about it.

"Hayden," I breathed and lifted my head up. "You can put me

down."

"No," he panted.

"I'm slowing you down. Please."

Hayden's gait slowed. "No," he said and picked up the pace again, not stopping until we were in the parking lot. Panting, he gently set me on my feet. "Can you climb?" he asked.

"Yeah," I answered automatically, though I had no idea what he was talking about.

"Good. Go first."

I nodded and blinked several times, willing my vision to focus. Ivan, Wade, and Brock gracefully landed on the opposite side of a ten foot chain link fence and helped Treasure over. Fuck. That's what I had to climb. Hayden pulled his keys from his pocket and stuck them through the fence.

"Get the truck," he told Brock.

My fingers grasped the metal fence. I stuck the tip of my boot in a link and hoisted myself up. Pain rippled through me, stinging and burning with every movement. I pulled myself up another foot and faltered.

"I'm right behind you," Hayden assured me. "Keep going."

"Ok," I breathed. My left arm was weak. Feeling as if my fingers were curling around metallic fire, I gritted my teeth and took another step up the fence. Hayden put his hand on my back to steady me.

"Come on, Riss," he encouraged. I moved up another foot. I paused to take a breath and slowly moved up again. My hands clasped the thick top of the fence. I cast a glance over my shoulder. A fire glowed in the distant hospital yard. I watched the flames flicker and swore I could smell burning flesh.

The fence wiggled dangerously when Hayden pulled himself off the ground. If I wasn't injured, it wouldn't be a big deal. But I lost my balance and almost fell.

"You ok?" Hayden asked, freezing.

"Yeah. Just, uh, wasn't expecting the fence to move so much," I confessed and put one leg over the top.

"Ok, I'll wait until you get done," Hayden told me and jumped back. My hands shook when I looked down, suddenly realizing that ten feet seems a hell of a lot higher than it sounds. I couldn't help but cry out when I flipped my body over. I closed my eyes in agony.

I opened them just in time to see a zombie stumble its way toward Hayden.

"Look out!" I cried, my body jerking of its own accord. Hayden spun around, pulling a knife from his waist. In a swift movement, he jammed it into the zombie's ear. My mind flashed to myself doing a similar thing to Rider. My heart ached and my stomach lurched.

"Go!" Hayden shouted when more zombies milled toward us. I swung my feet down, sticking the toes of my boots into a link. My ears started ringing again and my body screamed. I forced myself to step down.

Only I must have not taken the last steps properly...

* * *

"Riss, can you hear me?" Hayden asked.

"Yeah," I mumbled. "Where...where?" I failed at my question.

"I think she's dehydrated," I heard Treasure say.

I felt water against my lips and drank.

"We're going home," Hayden told me. "Try to rest."

"Ok," I agreed. My eyes closed and felt the truck moving; I struggled to stay awake. Every part of me hurt and it took every ounce of energy I had to take in air. Once my lungs were full of oxygen, a horrible, shooting pain radiated across my torso. Forced to take only shallow breaths, I could feel my body weakening by the minute. I knew something was wrong the minute I opened my eyes. My brain was fuzzy, as was my vision, and I wasn't aware of my surroundings. I had feeling in my feet and fingers but couldn't get them to work. Like heavy garage doors, my eyelids slammed shut. I fluttered in and out of consciousness for the rest of the journey home.

* * *

I woke up to a searing pain in my left arm. I couldn't open my eyes. "Hayden?" I murmured.

"I'm right here," he soothed and patted my hand. I curled my fingers around his.

"Where am I?" I feebly croaked.

"We're home," Hayden told me. "You're in the hospital ward."

"Orissa?" a deep, scratchy voice spoke. "Can you hear me?" It was the voice of someone who smoked—or used to smoke, since we didn't supply cigarettes on our missions—and I couldn't place it. I mustered up what little strength I had and opened my eyes.

"Yes," I croaked. My chest heaved as I attempted to cough.

"Orissa, it's Jack," he told me.

Jack? Who was Jack? I moved my eyes to the left. An older, gray-haired man was messing with my arm. Oh, right, Jack. He used to be an equine veterinarian.

"I'm putting in an IV; you're very dehydrated. It's probably why you're so confused."

I watched him tape the clear tubing to my skin and hook it to a bag of fluids. "And you said she has broken ribs?" Jack asked Hayden.

"Yes," he answered. "And she fell from about ten feet from a fence—after her ribs were broken. She's all bruised up." Hayden gently pulled my shirt up, folding it over my breasts.

Hayden gasped.

"Oh my," Jack exclaimed. He pressed his cold hand against my side.

I whimpered and winced.

"Brendan," he called. "I need you to get Dr. Sheehan. Tell him I'm sorry to wake him, but he's gonna want to see this."

"Am I that bad?" I whispered, my throat raw.

"Oh no," Jack lied. "Broken ribs can be tricky. If the bone breaks in the wrong place it could puncture your lung." He stood, his knees popping. "I'm going to run your blood work; I'll be right back."

I pressed my hands to my torso as I coughed. Moaning, I let my head fall back. "I'm cold," I told Hayden.

"It's probably from the IV," he said and grabbed a blanket off of an empty bed. "Here." He draped the blanket over me, pulling it up to my chin. "Try and relax." He sat on the edge of the bed and ran his hand through my hair. "You're burning up."

I coughed again and whimpered in pain.

"I've only bruised my ribs and it hurt like a bitch. I feel bad for you," he said with a frown.

I did my best to glare at Hayden. "You know I hate pity."

"And you know I hate seeing you in pain," he countered with a smile. He ran his fingers through my hair again, and, getting caught in a knot, he moved his hand to my face. He pressed his lips to my forehead.

"Alright," Jack said and pulled back the curtain. Hayden snapped up, but not before Jack saw. Jack flushed and made a big deal of opening a pale yellow folder. My name was written on the front in big black letters. "I'm going to get a second set of vitals while we wait for Dr. Sheehan."

When had he gotten the first? Must have been when I was unconscious.

He wheeled a little machine into my tiny curtained room and wrapped a blood pressure cuff around my right arm and put a little clamp with a red light on my finger.

"On a scale of one to ten, how would you rate your pain?" he asked and put a cover on the thermometer probe.

"Uh, a seven," I said. "Maybe more when I cough."

He nodded and stuck the thermometer in my mouth. I watched his eyes widen slightly when it beeped. Being nosy, Hayden leaned over and mirrored Jack's shocked expression.

"What is it?" I asked.

"One oh two point seven," Jack informed me. He picked up the folder again and wrote down whatever the machine told him. "Can I get you anything while we wait?"

"I have to pee," I told him.

Jack chuckled and looked at the IV bag. "It'll do that to you. Your blood pressure is still pretty low. I don't think it's a good idea for you to get up until we get the ok from Dr. Sheehan. I can bring you a bed pan."

"Hell no," I said, making Hayden laugh. "I can get up," I stubbornly spat and tossed the blankets back.

"Riss," Hayden started and put his hand on my shoulder. "Listen to Jack. You can wait until Padraic gets here."

"Can he take me?" I asked, looking at Hayden.

"Uh," Jack began and looked at Hayden. "If he doesn't mind."

"Good," I wheezed. Jack took the IV bag off of its hook and handed it to Hayden, who snaked his arm around me.

"Get up slowly," Jack instructed. Hayden held me tightly the entire walk to the bathroom, which was good because my legs were about as strong as Jell-O.

"You are so stubborn," he laughed as I sat on the toilet. He stepped out and closed the door as much as he could without kinking the IV tube. I wobbled back to the bed. Hayden had just pulled the blankets over me when Padraic walked in.

"Oh my God," he exclaimed when he saw me. "Orissa."

"Hi," I said weakly and smiled.

"What the hell happened?"

"Long story," I told him, trying to convey with my eyes that I couldn't discuss the details in mixed company.

Padraic held my gaze for a second before nodding. "Right. That's not the focus here anyway. Lift up your shirt."

"Padraic," I tried to say coyly but coughed instead. Giving up, I pulled up my shirt.

"How did this happen?" he asked. "This I need to know."

"I was kicked. Repeatedly."

"How long ago?"

"Um," I said and thought. "About two days ago...I think." I looked at Hayden; he nodded.

Padraic raised the bed up and lowered the head until I was laying flat. "I'm sorry," he said and put his hand on one of the bruises. "We don't have a way to X-ray so I'm going to have to feel for the fractures."

I closed my eyes and nodded. Hayden linked his fingers through mine. I squeezed his hand when Padraic pressed on my chest. He slowly worked his way up, tracing each rib with his fingers.

"There's a fracture right here," Padraic spoke. I wasn't sure who he was talking to. Jack hovered, watching Padraic work. "And here," he said and moved his hands up, pausing when his fingertips touched the base of my breast. Hayden's fingers tightened around mine when Padraic continued feeling for breaks. "I think there's another fracture here," he said and gently pressed his fingers down. "There's quite a bit of, uh, tissue over it so it's hard to tell."

He flattened his hand over the right side of my rib cage and told me to take a deep breath.

Taking in that much air hurt and I coughed. Padraic kept his hand pressed down. I dug my nails into Hayden's hand. Padraic repeated the processes with the left side, not finding any breaks.

"You have three broken ribs as far as I can tell," he said and picked up a stethoscope. "The bones seem to be staying in place, which is good."

"She fell, too," Jack told him. "A ten foot fall, right?" he asked Hayden.

"Yes. Onto pavement."

"What side did she land on?" Padraic asked.

"Uh," Hayden thought. "Kind of face down and to the right."

I cringed at the thought. Thank God I passed out.

Padraic removed the blanket and unbuttoned my pants. He asked Hayden to carefully lift me up while he gently wiggled my jeans down and off. I protested that I could undress myself, but I wasn't sure that was completely true. Padraic started to neatly fold my jeans but I stopped him from wasting his time, insisting that the pants were so bloody they weren't worth saving.

Worried that I had damaged my hip bones and knees, Padraic checked for breaks, painfully pressing into my bruised skin. I had a bit of road-rash on my right arm from falling; I wasn't even aware of that. Cleaning it was a fun experience. Finished with the physical part of the exam, Padraic covered me back up, placed the stethoscope on my chest and told me to breathe deeply. I could tell something was wrong by the little wrinkles that formed around his eyes. He had me sit up and lean forward so he could listen to my lungs from the back. "What are her vitals?" he asked Jack, who handed him the folder.

"You're gonna give me some cough medicine and ice and let me be on my way, right?" I asked hopefully, wanting to go into my room and be alone.

Padraic closed the folder. "No, Orissa. It's going to take more than that. You—"

Someone yanked the curtain back, and Dr. Cara popped her head in. Her brown hair was pulled into messy, uneven pigtails. "Blood work's done," she said and extended a paper to Padraic. "You look as bad as your labs," she told me and backed away.

All eyes feel on Padraic as he looked over the results. Hayden involuntarily tightened his grip on my hand.

"You're very sick, Orissa," Padraic finally said. He looked at me as if he expected me to object. There was no use denying it; I felt like shit and I knew I looked like it. "You have multiple fractures and lacerations. Your white blood cells are high, your red are low. Did you lose a lot of blood...again?"

I nodded and Hayden lifted up my left arm. "She has a pretty deep cut," he told Padraic and pointed at the bandage.

"Unwrap that, please," Padraic told Jack. "You have a high fever, very low blood pressure, are dehydrated, and your lungs don't sound too good."

"What?" I wheezed. "What's wrong with my lungs? I wasn't sick before."

"It's a common complication from fractured ribs," he explained. "You could easily develop pneumonia."

"She's gonna be ok, right?" Hayden asked almost desperately. "I mean, pneumonia isn't that big of a deal."

"With proper medical treatment, it wouldn't be that big of a deal for Orissa," Padraic admitted. "The broken ribs complicate things and I don't have everything I need here."

"What do you need?" Hayden asked. "I'll go get it."

"No," I said. "Don't leave." My eyes fluttered shut and I felt dizzy again.

"With some rest, medication, and some blood, I expect Orissa to make a full recovery." He turned to Jack. "Orissa tends to heal quicker than expected. She's always surprised me in how quickly she gets better."

"Blood?" I asked, opening my eyes only long enough to give Padraic a questioning stare.

"Yes. You could benefit from a bag of blood."

"I've bled a lot more than this before and didn't need blood," I stated, confused on why Padraic thought I'd need it.

"You're sick and injured, Orissa. Your body isn't able to work at its normal level; it's going to take longer than normal for you to produce a sufficient amount of blood."

"Oh. Ok."

Jack pulled the bandage off my arm; the gauze stuck to the hardened scab and prickled. "It looks infected," he said and held my arm up. Padraic moved around the bed.

"Yes, it is." Padraic let out a breath and stepped back.

"I'll clean it," Jack offered. He pushed the curtain back and disappeared.

"You look tired," I said to Padraic.

He flipped open the folder and began quickly writing something down. "I am," he admitted. "Natasha had her baby the day after you left. And it's been nonstop in here every since."

"How's the baby?"

"Wonderful," Padraic said with a smile. "And I did *not* have to do a C-section."

"Good." I had only seen Natasha a few times. She was one of the few pregnant women who took shelter in the compound. Being the only medical doctor here, Padraic felt the pressure to deliver healthy babies. He was a surgeon, but had no experience with live births. "I can go rest in my room and that way you can go back to bed."

"Nice try, but no." Padraic looked up from the folder. "You're very sick," he reminded me, and his brow furrowed.

I could tell something was wrong and he was working hard at covering it up. Even in my weakened state I knew it was odd that I became so sick so fast.

"And blood pressure this low isn't good, Riss. It's bad for your heart."

That frightened me a bit. "I'm sure I'll be fine," I blurted to ease my nerves. "I got blood poisoning and survived."

"Yes, but your heart and lungs were functioning properly then," Padraic countered.

Jack came back into the room and began cleaning the cut. The first thing he did was carefully scrape off the scab.

"What time is it?" I asked through gritted teeth. I closed my eyes and tried not to think about the sharp stinging coming from my arm.

"It doesn't matter," Hayden said gently.

"Mhh," I protested. "If it's not late, will you tell Ray I'm here," I panted, still unable to fully catch my breath.

"Of course," Hayden said and stood. "It is late, by the way," he told me with a half smile. Padraic followed him out, saying that he was going to come back with medicine. I closed my eyes, hoping Jack would finish quickly so I could sleep. A few minutes later the curtain was yanked back once more.

"Hi Orissa!" someone cheerfully called. I opened my eyes to see a big smile. "I'm Shanté. I'm the nurse on duty today." Her voice was chipper—too chipper. It irritated me.

"Hi," I said quietly.

She started pressing buttons on the IV pump. "Dr. Sheehan gave me all of the orders. I'm gonna give you some meds and then start a transfusion of blood. You were blood typed here, correct?"

"Yes. Dr. Cara did it," I told her. "I'm AB positive, I think."

"Yes, you're correct!" she said as if I had just given her the right answer to a final Jeopardy question.

It was late. Rider didn't come back with us. We were living in an underground bomb shelter while zombies roamed the earth. What the fuck was she so happy about?

"Can I get you anything?" she asked.

"Another blanket," I said, my teeth almost chattering.

"I will ask Dr. Sheehan about that. You have a high temp; usually we don't want you all bundled up. Hang on one second." She scooted out of the room and was back within a minute, holding an extra blanket. "Dr. Sheehan said you can have this until you feel warm so you stop shivering, since shivering consumes more oxygen and can raise your temp even more. And you need all the oxygen you can get so you can get better."

"Thanks," I told her after she spread the blanket over me. She left once again to prepare the meds.

"This might sting a little," Jack warned before he wiped the cut with an alcohol pad. I closed my eyes but didn't flinch. "You need stitches. I'll have Dr. Sheehan do them for you," he said with a smile, and I nodded. "You remind me of my granddaughter, Emma," he said quietly. "You both have the same blue-green eyes. And she was a tough cookie, just like you."

I almost didn't catch the 'was' in his statement. "I'm sorry," I replied just as quietly.

His lips curved into a slight smile. "She was one of the lucky ones, I suppose. Said she had a headache and an hour later..." he exhaled heavily. "You might think it's terrible I consider that lucky."

"No, not at all. I think the same thing. We can believe they're in a better place."

He taped a piece of gauze to my skin and stood to leave. "We can."

I couldn't help but think he was hiding something too.

* * *

I was close to sleep when Hayden and Raeya came in. Hayden set down a plate of buttered noodles and canned vegetables. Raeya flew to my side and wrapped her arms around my neck.

"Oh my God, Rissy!" she cried. "Hayden warned me you looked bad, but I didn't think it'd be this bad!"

I put my right arm around her and patted her back. My shoulder ached with the slightest movement. "I've been worse," I soothed.

She pulled away and looked over my face. "I can't recall a time you've been worse than this. Even when you had a concussion..." she trailed off and shook her head. "And you sound sick."

"I feel sick," I admitted.

"Should you have all these blankets?" Raeya asked.

"Yes," I responded.

"You have a fever," Hayden pointed out as if I didn't know. "You shouldn't be so wrapped up."

Raeya started to remove the top blanket. I groaned and put my hand in it. "Padraic said I can have it until I stop shivering."

"Where is Padraic?" Raeya asked me.

Shanté returned before I could answer. "He went to get something to eat. He'll be back when he's done," she said cheerfully. She set a bag of blood on the little nightstand by the bed and handed me a cup of water and three pills. She explained what each pill did and why I needed it in extremely simple terms.

"Did you work on a pediatric floor?" I asked her and set the water down.

"Yeah, I did! How did you know?"

"Lucky guess," I replied. Her annoying good mood made sense now. I spent a few minutes hacking up a lung before she took my vitals and hung the blood on the IV pump. "Can I sleep through this?" I asked.

"Of course you can. I'm gonna stay here with you for the first fifteen minutes," she explained. "And I'll be taking your vitals at that time, so I don't know how restful it will be. But go ahead and close your eyes.

Hayden pulled a chair close to my right side, and Raeya perched at the foot of the bed.

"You guys can go," I wheezed.

"I'll stay until you fall asleep," Raeya promised.

"Me too," Hayden said with a smile. Though I knew he would still be there when I woke up.

Shanté messed with the IV lines, hooking the blood to the port and wrote something on my chart. Hayden rubbed my hand, helping me relax. I closed my eyes and let my head fall to the side. Then something began to feel weird. I couldn't describe it. I just felt...wrong, almost as if my blood was itchy inside my veins.

"Your cheeks are really red," Hayden observed.

Shanté dropped the folder. "Orissa!" she exclaimed.

I couldn't open my eyes. Everything inside me was burning. The IV pump beeped and Shanté frantically moved around the little area.

"Go get Dr. Sheehan!" Shanté screamed. "She's going into shock!"

CHAPTER SIX

"Orissa."

I was floating in darkness; my body was weightless. Everything was calm, quiet. Time had no meaning and space didn't exist. It was just me and the dark.

"Orissa."

A voice vibrated around me, speaking in a language that I didn't understand.

"Can you hear me?"

The voice brought pain and awareness. I became *aware* that I had a body. And that body hurt. Something was in my throat, choking me. Suddenly panicked, I reached for it, though it took enormous effort to move my arms.

"Hold her hands down," the voice said. Why was it so loud? I fought against the invisible weights that pressed my arms down onto a soft surface. I tried to sit up. Whatever was in my throat made me gag. Heavy hands pushed me down. Red hot pain radiated across my chest and I screamed...or I thought I screamed. I had no voice. I frantically tried to free my hands.

"Orissa," the voice said.

Oh, right. *I* was Orissa.

The voice was talking to me. "You had a reaction to the blood. I had to intubate you. I just administered a sed..." the voice faded until it was nothing. I began to feel weak. My arms fell. Darkness crept over me again, swallowing me whole.

Images flashed through my brain, trying to put a face to that voice. Then I remembered him, walking down the hall of a hospital as I was wheeled into surgery to get my appendix removed. I was there with my aunt; other than my grandpa who was a state away, she was my only family in the country.

My mother, former drunk turned born again Christian, was off in another country with my stepfather, Ted. I guess she had forgotten that the Depression had left plenty homeless and hungry in her own country.

Then I remembered another face, this one handsome with hazel eyes. He brought us here, me, Padraic, my best friend Raeya, and a few others. He saved us. I had no idea I would fall in love with him when he rescued us from that barn months ago...

* * *

I woke up tired, and too weak to move. Everything hurt. Something rhythmically beeped. I listened to it, trying to figure out what it was. I opened my mouth; it was so dry. I pushed air out in an attempt to speak. I opened my eyes and saw a dark haired man wearing a mask. He was staring at something intently that he held in his hand. My eyes closed. I curled my fingers along the bed and dragged my nails across the sheet, trying to get his attention. It didn't work, and I was pulled back into black confusion.

Fingers gently traced circles on the palm of my hand. The skin on those fingers was rough. Rough and familiar. Hayden's face flashed in my mind. I opened my mouth to say his name. Air rushed out instead.

"Riss?" He stopped moving his fingers. "Orissa, are you awake?"

I opened my eyes for a second. Hayden was wearing a mask too, just like the dark haired man, who I remembered now was Padraic. "She's awake!" Hayden said. "Riss," he repeated. I could tell he was leaning over the bed. "Can you hear me?"

It took so much effort to open my eyes, and even more to keep them open. People shuffled around the bed. Hayden's hand left mine and my skin suddenly felt cold.

"She might need to be held down," Padraic said to someone. Heavy hands rested on my arm. "Hi, Orissa," Padraic said softly. "You're going to be in a lot of pain. Once you wake up and talk to us, I'll give you something to help with that, ok?"

"Mhh," I answered.

"Can you open your eyes, Orissa?" Padraic asked.

"Mmhhh," I groaned. My lashes fluttered open long enough to see the hope in Padraic's sky blue eyes. My head felt too heavy to hold up. I became more and more aware of the pain in my chest; breathing hurt.

"Why can't she open her eyes?" Hayden's voice cracked with fear.

"She's exhausted," Padraic informed him. "What she went though…it's going to take her body awhile to recover."

"Oh." A hand brushed my cheek. "Riss, if you're tired, it's ok," Hayden whispered. "But if you can, can you open your eyes?"

"Don't pressure her," Padraic snapped. "She'll open her eyes when she's ready."

Hayden exhaled and took my hand again. "I know she will."

I slipped back into sleep. Hayden's hand was still wrapped around mine when I woke up again.

"She scored higher than me on the SATs," a female voice said. I instantly knew that voice belonged to my childhood friend. "And she never studied! I spent weeks preparing for that test! She went with her parents to South America and got back a week before the test; I don't know how she did it! Orissa is a lot smarter than she gives herself credit for," Raeya noted.

"She is," Padraic agreed.

I hadn't thought about that trip to South America in years. It was the last mission my mother and step dad dragged me on. In all honestly, I enjoyed going to the faraway, remote locations. I liked wandering around the villages, meeting all kinds of interesting people, and learning about their sometimes unorthodox cultures. But I hated the violence, the way the women were treated, and the hunger. I hated that they didn't have medicine or money. And I hated that no matter how many times my mom read them passages from the Bible, brought them clean water and food, nothing made a significant difference.

Images from the trip flashed throughout my mind. I remembered walking down a river, watching a family of Giant Otters catch fish. That was when I had my first run-in with piranhas. One piranha wasn't anything to worry about. If you came across a group, you were fucked. A picture of a zombie flashed through my memory. A single zombie was not a big threat either. It surprised me that I hadn't made the connection earlier.

"Noise," I mumbled.

"Did Orissa just say something?" Raeya asked.

"Noise," I repeated and opened my eyes. *Noise and movement attracts* them, I had been told, but *blood and chaos excites them*. Padraic quickly stood. My eyes slammed shut again.

"Orissa," Raeya said softly. "I think you're dreaming." She

placed her hand on my arm. "Rissy?"

I opened my eyes and smiled weakly at my best friend. She was wearing a mask, just like the ones Padraic and Hayden had on earlier. "Piranhas," I wheezed, my throat burning, "are coming."

Raeya laughed. "You're drugged up and not making sense, Rissy."

"Good morning, Orissa," Padraic said with a smile. "Do you know where you are?"

"No," I whispered. My eyes weren't focusing. I could see Raeya and Padraic hovering over me. There was someone to my right. Hayden was bent over the bed, his head resting on his folded arms, sleeping. I squeezed his hand. "Hayden," I croaked. He took a sharp intake of breath and quickly sat up.

"Orissa," he breathed. "You're awake."

"Mh-hm," I moaned. I desperately wanted water.

"Riss," Padraic said and put his hand on the bed, leaning over me. "You're in the hospital ward at the compound. You're sick."

I nodded. "Water?" I croaked.

"As long as you have a gag reflex, yes," Padraic told me. He put on gloves and checked to make sure I wouldn't choke and aspirate on water. "Olivia," he called. "Can you bring me a cup of water and a cup of ice chips?"

I couldn't hear her answer but heard shoes squeaking on the tile floor. Raeya had tears in her eyes. She turned and wiped them away. Hayden stroked my hand again. I closed my eyes until I heard the familiar sound of the curtain being pulled back.

"Orissa!" Olivia exclaimed and walked in. "You're awake!"

I forced a smile. Padraic scooped a small ice chip out of the cup with a spoon and carefully put it in my mouth. Olivia was wearing a mask and gloves too. I waited until the ice melted, the cold water running down my throat felt amazing.

"Am I contagious?" I asked.

Padraic gave me another ice chip. "No," he told me. "You're very sick. We're wearing these to protect you from any germs we might have."

"Mmm," I said in acknowledgement.

"How are you feeling?" he asked me.

"I hurt," I said simply. "And I'm cold."

"I purposely lowered your body temperature to help your heart," Padraic explained, though his words confused me. He unfolded a blanket that had been at my feet and placed it over my body. Something tightened around my arm, startling me. "It's a blood pressure cuff," Padraic said quickly. "It's attached to this monitor and will do that every half hour."

"Oh," I mumbled and coughed. Searing pain made me cry out. "Fuck," I swore and put a hand over my ribs, pulling the IV tubing. "I forgot about that."

Padraic stood. "Would you like something for the pain?" he asked gently. I nodded and he left to get pain medication.

"Rider?" I whispered, turning my face to Hayden.

His hazel eyes pushed together and he rubbed his thumb on my hand. "We had a memorial service for him."

"It was beautiful," Raeya added.

"Why didn't you wake me up and take me?" I mumbled.

Hayden smiled. "You were in really bad shape, Riss. Once you're better, I'll take you to the memorial."

"Where is it?"

"It's in the back, next to where Jessica's ashes are buried," Hayden explained.

"Donald Richardson hand carved a wooden plague with Rider's name. His dog tags were fitted in too," Raeya told me. "It's gorgeous. Everyone here really liked Rider; we all miss him." A frown pulled down her face. "I'm so sorry, Rissy."

"Can I go?" I mumbled.

Hayden gingerly ran his fingers through my hair. "When you're better I'll take you," he promised. "Don't think about it now," he soothed. "You need to get better first."

I nodded, the heartbreak weighing on my physical injuries. Padraic returned and pulled a capped syringe from inside his pocket. "This will help with the pain, though I'm afraid it might make you rather loopy. Regular morphine for pain depressed your breathing too much; I made a concoction, if you will," he said with a lopsided smile. "It will make you tired too," he warned. "But, you are going to be very sore for a few days." He motioned for Olivia to come over. I watched as Padraic explained to her how to administer the medicine, telling her she had to push it slowly or else I could get sick. She nodded, wiped the IV port with an alcohol swab and administered the medicine.

"Thanks," I told her.

Olivia beamed. "I'm training to be a nurse. I've been following Karen and Shanté around for a couple weeks. And Padraic's been letting me help take care of you."

"You'll be a good nurse," I said honestly.

"Thanks," she said with a huge smile.

Padraic put his hand on her shoulder. "She's doing a great job. She's catching on very fast and is eager to learn. Those are the kinds of nurses I like to work with."

If possible, Olivia flushed even more because of Padraic's words. She looked at the floor, said a goodbye, and went to find Shanté. I closed my eyes.

"You were right; that is making me tired," I told my friends.

"Sleep," Padraic told me. "You need to rest after everything you went through."

"Ok," I agreed, not needing to be convinced. I was asleep in a matter of minutes.

* * *

My little curtained room was double the size it should be. It took me a second to realize that a curtain had simply been pulled, opening up one room into another. The other bed had been pushed over to the side; Hayden was laying on it, sleeping.

Padraic sat in a chair near me. He was holding a large book, tapping a highlighter against the page. I pushed myself up, which immediately got Padraic's attention. He closed the book and smiled.

"Hey, Riss."

"Hi," I wheezed. "Can I have water?"

"Yes," he said quietly and stood. He grabbed a water bottle from the nightstand, twisted the cap off, stuck a straw in it, and held it to my lips. "How are you feeling?" he asked after I took a drink.

"My chest hurts," I said and carefully swallowed another sip of water. I was dizzy from the medicine. I closed my eyes to prevent myself from getting sick.

"It will for a while," he told me with a frown. "Chest compressions are painful even without fractured ribs."

"Chest compressions?" My eyes flew open.

"Do you remember anything that happened?" When I shook my head, Padraic continued. "You were given blood."

"I remember that," I told him. "And I remember Hayden saying my cheeks were red. But that's it. Everything is blank after that."

"That's good," he acknowledged. "That wasn't a situation you want to remember."

"I've had a few of those recently," I said to myself.

"Your body had an allergic reaction to the blood. You stopped breathing and your heart rate dropped to almost nothing. That's why you were intubated and received chest compressions."

"Oh," I sighed. "No wonder I feel like shit."

"You were in bad shape to start out with," Padraic reminded me and shook his head.

"What time is it?"

Padraic looked at his watch. "Around midnight."

I coughed painfully. "Are the guys out of quarantine yet?"

"Who?"

"The guys," I restated.

Padraic's face went blank for a second. "Oh," he said with the look of pity. "Orissa, you were unconscious for three days."

"What?"

Padraic nodded. "It took a full day for the swelling to go down in your throat, and another two for you be stable enough to breathe on your own."

"Oh," I said and started coughing again, waking Hayden. He sat up and hurried to my side. I took another sip of water, panting.

"Is it really necessary for you guys to wear those...face thingys?" I asked. "You look ridiculous."

Padraic chuckled. "Yes. I'm not risking you getting another infection. I honestly don't know if your body can handle it."

I suppressed a cough.

"Don't do that," Padraic scolded. "You're coughing for a reason; you need to get that mucus up."

I grimaced but didn't object. Hayden leaned on the edge of my bed. I looked into his hazel eyes and had an instant flashback to him picking me up and carrying me to his truck. A fire burned behind us and angry shouts floated through the night air. The smell of death had been pungent all around us.

The rhythmic beeping sped up. My breath caught in my chest and I leaned forward as I frantically inhaled, painfully forcing air in.

"Did they follow us?" I croaked.

"No," Hayden promised and put his hand on my back. He moved his fingers in little circles. "They didn't even try. We don't think they saw us leaving at all."

"Good," I panted. "What are we gonna do about them?"

"We'll talk about it later," Hayden said calmly.

"No!" I objected with too much emotion and was thrown into another coughing fit. I leaned back on the pillows. "Please tell me we're doing something."

"Riss, you really shouldn't worry about it," he soothed, making me believe that Fuller wasn't going to act.

"We have to do something!" I begged and sat up.

"No," Padraic and Hayden said at the same time. Hayden put his hands on my shoulders and sat on the edge of the bed. I pushed against him.

"You're hurting me," I said.

"You're hurting yourself," he pointed out. "Riss, stop!"

"No!"

Padraic grabbed my legs. "Orissa, stop it. You're not going anywhere."

I remembered the feeling of the tip of my knife popping through Rider's skin. The blade silently entered his skull and punctured his brain. I remembered his body going limp and his cold, thick blood on my hands. The beeping quickened. I pushed against Hayden.

"Get off of me! We have to—" I gasped, cut off by a horrible cough. "They can't get away with what they did! Not to me, not to...to Rider!" A cough turned into a sob.

"They won't!" Hayden promised. "They won't get away with it."

I continued to struggle despite the pain.

"Riss! We're going back!"

I stopped fighting. "We are?"

"Yes!" He sounded exasperated and smoothed my hair. "We are. They will pay for what they did. To me, to you, and most of all, to Rider. We will get them."

Not only had they captured us and killed Rider, but a month or so earlier members of the same gang had shot Hayden and he...he had been very close to death.

I shivered and nodded. "They have to pay," I said, my voice breaking. "They have to." I couldn't help the tears that rolled down my face. My body was in horrible pain, but the heartache was worse. Hayden gently wrapped his arms around me. I buried my head in his neck and sniffled.

"It'll be ok," he soothed and ran his hand over my hair. "I promise." He held me for a few minutes before he leaned forward, carefully pushing me back until I was lying on the bed. Padraic had stepped back, and I noticed he had a syringe in his hand.

"You're always so eager to drug me," I pointed out.

Padraic smiled. "I thought I was going to have to, though

you're due for more pain meds soon anyway. Your heart rate sky rocketed. I'm not sure what happened on that mission but I'm sorry, Orissa," he said with much empathy. "I can't imagine what you guys go through." He shook his head, and traded the syringe for a stethoscope. "I'm going to listen to your lungs," he told me. Hayden helped me sit up and held my hand while Padraic assessed me.

"Any better?" Hayden asked.

Padraic was easy to read. His lips curved into a smile, but the little lines of worry around his eyes remained.

"It will take time," he said, avoiding Hayden's question. "Orissa being immobile for three days hasn't helped," he sighed.

"What's wrong with my lungs this time?" I asked.

Padraic glanced at Hayden, as if he was asking permission to tell me the truth. "You have a slight case of pneumonia."

"I do?"

"Yes," Padraic admitted with a frown. "It's from your injuries and lying still for three days. You're not fully expanding your lungs when you breathe."

"Don't worry guys," I coughed. "I'll be fine."

"Yes," Padraic affirmed. "You will."

* * *

Several days passed before anyone was certain that I *would* be fine. Though I was far from out of the woods, I felt a hell of a lot better than I did forty-eight hours ago. Since I was sicker than the average compound infirmary patient, Shanté and Karen had been switching off shifts every twelve hours. I almost felt bad for them for getting stuck with having to provide me with round the clock care. Luckily the only other patients in the hospital ward were a seven year old boy with a stomach bug and an older man suffering from gout pain.

Feeling guilty for ordering the blood transfusion that nearly killed me, Padraic insisted that he would stay by my side until I was better. It took Karen nearly an hour of convincing Padraic that she was more than capable of caring for me before he agreed to go to his room and catch up on his sleep. Raeya stayed too, saying that she was mostly there to provide company and entertainment. It took me nearly as long to convince her to get back to her job as an overseer. It was an important job; along with a few others, Raeya inventoried everything we had, keeping organized lists of what we needed to keep this place going, kept records of everyone here, organized sleeping arrangements, meal times, and jobs for everyone in the A, B, and C categories.

The A group was broken into three categories: A1s went on missions, A2s guarded the fields, and A3s stood guard in the watch towers. Bs worked in here with Padraic, doing medical stuff. He was the only B1. The nurses and Jack were B2s and anyone else with medical experience was a B3. And Cs did the everyday household chores that were very necessary, like cleaning and cooking. Though she wouldn't admit it, Raeya was the backbone of this place.

Hayden, on the other hand, refused to leave. When I woke up coughing that morning, he was slumped over in the armchair looking uncomfortable. "Do you need me to get the nurse?" he mumbled without even opening his eyes.

"No," I wheezed and swallowed a ball of mucus. "They're always right outside anyway. Go back to sleep. I think I will," I said slowly, still exhausted.

Hayden took my hand and gently rubbed this thumb in little circles on my palm. I feel asleep in minutes.

When I woke up a few hours later, Hayden was deep in conversation with someone. I opened my eyes just enough to see Fuller sitting in a chair near Hayden. Curious, I stayed still and listened to them talking.

"So there we are," Fuller said, his voice light with amusement, "frozen from the rain and scared shitless thinking we had found the bear again. But Aaron was so damned determined to shoot the thing we kept on the tracks. We were behind a mess of rocks and bushes; we couldn't see what the hell was in front of us. We hear more rustling so we dive around the weeds with our guns cocked and aimed."

"Did you get it?" Hayden asked.

Fuller laughed and shook his head. "Not the bear. We scared the shit out of some Girl Scouts. Turns out, there were never bear tracks. We had been hunting a troop of twelve-year-old girls the whole time." Both he and Hayden laughed. Fuller let out a breath and shook his head. "They were being taught how to distinguish different prints; their troop leader randomly stamped the ground with different animal prints for the girls to identify."

"I would have loved to see that," Hayden chuckled.

Fuller shook his head, the smile still on his face. I had never seen him look so genuinely happy before. Little wrinkles pulled up the skin around his gray eyes. He let out a breath and nodded. "You sure you're doing alright?" he asked Hayden, who quickly nodded. "You look like hell," he continued.

"I'm tired," Hayden confessed. "And stressed. And pretty fucking worried."

I closed my eyes when he turned to me.

"I should have been there," he said bitterly. "I should have kept her safe."

Fuller leaned forward, his face gentle and reassuring. "You can't blame yourself."

"Yes, I can," Hayden protested.

"I won't argue; I felt and still feel responsible for Carol's death." He paused and looked at me; I sensed his eyes on my face. "But Orissa is still here. She's strong. She's made it this far," he assured Hayden. "But I know how much she means to you. It's not easy to sit back and watch someone you love suffer. Believe me. There were so many times I prayed to switch places with Carol, so many times I wished I could take her cancer away." His voice grew softer as he spoke. "All you can do is be there with them; let them know you care. Carol told me that just knowing I was sitting by her side was better than any gift I ever bought her."

"You're right," Hayden agreed. "You really think she'll be ok?"

"She looks considerably better than she did a few days ago so yes, I do," Fuller said definitely. "She's a fighter, that's for sure," he said with a chuckle. "From the moment I met her I knew she was a tough one. She's a good match for you."

Hayden leaned back in the chair. "She is."

Fuller stood and took a few steps toward the curtain. "Let her know I send my thoughts and prayers. And let me know if you need anything. Seriously, Hayden. You're not alone here. Don't forget that."

"Thank you, sir."

Fuller shook his head. "You don't have to call me 'sir'," he reminded Hayden. "Take care." He smiled at Hayden and left the room.

I was rather shocked at just how close and open Hayden and Fuller were with each other. The Fuller I knew, and didn't like, was cold and cut throat. I never heard him talk about his family before. It was odd, kinda sad, and a little touching.

I coughed, blowing my cover of being asleep. Hayden immediately came to my bedside to see if I was ok. I sat up and assured him I was fine. He gave me my cup of water and fussed over me for a minute before leaving to go to the bathroom. I slowly shifted my weight to the side, trying to find a comfortable position. I huffed, growing more annoyed with my painful ribs each day. Shoes on the polished tile floor caught my attention. Hayden had only been gone a few seconds; I assumed it was Raeya or Padraic coming to tell me good morning.

"Morning," Dr. Cara said flatly and appeared beside the curtain.

Dammit. I was wrong.

"Morning," I replied, my voice breathy.

"You need blood work," she informed me.

"Again?" I asked, taking in her odd outfit of neon green leggings, a pleated, knee-length black skirt, and an oversized sweatshirt with the faded words 'World's #1 Dad' printed on the front. Her normally messy brown hair was brushed today and pulled into a tight bun on the top of her head.

"Yes."

"Why?" I questioned and pulled my arm out from under the covers so she could stick me.

"To see if the antibiotic helped. And to check your labs." She set a plastic pail on the bed and grabbed her supplies. "If it's good you can be disconnected from all this." Her eyes swept over the equipment. "And we won't have to wear masks around you anymore."

"Thank God," I sighed. I watched as she cleaned my arm, felt for a vein, and push the needle into my skin.

"Have you ever been exposed to the virus?" she asked suddenly.

I bit my lip. "Never directly," I said slowly.

"But you have?"

"I think so." I waited for her to continue until after she extracted the needle and put the little vials of blood in her pocket. I opened my mouth and then stopped. I had no reason to not trust Dr. Cara, but I had no reason to trust her either. "Why does it matter?" I finally asked.

"Just a theory," she mumbled and gathered up her supplies. "You had an anaphylactic reaction to something foreign," she explained shortly, not answering my question. "And your body was responding to some sort of infection before that." She shook her head. "But I couldn't find anything foreign in your blood."

My eyebrows pushed together. "What?"

"You had multiple infected injuries, but it wasn't bad enough to cause that kind of reaction. It was as if you were septic again if I've read your chart right."

"Oh," I said in response. My mind was too hazy to let the scary implications sink in. "Could it help if I had been exposed?" I started. "Help you with your research about the vaccine, I mean."

"Possibly. Have you been exposed to the virus?" she asked again, her voice picking up speed. I could tell that whatever theory she had made her excited.

"Well, I think so," I repeated. Not that long ago, Padraic told me that Hayden *is* infected with the zombie virus. It just doesn't make him sick. He was worried about me being around Hayden on missions since there was pretty much a guarantee that one of us would end up bleeding and had warned me on the dangers of coming into contact with Hayden's blood. I didn't tell him that I had come into contact with Hayden's blood many times…as well as his other bodily fluids.

Dr. Cara tipped her head. "What do you mean?"

"Hayden's infected," I began.

"I know that."

"Can he…" I cast my eyes down. "Is he contagious?"

She nodded. "Yes. Or at least I believe so. Unfortunately, I don't have a way to test that. But only through his blood. I have tested his saliva and not even a trace of the virus shows up. The virus is dormant inside him. The virus looks like this," she said and pulled out a sketch from her skirt pocket. An alien-looking chain of nastiness was messily drawn with smeared ink. "In a live—or dead, I guess—sample, the virus moves when looked at under a microscope," she simplified. "It's not alive or moving in a sample taken from Hayden."

"Oh, ok," I nodded. It made a little sense to me. "So if I got his blood on me, you're not sure if it would infect me?"

She shook her head. "It might stay dormant or it might come to life. Have you had blood contact on an open wound?"

I was sure I had, though I couldn't think of a time where I was positive that Hayden bled into a cut that I had. "And only his *blood* can transmit the virus?" I asked slowly.

Dr. Cara's eyes narrowed and she shook her head, not understanding. Then she inhaled sharply. "Oh. *Oohhh.* Well," she said causally. "I can ask him for a semen analysis. Then I'll let you know."

"I don't think he'll be too keen on that idea," I said softly and tried not to laugh at the thought of Dr. Cara handing Hayden a cup and a *Playboy*.

"How many times have you been exposed to his semen?" she asked professionally, not at all bothered by the subject matter.

I, on the other hand, didn't feel comfortable discussing my sex life with Crazy Cara. "Uh, more than once."

"Twice, three times?" she probed. "Because there could be a chance, like when Brad got bitten by the S1."

"Brock," I corrected. "And more than that. More times than I could, uh, recall."

"You better hope you don't get pregnant," she scolded and picked up her pail. "I won't mention it," she added before she left. "Girl Code Promise." For the first time, I saw her smile. With normal clothes and brushed hair, I thought she would look pretty.

"Thanks," I said and returned her smile. My body relaxed considerably when she left. I never wanted to have that talk again. It was almost as uncomfortable as the sex talk I got from my mom and stepdad when I was fifteen.

Hayden returned, with a bewildered expression on his face. He was holding a little plastic cup out in front of him as if it was full of red ants. He set it on the nightstand next to my bed and sat in the arm chair.

"Why?" he started, looking at the wall. "I'm confused."

"About what?" I pushed myself up.

"Dr. Cara told me I needed to make a, uh, deposit for her to analyze."

The horrified look on his face made me laugh—and then cough.

"What?" he asked and leaned forward. "Is there something wrong with me?"

"I'm sure everything is fine," I chuckled. "She didn't tell you why?"

Hayden quickly shook his head.

"She wanted to see if the zombie virus is the newest STD."

"Oh," he said, taken aback. "If it is then you're infected too."

"I know." I reached for my water. "Which is why I don't think it is. I'm honestly kinda curious," I admitted, gaining a scowl from Hayden. "My blood's been tested; there's not a trace of the virus in it."

Hayden nodded. "Good enough for me."

"What time is it?" I asked, hating not having a clock to look at.

"Almost eight," he told me. "Stop asking."

"I'm surprised I slept that long. Go get breakfast," I encouraged.

"Nah, I can eat in here."

"Go. Tell everyone 'hi' for me or something lame like that."

Hayden shrugged. "Alright. Want anything?"

I shook my head.

Hayden ran his hand over my cheek and pressed his forehead to mine; he still couldn't kiss me with the stupid mask on.

* * *

"Morning," Hayden said to me when I woke the next day. He had slept in the extra bed, doting on me all night. I vaguely remembered him leaving for breakfast.

"Up for some visitors?" he asked, pausing at the curtain.

"It depends on who it is," I said honestly.

Hayden smiled. "I think you'll like these guys."

I pushed myself up. Hayden slipped into the room and sat on the edge of the bed. Ivan, Wade, and Brock shuffled in, filling up the small room.

"Hey guys," I said with a smile. I had come to trust and rely on them; I felt almost brotherly bonds of friendship with the guys.

"Hey, Orissa," Brock replied. "You're looking better."

I nodded. "Thanks. I have no idea what I look like," I said as the thought dawned on me. I could feel the cuts and bruises on my face. If I looked *better* now then how horrible did I look before?

"Uh, you're not at your best," Ivan teased and flashed me a bright white smile.

"How are you feeling?" Wade asked and leaned against the nightstand.

"Shitty," I said, making them laugh. "They keep me pretty drugged up so I've been sleeping a lot."

Ivan and Brock sat in the two chairs near the bed.

"As if getting kidnapped, beaten, and making a narrow escape weren't enough," Ivan started, "you have to go and have a life threatening reaction. Admit it: you like torturing us."

I laughed, which turned into a cough. Wade elbowed Ivan. "Asshole, look what you've done," he teased.

Being around the guys brightened my mood, but it wasn't long before we all felt the sting of our incomplete group. Carefully, the conversation turned to Rider and his last moments.

Wade, who had become the closest to Rider, was having a hard time dealing with the loss of his friend. He wanted to know his partner went down fighting.

"He did," I assured him and my heart started to beat faster as I lied. "If it wasn't for him, I think they would have killed me too."

Wade blinked back his emotion. "He would have done anything for you—for any of us."

Brock nodded. "Yeah," he said heavily. "So would I."

Hayden slipped his fingers through mine. "Me too," he said.

Ivan nodded as well. "Semper Fi. And Penwell...what you endured for us, for all of us here at the compound..." he trailed off and looked away. "You're a damn fine Marine, Orissa," he concluded.

I smiled, unable to help the tears that pooled in my eyes. I looked down to hide them. Noticing my pain, Hayden gave my hand a gentle squeeze. I shook my head and wiped the tears away.

"I remember the first time I met you guys," I reminisced. "Rider had cut his leg on something. I thought he was a little asshole," I added with a laugh. "He must have been in a bad mood or something when we first met."

Wade smiled and looked into my eyes. "Oh yeah. He sliced his calf open on blades on a tractor. He was so pissed! We drove straight through that mission and we had literally just set up the camp and set out in search of survivors. And within fifteen minutes he was on the ground bleeding."

Ivan chuckled. "I think he was more pissed about ripping his camo pants. But he didn't let it slow him down. If he hadn't cut himself, we wouldn't have been forced to turn around and go back to our camp."

"And we wouldn't have found you," Hayden finished and looked at me. "I never thanked Rider for that," he added softly.

The guys stayed with me, talking about Rider and the revenge we couldn't wait to take on the assholes who'd killed him. After awhile Shanté nicely reminded them that I needed to rest. Hayden stayed with me for a while longer, not leaving until I was fast asleep.

I woke up covered in cold sweat from a nightmare about being locked in a padded room wearing a straightjacket. A zombiefied Rider crawled toward me, and I was unable to fight him off. I must have thrashed around because my blankets were on the floor. It took too much effort to pick them up so I just gently curled my legs up and waited for someone to come back into the room, the whole time replaying the horrid dream over in my head.

"You're shivering," Hayden's soft voice came from the hallway. I was so caught up in reliving my nightmare I hadn't heard him coming.

"I dropped the blankets," I said, hardening my expression. The air conditioner kicked on and the cool, crisp air made goosebumps break out across my skin. Hayden picked the blankets up, shook them out, and spread them over my body.

"Any better?" he asked.

"Yes," I lied and huddled under the covers. I coughed up sticky phlegm and reached for my water cup. I groaned when I remembered it was empty. Hayden snatched it from my grip and hurried to fill it up for me.

I took a long drink when he returned.

He set the cup back down and laced his fingers through mine.

"Your hands are cold," he told me.

"I can't get warm," I admitted.

"I'll get you another blanket," he offered. "Or put one in the dryer to warm it up."

"That would be nice."

Before Hayden could get up to leave, someone approached the curtained room. "Knock-knock," a voice spoke. A second later the curtain pulled open. "Hi, Orissa! Glad you're awake," Shanté exclaimed. "I've got good news; your labs came back *almost* normal!"

"So you can get rid of all this?" I asked hopefully, eyeing the many tubes and cables I was hooked up to.

"Everything but your IV, dear." She pushed a button on the heart monitor. "It will make getting up a lot easier."

"Yes," I agreed. Though my ventures were only to the chair across the room, I had almost tripped more than once. It only took a few minutes for her to remove the annoying lines. She reminded me twice that since I now needed to get up and walk to the bathroom, I was to call for help and *not* attempt to go on my own, which was bound to be annoying. But she delivered good news as well: my high white blood cell count was down and the masks weren't necessary anymore.

"Would you like anything for pain?" she asked.

I shook my head. "I'm ok right now," I told her, not wanting to be in a drug induced fog again.

"Do you need anything else before I go?" she asked.

"She's cold," Hayden answered for me.

"I noticed the goosebumps," Shanté said. "I'll put your blanket in the dryer. In the meanwhile, why don't you hop up there and cuddle with her? It'll help her warm up and make her happy," she directed toward Hayden.

"What? I-we-uh...we're not like that," Hayden sputtered.

Shanté put a hand on her hip and raised her eyebrow. "You think I haven't noticed? You haven't left her side since the moment you brought her down here. You offered to race off and get any medical supplies she needed. I've seen the way you look at her and," she said, opening the nightstand drawer to grab something, "she was wearing this." Hayden's dog tags dangled from her hand.

I wasn't even aware that my necklaces had been removed.

"You don't have to pretend around me. It's actually nice to see that something good came out of this mess." She set the tags down. "Keep her warm until I get back," she ordered with a smile. "Watch the IV line; she won't appreciate it if you pull them out." Shanté took the extra blanket and left the room.

I slowly moved to the left, giving Hayden enough room. He took off his shoes and got under the blankets with me. His body heat felt wonderful. Carefully, he put his arm behind me. I rested my head on his shoulder, feeling almost comfortable...until I coughed. I moved around again so I could put my hand on top of Hayden's. He stayed with me even after Shanté brought the warm blanket, keeping me company until he left for lunch.

CHAPTER SEVEN

I woke up the next morning with a start, my body painfully rigid. I sharply exhaled and winced, feeling the effects of the nightmare. My heart pounded and I ran shaky hands over my face. I had to remind myself that I wasn't in Eastmoore anymore. I could feel the IV line tug on my skin. I was in the hospital ward at the compound, safe and sound.

I shook my head; why was the fear still coursing through my veins? With a new appreciation of the strength it took Hayden to pull himself from his hellish nightmares, I drew in a ragged breath and leaned back.

"I still have nightmares, too," a soft voice came from beside me. I startled and Olivia apologized. "Was it about Delmont?" she asked softly.

I shook my head, not wanting to think about Delmont, the inbred creep who tried to hold me hostage, thinking it was his duty to repopulate the world. That's how I met Olivia; she had been taken captive there weeks before I showed up. I got us both out just in time. "Someone else."

I took another breath, not as deep as I'd like since pain stopped me. "I have had dreams about them, though. Usually I slit their throats."

She gave me a small smile. "That would be nice." With careful grace, she sat on the edge of the bed. "Who were you dreaming about?"

I bit my lip and cast my eyes down. "The people who kidnapped me," I said simply, not wanting to burden Olivia with my troubles.

"You've been kidnapped *and* held hostage," she said seriously.

"I know. What the fuck?" I asked rhetorically and with a shake of my head. I looked up into Olivia's green eyes and smiled. "I've been abandoned, held hostage, kidnapped, and tortured all while killing zombies and living in a bomb shelter." Suddenly my fear twisted into amusement and I burst into laughter. After a few seconds of looking at me as if I was infected and had gone crazy, Olivia laughed too.

Chest hurting, I put a hand over my broken ribs and stopped. "You know," I said to her. "I never put much thought into my future. But I never thought it would turn out like this."

She shyly put her hand on mine. "You've done pretty well. Besides ending up in here, I mean."

"I think that's debatable," I said with a sour frown.

She shook her head. "No, it's not. I wish I was more like you."

"No you don't," I snorted. "I've made a lot of mistakes."

"Who hasn't?" she pressed. "And I don't think you have since I've known you at least."

"I suppose that's true," I told her. "Still, there is a lot I wish I could redo."

"Me too," she said with too much emotion. It tugged on my heart to see someone so young and innocent want a do-over on life—already. She chewed the inside of her cheek and cast her eyes nervously at me. I could tell she wanted to say something but was afraid to.

"What's wrong?" I asked.

She shook her head. "It's just something Sonja told me last night. It doesn't matter, I suppose."

"That's not an 'it doesn't matter, I suppose' face," I egged on. "You can tell me, Olivia. I won't say anything if you don't want me to."

"Oh, I know," she promised as if she had offended me. "I trust you, totally! Probably more than anyone," she added with a nod. "It's just that...well..." she trailed off and tightly crossed her arms over her chest. Her body language let me know she was embarrassed to say what she was about to. "Are you a virgin?" she finally asked.

I almost laughed. "No, I'm not."

"I don't think I am, either."

"Think?" I questioned before it dawned on me that her first time hadn't been by choice. Delmont's brother Beau had the same womanizing ideations about repopulating the world. I got out before Del put his plan to action but Olivia...Olivia hadn't and she had been raped. Repeatedly. Rage flowed through my veins.

My hit list was getting long. I needed to start picking off the assholes who were on it. "Oh, well I guess physically you're not."

Tears brimmed her green eyes. "That's what Sonja said. I want to think I am since I didn't have control over it. I want my first time to be special and now it never will be because he took it from me!" Fat tears rolled down her cheeks. I scooted forward and wrapped my arms around Olivia. Her body shook as she tried to control the volume of her soft sobbing.

"It's ok," I said automatically and lifted my left hand to run it over her hair. The IV line was pulled as far as it could go and I awkwardly had to stop my hand at her ear. She leaned into me, her tears soaking the front of my make-shift hospital gown. "It's ok," I soothed again before realizing how stupid it was to say that. It wasn't ok. What was done to her was *far* from ok. With a heavy sob, she untangled her arms from around herself and placed them around me in a hug. I tensed when her arms brushed my sore ribs.

"It's good to get those things off your chest," I told her, feeling like the world's biggest hypocrite. I shoved the horrible memory of killing Rider down into the place where the rest of my repressed memories were stored. "And to be honest, when you do find someone that you, uh, want to get close to, it will feel just as special. Not because it's the first time, but because you care about that person so much it makes it special, no matter what."

"Really?"

"Yes," I said definitely, thinking of the first time Hayden and I slept together. It happened in a burst of long awaited passion and we were both focused on desperately removing each other's clothes as fast as possible, but there was something else I felt too. Nerves maybe? Though I felt nothing but comfortable around Hayden. No...it was something else. Something that made my body tingle in a different way than from his touch.

"Do you remember your first time?" she asked rather sheepishly.

"Yeah," I said with a smirk. "I was a senior in high school. I was dating this guy named Chase. He was older than me and had an apartment in town; I thought he was hot shit." I laughed. "Anyway, my first time was on his nasty apartment floor. He was heavy on top and kept breathing in my face; his breath smelled like the burrito he just ate."

Olivia laughed.

"It was awful."

EMILY GOODWIN

I coughed and leaned back against the bed. "Really, though, if you find someone you want to do that with, they should care about you enough to overlook the past and not hold it against you. If they do, well, then they are a dick and you deserve better," I said, wondering if she was crushing on a boy at the compound.

She nodded. "I want to be in love if I ever do again."

"It's better when you are," I blurted and felt my cheeks redden. "But it's slim pickings. Damn you, zombies," I joked and held up a fist. "But who knows? Maybe you'll find someone now. It's possible, I suppose."

She cast her eyes down and tried not to smile.

"What?" I finally pried.

"I know," she said so quietly I almost didn't hear her.

"Know what?" I asked. The curtain was pulled back suddenly. We both jerked up to see Raeya's smiling face.

"Hey guys," she said brightly. "How are you feeling, Riss?"

"Ok," I told her.

Olivia withdrew her hand and smoothed her hair. She smiled at me before quietly excusing herself.

"Is she alright?" Raeya asked.

I nodded. "It's gonna take her a long time to heal." I locked eyes with my best friend. "After I kill every single prick at the state hospital, I'm going back for those inbred, nasty waste-of-human-life hillbillies."

"Yes," she said shortly. I had expected her to object and to tell me to be reasonable. "Can you just lead a herd of zombies to them and safely escape this time?" she asked with a half smile.

"I like that plan," I told her. My arms went around myself as I was pushed into another coughing fit. "Ew," I said as I spit a ball of phlegm into a tissue. Raeya grimaced and looked away. She handed me my cup of ice water. "Thanks," I said and took a sip.

She smiled and looked at something next to me. "That was really sweet of him," she said quietly.

"What was swee—" I cut off when a bouquet of dandelions came into view. I twisted around to get a better look. What had to be over two dozen bright yellow weeds had been tied together and stuck in a water glass. The corners of my lips pulled up in a smile. Only two people in the compound knew my odd love for dandelions and how I considered them flowers and not weeds, and one of them was in the room with me. "Ok, that is sweet," I admitted.

"He really loves you," Raeya stated. "Speaking of, where is

- 88 -

he?"

"Fuller made him go back to training. Ya know, since I'm not actively dying anymore he said it's 'unprofessional and unnecessary' for Hayden to stay down here with me all day."

Raeya frowned. "I thought he knew about you guys."

"He does," I assured her. "But I kinda agree with him. Not that it's unprofessional or anything. Hayden has to be bored out of his mind just sitting here."

Raeya opened her mouth to tell me otherwise when Karen came into the little room. She did a quick assessment; she said my lungs sounded a little better than yesterday.

"Good," I said genuinely. "Can I shower then? I haven't since…since before I left for the mission." I shook my head and wrinkled my nose in disgust.

Karen straightened up as she thought. "You did get a bed bath when you were unconscious," she informed me. "But I don't blame you for wanting to shower. But it would make me feel better if someone helped you in and out."

"That's fine with me," I said, feeling so grimy I didn't care if she assisted me. I mentally yelled at myself for not waiting until Shanté was my nurse; I was sure she would have had no problem if Hayden was my shower assistant.

"If you'd feel more comfortable with your friend helping you, that's fine with me," Karen suggested.

I turned to Raeya.

"That's fine with me, too," she informed us.

"Great," Karen said and lowered a side rail. "Do you feel up to moving to the chair?" she asked hopefully. I nodded and let her assist me to the uncomfortable armchair. She said she would come get me for a shower in about an hour.

Olivia came back in and changed the sheets and blankets on my bed and Raeya filled up my water cup the second it was empty. As annoying and impractical as it was to be out of commission, it was almost nice to have everything done for me.

Raeya was showing me the layout of the cabins that were currently being built when Hayden entered the small room. He was still hot and sweaty from working out and his ear buds hung around his neck, playing country music.

"Hey, Riss," he said with a smile.

I smiled back, instantly reminded of how attractive Hayden was when he was doing something physical. "Hi. How was training?"

He shrugged. "It kinda felt good to get back into it."

"I'm looking forward to it," I groaned. "Though it won't be for a freaking long ass time."

He gave me a reassuring half smile. "I'll start you off slow."

"You stink," Raeya observed.

"That happens," Hayden laughed.

"Ray is one of those people who likes to quit her workout *before* she gets too sweaty," I teased.

"I am," she admitted. "I hate feeling sweaty. It makes my skin all itchy!"

We all laughed...well, they laughed and I coughed.

"I just wanted to stop by before I went upstairs," he said. "Do you need anything?"

"Actually, yeah," I told him. "Can you bring me clean pajamas? I'm allowed to shower today. Finally!"

He smiled. "Yeah, I can do that. I'll be right back."

Fifteen minutes later, Hayden returned. "Sorry," he told me. "Theresa stopped me."

"Treasure," I said. "Her name is Treasure, Hayden." Then I felt the blood drain from my face and ice shoot through my veins. Had she told Hayden about what she had seen me do to Rider? Suddenly, I saw doubt and question in his eyes. My heart sped up with nerves. What would he think of me, knowing what I had done?

"She says 'hi'," he said dryly. "She really is annoying and very odd."

"Yes," I said with a breath of relief. "She is."

"Here." Hayden layed the pajamas at the foot of the bed.

"Those are yours," I dumbly stated.

"I know," he said with a grin. "You had no clean clothes. I already put your laundry in the washer."

"Thanks." I yawned. "I had intended to do laundry when we came back," I lied.

"Oh yeah, sure," Hayden said sarcastically. He bent over the chair and kissed me. His lips were salty with dried sweat. "I'll come back later."

"And I'll be clean," I reminded him. After he left, Raeya dove back into explaining the cabins and gardens. Finally, Karen came in to tell me I could shower.

* * *

Once in the shower, with Raeya waiting just outside the curtain, it didn't take long before my breath caught in my chest and my lungs ached. After washing quickly, I pushed myself up and turned the water off.

"You're done already?" Raeya asked.

I muttered an incoherent reply and wrapped my arms around myself.

"Riss?" Her voice carried an undertone of worry.

I inhaled, choking back a sob. Without warning, Raeya pulled back the curtain, towel in hand. She wrapped it around me. "Are you hurt?"

I shook my head and gripped the towel, pulling it tightly around myself. My lip quivered in my attempt not to cry.

"You're scaring me, Riss. Should I get Karen?" she asked and turned to the door.

"No," I whispered. I looked up into her frightened brown eyes. "Rider," I mumbled in explanation.

"Oh, Rissy. I'm so sorry."

I cast my eyes down, my vision blurring with tears. "I...I..." I trailed off. I took a breath to steady my emotions; the pain was sobering. "I killed him," I whispered harshly and closed my eyes. Tears ran down my cheeks.

"No, Riss, you can't take the blame for it. Ivan told me what happened. He heard the shot. It must have been so terrible, Riss, but it's not your—"

"I killed him!" I said through clenched teeth. "I stuck a knife in his brain!"

Raeya shot back. "No. W-why would you...oh my God. Did he...?"

I shivered. "He turned."

"Oh. Oh my God," she said to herself. Stunned, she stood with her hand over her mouth for a few seconds. Then her arms flew around me. Shaking her head, she soothed me. "Orissa, I am so, so sorry. He turned," she repeated. "Oh my God." She let go of me and straightened up. Putting her hands over mine, she looked me in the eye. "You didn't kill him. You let him die. He's free now; in a better place. Remember," she said quickly, her eyes going misty, "that we promised to do the same for each other."

I nodded. "I should have brought him back. We could have done something!"

"No," she said gently. "There is nothing we could have done.

Rider wouldn't have wanted to be in that...in that condition. If he could, he would thank you, Riss."

I nodded again. Raeya was right. I knew it; I had known it all along. I closed my eyes again and exhaled. "I feel better telling someone."

She tipped her head. "Hayden doesn't know?"

"No. I didn't tell anyone."

"Riss," she scolded with motherly love. "Will you stop being such a martyr?" When I didn't reply she laughed. "You don't have to hold in all this pain. You need to open up. And...I think Hayden will be hurt if you don't tell him."

I shook my head. "I don't want him to know what I did."

"If the roles were reversed would you think less of him?"

"No, but—"

"See?" she butted in. "Now come on, you're cold."

I nodded.

* * *

Later, after I was dressed in Hayden's pajamas and tucked into my hospital bed, Raeya stood. "I'll stop by tonight," she promised. "Make sure you tell Hayden about Rider," she added.

"No," I said stubbornly.

"Tell him or I will," she threatened. "Keeping that from him will start to bother you—we both know it will."

The hospital ward door opened and clicked shut. Footfalls echoed off the empty walls. "He doesn't need to know," I urged.

"Yes, he does. Hayden will be mad if you *don't* tell him."

"What will I be mad about?" Hayden asked, stopping outside the pulled back curtain.

Dammit, Raeya.

A grin was plastered on his face, but his hazel eyes showed concern.

"Nothing," I muttered.

Raeya pressed her lips together and gave me a wide-eyed stare. "See ya later, Rissy."

"Bye," I sighed.

Hayden was carrying a tray with a can of pop, a bag of microwaved popcorn, and a plate of sliced tomatoes. Previously, I would have thought it was an odd combination, but here at the compound it didn't faze me. "Can I have some?" I asked, eyeing the tomatoes. I hadn't eaten anything grown from our gardens yet.

"Yeah," he said and set the tray down. "I salted them."

"I only eat them with salt," I informed him. I reached for one, picking the biggest slice. It tasted wonderful. Fresh fruit and vegetables were definitely something I had taken for granted. I had been having a hard time stomaching all of the preservatives and added crap in the prepackaged and canned food we had been eating. Chewing the locally grown tomato amazing.

"What was Raeya talking about?" he asked and popped a slice in his mouth.

"Nothing," I said with my mouth full. I wiped tomato juice off of my chin and reached for another piece.

"I don't believe that," he said shortly.

"Fine. Don't believe me." I bent my slice in half and took a bite.

"Riss," he urged.

"Hayden," I spat back, getting angry. I finished my slice and sighed. "Sorry," I told him and shook my head. "It's just something that happened. I don't want to talk about it."

"Oh, wow, really narrowed it down there," he snapped sarcastically. "I'm not going to play that stupid game."

"What stupid game?" I asked and licked the tomato juice and salt from my fingers.

"The game you women play where you say something is wrong but you don't want to talk about it. Though really you do. I'm not prying it out of you."

I felt angry again. "No. You asked me. I didn't bring anything up. *You* did."

"You're the one that said 'it's something that happened.'"

"So?" I crossed my arms, realized it was painful to do so, and folded my hands in my lap. "Something did happen. And I *don't* want to talk about it."

"Yeah right," he said with a roll of his eyes. "I know how this goes. You say that, I listen to *exactly* what you say, and you'll be complaining to Raeya how I don't care about your feelings."

"I'll be complaining to Raeya about how you're an—" I was cut off by Karen clearing her throat.

"Hi, Orissa," she said softly. "I'm just checking on you; do you feel any pain?"

"No," I lied, not wanting my brain to slip into a murky haze of confusion.

"Alright." She nodded and said she'd come back to check on

me later.

I coughed and looked at Hayden. His face was set and he looked pissed...or maybe scared. Scared that whatever I was going to tell him was bad.

"It was something that happened at Eastmoore," I said quietly.

"What happened? Did they—" He jumped up and moved to the bed. "Did they—they touch you?" he asked looking as if he might get sick.

"No," I said quickly, shaking my head. "Well they did, but not like that."

Hayden put his hands on my shoulders and locked eyes with me. "Are you sure?" His voice shook with anger.

"Yes. They didn't rape me," I said slowly, knowing Hayden needed to hear what he couldn't bring himself to ask. "It was something I did."

Hayden slid his hands down my shoulders and onto my wrists.

I turned my head down. "I saw Rider get shot. Then they took me away." I felt too numb to cry. "I assumed he died where they left him." I shook my head. "He didn't. And..." I took a breath. "He must have gotten away because...because he turned."

"Turned?" Hayden questioned. "What did he—oh, shit." He tightened his hands around mine.

"I didn't want to do it," I said and unwelcome tears pooled in my eyes. "But I couldn't leave him like that."

Hayden moved next to me and gently cradled me in his arms.

"I killed him," I whispered.

"Shh," he soothed. "No you didn't." His voice was tight and his body was tense.

"Yes," I protested. "I plunged a knife into his brain! Through his ear."

Hayden's breathing became rapid and he grimaced at the thought of what I had done.

"I didn't want to tell you because I didn't want you to think I was a monster," I said, my voice breaking.

Hayden hugged me tighter. "You're not a monster, Orissa," he said so softly I could barely hear him. "I'd want you to do the same for me....and I'd do it for you. We talked about it, remember?" He shook his head. "I hate that you had to do that. I hate that you have to do any of it." He rested his head on mine. I was on the verge of coming unhinged. I snaked my arms around

Hayden, focusing on the physical pain I was in. More phlegm worked its way out of my lungs and I was forced to let go of Hayden and lean forward to cough it up. We resituated and Hayden resumed holding me.

"You're not a monster," he repeated. "You did the right thing," he affirmed.

Hearing it from him brought me more relief. I rested my head on his chest. Exhausted, I closed my eyes. Hayden stroked my hair, relaxing my stressed body. I tried to fight it but was asleep in minutes.

What a fucking emotional day.

CHAPTEREIGHT

The first place I went after my unofficial discharge from the compound's hospital was to Rider's memorial. I lost track of just how long I was in there, but it felt like forever. Padraic didn't want me to leave until the pneumonia cleared up. I still had an annoying cough but I felt much, much better. I had been told—repeatedly—that I was to spend most of my time resting and to avoid strenuous activates. Since I was still in pain from my healing fractures, I had no issues obliging.

Hayden held my hand as we slowly walked through the tall grass. We sat down in the sun several feet in front of the wooden plaque. Raeya was right; the carvings were beautiful. Squinting in the sun, I stared at it, mentally thanking Rider for everything he had done for us.

Not worn out just yet, I detoured to the outside dog runs to visit with Argos. I sat on a bag of dog food and watched Hayden throw a ball. Several other dogs joined in on the game, which turned into playful fighting over the tennis ball. Hayden's favored dog, a female German Shepherd named Greta, nuzzled against him as the other dogs ran around. When the weather was nice, the dogs spent most of the day outside playing. They all seemed to enjoy it, and Jones, an A3 who was the primary caregiver for the dogs, had told me that it was really interesting to see that a pack had formed.

But keeping the dogs outside had another benefit; they had the keen ability to detect zombies from far away. Even little dogs were able to sense the undead. If the dogs weren't outside playing or unknowingly keeping watch, they were inside with their families. It wasn't uncommon to go into the community rooms and see several dogs lounging around.

Though I was no big fan of Fuller, I had to give him credit for allowing people to bring their pets. If I had been told Argos wouldn't have been allowed in with me, I doubted I would have come at all. We had dogs, cats, ferrets, and two guinea pigs inside the compound walls. Raeya told me she thought someone had a parrot, but we'd yet to see—or hear—it.

"Do you still want to shower before dinner?" Hayden asked me. I nodded. "Then we better get going." He helped me up and inside, and insisted on sneaking into the shower with me, though he didn't have to sneak. Alex, Mac, Noah, Jose, Gabby, and Mike—a newly promoted A1 who was taking Jessica's place— had come back from their find-animal-feed mission with exciting news and were still in quarantine.

They had discovered a farm several hours north of here that was void of people but full of animals and a barn and hay. Fuller was more than eager to expand our own supply of milk, eggs, and meat. It would take several days to haul the animals, farm supplies, and feed and hay, but it was worth putting off the 'kill the bastards at Eastmoore' mission. Plus, it gave me an extra week to heal and hope to tag along.

I ate dinner in the cafeteria for the first time since the mission. It was also the first time that the residents of the compound got to see me. Padraic had created a strict 'no visitors' rule since he knew that there were only a handful of people I wouldn't be annoyed with. I was forever grateful for that.

I was bombarded with condolences and well wishes by almost everyone who saw me. I smiled politely and said a pressed 'thank you' and wished to be left alone. My ribs still hurt and I was tired; the last thing I wanted to do was please a bunch of people who really didn't know me.

I was looking forward to stretching out in my own bed. The small hospital bed was less than comfortable. Both windows in our room were open, allowing the fragrant night air to softly blow in. A chorus of crickets and frogs surround the large, old estate. Being above ground felt so right. I didn't know how some of the residents handled staying down in the safety of the bomb shelter. It would drive me to insanity.

I kicked off my shoes and slowly tugged my jeans off, still having difficulty bending over. I took a breath and braced for pain as I pulled my shirt over my head. In only my bra and underwear, I climbed under the blankets, thinking about how much I missed the outdoors.

Raeya had told me that there were a handful of people who

refused to leave the C and B levels of the compound. A while ago, a very secure fence had been added to the already fenced in property of the old estate to allow the residents a chance to get some fresh air and not feel so trapped. Those same people weren't happy that whoever got to go outside wasn't considered a threat for infection.

She told me of one family in particular who had three children. She had seen the children begging and crying on more than one occasion, wanting to go outside with their friends. Both parents refused. It boggled my mind how they could be so ignorant about the virus. Yes, what we knew was extremely limited, but we narrowed it down enough to know that you needed person to zombie contact to get it. Or person to zombie body fluid covered object contact…they didn't need to know that.

"Going to bed already?" Hayden asked as he stepped into the room.

"I still have to brush my teeth," I replied. "Then yes."

"It's eight-thirty," he said with a laugh.

"I'm used to doing nothing all day," I reminded him. "I'm tired," I said shortly.

"Alright, fine. Go brush your teeth now; you'll want to do it even less five minutes from now."

I groaned but knew he was right. I pushed the blankets off and slowly stood. I felt Hayden's eyes on me.

"What?" I asked and went to the dresser to get a pair of pajamas. He stepped over to me and tipped his head.

"You look good."

I raised an eyebrow. "Why do you sound so surprised about that?"

"Because I keep expecting you to still be covered in bruises and cuts. It still surprises me how fast you heal."

I shook my head and looked down at my torso. "They're almost gone." I traced my fingers lightly over the greenish-blue marks. "But this," I said and held up my left arm, "will be scarred for life." A nasty pink line ran almost the entire length of my forearm. I frowned at it, hating that every time I saw it I would be reminded of what I went through. I flipped my arm over and looked at the white line on the inside of my wrist. That cut had been my own doing, but by almost bleeding to death, I'd distracted a herd of zombies and saved Hayden. This had been awhile ago now.

He put his hands on my waist, careful not to press his body

against mine. "I wish you were better," he exhaled. I smiled and wrapped my arms around his neck.

"I'm good enough," I whispered and leaned in to kiss him. He tipped his head and pressed his lips to mine. Hungry for more, I moved my hand to the back of his head and pulled him closer, exploring his mouth with my tongue. Hayden's hand slipped from my waist and onto my butt. Giving it a squeeze he inched closer.

A soft moan escaped me and I let go of Hayden for an instant. I resituated my hands on his waist, working on unbuttoning his jeans. Once the fly was down, I stuck my hand inside and took a hold of him. He exhaled and took a step back, pushing me against the dresser.

He moved his mouth from my lips to my neck as I worked my hands. I tipped my head back and shivered in pleasure. With my other hand, I tried yanking Hayden's pants down but wasn't having much luck. Impatient, he let go of me and pulled them off. Stepping out of them, he took me in his arms and lifted me onto the dresser.

My body tensed in pain and a strangled cry escaped my lips. Hayden froze, his breath still hot on my neck. The pain subsided after a few seconds and I resumed right where we left off. But Hayden didn't.

"What's wrong?" I asked.

"I hurt you," he said guiltily.

"I'm fine now," I promised and wrapped my legs around him. I tightened my muscles, wanting to pull him close. He resisted, and the slight strain was painful. "I'm fine," I repeated.

"I don't want to hurt you," he said but continued to nuzzle my neck.

"You won't." I closed my eyes and urged Hayden closer. This time he took a step, pressing himself against me. I liked the position we were in. But leaning slightly back to avoid crushing my fragile rib cage wasn't comfortable at all. "But let's move to the bed," I begrudgingly stated. Hayden hooked his arms around mine and helped me make a graceful landing.

We got under the covers; Hayden angled his body so he was slightly over top of me. Holding himself up, he kissed me. I took a hold of his waist and pulled him over before pushing him down. His skin against mine sent more shivers. I closed my eyes at the pain it caused to arch my back and remove my underwear. Panting, I dropped myself back onto the bed.

And then I had to push Hayden's face away as I suddenly

couldn't resist the urge to cough.

"Sorry," I mumbled.

Hayden laughed. "This is so romantic, isn't it?"

"Oh yeah," I agreed with a chuckle. "I'm coughing in your face and you're worried about my broken ribs. Such a turn on."

He lowered his head and sucked at my neck. "It's not a turn off," he whispered and I laughed. "Is that bad?"

"No," I whispered back. "Because it isn't for me either."

He grabbed a condom from inside his nightstand and quickly put it on before laying over me again. I opened my legs wider and pulled him to me. I ran my nails over Hayden's back, down along his sides, and over his butt. He quietly groaned and lowered himself onto me.

If I kept my upper body relatively flat and still, I felt no pain. Awkwardly, I pushed myself up so I could reach Hayden, my lips finding the side of his neck. I gently bit at him, knowing he loved that. He rubbed himself against me until I couldn't take it any longer. I reached down and guided him inside.

Hayden kept his body close to mine but was careful not to inflict pain. I wrapped my hands around his biceps as my breathing quickened. He continued to kiss me, which wasn't something we usually did...unless he was trying to get to me stop loudly moaning. Though this time, I coughed more than moaned.

I tightened my legs around Hayden's waist, pushing him deeper inside. My body hummed with pleasure that soon grew to the point of blocking out any pain. Hayden stopped kissing me and lowered himself onto his forearms. He tangled his fingers in my hair.

I began rocking my hips, too deep into bliss for pain to register. I pressed my nails into Hayden's back, dragging them down when he kissed the base of my neck. I snaked one arm down and put it on the back of his head, gently running my fingers over his hair. Hayden let out a deep, satisfied breath and put his mouth over mine.

I broke apart for air and slid my hand down to cup Hayden's face. I opened my eyes and looked at him; the feeling I had been trying to describe to Olivia welled inside of me. A moment later Hayden's eyes opened, locking with mine.

"Orissa," Hayden breathed. Hearing the allure in his voice almost pushed me over the edge. "I love you," he whispered. Our bodies rocked in perfect rhythm. I closed my eyes and clung to him. My legs squeezed against Hayden's waist and my back arched in pleasure. Hayden came just seconds after I did.

Panting, he rested his body on top of mine out of habit. I flinched; he quickly rolled off. I resituated so he could wrap his arms around me. I folded mine on top of his, intertwining our fingers.

"I love you, too," I said quietly.

Hayden kissed my cheek and I smiled. Pain was starting to filter through the pleasure- drunken endorphins and I couldn't catch my breath. But for the first time in a long time, I felt content. And I knew it just wasn't from the physical aspect of it all.

Hayden pulled the blanket over us, making sure I was tucked in. He ran his hand over my hair and kissed me once more. Happy to be in my own bed next to the man I loved, I drifted into a comfortable, peaceful sleep.

* * *

"Riss!" Raeya called when she walked into the cafeteria the next morning. Ivan was by her side. "It's so good to see you down here again!"

"I'm glad to be back," I said honestly and sat down at my usual spot in the back. "I forgot how much I missed the florescent lights and tasteless food," I joked. She sat down next to me. "Aren't you gonna get a tray?" I asked.

"Ivan said he'd get it," she told me casually. I smirked and raised an eyebrow. Ray kicked me under the table. I flinched, pretending like she actually hurt me. Her cheeks flushed and she apologized. "Stop," she whispered. "It's not like that."

"Like what?" I teased and stirred my oatmeal. I had decided to save my single strawberry for last. "You guys were getting it on last night too?"

"No!" she said loudly. Hayden glanced up and Raeya shook her head at him. "And what do *you* mean, 'too'?"

"We had sex," I told her. "Nothing new there."

"Should you be doing that?" She was suddenly concerned. "You're supposed to rest."

"Relax," I told her and downed a spoonful of oatmeal. "I was on the bottom."

She sighed and shook her head. "You would, Riss."

I laughed, coughed, and winced. After clearing my throat and getting a drink, I assured her I was ok. "Actually," I whispered, "it was the most intimate sex we'd ever had. It was weird and...and kinda nice."

Raeya rolled her eyes and smiled. "I'm starting to get jealous of you two."

"Why be jealous? You can have your own zombie-killing solider." I turned my head in Ivan's direction.

"No." She shook her head. "He's nice and attractive and I like him, but I'm just not..." she trailed off. She wasn't ready for a new relationship yet. I knew Raeya would have a hard time starting something new when she had lost her long-time boyfriend Seth not that long ago.

"Time," I said and turned back to my food. She stiffly smiled and nodded. Ivan joined us, giving Raeya her tray. The guys talked about their 'awesome' video gaming last night while Raeya and I chatted about mundane, compound business.

"I don't like those two hanging around each other," Brock said, catching my attention. "I get a bad feeling about it."

I followed his eyes and saw Treasure walking next to Jarrod, a young man who attempted to shoot us and take our supplies a awhile ago. Ivan shot and killed Jarrod's partner in crime and I landed an arrow through Jarrod's arm, rendering him useless in trying to harm us. We didn't know what else to do with him so we brought him back and left his fate up to Fuller. He had decided to give Jarrod a chance since, after all, the residents had no access to weapons and Jarrod was out numbered over three hundred to one; Fuller didn't view him as a threat. Still, Jarrod made no attempts to socialize with anyone and even avoided the group he had spent months surviving with.

"It is odd," Raeya noted. "Of all the people, why would she buddy up with him?"

"Maybe it's because they're both outcasts," Wade suggested. "Though Treasure never tried to kill us."

I waved my hand in the air. "Let 'em. She's annoying anyway."

Brock spent another few seconds watching Jarrod and Treasure speak in hushed voices before he shrugged and went back to his food.

* * *

I spent the rest of the morning with Raeya, Sonja, and Olivia. We sat in the community game room, attempting to play poker. Treasure and Jarrod slunk in the room almost unnoticed and took a spot in a corner by a bookshelf. I felt eyes on me and looked up to find Jarrod starring. He quickly turned his face down. Treasure's eyes went wide and she madly shook her head. Jarrod put his hand on hers and whispered something to her.

Part of me was curious as to what they were talking about. The other half didn't care. Brock's words echoed in my head. I didn't get the best feeling about those two being BFFs either, but I didn't see how it could cause any harm.

When my friends and I stood and put the cards away, Treasure scuttled over.

"Hey Hay—Orissa," she said quietly. "How are you feeling?"

"Not great but not terrible," I said honestly. "It's nice to get back to normal...well, if this were normal."

"That's good," she said and nervously picked at a scab on her elbow. "So you're probably planning on going back out, right? What are you gonna do?"

Raeya smiled. "We don't discuss missions openly," she explained with perfect grace. "I don't even know the details and I help determine where the A1s go and what they bring back."

"Oh," Treasure said with a deep exhale. "What about Eastmoore?" she blurted.

Thinking she was scared, I assured her, "They won't hurt anyone anymore."

Terror flashed over her face for just a second. "Oh, good." She forced a smile and turned around, shuffling her feet as she hurried toward Jarrod.

"What was that about?" Sonja asked me in a hushed voice.

"Beats me," I told her. "I would have thought she was scared the guys at the asylum would find her, but her body language says otherwise." I shook my head. "Who knows? Her brain is so fried from drugs it's hard to read her." I watched Treasure twitch and pace as she talked to Jarrod, unable to sit down.

"Come on," Sonja said with a wave. "Let's go to lunch; I'm hungry."

The four of us filed into the cafeteria, taking our trays and joining Padraic and a young woman named Maya at a table. Maya had long, flowing hair, fair skin splattered with pale freckles, and believed that demons were the cause of the zombie outbreak. It surprised me to see her and Padraic deep in conversation.

Not liking my back facing the door, I sat on Padraic's other side. Maya was talking to Padraic about herbal remedies. As much as I wanted to scoff at her, my grandma swore by her homeopathic medicine. Slightly interested, I paid attention to what Maya was saying while keeping an eye on the door.

I smiled involuntarily when Hayden and Ivan walked in, talking and laughing. They took their trays and sat in the back. Hayden waved me over. I dumped my tray and sat down across from him.

"Fuller wants to talk to you tonight after dinner," he said with his mouth full.

"About Eastmoore?" I asked hopefully.

Hayden nodded and finished chewing. "Yeah. Now that the others are back, things are a-go."

"Yes," I said with a wicked smile.

"Don't get too excited," Ivan reminded me, his voice smooth and professional. His dark eyes were apologetic. "You're not ready yet, Penwell."

I shook my head and rolled my eyes. I was really getting sick of being reminded that I wasn't healed. As if the constant pain wasn't enough.

* * *

Time crept by. 'After dinner' turned out to mean after *everyone* was done eating, not just us. I didn't have much faith in Fuller; I had been mentally preparing my arguments while I ate my spaghetti. Not everyone ate at the same time since the number of residents had grown too big for the cafeteria. Technically, A1s didn't have a set schedule since we couldn't guarantee everyday would be the same, but we usually ate with the first group since I was always hungry and my friends ate then as well.

I didn't know everyone's name, but I was familiar with their faces. Unfortunately, Lauren Hill was scheduled for this hour, the most selfish person I'd ever rescued. I momentarily considered using her as bait in our plan of attack on Eastmoore. I sighed, knowing no one else would go for it.

Speaking of the residents from Eastmoore, where was Treasure? I looked around the sea of faces and didn't find her. I assumed everyone who ate breakfast and lunch first would also eat dinner first. Maybe not. I let the thought go and focused on the best ways to surreptitiously ensure the deaths of everyone in Eastmoore.

The A1s moved to the theater room after dinner to wait for Fuller. Jason approached me, making polite small talk before carefully asking if I knew when a new A1 would be picked.

"I'm not sure," I said honestly. "It took a while for Mike to move up after Jessica died," I added softly.

"Do you think I have a chance?" he asked hopefully.

I smiled and internally groaned. I liked Jason. He had been with me since the beginning of this whole mess. He was a nice boy; young, innocent, loyal, and willing to do whatever he could to take care of his friends. And I knew his sister, Sonja, desperately did *not* want him out in the zombie-infested world. I couldn't blame her. "Probably," I told him.

He beamed. "Awesome. It would be great to go back out with you, Riss."

"Yeah, awesome," I said distantly. It was awesome to see your friends die.

"Fuller's here," Jason whispered and stood, formally nodding at the former Marine Coronel. I stood as well, impatiently waiting as Fuller made nice with the residents. Finally, he waved at me to follow him into his office. Being polite for once, he pulled out a chair for me to sit in.

"Alright. Tell me what happened," he began and moved to the other side of his desk.

"Ok," I said and closed my eyes, forcing any emotion from my heart so I could flatly tell the story.

"What did you tell them?" Fuller interrupted when I reached the part where Dre had me tied up and tortured for info.

"Not a damn thing," I spat. "Or else I wouldn't have been beaten within inches of my life!" I stared daggers at Fuller. "I stuck with the story that Rider and I were alone."

"And they didn't believe you?"

"Of course not." I raised my eyebrows. "Hence the beating." My heart was thumping in anger. I shook my head. "They are ruthless and will do whatever it takes to get what they want. And what they want is supplies and weapons. They're desperate."

"How do you know?" Fuller asked, though this time his tone carried curiosity, not questioning.

"When Rider—" I stopped, realizing I'd have to tell the entire truth. My brain buzzed with a way to avoid the subject all together. "They kill their own. I saw a guy kill his friend to cover up his own mistake. And they locked up another guy who wanted to leave, with the intentions of letting him starve to death. I think they're afraid of anyone knowing their location."

Fuller nodded. "The girl you brought back," he started,

"assumed there were about a hundred people there."

I shook my head. "I don't know. I didn't get to see much of it being locked in a seclusion room."

Fuller sighed and rubbed his left elbow. "Before you get upset, know that I already spoke to Underwood, as well as the others on your mission, about going back and eliminating the threat. *But*," he said pointedly. "You need to understand that we are extremely outnumbered."

I couldn't argue with that. Technically, the number of residents at the compound more than doubled the residents at Eastmoore, but when it came down to residents who could use a gun and who would willingly go into a battle, we were *grossly* outnumbered.

"I don't want you to think I'm siding against you," Fuller promised me; I could hear the sincerity in his voice. "You need to understand," he repeated, "we just can't take them down."

"And *you* need to understand that they recognized me! They knew I was the woman who was with that guy they shot who had the nice black truck with the gun mounted in the back."

Fuller's face went black. "They what?"

"They fucking remembered me—us! Twice they've tried to kill me and *twice* I got away. I know we're far away, but don't you think it's a possibility they might come looking for us?"

Fuller turned away from me, inspecting the picture of his son. "We're underground."

"We are, yes, but our animals and fields aren't. If that's not a red flag for a large group of organized, armed people, then I don't know what is," I spat.

"Penwell," he said sternly. "I didn't bring you here to argue. Don't think for a second I want to brush this off. We simply don't have the means to kill them!"

I huffed and leaned back heavily in the chair, accidentally hurting my torso. For the last several days, I had dreamed about destroying Eastmoore and single handedly killing every last son of a bitch inside.

"We don't have to *kill* them to kill them," I said flatly as the thought entered my head.

"And how would we do that?" he asked dubiously.

"Take out their means of survival. Destroy the generators. Slash their tires. Destroy the fences that keep zombies out. If they've planted any crops, drive through the fields. It won't kill them, but it will leave them to suffer."

Fuller looked above me, letting my idea sink in. "We take away what they need to survive, and they won't," he finally said. "It's something to consider." He nodded to himself and paced around his office. "It's not set in stone," he reminded me. "And it will still be the most dangerous mission I will send you on."

"I'm aware."

"All right," Fuller said and moved back to the table. "Find the rest of your group, bring them here, and we'll come up with something."

I smiled and rose from the chair, turning around just in time to see the door fly open. A very winded A3 stepped inside. "Sir," he panted, "we have a situation. That woman—Treasure—is gone."

CHAPTER NINE

"What do you mean, she's gone?" Fuller's voice rose.

"She was assigned to the farms," the A3 started and closed the door. I caught a glimpse of his name tag. "Just feeding and brushing the new horses," Pete stated. "Lenard and Kyle were with her, keeping an eye on everything while the cows were rounded up for the night."

I was tempted to tell Pete to get the fuck on with his story; we didn't need to know the details. I pulled on my hair and waited instead.

"They don't remember what happened," he stated, shaking his head. "We think she drugged them."

"How?" Fuller demanded.

"Lemonade. We saved a sample for testing," he added, earning a nod of approval from Fuller. "I found them passed out on the barn floor. Several people said they saw a truck driving away but no one thought anything of it. It was almost time to go in," he reminded us. "We thought she might have come back here, but nobody has seen her. She could still be here, I suppose."

"Why would she drug the two guys she's with just to come back here?" I questioned.

Pete slowly shook his head.

"She has a point," Fuller agreed. "Penwell," he ordered. "Get the others out of quarantine. I want every A1 out there searching for her; we don't know what she's up to. Tell them teams of two. And," he boomed. "You're not going. Do not try and argue with me. We both know you're not well enough."

"What? No! I can be in the car searching for the bitch!" I protested and stood. "I know her best!" I tried, though I hardly knew her at all.

"Then where the hell would she go?" Fuller asked in a patronizing tone.

"Back to Eastmoore," I said quietly as the thought dawned on me.

"I beg your pardon," Fuller exclaimed.

"She's going to warn them about our attack." I stared at the table.

"Why would she do that? She hated everyone there," Pete shyly began.

"No, not everyone," I interrupted. "She had a few friends there." My mind whirled. "And...and I don't think it was her idea." It was something Brock had said. "Jarrod."

"Jarrod?" Fuller questioned.

"They've been talking," I clued them in. "He's always hated us."

"Do you think he would really leave?" Pete asked me.

"We're wasting time, here," Fuller said, exasperated. "Kosteka." He looked at Pete. I uselessly wondered how Fuller was able to remember everyone's last name. "Get that sample to Dr. Cara. Tell her it's a priority. Penwell, I need you to go get your overseer friend to do a role call to look for Jarrod. Now!"

Pete and I rushed out of the room, followed by Fuller. He pulled a walkie-talkie from his belt and muttered something into it. I took off in the opposite direction, jogging to Raeya's room. I felt winded before I was even there.

"Riss!" she exclaimed when I stood in the doorway panting. "What's wrong?"

Lisa looked up from the book she was reading, worry apparent on her young face. Lisa was one of the two children I had rescued early on from the hospital.

"Nothing," I lied with a smile. "I just had a question about inventory and what we will get on our next mission."

"Oh," she said, knowing that wasn't the truth. "I'll, uh, come show you my sheets."

"Great," I enthused and waved to Lisa. Once Raeya was in the hall, I dragged her down and away from the resident's rooms. Not taking any chances, I quickly whispered the situation.

"Oh my God!" she exclaimed. "You think she—"

"Shh!" I reminded her. "And yes. Where else would she go? We need to find Jarrod."

She nodded. "Ok, come with me." She led me down the hall and into one of the supply rooms. After selecting a binder, she sat on the floor and flipped through the pages. "Ok, he's housed in room two forty-one. Let's go see if he's there."

"There's a list of where everyone sleeps?" I asked.

"Yeah. It lists their age and sex too. It helps us decide where to put the new residents."

"Interesting," I noted.

Not surprisingly, Jarrod wasn't in his room. His roommate, however, was. He told us that he had just seen Jarrod about fifteen minutes ago. He suggested we look in the game room. "Jarrod!" I called as soon as I spotted him. Jarrod looked around as if I was calling for someone else.

"Yes?" he sneered.

"Come here." I demanded. Everyone in the room was looking at me.

"Why?" Jarrod crossed his arms.

"You know why," I retorted. "Come. Here."

With a sigh, Jarrod begrudgingly trudged over. I grabbed his arm and yanked him out of the room, ignoring the pain it caused my still-tender torso. "What the fuck did you do?" I asked as soon as we were out of ear shot.

"I don't know what you're talking about," he said with heavy innocence.

"Do you want me to shoot an arrow through your other arm?" I threatened. "You know *exactly* what I'm talking about." I took a step forward and glowered at him. "Where is Treasure?"

"Oh, she left?" He faked surprise. "I wonder why?"

"You've been feeding her lies. You convinced her to go back. I know you did, you piece of shit!" I raised my hand.

Raeya gasped. "Maybe we should take him to Fuller's office," she suggested.

I unclenched my fist. "Sure," I agreed, knowing it would most likely be painful to act on my aggression. We made it several yards before Brock and Ivan rushed down the hall. I could tell by the looks on their faces they had already been filled in on the situation.

"He's here," Brock stated in shock.

"Yes, he is," I said through gritted teeth. "And he's not talking."

"Let us handle it," Ivan offered. "You go...go say goodbye."

"Goodbye?" Raeya echoed.

"We're leaving," Ivan explained. "To find Treasure."

"Now?" Ray asked, with just a slight panic in her voice. She looked up at Ivan.

"Yeah," he told her gently. "Underwood is waiting," he said to me. "In the weapon storage room. Go. We don't have much time."

I took off, but not before I saw Raeya give Ivan a hug goodbye. The fact that Hayden was leaving the compound without me was starting to sink in as I hurried down the long hallway.

The weapons room door was propped open. I heard multiple voices coming from inside.

"Hayden?" I called softly.

"Riss," he replied and set down a machine gun. He cast a glance over his shoulder. He slipped his hand into mine and led me out of the room, stopping in the hall.

"I don't want you to go," I blurted.

"I don't want to go," he replied. Acting impulsively, we hugged. "I'll come back, don't worry."

"What if you don't?" I asked, my voice breaking.

"I will," he promised and tipped my head up. "I have to go. We have to find Treasure before she gets back to Eastmoore. If she gives away our location..." he trailed off and shook his head. "We'd be fucked."

I looked up and blinked away the tears. "You're right. She can't have gotten far. She's not very smart."

"I'm banking on that too." He turned his face down and kissed me. His tongue slipped past my lips as he dipped me back. I pulled him closer and wished we had time to take things farther one more time.

"Real inconspicuous, guys," Wade said with a raised eyebrow, his voice coming from only feet down the hall. Hayden and I broke apart and I turned to Wade.

"Be careful out there without me," I told him. "Come back in one piece."

"I will," he stated definitely. "*We* will. If we don't find her in forty-eight hours, we'll come back and regroup."

"And then what?"

"We go after the guys at the hospital before they come after us," he said coldly.

Gabby rushed down the hall. "I put our food and water bags in the foyer," she told the guys. "I'm getting more water and then we're off." She looked at me and quickly glanced at Hayden. "I'm sorry, Orissa. I wish you could come with."

"Me too," I told her. My heart started to beat faster as each second passed. I didn't want to stay. I couldn't stay. I *wouldn't* stay. I followed Hayden and Wade upstairs and outside, carrying extra weapons to be put in the back of Hayden's truck. I watched as our A1s scrambled into their vehicles. The line of cars began to file away from the compound and to the front gate. Hayden pulled the truck keys from his pocket.

"If you don't come back I'll kill you," I threatened with a forced smile. My body trembled with dread. Hayden only nodded. Aware everyone could see us, I kissed him once more before regretfully letting go. I wrapped my arms around myself, suddenly shivering in the humid night air, and watched the truck disappear.

* * *

I was a tight wound ball of anxious nerves, snapping at everyone who tried to calm me down. After putting up with my short temper for several hours, Raeya dragged me upstairs and into my room. She made me sit on my bed and went to the closet.

"What are you doing?" I asked, crossing my arms.

"Getting you something," she called from over her shoulder. "You're not still taking any pain meds, are you?"

"No."

"Ok, good." She emerged from the closet with a bottle of rum and a bag of cheesy potato chips. She thrust her arm forward, holding the bottle in my face. "Drink."

I raised an eyebrow and took the bottle. "Really?"

"Yes," she sighed. "I'm worried about him, Rissy. I can't imagine how you feel."

I unscrewed the lid. "It's awful. I can't stop thinking about all the bad stuff that can happen. What if they run into a herd? What if the truck breaks down and Hayden can't get away? And then there are the people, Ray. What if Hayden gets shot...again?"

She gave me a half smile. "It sucks, doesn't it, worrying about someone you love?"

"Yes!" I said, exasperated. There were of course people I had loved before, Raeya included, but Hayden was the first person I ever felt *in love* with.

"Drink," she repeated and sat next to me, opening the bag of chips. "You know how much Seth loved that stupid motorcycle," she recalled, her eyes distant as she spoke of her long-time boyfriend. "I worried every time he went out on it." She dug her hand into the bag. "Especially if he said he'd be home at a certain time. I'd call wanting to make sure he was ok and get his voicemail." She laughed. "I'd go crazy with worry and call again and again until he finally answered. He always freaked out too, thinking something was wrong and that's why I called so many times."

"I remember," I said and pressed the bottle to my lips. I closed my eyes as the liquor burned my throat. Almost instantly, my stomach felt warm. I took another drink.

"I want this to be over," she admitted quietly and took the bottle from me. "Do you think it ever will be?"

"It has to end sometime." I shook my head. "It just has to. But nothing will be the same."

"No," she said, shuddering as she took a drink. "What do you think we'll do? Start a government again? Will people have to pay for things?"

I turned to better look into Raeya's dark eyes. "I have no idea. I never thought about that."

She nodded. "I think it will be like when the English settlers came all over again."

"Hayden said something similar," I recalled. "He said this country was built from nothing so we could do it again."

"We can."

I made a face and took the bottle of rum back from Raeya. "Do you *really* think so?"

"Yes!" she affirmed. "We have a good base here. We will only grow stronger. You guys are still finding people! Alex and his group found two more people on the way home!" She looked at her wrist then shook her head, forgetting she wasn't wearing a watch. She searched the room for the alarm clock. "They should be out of quarantine by breakfast."

I smiled and resituated so I could lean on my pillows. "Good."

"Do you still hate Alex?" she asked lying back and propping herself up with her elbows.

"Hate him? Oh no, of course not. He only left me for dead and lied about my chance of survival. Why ever would I hate him?"

"Alright, alright. I'm still mad at him, but don't you think you should let it go?"

"I'll let it go the day we are running from a herd and he trips and falls."

She shook her head. "That's why I love you, Rissy."

"Want to watch a movie?"

"Sure," she replied. I let myself into Brock and Ivan's room to pick a movie from their collection; I had seen everything Hayden and I had in our room at least three times. With the help of the spiced liquor, I passed out by the end of the movie. I remembered Raeya pulling the blankets over me and whispering that she was going to her room. I quickly fell back asleep and didn't wake up again until a little after five in the morning.

* * *

"You're up early," Jason said with a smile when I walked into the cafeteria.

I shrugged. "I guess. I'm hungry." I stepped in line behind him to get a tray.

"Hey, Riss," he said suddenly and whirled around. "Do you think I can borrow your bow? I really want to get in some more archery practice."

"Sure," I told him. "And there should be more bows and a shit ton of arrows in the weapons room, too. We raided a sporting goods store a while ago."

"Awesome!" he exclaimed. "Can you let me in? I don't know the pass code for that room. Yet," he added.

"Yeah, I can," I said, surprised the A2s didn't have access to the weapons. I supposed it was good, but would be a bitch in a bad situation. "We can go after breakfast. And I can coach you if you want," I offered, eager to keep busy and to spend time with Jason.

His dark eyes widened. "That would be amazing! Thanks!"

"Don't mention it," I said and shuffled forward.

"Want to sit with us?" he asked hopefully.

"Uh, sure," I said. He motioned to the seat next to him. Begrudgingly, I sat, not liking that I couldn't see the door. Two other teenage girls, who I thought were named Megan and Felicity, were already sitting.

"Oh my God, Orissa!" one of them gushed. "Hi! How are you feeling?"

"Ok," I said with disinterest. The last time I had any interaction with those two, they had cast me fan-girl jealous glares because I'd been partnered with Hayden. Hah. If they only knew.

"Oh great!" the girl with the shorter, dark hair exclaimed. "We were all so worried! But I knew you'd be ok." She leaned forward.

"Don't tell anybody, but you're my favorite."

I bit into my toast. "Favorite what?"

"A1," she replied, her voice obnoxiously high pitched. "I know there are now only two girls that go out on missions, but you'd still be my fave even if there were more! You're so pretty, and I'm totally jealous of you for getting to spend so much time with Hayden!"

"And Brock," Felicity—or maybe Megan—added. "He looks so good with a tan right now!" Both girls giggled.

I stared at them for a few seconds, trying to wrap my head around the fact that they had dehumanized us to the level of Hollywood celebrities. For the first time in a long time, I was speechless. I folded my toast in half and took another bite.

The loud clattering of someone dropping a tray pulled me away from my breakfast. With everyone being protective of their food, the dropping of trays didn't happen too often. I looked up to see Olivia standing at the end of the line with food and juice splattered across the hems of her jeans. But then I noticed something else...

Her green eyes were filled with terror and her already-pale face had gone completely white. A tremor ran through her body and I turned around, following her stare.

And my body became rigid with terror. Standing at the threshold of the cafeteria, was Delmont.

CHAPTER TEN

Without thinking, I grabbed my fork and sprang up, racing to get in front of Olivia. I slipped on the spilled food and jerked to stay upright. I put a hand behind me and pushed Olivia back, stepping away from the mess. She bumped against the wall.

With wide eyes I watched Delmont cock his head and look at us. Then a sickly smile of remembrance pulled the corners of his lips up. He turned around and called to someone. Olivia whimpered when Beau appeared at his brother's side.

"Well, what'd ya know?" Delmont said and crossed the front of the cafeteria. He was missing a tooth; I was pretty sure I had done that. "Orissa and Olivia."

I tightened my grip on the metal fork. "Get the hell away from us!" I threatened as they drew near.

"I don't believe it," Beau dumbly spat. "Of all the places to end up."

"Take another step and I swear to God..." I raised the fork.

Beau looked at it and laughed. "You'll what?"

A sob escaped from Olivia, fueling my body with rage. Delmont grinned and glanced around the cafeteria. Quiet chatter surrounded us; only a few people were watching our confrontation.

"I'm warning you. Keep your inbred, fucked up, hillbilly asses away from us."

Delmont laughed quietly. "We won't hurt you," he said, as if to sooth us. "Not here."

"And I won't hurt you—again—if you don't take another step," I said through gritted teeth.

Delmont's eyes twitched ever so slightly. "You got lucky, ya dumb bitch. You won't get away with it next time." He slowly picked up his foot with a sick smile. His eyes were latched onto mine as he extended his leg, taking an exaggerated step in our direction.

Olivia covered her head with her hands and sank to the floor, cowering like a scared puppy. A few more tables had noticed what was going on at the front of the cafeteria, but it did nothing to stop me. I raised my arm as Delmont shifted his weight, moving another few inches in our direction. Once he was close enough, I brought my hand down, sinking the fork into his shoulder. He yelled and took a swing at me. I ducked out of the way, bent my right arm and, with a pivot of my hips, used my elbow to strike him in the face.

He doubled over, his hands flying to his nose. Beau grabbed my wrist and yanked me back. Pain rippled across my torso but I ignored it. I turned, reached over his hand and jerked his fingers up, twisting his arm off of mine, circling it around until I had him in a wrist lock.

"Orissa!" Jason yelled and jogged over. "What the hell are you doing?"

"Justice," I spat and kicked the back of Beau's knees. Jason wrapped his arms around me.

"Let him go, Riss!" He took a step back, pulling me off my feet. I could have easily released Beau from my grasp and flipped Jason over. I had to stop myself mid-blow. I didn't want to hurt Jason; he didn't know what was really going on.

Beau rose to his feet and rushed to his brother. Delmont shoved him off, sniffling up the thin trail of blood that oozed down his face. Padraic stood behind him, his blue eyes open wide.

"Olivia!" I called, struggling against Jason. "Stop! Jason, stop! Those are the guys." Giving up, I let my knees buckle. Jason fell to the ground with me, losing his grip around my chest. I crawled forward to Olivia, protectively wrapping my arms around the girl. "Those are the guys who hurt her!" I sneered, staring daggers are Beau. Jason followed, putting himself between us and Beau.

"What?" Jason asked, looking from me to the brothers. The fork was still sticking out of Delmont's shoulder. Beau leaned forward, trying to look like he was ready for another fight. I could see the slight fear in his eyes. It gave me *some* satisfaction. "You mean he...?"

"Yes!" I screamed, and ran a hand over Olivia's hair. She broke down into sobs and clung onto me.

"Shit," Jason said under his breath. His dark eyes met mine and I nodded. Subconsciously shaking his head, Jason rose and turned. With his feet slightly apart, he drew back his arm and punched Beau in the jaw.

Beau stumbled back into Delmont, who shoved him off. Del huffed and stomped over. I sprang to my feet, searching for Padraic.

"Get her out of here!" I called, finding him only a few feet away from where he'd first been standing. With my head turned, I didn't notice how fast Del was approaching. His hands wrapped around my throat and he shoved me against the wall.

The last time somebody had me in a choke hold, delivering blows of pain had no effect. Adrenaline flooded my body and I fought to stay calm. I put the palm of my hands together and brought them up through Delmont's arms.

My throat burned and the feeling of being suffocated made my body want to go into a panic. I opened my arms, pressing against Del's. Then I brought my hands up, pushing my thumbs into his eyes. He screamed and gripped my neck even tighter. I sank my nails into his scalp, leaned my head forward, and brought his face down against my forehead.

It took two more blows to the head for him to let me go. I kneed him hard in the balls, grabbed his arm, and spun him around. I used my free hand to shove him into the wall.

"I told you to stay the hell away from us," I said through gritted teeth.

"What the hell is going on in here?" Fuller's voice bellowed from behind. "Penwell!" he yelled. "What are you doing?"

Out of the corner of my eye I could see Olivia holding onto to Padraic, who had her safely wrapped in his arms. Sonja put an arm around her friend, glaring in our direction. Jason was in front of Beau, his arms held a few inches from his sides, ready for his next move.

Fuller hurried over. "Let him go, Penwell," he boomed.

"No." I said and yanked Del's arm up.

"Orissa!" Fuller hissed. "Whatever he did, it's not worth it," he added almost gently. "And everyone is watching."

"Good," I spat. "Public executions used to be entertaining."

Fuller extracted something from inside his jacket. "If he comes after you, I got this," Fuller soothed. "Don't hurt yourself," he added quietly. I heard the all too familiar buzzing of electricity. The hair on the back of my neck stood up and my heart plummeted. Great, now I had a fear of tasers.

Reluctantly, I let Del go. He pushed himself off the wall and turned around. He looked at Fuller; even his dumb ass was able to recognize that the man was in charge. He glanced at him and then at me, smiling as if he had just gotten away with eating a cookie before dinner. I let him take two steps away before I punched him.

"Yes!" I heard Megan and Felicity whisper.

"You three, in my office," Fuller ordered. His face was set and his eyes reflected his anger.

"I'm not going anywhere with them," I said defiantly.

"Fine," Fuller snapped and looked at Del and Beau. "Get yourselves to the medical ward; you're bleeding all over my floors. And stay there. You," he said to Jason. "Escort them. I will get you when I'm done with Penwell."

"Don't leave her!" I shouted to Padraic. Still stunned, Padraic only nodded. Fuller dragged me down the hall and into his office. The door slammed shut and he let me go.

"What the hell was that?" he sputtered, his face growing red. Seething, he leaned on his desk. "I don't even think *you* can explain that! People will think you've gone crazy," he bellowed. He pushed off of his desk and paced around. I stood, rooted to the spot and let him shout.

"Those are the guys who held us hostage and raped Olivia," I said calmly when he was done.

Fuller faced me, blinking several times. "What?" he asked in disbelief.

"Delmont and Beau are brothers. Beau repeatedly beat and raped Olivia, trying to knock her up so he could 'repopulate the world.' Delmont tried to do the same to me. We got away just in time."

The fear of being trapped in the house full of people who viewed us as breeding stock and nothing else cloaked my heart. It was terrifying. I had been sick and defenseless against them for a long time. Waiting to get better to make our escape had been awful.

"Are you serious?" Fuller asked, looking sickened. He strode to his desk again.

"Yes. I'm not crazy," I reminded him. "And you're not either. You talk about the kind of people you *don't* want here. I'd say kidnappers and rapists sit pretty high on that list."

Fuller put a hand to his chest, rubbing away discomfort. "Yes. You're right." He stared off into space for a few seconds before looking up at me. "Penwell, I am sorry," he said sincerely.

Taken aback, I didn't reply for a second."Thanks," I finally said. "The compound is supposed to be safe. And it's not safe with those two here."

"You're right," he agreed without hesitation. He clasped his hand over his left arm, grimacing at the pain. I was going to ask him if he was alright but he let go and said, "Still, I wish you wouldn't attack people in the cafeteria. That's the second time."

"What was I supposed to do? Wait and attack them in a dark hallway?" I bit my lip and nodded. "I should have. That way I could have finished the bastards."

I expected Fuller to object and tell me to grow up. But he only nodded. He looked at the picture of his son then around the room, avoiding my eyes.

"I can't imagine what you went through," he said distantly. "Olivia either. She must be terrified."

"She is," I stated. "Didn't you see her?"

"What do we do?" he asked quietly.

I wasn't sure if he was thinking out loud or really asking me for advice. "Take those fuckers outside and feed them to the zombies," I supplied anyway. "No one is safe around them."

Fuller sighed heavily. "I highly doubt they'll attack anyone here; there are too many people."

"That didn't stop them from coming after us in the cafeteria."

"You didn't start it?" he asked, clearly shocked.

"No!" I said, though I think I really had. "I told Delmont to stay away and he didn't listen."

"So you stuck a fork in his shoulder?" Fuller asked with a slight tone of amusement.

"Just be glad I didn't have a knife."

He exhaled deeply and sighed. "You can go back to breakfast as long as you're not hurt."

"I'm not," I stated with mild surprise. Was adrenaline the culprit or had I healed faster than even I thought possible? I shook my head. "And you will get rid of those two assholes, right?"

Fuller pushed off his desk and paced around the office. "Eventually. We won't do anything right now."

"Why not?" I demanded and resisted stomping my foot in frustration.

"They just got here. Let them eat one full meal before we...we decide what to do."

"I've already decided what to do," I countered.

"Orissa," he spoke with authority. "We are not having a public execution."

"Fine. Take them out behind the barn." I rolled my eyes. "Or drop them off in the middle of the woods. Let them fend for themselves. We can even give them food and water if it makes you feel better."

He clasped his hand on his left arm again. "We can keep them separated for now."

I threw my hands in the air. "Why take that chance?"

"We have bigger issues to worry about," he reminded me. "And I have no soldiers to take them off in the middle of nowhere," he reminded me. "Once the others return, we will take care of it. I promise. We just have to wait until the other group returns," he repeated.

Seething with anger, I shook my head and turned to leave. I thrust the door open and stopped. Turning to Fuller, I said, "For months, Beau held Olivia down every night and raped her. Then he beat her when she didn't get pregnant. They dressed us up like baby dolls; forcing us to wear these hideous, short silk dresses and thigh high tights. They didn't think they did anything wrong." I lifted my gaze to meet Fuller's. "And you want to let them stay here for another day? How did we get so lucky to have you be in charge?"

It took every ounce of self control not to slam the office door. I was only a few steps down the hall when someone called my name. I whirled around to see Raeya jogging toward me.

"I just heard what happened." She took my hands. "Are you alright?"

"Yes," I spat. "Sorry." I shook my head and exhaled. "I'm pissed but I'm fine—physically. Have you seen Olivia?"

Raeya nodded. "She's in the game room with Padraic. She wants you." We hurried down the hall and down another flight of stairs. "Everyone's gonna know," Raeya promised. "And they will want them out. I know I do. I don't feel safe knowing people like that are living with us."

"A lot of people here probably have shady backgrounds," I said with sudden realization. "We just don't know about it."

"That's creepy," Raeya noted as we passed through the game room doorway. "And very true."

Olivia and Padraic sat on a couch, her hand was in his, squeezing her fingers into his skin. She had stopped crying but her eyes were red and puffy. I sat next to her; she immediately wrapped her arms around me.

"Thank you, Riss," she stammered.

"You don't have to thank me," I soothed.

"You keep saving me," she sniffled.

"You're worth it," I promised and smiled.

"I brought your food," Jason said as he and Sonja entered the room carrying trays a few moments later.

"Thanks, I'm hungry," I told him. Padraic, Sonja, and Jason huddled around Olivia. Raeya dragged a table up to the couch, making it easier for us to eat. Padraic stood and moved around the table.

"Are you hurt?" he asked me.

"I'm starting to feel a little sore," I admitted and put a hand on the right side of my rib cage. The corners of my lips pulled into a smile. "It felt good to kick some ass again." I finished my toast and downed the small glass of milk.

"You make it look easy," Olivia commented.

"I started taking martial arts lessons years ago," I explained. "It takes a while to learn it all. I could teach you."

"Really?"

"Yeah. I'd love to."

"Oh!" Sonja exclaimed. "You should teach a self defense class! I always wanted to take one."

"It's a good thing to know," Padraic agreed. "Especially now."

I nodded. "And I think you girls should know how to use a gun. You never know when you'll need to." I peeled off the shell to a hardboiled egg and sprinkled salt over it. "How about once I'm better I'll give you two private lessons?"

Sonja beamed and a bit of tension eased out of Olivia's shoulders. "I'd like that," she said quietly and picked up her fork. I noticed she hadn't eaten a single piece of her breakfast.

"And I can show you different ways to kill someone," I added with a smirk.

"I'd really like that," she agreed and returned my smile. "Riss?"

"Yeah?"

"Will you stay with me for the rest of the day?"

I nodded. "Of course."

* * *

I punched in the passcode and opened the door, holding it

back so Olivia could walk through.

"You sure you don't mind?" she asked and hugged her blanket.

"Not at all. I have an extra bed while Hayden's away," I told her sincerely. Saying his name caused my heart to flutter. I let out a slow breath and pulled the door closed, waiting until I heard the lock click before moving. Olivia had stayed glued to my side the rest of that day while we carefully avoided running into Delmont or Beau...and Fuller. I wasn't sure if I could keep from losing my temper if I saw him again.

"Thanks, Riss," she said with a small smile.

"No problem. I'll look after you," I promised.

Her green eyes met mine and I was reminded of Zoe. I'd tried looking after Zoe, but there was nothing I could do to keep the cancer from killing her small, fragile body. Zoe was a little girl I'd rescued from the hospital during the early days of the outbreak. Olivia was different, and I'd be damned if I let anything happen to her.

"Your room is nice!" she said as she stepped inside. "You have windows!" She moved to the dresser and looked outside. "And they're open! Can we leave them open at night?" she asked hopefully.

"We always do now that's it's nice out. It can get kinda cold sometimes, though," I told her, missing Hayden even more. It was my second night sleeping without him. I pulled on my braid and looked at Hayden's empty—and unused—bed. We now always slept together in my bed. Olivia and I changed into pajamas, turned on a movie, and ate a ton of junk food.

I lay in bed worrying about Hayden, paying no attention to the movie. Horrible situations flashed through my mind. I was worried about the other guys too, of course. I hated not being out there with them. I was so anxious and scared for their lives, and I felt guilty, as if I should have healed faster or not gotten hurt in the first place. And as much as I didn't want to blame myself for her choices, I felt like the whole situation was my fault for bringing Treasure back with me.

"You love him, don't you?" Olivia asked suddenly. She turned her attention away from the cheesy romance movie she had picked out and curiously looked at me.

I swallowed and took in a breath. "Yes," I finally said.

She smiled. "I knew it." Crossing her legs, Olivia turned to me. "Does he know it?"

"Yes," I said again.

"Does he love you?"

I nodded, my hand subconsciously pulling the dog tags from under my shirt. The metal was warm from being against my skin.

"Are you guys *together*?"

"Yes," I repeated. "We have been for a while."

Olivia smiled. "Did you know that there are rumors about you guys being lovers?" she asked with a giggle, her cheeks flushing.

I smiled back and rolled my eyes. "Everyone needs to get a hobby and stop gossiping."

Olivia shrugged. "There's nothing else to do here."

"True," I agreed. I leaned back on the pillows and sighed. I desperately wanted Hayden to open the door, safe and in one piece, and tell me their mission had been a success.

"How long have you been together?" she questioned.

I pushed myself up and went to the closet. My hands almost shook with nervous fear. I pulled out a can of Coke and the rum. I rooted around the box of junk food and candy until I found the plastic cups I kept stashed inside. After blowing the dust off, I divided the Coke up into each cup.

"I don't know," I said honestly. "I don't really keep track of time anymore. It, uh, became official after I came back with you." I poured a liberal amount of rum in my cup. "Have you ever drank before?"

"My grandma shared a margarita with me once," she told me.

I put a splash of rum in her drink.

"This isn't illegal anymore," she speculated and took a drink. "Right?"

"No rules or laws," I said with a shrug. "Don't go crazy though. You'll regret it in the morning." I took a long drink and waited for the effects of alcohol to warm me. Olivia was very curious to find out more about Hayden and my love life, and the more I drank, the more willing I was to share the details.

Tipsy, but not drunk, I grew tired and fell asleep in the middle of Olivia's questioning. What felt like only minutes later, Olivia shook me awake.

"Riss," she hissed. "Wake up!"

"Mmm," I groaned. "What?"

"There was someone in the hall! I heard them!" she whispered.

I sat up and listened. "I don't hear anything. Stay here," I instructed. I had to pee anyway; I figured I might as well check it out. "No one," I said when I returned. I closed the door. "Maybe you were dreaming."

"I know what I heard!" she cried. "What if Del and Beau sneaked up here?" Her body trembled. I flicked on the light and opened the closet. I shoved a magazine into my Berretta and held it up.

"I hope they did sneak up here," I grinned. I double checked the safety and crawled over Olivia, safely placing the pistol on the windowsill. "We will be safe. Really, they have no way to gain access to the upper levels. At all."

Olivia nodded; her head moving so fast it looked like a nervous tick. I lay back down and pulled the blankets over me.

"Can you hold my hand?" she asked shyly, reminding me of our adventure through a zombie filled haunted house. She insisted she hold my hand then, too.

"Sure," I said.

She moved closer to me and rolled over, with her face to mine. Not liking the close contact, I reminded myself of how terrified the poor girl was. Hayden and my grandfather suffered from PTSD because of the terrible things they had witnessed during war; I wondered if it was possible for Olivia to have it from the terrible things that were done to her, too.

We both fell asleep within an hour. I dreamed that Hayden and I lived together in my grandparents' Kentucky farmhouse. There were still zombies, but not as many. Everything was so realistic it seemed as if could really happen. I didn't want to wake up from that dream.

But I did. The mattress sank down and someone's breath warmed the skin on my neck. My eyes flew open and I tried to sit up. My body hit another's and panic flooded my brain. A man was hovering over the top of me, pinning me to the bed.

CHAPTER ELEVEN

"Replacing me already?" he whispered.

"Hayden?" I hissed.

"Who else, dummy," he teased.

My stomach fluttered and my heart raced. "Hayden," I repeated and wrapped my arms around him. Emotion choked me and tears filled my eyes. "Is this real?"

"Yes," he laughed and hugged me. He pulled me up and into his lap. "Shhh, don't wake Raeya."

I pressed my lips to his before saying, "That's not Raeya."

He pulled me to his body, tightening his embrace. I winced and he loosened his grip. "Who else would be in bed with you?" he whispered.

"Olivia," I said softly.

"Why?" he started. "Never mind." He put his mouth on mine. I moved a hand to his face, gently running my fingers through his hair as we kissed. "I missed you."

"Saying I missed you is an understatement," I confessed, too caught up on the joy of his return to ask how things had gone. I rested my head on his shoulder.

Olivia suddenly sat up. "Riss!" she cried, feeling the empty spot on the bed.

"I'm here," I said and moved out of Hayden's lap. "It's ok. It's Hayden," I assured her before his dark shadow freaked her out.

"Are you sure?" Her voice trembled and she took my hand.

"It's me," Hayden said quietly. "Who were you expecting?"

"Beau," Olivia blurted.

I pulled Olivia into a hug. "It's not Beau, I promise. Here," I said. "Turn on the lamp," I suggested. Olivia twisted and ran her hand up the bedside lamp until she found the knob. The three of us blinked in the bright light. "Did you find her?" I asked Hayden.

"Yes," he replied.

I closed my eyes and let out a breath. "Thank God." Hayden put his hand over mind. "Was she hard to find?"

Hayden snorted a laugh. "She ran out of gas. We actually drove past her—not literally *right* past—but we went farther, thinking she'd make it at least fifty miles out."

"Where is she?"

"The quarantine barn." With a smile, Hayden faced me.

"What is this?" I asked, gently putting my finger on a cut. Dry, crusty blood was matted in his hair.

"Nothing," he said with a shrug and leaned away from my inspection.

"I thought you said finding her was easy."

"It was, but I didn't say *how* we found her," he added with a grin.

"How?" Olivia asked shyly. She had her hands clasped on her elbows and was shivering, though the night air hadn't chilled the room below sixty degrees.

"The dumbass ran out of gas," Hayden began. "And decided to get out and walk." He grinned and shook his head. "We found her inside a bank, completely surrounded."

"So you took down the zombies," I finished.

Hayden nodded. "Not a moment too soon. Gabby and that new kid, Mike, helped. He was scared shitless," he added with a laugh. "Who's Beau?"

I swallowed hard and glanced at Olivia. "You know the two guys Alex and his group picked up when they were on their way back from getting the farm supplies?"

Hayden nodded.

"Well, those guys are..." I took Olivia's hand, not sure how hearing the words out loud would affect her. "They are the guys who held us hostage in Iowa. Their names are Delmont and Beau."

Hayden's hazel eyes went wide. "Are you fucking kidding me?"

"I wish I was."

He looked over my head and clenched his jaw. "I won't let them hurt you—either of you."

"I can look after myself," I reminded him. "But thanks."

"You're still hurt," he replied.

"That didn't stop her from sticking a fork in Del's shoulder," Olivia said with a grin.

"Figuratively stuck a fork in him?" Hayden asked.

Olivia's grin grew and she shook her head.

"You would," Hayden teased before his face went serious. "What happened?"

"Uh, nothing really," I admitted. "Del needed to learn his boundaries."

"Can we talk about this later?" Olivia asked suddenly. "It makes me want to puke."

"Of course," Hayden and I said at the same time. I looked Hayden over one more time, still so thankful he made it home in one piece.

"Shouldn't you be in the quarantine room?" I inquired.

"Yeah," he said. "I, uh, wanted to come and let you know I was back."

"Oh," I replied, knowing that was a variation of the truth. "Thanks." Hayden pressed a smile and nodded. He stood.

"Do you guys want some alone time? I can leave," Olivia offered with a giggle.

"That'd be nice," Hayden said over me telling her 'no'.

"Really," she pressed. "I'm a teenager. I know he didn't come up here just to tell you he was back."

"It's ok," I assured her. "I don't want to make you be alone."

She laughed again. "Really, Riss, it's ok. I kinda feel silly being so scared before. It's just..." she looked down. "There's something creepy about the dark."

I had never understood that fear. Yeah, it was hard to see if someone was lurking in a dark corner of your room. But unless they had night vision goggles, they had a hard time seeing you too.

"I'm tired anyway," Hayden lied. He stood and pulled me up. I walked with him to the top of the stairs. Suddenly, he grabbed me and pushed me up against the wall. I wrapped my arms around him, ignoring the slight pain his body against mine caused. He pressed his lips to mine and kissed me. I stuck my hand under his shirt and pulled him closer. He moved his lips to my neck before stopping.

"Are you sure we can't leave her for just a few minutes?" he asked.

I rested my forehead against his. "Maybe," I began, being pulled under by desire.

"No," he decided. "It's wrong. I can have you tomorrow."

I nodded and kissed him once more. "It's pointless for you to be quarantined," I stated.

"I know," he agreed with a sigh. "Not everyone knows I'm immune."

"Resistant," I corrected.

"I should go," he said but made no attempt to let me go. I kept him in my embrace, not wanting him to leave. Eventually he pulled away with a sigh. I watched him go downstairs before turning to go to my room.

"I could have waited in the hall," Olivia told me with a smile when I sat back down in bed.

"Nah," I said with a wave of my hand. "It's fine. It'll be even better since I made him wait."

Blushing, she attempted to tease me about having sex with Hayden. When she asked me how it felt to sleep with someone you love, my heart broke and I knew that—no matter what—Beau and Delmont were leaving the compound. Dead or alive.

* * *

As soon as the sun was up, I got dressed and took Olivia downstairs to safely stay in the hospital ward with Padraic for a little while. I skipped breakfast and quickly went up the stairs to the ground level of the old estate. I smiled and nodded to the A3 on duty as I pushed open the front door. Warm morning sunlight caressed my face. I held my hand over my eyes for shade and made a beeline for the quarantine barn.

In the end stall, Treasure lay curled up on a cot, sleeping. I hit the stall door with my foot. She woke up, looking around as if she couldn't recall where she was.

"Hayden," she breathed when she saw me. She quickly shook her head. "Sorry, Orissa."

My face set, I stared at her, unblinking. She pushed herself up and moved to the font of the stall, stopping mere inches from the electrified bars.

"What are you doing?" she asked. "You're creeping me out."

I shook my head and forced myself to slowly exhale. "You betrayed us," I said slowly.

"No I didn't!" she blurted. "I swear! I didn't want anything bad to happen to you!"

"Bullshit."

"Really, Orissa! I like you!"

"But you like them better, don't you?"

"I...I...yes." Her eyes dropped.

"Was that your plan this whole time?" I asked through clenched teeth. "To win my trust and play the double agent?"

"No," she confessed. I believed her; I didn't think she was smart enough to plan this far ahead. "You're my friend!"

"Do not call me that."

"You are! We got out together. We—we fought! We survived!"

"They why go back?" I yelled. "If we're such good buddies then why the hell did you leave?" My heart pounded and I wanted nothing more than to slide the wooden door open and smack the shit out of Treasure. "People I love put their lives in danger to find you. What the hell is wrong with you?" I shook my head, disgusted.

"You're not the only one who loves someone," she said quietly.

I narrowed my eyes. "Is that what this is about? You left to find someone you love?" I asked incredulously.

"Yes!" she exclaimed. "If I went back and warned Dre, then he would love me too! He would forget all about that whore, Kisha. I would be important. I would be the one to save him!"

"What?" was all I could say. "You wanted to go back there and fucking *warn* Dre? Warn him about what?"

"That you guys were going to attack! I just wanted to tell them! I swear, Orissa, I wasn't gonna tell him where you live!"

I could feel my blood boiling. "You are a damn fool." Seething, I spun on my heel and marched out of the barn. Treasure called after me, begging for me to forgive her and let her out. She could rot in there for all I cared.

Too pissed to go inside, I walked—ok, stomped—around the outside of the barn. Guilt weighed on me, making me want to throw up. I had no idea she had it that bad for Dre. And even if I had, I would never assume *anyone* would be dumb enough to pull what she attempted to pull.

I closed my eyes and turned my face up to the sun. She's here. She didn't go to him. Hayden was home, safe and sound. We would get our justice on the guys at the hospital and there was nothing Treasure could do to stand in our way.

CHAPTER TWELVE

Hayden crossed his arms and glared at Fuller. For the last hour, we had been arguing about Delmont and Beau's fate. After Hayden got out of quarantine, we went to Fuller with the same request: get those two bastards far away from us.

Alex had surprised me by apologizing; he said he had no idea those were the guys who had held Olivia and me against our will. I still thought of him as an emotionless prick, but there was something in his eyes that conveyed his true sincerity. Mike—the newest A1—looked sick with guilt. After zombies ravaged their house and killed the other members of their family, Del and Beau made an unfortunate escape and wandered quite a ways south, ending up far away from Iowa where Alex and his crew stumbled upon them.

I shifted my weight, uncomfortable in the folding metal chair. I loudly exhaled and realized that, for the first time, it wasn't painful.

"I would think you, of all people," Fuller directed toward me, "would go for the more recent vendetta."

"Oh, I'm gonna kill those fuckers at Eastmoore," I assured him. "As well as Del and Beau."

Fuller shook his head. "Didn't anyone tell you that a lady shouldn't swear like that?"

"Oh yeah." I rolled my eyes. "The same day they told me that *ladies* don't compete in martial arts, shoot guns, or kill zombies."

Dismissing my retort, Fuller clasp his hand over his left elbow and continued. "We have enough going on right now. Treasure," he said pointedly, "almost escaped. She was fleeing back to Eastmoore. We can already assume those men are on the lookout for us. We have to deal with her and that man...Jarrod. The safety of the compound is the most important."

I threw my hands in the air. No matter what Hayden and I had suggested, Fuller came back to protecting the compound, as if doing anything but would leave the residents in harm's way.

"Sir," Hayden began, somehow able to stay calm the entire time we had been discussing our plans. "I feel that the residents are *not* safe with a known rapist living amongst them. And it is a waste of manpower to assign a guard. If we go with the original plan—"

"—Public execution?" I quipped. That *had* been my first idea of how to deal with them.

"No," Hayden stated, annoyance building. "The plan of driving them far away. You said it yourself," he spoke smoothly and straightened up. "They arrived at night and do not know the fine details on where we are. We'll give them a few days' rations and they will have a fighting chance. What they did to Orissa and Olivia can't be forgiven."

Fuller cleared his throat. "Don't let your feelings get in the way of this, Underwood." he ordered. "We do not have the time to waste driving to the middle of nowhere."

"Yes we do," Hayden insisted, slowly losing his patience. "Nobody wants them here," he reminded Fuller. It was true; everyone at the compound knew what Del and Beau were guilty of by now. Fuller gripped his arm once more and sighed.

"What would you do?" he asked Hayden.

"What?" Hayden asked, taken aback.

"If you were in charge. What would you do?" Fuller clarified.

Hayden shook his head in disbelief for a second before answering. "I'd blindfold them, cuff them, and take them over the state boarder. It would only take a day at the most."

Seconds of silence ticked by. Finally, Fuller nodded. "Sergeant Brewster will not be happy about leaving again," he finally decided. He held up a hand before I could protest. "Penwell, find Doctor Sheehan and see if you are medically clear to begin training." He shook his head. "After seeing you take on those two I'd find it hard to believe you're not. I want you out there when we infiltrate Eastmoore."

I smiled, but knew it wouldn't go over well with Padraic.

Hayden walked me to the door and stepped into the hall. He pulled Fuller's door partially closed and kissed me.

"We'll be back before night," he promised.

"Be safe," I whispered, hating the fact that Hayden was leaving without me—again.

"I will." We wrapped our arms around each other for a quick embrace. "And I'll make sure those guys are *never* coming back. No one hurts you and gets away with it."

I let my hands slide down Hayden's shoulders and settle on his waist. I slipped my hands under his shirt and tipped my head up to kiss him once more. "Hurry home."

* * *

I tapped my foot against the exam room bed, anxiously digging my nails into the hard foam. I made a quick detour to find Olivia and tell her the good news, before heading to the hospital ward to wait for Padraic. Impatiently, I stared at the door while I waited for him to materialize. The air conditioner rattled to a start and the quiet, persistent buzzing filled the room. Goosebumps broke out across my arms.

I unbraided my hair and flipped my head upside down, shaking out the long locks. I hadn't had a haircut since months before the outbreak; my hair was no doubt full of terrible split ends. Not caring enough to do anything about it, I flipped my head back just as Padraic walked through the door.

It was his day off. Wearing black athletic pants and a gray sweatshirt, Padraic looked out of place. He carried my patient file in his left hand.

"Hello, Orissa," he said with a smile.

"Hey," I replied.

He set the file on the bed and leaned on the counter. "Why are you doing this?"

"Doing what?" I asked, thinking he meant flipping my hair around.

"Going back out there."

"It's my job," I said simply.

"Do you *want* to go back out?"

"Uh, yeah."

He shook his head. "Ok," he responded dubiously. "I don't know why you would since that's twice now you've almost died at the hands of humans."

"Funny, isn't it?" I asked with a shiver. "That the world has gone to shit and is overrun with zombies and it's good-old humans who torture and kill for no reason. At least the zombies don't know any better."

"You make a good point," he said and picked up a

stethoscope. "No matter what tragedy we face, human nature will never change at its core. We will be our own self destruction."

I nodded as I thought about the truth in his statement. "And I almost died once. But, as you said, if it wasn't for the extreme dehydration, I wouldn't have been that bad." Padraic cast me a quick glare and didn't say anything.

I passed the physical exam with flying colors. Next, Padraic had me lie down and pull my shirt up. Like Hayden, he was impressed with my quickly fading bruises. But they were *fading*, not gone. It was uncomfortable, but not painful, when he put his hands over my ribs and gently pressed down.

"How are things with Hayden?" he asked casually. My face went blank and I didn't respond. Padraic chuckled. "Don't play dumb, Riss. You're anything but."

"Oh, um, right. Things are good."

"I'm glad. He seems to really care about you."

"He does," I agreed. "And I care about him. How long have you known?"

Padraic smiled. "I've had a feeling for a while now that was confirmed when you were sick."

I felt my cheeks grow a little warm. "I guess him not leaving my side was a dead giveaway."

His smile broadened. "And hearing him tell you he loves you."

I pressed my lips together, refusing to let a school-girl-crush grin pop up on my face. "Yeah, doesn't get any more obvious than that."

"I'm happy for you, Orissa," he told me genuinely. "After all you two have been through—"

"Save it," I said and put my hand up. "No chick-flick moments."

Padraic chuckled. "My point is, Riss, you don't have to go out just because he does. He served in the Marines for almost ten years; he knows what he's doing."

"I know he does," I agreed. "But I do too. It's not like the military received special zombie training. We're all new to this."

Padraic sighed heavily and moved to the left side of my body. "I'd rather you stay here with us where I know you're safe. Call me selfish, then."

"That's not selfish," I admitted. "But you know staying locked in this place would drive me crazy. Everyone would think I'm infected."

Padraic laughed and helped me sit up.

"Am I good?"

"You can start doing light work. And I mean *light*, Orissa. I can't be sure if you're completely healed without an x-ray. And even if you were, your body isn't used to working out. You need to take it easy."

I nodded. "I will," I promised and meant it. Padraic walked with me to the game room, where I found Olivia and Sonja cutting apart magazines. We sat with them for a while, sorting out pictures to be made into a collage. I could tell Olivia was relieved that Del and Beau were out of the compound, but I knew she would forever fear them until death made it impossible for them to do any more harm.

"I used to have shoes like that," I said as I pointed to a model in the magazine. "And dress up."

"Really?" Sonja and Olivia asked at the same time.

I nodded. "I liked going out."

"Going out?" Sonja quipped.

"To bars." I turned Sonja's magazine around and tapped the page. "I would have worn this, too."

Olivia wrinkled her nose. "That doesn't look comfortable," she observed, scanning the tight black and red dress the overly thin model had on. "Why would you wear something like that?"

"To get free drinks," I admitted.

Padraic quietly laughed.

"I don't have the boobs to pull that off," Sonja stated. "I wish I could have gone to a bar."

"It's overrated," I promised. "They're loud and smoky and full of losers."

"Then why go?"

I liked the attention I got when I put on something short or tight. It was a temporary self confidence booster that reinforced the fact that I looked good—or just easy—that never lasted longer than the night. "It let me ignore a lot of personal issues," I confessed and raised my eyebrows. "Not a healthy way to cope, I know now."

"I like pubs," Padraic spoke. "There needs to be more of them here. Low key, low lighting...you don't have to dress to impress to go have a good time."

"Open one, then," I joked. "When this is all over."

He winked at me. "I just might."

I stayed in the game room for a while longer. Once I was too bored to just sit, I went upstairs and straightened up our room, thinking it would make Hayden happy to come home to an organized closet and clean sheets. I carefully did twenty minutes of yoga after lunch and spent the rest of the afternoon playing with Argos. I was starting to feel stir crazy from being stuck at the compound when Hayden and Ivan returned.

I was sitting at the back table talking to Wade and Brock when they walked in. I snapped my head up when I caught movement, not expecting it to be him. Instantly, I smiled. Wearing jeans and a light blue t-shirt, Hayden smiled back. He and Ivan grabbed trays and joined us.

"So?" I asked before Hayden even sat down.

"So, what?" he responded. I playfully smacked him.

Laughing, he put his tray down and took a seat.

"What happened?"

"We had a successful, non-eventful mission," he said in a monotone voice. I could see the amusement behind his eyes.

"Yeah, ya know," Ivan joined in. "We took them over the state line, found a nice-sized city, and dropped them off on Main Street." He smiled, flashing perfectly straight, white teeth.

Hayden dug into his pasta. "You won't have to worry about them ever again."

"Did you shoot them? Run them over? Hang them upside down from trees and let zombies eat their faces?" I asked.

Hayden raised an eyebrow, turning his head to me. "Uh, no." He stuck a forkful of pasta in his mouth. "Those are good ideas, though."

"We made sure they weren't alone," Ivan added with a wink. "There was a herd not far from where we dropped them off."

"I'd imagine they're nothing but piles of skin and blood in zombie stomachs by now," Hayden finished.

I smiled. "Good." Should it have sickened me that I took satisfaction in knowing the Del and Beau were violently ripped apart? Maybe. But I didn't care. Relief washed over me and I felt an odd sense of warmth to know that Hayden would go to extremes for me.

Wade nodded. "I'm not a fan of the death penalty, but those fuckers deserved a slow, painful death."

"And so do a few others," Brock added. "I can't wait to get my hands on that guy...what did you say his name was...Cutter?"

"He's mine," I stated. "Unfortunately, he cannot withstand all the pain I want to inflict on him."

"Hey guys," Raeya's voice came from across the table. Ivan

straightened up and pulled out a chair. "Whatcha talking about?" she asked as she sat.

"Murder," I told her with a casual nod.

"Oh, that's joyful."

I laughed and shrugged. "Done with your overseer duties for the night?"

"Yeah," she said enthusiastically. "We're actually pretty good on human supplies but kinda low on cattle feed. And the gardens are doing so much better than I ever expected!"

"Well, since you're done, do you want to join us?" Ivan asked. "We're having a video game tournament tonight."

"I suck at games," she informed him.

"So does Riss," Hayden teased.

"Fine," Raeya said with a smile. She *didn't* suck at video games. Seth had been a big gamer, and Raeya, being Raeya, had to be just as good. I had yet to meet another female who could dominate *Call of Duty* like Ray. "Where are you playing?"

"Our room," Ivan said and motioned to Brock.

"Sounds fun." She broadly smiled and her cheeks turned the slightest shade of red. I knew that Ivan had been interested in Raeya for a while now. I hoped she was finally starting to return his feelings. The topic of death and murder was dropped for the rest of the evening, and the night had a different air to it...almost as if we were normal.

Since Hayden and I had yet to have a night alone since his return from hunting for Treasure, we checked out of the video game party early. Knowing that all our friends were in the room right next to us, Hayden and I made an effort to keep quiet. We fell asleep naked and tangled together.

I didn't hear the alarm going off until Hayden rolled me off of him, our skin uncomfortably sticking together.

"What are you doing?" he asked when I slowly got out of bed.

"Going to training," I grumbled.

"Why?"

"I miss seeing you guys get all hot and sweaty with your shirts off," I replied. Hayden sleepily exhaled and stared at me. "Why else?" I stretched and opened the middle dresser drawer. "To train."

"Can you?"

"After last night, you should know what I'm capable of," I said flatly.

"Oh, right," he said with a smile. "Just...be careful, ok?"

"I'll be fine. Padraic even said so."

And I was fine, until I got about halfway through my workout. I was so tired and worn I had to stop early. Pissed and annoyed, I trudged upstairs to shower. The next day's workout was the same, though by day three, I was able to complete an entire cardio routine.

Every night for the next week, Hayden, Brock, Ivan, Wade, and I met with Fuller to discuss exactly what would go down when we left in a few days. Fuller was torn between sending the other A1s with us for reinforcement or leaving them here in case of an attack. We all agreed it would be nice to have backup, but none of us were comfortable with the idea of leaving the residents unguarded, especially with the risk of retaliation.

There were ten people in training to become A3s, whose main job was to secure the perimeter and alert us if danger lurked. That would enable several current A3s to bump up to A2s.

"...and," Fuller continued his long explanation. "You are in need of a new teammate. I only had one A2 request to be moved up."

I swallowed my beating heart. No, please...*no.*

"Jason Atterby," Fuller confirmed my fear. "Will be joining you on this mission."

I put my hands on my thighs, pressing down into my skin. "Don't you think this mission is too important to bring a noob along?" I asked.

"Atterby is well aware of his status on this mission," Fuller informed us. "He knows how to obey orders and do what he's told." Fuller's gray eyes met mine for a split second. "And it's my understanding that you and Jason had carried out missions together before."

"If you call it that." I shook my head. "Jason's just a kid."

Fuller rubbed his forehead. "We're aging faster now, Penwell."

I couldn't argue with him there. Jason was no solider—but neither was I—and had no training other than what was offered here. We had survived together, and I grew to *almost* depend on him to back me up. He was willing to learn and turned out to be a decent shot; I'd seen him in training a few times.

Jason sat with us for lunch and dinner, excitedly talking with the guys about joining us on the mission. I saw the disdain in Sonja and Olivia's eyes as they glared at him, angry that he'd decided to leave against his sister's wishes. He went to training with us in the morning and followed me around the entire time. I knew it was because he was familiar with me, but it quickly got on my nerves. I wasn't so much annoyed with Jason as I was with my inability to function at my optimal level. I wasn't sore, I was weak. I knew it wouldn't take long to get my strength back, but every day that ticked by was wasted time. Able to sense my short temper, Hayden stepped in and offered to take on the role of personal trainer.

The days left until we set out went by quicker than I expected. We had a lot to do, and our days were filled with working out, going over weapon use and safety with Jason, and mapping out the state hospital with Fuller. Anxiety began to grow among the six of us about our mission; the danger became more and more real as each day passed.

With only a few hours of daylight left, I grabbed my bow and arrows and went outside to get some practice in before we set out in the morning. I waved an arrow back and forth in the air, breaking up a swarm of gnats as I walked past the quarantine barn. My foot froze and I hesitated. Shaking my head, I continued. I had nothing left to say to her.

I slowly let out the breath I was holding and walked past the barn. With chalk, I drew an uneven bull's eye on a bag of cattle feed and stuck it to a bale of straw. I walked backwards until I was satisfied with the distance I had put between myself and the target. I picked up my extra large homemade quiver and slipped it over my shoulder. I grabbed out and arrow and pulled back the string of the bow. I exhaled, steadied myself, and released the arrow.

And missed the target. Cursing, I tried again. I hit the hay bale this time, but it was a few inches above the biggest chalk circle. I was tempted to take a few steps closer.

"No," I mumbled to myself. I closed my eyes and focused, trying to center myself like I did while doing yoga. Moving slow to remain calm, I reached behind my neck for another arrow. It landed inside the target. "Finally."

Without stopping that time, I quickly grabbed another and shot it. And another, and another, pulling and shooting as fast as I could. When five arrows crowded around the bull's eye, I stopped and jogged over to yank them out. I continued to practice, increasing the distance from the target and walking and running at the same time as shooting until the sun began to set.

CHAPTERTHIRTEEN

We left as the sun rose the next morning. We drove in pairs, with Ivan and Brock in the Range Rover, Wade and Jason in a Jeep, and Hayden and me in his truck. We had to ditch the truck—somewhere safe, as Hayden repeated over and over—several hours before Eastmoore since it was not only highly recognizable but also an object of desire to the inmates.

As usual, Hayden and I bickered over music until we agreed to set the iPod to shuffle and listen to whatever came on. We were speeding along a back road with the windows down. Save for the occasional dead body or charred building, it was a beautiful summer day.

Movement caught Hayden's attention. He let off the gas and motioned for me to look out my window. I grabbed my new pistol, slightly annoyed that my preferred Beretta had been lost somewhere at the state hospital, and flicked the safety off. I unbuckled and twisted in the seat, putting one hand on the door to steady myself.

A small herd of zombies staggered through a weedy field to our right. The sound of the cars got their attention and they tripped over the uneven ground with arms out in front of them as if they could grab us.

I aimed and shot one in the shoulder. I fired again and hit the same gummy in the jaw. Third time's the charm; I got him in the eye. He dropped and a female zombie wearing a long gown stumbled over his body, disappearing from view behind tall grass. I pulled the trigger once more and watched chunky blood spray out of the bullet wound of another gummy. Her body stiffened, before she too collapsed into the weeds.

"Four points," Hayden grinned as he spoke into the walkie-talkie.

"Two," Wade corrected. "Those were all S3s."

"And you're in front," Ivan added. "It doesn't count."

I took the walkie from Hayden. "There were still plenty left for you guys. Don't be a sore loser. You know I'm gonna win. Gotta make up for lost time," I added with a laugh.

"It's on, Penwell," Ivan declared. "And your ass is about to get whooped."

"Oh sure," I said with heavy sarcasm. "I'll believe it when I see it." I shook my head and smiled. I settled back into my seat and clicked the seatbelt into place.

About five hours had passed since we left the safety and security of the compound. Hungry, and ready for a bathroom break, we drove off the road and into a grass and weed-speckled field. A green Jon Deere tractor had been abandoned a few yards away from us; the door was ajar and a decaying body hung inside. The crows that had been eating the maggots and worms from inside the long-dead farmer's skull took flight when we closed the truck doors.

Wade explained our method for scoping out our surroundings to Jason. Jason nodded; his dark eyes were wide with excitement and fear. I wandered through the field and around the tractor, using the large wheel for privacy from the guys when I pulled my pants down. The sun was hot, and I was sweating by the time I returned to the truck. Hayden and Ivan were looking over the map. They marked our approximate location and calculated how much farther we should go before we had to assume battle-mode.

I swung up into the bed of the truck and looked around, holding my hand over my eyes to shade the bright sun. The road stretched ahead of us; sunlight reflected hazily off of the pavement. There was a cluster of houses around a cul-de-sac across from us, all with matching brick mailbox stands and tall, black lampposts. After a full spring and touch of summer of not being mowed, the neat little houses were surrounded by overgrown lawns. Behind us, dark green leaves shaded the land under a tree-filled forest.

There was something about a dense tangle of trees that always appealed to me. I wanted to go into it, to explore it and see what I could find. Though I still felt the desire to enter the woods, I wasn't eager to run across a herd just yet.

A bead of sweat rolled down my forehead. I wiped it away with the back of my hand and exhaled heavily. I slipped the quiver around my shoulder, grabbed my bow, and jumped out of the bed of the truck. Leaving the guys to put together a craptastic—and hot—lunch, I crossed the street. Loose stones crunched under my boots. I paused at the end of the street to pull my ponytail out from under the quiver strap; my hair stuck to my sweat soaked back. I yanked the hair tie up and looped my hair through, creating a very unattractive yet practical blob on the back of my head.

A lone gummy meandered through the back yard of a light blue bi-level. I turned around; the guys were busy patrolling the other side of the street and preparing food. I quickly pulled an arrow from the quiver, strung it on the bow, pulled back, aimed, and released. It hit the zombie in the shoulder. Pissed that I'd missed, I grabbed another arrow. I let my breath out to steady my arms. That time I got her in the face.

Smiling, I lowered my bow and stepped into the yard. I flicked a spider off my arm and swatted a swarm of gnats from my face. The zombie lay several yards from the street. I put my foot on her chest and yanked out the arrows. Before I wiped the blood and muscle fibers off on her clothing, I looked her over. She was wearing a filthy and tattered pink sundress. Only one of her matching platform shoes was on; it was worn and coming apart as well. She was missing a diamond earring but the string of pearls was intact around her neck.

"Holy crap," I said when I saw the fist-sized diamond in her engagement ring. "I bet you were a bitch when you were alive." I put the arrows back in the quiver and stood up.

"Riss!" Hayden called, standing in the middle of the street. "What are you doing?"

"Zombie," I responded and held up an arrow. "Well, S3," I admitted when I joined him on the hot pavement. "But with this," I held up the bow, "it's still two points."

Hayden smiled. "That's why I love you." We walked back to the truck, stopping at the driver's side. Hayden opened the door and grabbed his water bottle. "Did I ever tell you how hot you look when you're using that thing?" he asked and eyed the bow.

"No," I said with a snort of laughter. "I'm sure I look really hot right now, all sweaty with messy hair."

Hayden hooked his fingers through my belt loops and pulled me close. "All you need is some zombie blood splattered across your face and you'd be irresistible," he joked.

"Oh yeah," I said coyly. "And you can be the brave, sexy

soldier who comes and saves me."

"Aren't I already?" He grinned and I laughed.

Wrapping my arms around his shoulders, I nodded and kissed him. When we broke apart, I saw Jason's stunned face looking at us through the open passenger window.

"Jason," Hayden called. "I forgot to tell you the best part about missions." He pulled me closer. "Orissa takes turns sleeping with everyone. I get first dibs because she's my partner."

Jason's eyes went even wider. I made a face at Hayden and pulled away. "He's joking, Jason," I assured him.

"No he's not," Ivan quipped. He winked at me. "I call second. I hate getting her last when she's all worn out and tired."

"You guys are pigs," I laughed. "Hayden and I are together," I quickly explained.

After a second of stunned silence, Jason nodded. "I knew it."

"Told you," Ivan said to Hayden. "It's obvious."

"No it's not," I countered.

"Yes it is," Ivan and Jason said at the same time. Hayden laughed and let his hands fall off me.

"Why do you keep it a secret?" Jason inquired.

"It's just easier not to deal with the drama," I admitted, since our original fear of Fuller finding out and separating us had come and passed. Hayden closed the door and walked to the bed of the truck. He extended a hand to help me up.

"How are you feeling?" he asked.

"Good," I said right away. He shot me a dubious stare. "Ok, I'm kinda tired, and I'm not a fan of this heat, but I'm fine."

"Heat?" Brock, who was born and raised in Texas, said, and folded his peanut butter sandwich in half. "This is nothing! Be glad we're not here at the end of summer."

"It got hot in Kentucky too," I assured him and rifled through the bag for a bottle of hand sanitizer. "But the sun feels so much closer."

"It's probably because no one has been around to fill the air with pollution," Wade joked, though it made sense to me. "It has no smog filter anymore."

We chatted about the environmental changes while we quickly ate, all eager to get out of the sun. We drove for what felt like forever before breaking out of the mundane farmland and turned down a curving road. This one was speckled with trees, which was a welcome sight. The trees became closer together the farther down we went.

"What is that?" I asked, squinting my eyes as it zoomed into my vision. A dark shape loomed ahead, its true form masked by the swirling heat coming from the road. Hayden let off the gas.

"I'm not sure," he said and leaned forward. "It's a car."

"Thanks, Captain Obvious," I retorted since it was clearly visible now. A dark green SUV was pulled over in the shade of a large maple tree. The entire thing was coated in dust, and grass grew around the tires, twisting into the metal rims. This thing had been here for months. We were only feet away when a face popped up, staring at us through the rearview window.

"There's someone inside," I exclaimed. Hayden slammed on the brakes and grabbed the walkie.

"Stay here and cover me," he instructed and opened his door. I shook my head and unbuckled. Ivan and Brock rushed over, machine guns in hand. Hayden grabbed his from the back of the truck and made some sort of hand gesture that I didn't recognize to the others. Wade and Jason stepped out of the Jeep but stayed close to it, using the doors as shields.

Following Hayden's commands, the three swarmed the car in a very organized—and military—fashion. The person in the SUV jumped from the back to the front, screaming incoherently. She scrambled to the side and banged on the window, growling at Brock.

"Crazy," I muttered and grabbed my bow from the back seat. Hayden lowered his gun and shook his head. Brock lowered his weapon as well. Ivan came around to the driver's side, hooked his gun over his shoulder, and held out a knife.

"Riss," Hayden said quietly. He inclined his head to Ivan and I knew he wanted me to cover him, using the bow. He looked at Wade, motioned to his eyes and then the woods, and turned his attention back to the SUV. Brock had moved to the passenger door. He stood to the side, so when he opened the door he would be guarded from the S1.

Ivan nodded and took a defensive stance. Brock put his hand on the door and tested the lock. The door opened, ever so slightly. He pushed it closed and silently counted to three before thrusting it open. The crazy spilled out, sputtering and snarling.

She was pretty, with tight red curls and light colored freckles covering her nose and cheeks. She made a mad jump for Ivan, who greeted her with a knife to the chest. She let out a high pitched whine, much like an injured dog, and went limp. Ivan shoved her off and flicked the fresh blood from his knife.

I relaxed my arm and lowered the bow without taking my fingers off the arrow. I stepped closer and looked inside the SUV. No windows had been opened or even cracked. Yes, the trees offered shade, but there was no way anyone could survive an extended period inside a dark car in this heat. Had she let herself in? Or had someone trapped her inside?

Wade whistled, getting our attention. Weapons at the ready, we silently slipped down the road, our boots echoing in tandem. He pointed to a fresh pile of dirt. Sticks had been laid over it in the shape of a cross. Dry vegetation crunched behind us. The hair on my neck prickled and I knew we weren't alone.

I spun around, holding my breath as I waited for someone to emerge from the trees. My heart pounded and sweat rolled down my back. Thirty seconds passed and nothing happened.

"Someone was recently here," Hayden stated. "With the tools to bury a body."

"Do you think they're still close?" Jason asked hopefully, looking around for a group of survivors.

"They'd have to be," Brock said and nudged the S1 with his foot. "Or else this crazy would be cooked."

"You think someone put her in there?" I asked.

Brock nodded. "Why would she go in it on her own?"

"Uh, cuz she's crazy," Wade pointed out. "Why do they do anything?"

"For food," I said. "They're always looking for food."

Jason walked back over to the SUV and looked inside. "It's empty," he said. "Nothing for anyone to eat."

"Then she was shoved inside and left to die," Brock assumed. "And whoever did it has to be within a few miles from us."

I looked into Hayden's hazel eyes. He nodded slightly, silently agreeing with me. We were on a mission, and meeting up with a group of rag-tag survivors would only get in the way. That, and I wasn't willing to trust anyone. Yes, the good people we'd come across outnumbered the bad, but the bad were really bad. I didn't want to take any chances.

"Let's go," Hayden instructed.

"We're not gonna look?" Jason asked, his face stricken.

"No," Hayden explained. "We're on a mission to destroy the hospital. We can't tote around civilians...if that's what they are."

"Underwood is right," Ivan agreed. "We're not picking anyone up. After the guys at Eastmoore, Treasure, and the assholes who tried to control Penwell and the redhead, we're not taking anyone back with us. The compound is full."

"The compound is full?" Jason echoed, the horror that we were closing the doors to anyone alive apparent on his face. I stepped forward to talk to Jason before he could start an argument. A bad feeling was churning around in my stomach and I wanted to get out of here as soon as possible.

"If they're still here—" I started, but cut off when something blundered through the trees. I looked across the street, arrow pulled back, and watched a zombie quickly stumble out of the woods. Bright, shiny blood glistened in the sun, covering his mouth, chest, and hands. Jason raised his gun but Wade quickly held up his hand.

"If anyone is close, they will hear a shot for sure," he whispered. As soon as I had a clear shot, I released the arrow, which quickly found a new home in the forehead of the zombie, splitting his skull open on impact.

I crossed the street and hopped down the small embankment to retrieve my arrow. I put my foot on the zombie's chest, holding his chin down with my toes. I yanked the arrow out; bits of broken bone and browning brain stuck to the point. I flicked it off and wiped the tip in the tall grass. I knelt down next to him, looking at the sticky red goo on his face.

I stuck the tip of the arrow in his mouth and pulled a blackened, necrotic lip and recoiled at the smell.

"Animal," I said, careful not to inhale the stench of rotting breath and fresh blood. "There's fur in his teeth. Squirrel...maybe?"

"That really makes me feel bad about my hunting skills," Brock said seriously. "He's not exactly the epitome of stealth."

"I know." I wrinkled my nose and stood, shaking the urge to vomit. "How the hell did he catch anything?" A light wind rustled the sun warmed leaves. It would have been welcome on this hot day but it blew the decaying smell of the zombie right into my face. "Ugh," I complained. "I will always hate that smell."

The trees became still once more but the rustling didn't stop. I turned to hike up to the road when a zombie ran through the trees and nearly collided with me.

"Riss!" Hayden yelled and raised his gun. Still holding the arrow, I ducked out of his death-grasp and raised my arm. He was open mouthed and moaning, and the point of the arrow easily lodged in the back of his throat.

"*And*," I added. "I hate when they do that. Don't these fuckers know they're supposed to be slow?"

"He just ate too," Ivan observed. "Animal again?"

Hayden walked a few feet over, stopping in front of me. "No," he answered as I pulled the arrow backwards out of the zombie's mouth. Blood splattered on my pants. "Human." His voice was hollow. Using the end of his gun, Hayden nudged the S2's hand open and carefully picked up an ear. Blood and dirt crusted over a purple gemstone.

"I guess we don't need to look for those survivors anymore," Wade muttered.

"Anyone else getting a bad feeling from this?" Brock asked, spinning around as if he expected us to suddenly get surrounded.

"Yes," Ivan and I answered at the same time. His brown eyes met mine and he nodded.

"Let's get out of here," Brock suggested.

"Yeah," I agreed. Hayden dropped the ear, wiped his hands on his pants, and put his hand on the small of my back, ushering me up the drainage ditch. A branch snapped and a flock of birds took flight, their shrill calls of danger echoing in the distance. I strung the arrow and turned around, bending slightly back to avoid hitting Hayden.

A zombie, with sun-hardened gray skin, tripped over the trail of intestines he was shoving into his mouth. The shreds of a blood stained, pink shirt were tangled around his arms. Strands of hair clung to his mouth. His faded eyes spotted Hayden and he struggled to right himself. I let the arrow go; the zombie stopped moving. Hayden grabbed the arrow and stuck it back in the quiver.

"Is it always like this?" Jason asked, trying to causally hold a crossbow at his side.

"Like what?" I glanced at him.

"Stressful. I've been on edge since we left. And seeing that..." he trailed off and shook his head. "I knew what we'd come across. I didn't think it would...it would cause so much anxiety."

I laughed. "Yup. Always. I feel like my heart is constantly pounding. Anything and everything is possible out here. It's crazy, isn't it? The world we used to be so careless in is now a death trap." I let out a deep breath and rolled my shoulders. "But there are moments where you don't feel like shitting yourself. The guys are a good group. I know we're not invincible, but we're careful...mostly." I bit my lip, thinking of Rider. I willed the sting of tears away and stared at the cloudless sky, taking a few quick steps down the road away from Jason.

The smell of something putrid hit me. "Eww," I grimaced. It was a different kind of nasty smell than what I was used to, though it was still familiar. I had become very accustomed to horrid smells over the last few months. I rolled an arrow between my fingers, prepping myself to string it back in a flash if need be.

My heart skipped a beat when I found the source of the smell. I turned my head, not wanting to look at the pile of human puke. Not too many things can rival the putrid smell of a walking, decaying human being, but a puddle of vomit on hot pavement in the mid-afternoon during a Texas summer took a close second.

I covered my nose with my arm and stole another glance. It was rather fresh as far as I could tell, which meant whoever had spilled their cookies might be close. I whirled around, swallowing my own urge to vomit and hurried to Hayden.

"Someone's—" I started. Hayden held up his hand.

"Do you smell that?" he whispered and tipped his head up. The last thing I wanted to do was take a deep breath. As soon as I did, another familiar smell hit me. Though this time, it wasn't unpleasant.

"Campfire," I whispered back.

"Look," Ivan said quietly. An empty water bottle and a granola bar wrapper sat buried in the tall grass. I scanned the trees and found an entrance. A spark of adrenaline shot through me. Yes, there were definitely people not far from us.

* * *

Soon we were on their trail.

"They walked through here," I pointed out. "And there was more than one person."

"We should avoid them all together," Brock suggested.

While I definitely liked his plan, it bugged me to not know what we were up against. "I can go through unnoticed and see who they are. All I have to do is follow the tracks."

"No," everyone said at once.

"No one is splitting up," Brock said sternly. "We should turn around and take a different route."

Hayden nodded, and then shook his head. "If there's away to sneak in from behind and get a visual, I think we should do it. I don't know about you, but I don't want to be surprised again."

"Yeah," Wade agreed. "We underestimated the last group we

came up against. If there is *any* chance we could have a meet and greet with a group of strangers, I want to know what I'm going up against."

"Ok," Ivan said slowly. "How do we do this?"

"Follow me," I suggested. "Quietly."

Several bad situations were likely and possible. We could run into a herd in the woods and be screwed that way, unless the guys could scramble into a tree; it had saved my life more than once. Or we could run into the humans we were tailing. And that could end badly in more than one way.

I armed myself with the bow and arrows as well as two knives, a loaded M9 and extra rounds that I shoved in my leather bag. One knife attached to my belt and I fastened the other to my thigh. Hayden checked the scope of his machine gun and nodded us forward. Our plan was to go in twos with Hayden and me leading the way. I schooled Jason for all of five minutes on how to walk heel-toe through the noisy forest floor.

"If there are branches in your way, move," I said quietly. "Not only can pushing them out of the way be heard, it can get you seen. Unnatural movements of plants are a dead giveaway that something is moving through the woods...or anything for that matter." I paused to make sure Jason was following. "Do not take a step you haven't already thought about. Know where your feet are and where they are going. Keep your weapons down and remember that they can easily get caught, ok?"

"I got it, Riss," he promised.

I nodded and took a step forward before stopping. "Show me."

"Huh?"

"Show me how you're going to walk," I whispered impatiently.

"Uh, ok." Jason hunched his shoulders forward and stepped across the drainage ditch and into the trees.

"Don't look down," I instructed.

"But you said—"

I shook my head. "Look everywhere. Watch your feet but don't keep your eyes on the ground. You have to know what's around you."

"How the hell am I supposed to do that?"

I threw a hand in the air. "Figure it out. I did." I pulled an arrow from the quiver just in case. "Ready?" I asked Hayden. He adjusted the M16 that hung around his back and nodded. Once we were several yards in, Ivan and Brock followed. "They're going to give us away," I muttered. Hayden held up his hand and pulled out his walkie-talkie.

"Give us a few more yards," he whispered. After Ivan agreed, we moved forward again. The smell of campfire grew stronger as we deepened into the forest. The trees weren't as plentiful as I'd prefer when sneaking up on an unknown group of strangers, but the leaves were full and the slight breeze every now and then masked the sounds of human footfalls.

My pants snagged on something prickly. I used the shaft of the arrow to break free, carefully moving it away from my body in such a way that I could dance around it without having to let the prickers swing to a stop. Itchy sweat rolled down my back and a bee buzzed around my head. I paused and closed my eyes, waiting for it to go away.

Hayden was a foot behind me. I could sense his presence and feel the heat radiating from his body.

"I think I walked through poison ivy," he whispered.

I smiled and shook my head. I let out a steady breath, opened my eyes and continued onward. I walked through a spider web; the thin, translucent string wrapped around my neck and got tangled in my hair. Both of my hands were full, and I wasn't risking setting the arrow down. I used the inside of my arm to brush it away.

The wind blew again and I froze. Chest tightening, I whipped around to face Hayden. His eyes were wide and his jaw set. He gave me a curt nod and then looked ahead. Voices had been carried to us through the breeze. Whoever was talking was upwind from us, which was to our advantage.

Hayden whispered a code word over the walkie-talkie before turning the dial and clicking the device off. Painstakingly, we eased forward. The trees thinned out, replaced by thick, tangled bushes. We dropped to the ground and crawled the rest of the way, stopping a safe distance from the cluster of people who stood in front of us.

My arm brushed against Hayden's. Inside, my body was shaking uncontrollably. Outside, my fingers only trembled. Hayden noticed and put his hand over mine and gave it a reassuring squeeze. My heart thumped in my throat and my breath came out in loud whooshes that were sure to give us away. I parted my lips to slow down my breathing as I raised my head.

There were three people standing just feet from us. An older, gray haired woman held a shovel and an adult male held a shotgun causally at his side. The woman closest to us was facing the other direction. Her brunette hair was pulled into a messy bun and twigs and leaves were stuck to it as if she had recently tumbled around the leafy underbrush. A handgun was strapped to her waist and by her stance I could tell she was holding another weapon, though I couldn't tell what it was.

Behind them was the gray silhouette of a large building with a flat roof. The campfire burned not far from it.

"That takes care of that," the woman with the messy bun spoke. "Figures, they pick the hottest day to die." She exhaled and swallowed a sob. "I miss him already."

Hayden turned his head, allowing himself to hear better. An odd look of desperation took over his face. It was unnerving. I shot him one questioning stare that he didn't return.

The old woman sighed heavily. "At least he went quickly."

"Right," the man agreed. "Felt little pain."

"But a lot of fear," the lady with the bun said grimly, her voice full of sadness. "We barely got out of that one." She slapped a mosquito off her neck, turning slightly. I caught a glimpse of her face and—more importantly—of her crossbow. I could tell right away that it was made for a youth; if the purple and pink paint job didn't give it away then the smaller size did. Still, the thing packed a punch and had the power to kill. "And I'm out of bullets."

"We'll get more," an older woman with the shovel assured her. She speared the spade into the ground and leaned on it. "Whew," she said and wiped sweat from her forehead. "It sure is hot."

Hayden's fingers tightened on mine when Bun Lady turned around. My heart slowed and I felt like I was pulled backwards into a frozen lake. Her eyes flicked over our hiding spot. My gray t-shirt wasn't exactly the stealthiest thing to have on.

She had to have seen us. I just knew it. All within a split second, I debated if I should spring up with my weapon raised and confront her before she confronted us. But Hayden beat me to it. Only he had dropped his gun. His eyebrows pushed together with concern and he crashed into the bush.

"Hannah?" he asked, his voice shaking.

The woman he called Hannah lowered the crossbow and gasped as she looked at Hayden.

"Hannah," Hayden said again.

CHAPTER FOURTEEN

"Hayden?" Hannah spoke, her voice just a soft whisper. "Oh my God, Hayden!" The crossbow slipped from her fingers.

Hayden walked through the bush until he was in front of the girl. He shook his head in disbelief before throwing his arms around her.

"Oh my God," she cried again, burying her face in his chest. "I never thought I'd see you again! I thought you were dead!"

I grabbed Hayden's weapon and slowly stood up, eyeing the rest of the group nervously. The older woman gripped her shovel as if she was ready for an attack. When I noticed the shotgun aimed at me, I raised my bow.

Blinded by their embrace, neither Hannah nor Hayden saw the nonverbal exchange of threats. The string groaned in protest next to my ear, begging for me to release the arrow. Footsteps crashed behind me. I didn't have to turn around to know that Ivan and Brock were coming in for backup.

"Hannah," Hayden breathed again and placed his hands on the young woman's face. He inspected her and shook his head in disbelief. "Heather and Mom?" he asked quietly. My heart skipped a beat when I realized Hannah was his sister.

"No," she said, her voice breaking. Hayden's body tensed before he hugged his sister again.

"Hannah," the guy with the shotgun spoke. "We have company."

"I know," she said and sniffled, breaking away from Hayden just enough so she could look into his eyes. "This is my brother," she mumbled with another sob. "Hayden."

"What?" the guy questioned. "Your brother that was in Afghanistan?"

"Yes, but he's—" she cut off when she took in the sight of

Ivan, Brock, and me standing behind the bush with our weapons aimed.

Hayden whirled around and held up his hand. "It's ok," he assured me and turned back to his little sister. Wade and Jason crept behind us. If I wasn't so shocked, I would have told them they were going a good job with the whole sneaking through the woods thing.

"What's going on?" Wade asked me.

I shook my head. "That's Hayden's sister."

"No way," he whispered. "Holy shit."

Hannah pulled away from Hayden. "Are they with you?"

"Yes," Hayden answered, shaking himself back to reality. "Sorry," he told Hannah's companions. "Once I realized it was Hannah I couldn't..." he stopped and shook his head. "I'm Hayden. These are my friends. We won't hurt you."

"Hannah," the older woman hissed. "Come here."

Hannah scuttled away from Hayden. Stunned, I watched their little group huddle together. Taking the initiative, Ivan stepped around the prickly bush.

"Underwood, what the hell?" he asked.

"It's her," Hayden replied, sounding star-struck. "That's Hannah. My sister." I wanted to rush to Hayden's side and question him as well, but I didn't trust those people just yet. I relaxed my arm but kept the arrow in my grasp. "I don't believe it, but it's her. I just...It's..." he trailed off and shook his head. "We have to take her back," he said suddenly. "It's not safe here."

The wind blew again, making it impossible for me to hear what Ivan said in response. Whatever it was, Hayden didn't like it because he shook his head and turned his gaze to his sister. Awkwardly, the rest of us just stood there, watching the silent debate going on between the strangers. So focused on what was going on in front of me, I forgot that we were surrounded by the forest. A gust of air rattled the branches and a flock of birds took off, their cries echoing above.

Heart racing, I whirled around and let my eyes scan the brown and green surroundings. Two small, white moths fluttered in unison, hovering over a patch of flowery weeds. Pins of adrenaline poked my muscles when my sight rolled over a moss-covered fallen tree; it was about the size of a man and for a second I mistook it for a zombie. I shook my head and faced the small group once more; they scared me more than not knowing what this vast forest could be hiding.

Finally, the man broke away and waved Hayden over. Like me, Ivan didn't trust them, and stepped in behind Hayden. They exchanged a few words before Hayden turned to us.

"Riss," he spoke and moved his head, motioning for me to join him. Wade and Brock nervously followed, keeping their eyes on our surroundings. Jason, however, seemed excited to have stumbled upon a band of rag-tag survivors.

We stepped out of the shade and into the blindingly bright sun. Hannah introduced us to Jon and Lupe, the older woman with the shovel. Both seemed rightly curious about our clean, well dressed and fed group.

Hannah linked her arm through Hayden's. "Come on," she spoke to him. "I'm sure you want out of the sun just as much as I do." Hayden only nodded, still too shocked to form a coherent thought. "We have water! It's warm, though. Oh my gosh, I can't wait to introduce you to the others! I've talked about you before!" She took a step forward, ignoring the fact that anyone else was around. Jon and Lupe exchanged sideways glances. I saw Jon's eyes narrow ever so slightly and Lupe give her head a small shake.

When Hayden walked forward without a look back, Jon and Lupe followed. Ivan fell in step behind them and the rest of us brought up the rear.

"So," Ivan began. "How many are in your group?"

"About a dozen," Jon replied.

"A dozen?" Brock echoed.

"More or less," Jon said ambiguously.

"Are the others inside?" Ivan asked, eyeing the gray building.

"Some are," Lupe answered but didn't expatiate.

"What happened back there?" Wade questioned, using his thumb to point behind us. "Was that one of yours?"

"Yes," Jon said shortly.

"What happened?" Wade asked again.

"We ran into a bad situation and—and they died," Jon summed up.

"No shit," I spat, not understanding why he was being so secretive. "We lost someone recently," I quickly recovered my manners. "It's hard. I'm sorry."

"That crowd of zombies came outta nowhere," Lupe muttered under her breath. I thought it was oddly nonthreatening to call a herd a 'crowd.'

"How many did you lose?" Ivan asked. We had seen one

other fresh grave and found the crazy in the car. I knew it was at least three.

"Two for sure," Lupe admitted. Jon shot her a 'shut the fuck up' glance.

"Three," I told her. "You lost three for sure."

"What?" Jon demanded. "How would you—"

"That girl you left to cook in the car," Wade explained. "She's dead."

"Keaira," Lupe gasped. "She got bitten. We knew she was sick!" Jon put his hand on her shoulder as if he was consoling her. He quickened his pace and whispered something in her ear.

"Anyone else get a funny feeling from them?" I asked.

"Kinda," Brock agreed. "They seem to be handling the death of their friends pretty well," he said quietly.

"Shock?" Jason suggested.

"Maybe," Ivan agreed. "Or maybe they're used to it." He shook his head. "Who knows how long they've been out here."

I rolled the arrow between my fingers and looked past Jon and Lupe to Hayden and his sister. Her arm was still through his and she was talking to him; he smiled and laughed at something she had said. I could only imagine how he must feel, thinking that everyone in his family was dead and then randomly stumbling upon a band of survivors containing his little sister.

Tall, browning grass cracked and snapped under my boots, sending a grasshopper frantically flying through the air. Birds busily flew back and forth from the surrounding trees, chirping and chattering loudly to each other. The comforting smell of smoldering logs became stronger with each step. But I didn't stop to enjoy the little things that had the makings of creating a picturesque summer day. My eyes nervously darted around the forest on the lookout for zombies.

"Come in," Hannah beckoned, turning around. We all shuffled into the ramshackle building. Shaded by trees, it wasn't as hot and awful as I expected. Large screen windows lined the front of the building, allowing the minimal breeze to occasionally pass through. Thick cobwebs draped the rafters and dusty piles of rusted crap had been shoved out of the way. Three bloody, bruised, and broken people sat on dirty blankets and rags that were spread over the dusty concrete floor.

A teenage girl with curly blonde hair pulled into a pony tail knelt on the ground next to another young-looking boy, pressing a dirty rag to his shoulder. She jumped up when she saw us, her mouth opening in shock.

"What's going on?" an older man demanded and struggled to his feet. He limped over to Hannah.

"Guys, you're never going to believe it," she started with a huge grin on her face. "This is Hayden—my brother!"

"What?" the blonde girl asked, her voice was delicate and soft, sounding oddly out of place in this cruel world.

"I know," Hannah said with a laugh and pulled Hayden forward to show him off. "We were in the woods and I looked up and he was there. I feel like I'm dreaming."

The blonde wiped her bloody hands on her jeans. "You're not dreaming," she spat dryly.

"Hayden," Hannah spoke, turning to his again. "This is Madison, Gage, and Daniel," she pointed to the older man who was now speaking in a hushed voice to Jon. "Guys, this is Hayden. And they are..." she trailed off, looking us over. "Well, I don't know who they are. But they're with my brother so they're ok!"

I gave Madison a small smile, mentally approving of her apprehension. Ivan stepped forward and introduced us with professional grace. Gage stayed seated on the ground, either too weak or too shocked to get up. I let my eyes wander as Ivan spoke, noting the lack of weapons. Daniel looked as if he had seriously twisted, if not sprained, an ankle and Madison kept her left arm close to her body. She winced every time she moved or turned and I got the sick feeling something was broken. Jon was right by saying the 'crowd' came out of nowhere. By the looks of it, the remainder this group was lucky to get out alive.

"Are you hungry?" Hannah asked Hayden rather suddenly.

"No," he told her with a shake of his head. "We have food."

"Oh, we do too."

Jon cleared his throat. "We don't have much," he muttered to Hannah when she approached an old, warped table. She waved him away and opened a cardboard box, pulling out two cans of fruit and a bottle of water.

My heart was still pounding hard enough to feel my pulse in my fingertips. I held up the arrow and ran my hand over the fletching, waiting for Hayden or Ivan to make the usual speech about coming back with us to the safety and security of the compound.

"I'm going to keep watch," Brock informed us. "I don't like not being able to see what's going on."

"I'll come with," Wade offered. He nodded at Hannah and followed Brock out of the building.

"So," Jon spoke, drawing his words out. "Where did you come from?"

"A ways northeast," Ivan answered.

"How did you make your way this far south?"

"We drove," Ivan responded and flashed a small smile. "We leave our base every now and then in search for supplies and other civilians."

"Ain't that nice?" Jon laughed. "You bring back those civilians?"

"If they are willing to come with us, yes," Ivan politely told him.

"You got cars?" Jon probed, his eyes leaving Ivan's face and taking in the M16 strapped to his back.

"That we do," Ivan continued. He drew his shoulders back ever so slightly and turned his head down, subconsciously tucking his chin into his throat. Ivan was growing uncomfortable with the tone of Jon's questions.

"Must be nice," Jon sneered. "What kind of cars you got?"

"Where is the rest of your group?" Ivan asked and avoided answering his question.

Behind me, Jason and Hayden helped Hannah open the cans of fruit and dish it out to her injured companions.

"We got separated."

"You said that already," Ivan reminded him. "You went out for supplies." He shook his head. "We can help you get to them."

"Can you really?" Madison spoke up.

"Yes, we can," Jason assured her.

"We should go now," Madison suggested. "Before the sun sets."

"Yeah," Jason agreed. "And if you want to come back with us, we can take you to our compound." He beamed at Madison.

"Compound? Like a military base?" Jon asked. His voice was flat and raspy. I didn't like it.

"No, a bomb shelter," Jason told him eagerly. "It's all underground and completely safe!" I wished I had a desk to slam my head against. Clearly Jason hadn't picked up on Jon's suspicious vibes.

"But we need to find your friends first," I added quickly. "Before we can even *think* about the compound," I stressed, hoping Jason would take my hint.

"We don't know where they are," Madison confessed. "Well, not exactly I mean. They're in a church. We, uh, ran into some car trouble and came this way on foot. They can't be too far, though."

"It doesn't help that Flint had our map," Gage said quietly. I assumed Flint was among the dead.

"It's somewhere that way," Madison concluded, pointing to the front of the building. "Through a *lot* of trees. We drove for a while and then detoured through the woods on foot once the engine started smoking."

"Madison," Jon said harshly and waved her over.

"Riss," Jason said excitedly. "You can track stuff, right?"

I nodded. "I might be able to retrace the steps. But if a herd of zombies trampled through the woods after you, your tracks will be gone."

"Could you try?" Hannah asked.

I opened my mouth to tell her 'no' because I knew the human prints would be indiscernible once zombies had made their way through. But the hope and happiness in Hayden's eyes changed my mind.

"I can try," I offered and even managed to fake a half smile. "Do you at least have a rough idea of what direction you came from?"

"Kinda." She stood up and looked at the front door before shaking her head. "We barricaded it," she said to herself and motioned for me to leave out back. I nodded at their effort to make this little, old building safe and headed outside. "I think we went this way," she told me once we were in the front. "The church is off of a little gravel road. There's not much in this area at all, which is why it seemed so safe."

"That's usually when it's not," Hayden added. "You can't assume anything anymore."

"Obviously," Hannah sassed. "Anyway, there is a brick house surrounded by a stone fence probably in about midway between here and the church. Jon has the key; I'll get it for you so you can have a safe place and so you can drop the others off. I think it's a summer house or something because, other than furniture, it's empty, but safe. Our plan was to go back with supplies and move the others in, but not all of us can walk right now. We have to wait at least until tomorrow." She shook her head. "That is, if we all make it 'til then."

"Is there a road that takes you to this house?" Hayden asked.

Hannah nodded. "It's too overgrown to drive on. And I

actually think it was some sort of drug dealer or sex slave trader's house. The fence is solid and way too high to climb. Or maybe some European royalty's getaway." She shrugged. "You can tell there used to be tire tracks but there are too many fallen trees and just nature-crap in the way."

That was something I could go off of. "Do you think the tire tracks could have feasibly led to that gravel road? It would be easy to follow," I said.

She quickly inhaled. "I never thought of that! It would make sense. Oh, I wonder if that house belongs to someone in the church and they used it too—"

"Hannah," Hayden scolded. "Focus."

She bit her lip and nodded. "Right, right. The path. It's really over grown. I could barely even tell it was a path. But from there, we drove for only a few miles before the engine overheated. We weren't *that* far from the church."

I wanted to ask her why they weren't logical enough to backtrack and get another vehicle, well *if* they had another vehicle that is. "I should be able to follow it and then find that church. Do the others in your group have a car?"

"Yes," she answered. "More than one."

"Will everyone fit in them?" Hayden asked his sister.

She tipped her head in thought. "Yeah, they will. I don't think our stuff will, though."

"You don't need your stuff," Hayden told her quickly. "You can get new stuff when you come home with me."

Hannah frowned before nodding. "I know."

"I'll find your friends," I promised. I just hoped I'd find them alive.

"You're not going alone," Hayden informed me, the dubious look on his face telling me that he already knew my plans to go solo. "I'll go," he offered.

"No," I said quickly. "I'll...I'll take Jason," I told him. Though the boy's intentions were nothing but good, I didn't want him to give away the compound's exact location, and it had more to do with not trusting Jon. What if we ran into some guys from Eastmoore? Jon would have nothing to lose blurting out coordinates and directions to our safe haven.

"Ok, great!" Hannah exclaimed. "Are you any good with that?" she asked suddenly and eyed the arrow that was still in my grasp.

"I'm alright," I said as modestly as I could.

Hayden laughed. "Yeah, just alright."

"I used to want to learn archery," she told me. "I've gotten pretty good with my crossbow. It's hard to find bullets. Do you guys have a lot of bullets? Oh, Hayden! Did you know about this? Is this why you came here? Did you have zombie training practice?"

"Hannah," Hayden spoke, his voice heavy with fatherly annoyance. "We need that key."

"Right," she said and spun around.

"I always wondered what she'd be like without medication," Hayden muttered under his breath and I laughed.

"She seems to be doing well enough," I said. "At least she can channel that energy into survival."

"Good point," he agreed. He slipped his hand in mine and gave it a squeeze before letting go. Hannah disappeared into the old shelter. Wade and Brock were outside, standing guard several yards into the forest. Hayden waved them over.

"I'm going to get the rest of their group so we can get the hell out of here," I quickly summed up.

"Good," Wade said right away.

"Are you sure that's a good idea, Riss?" Brock, of course, had to ask.

I nodded. "It's not safe here and we have something important to do."

"I'll go with you," Brock suggested. "I don't like any of us splitting up, but you're not going alone."

"I'd rather have you come with," I said ruefully. "But Jason needs to get away from these people before he draws them a map back to the compound."

Brock made a face but nodded. "So I'm not the only one who feels like that Jon guy is plotting to mug us and steal our car keys?"

"Let him try," Wade sneered.

"Guys," Hayden intervened. "He's not gonna do anything."

"He gives off the shady vibe," I retorted. "I don't like it."

Hayden shook his head. Of course he wouldn't see it; he was blinded by his family ties. "Hannah's a smart girl. She wouldn't stay with anyone *shady*."

"Unfortunately," Brock said gravely, "the shadier you are in this world, the better chance you have at survival."

"We're not shady," Hayden argued.

"Exactly," Wade said pointedly. "We went into that state hospital thinking we could do some good. And look where that got us."

Hayden sighed and crossed his arms. "Yeah," he muttered. "But Riss is right; we should get out of here. This place isn't safe. And Brock should go with. No offense to Jason, but I'd feel better knowing Brock was with you instead."

"Fine with me," I quickly agreed.

The door to the old building creaked open. Hannah, Jason, Ivan, and Jon emerged and joined our little gathering.

"Well, our Hannah just filled me in on your plan," Jon began, carrying just a hint of mocking in his voice. "You're going out in the middle of the woods to look for strangers."

"Yes, I am," I said sternly.

"That's very nice of you," he cooed.

"Yep. I'm awesome." I pressed a smile. Really, I knew that Hannah wouldn't leave without the rest of her group and Hayden wouldn't leave without Hannah...and I wouldn't leave without Hayden. So there was no way around this.

"And Hannah's war-hero big brother is staying, right?"

"Yeah," Hayden told Jon. "I am."

"Well isn't that nice," he said through a smile. "You two can have a little family reunion." He pulled a pack of cigarettes from his pocket and lit one. "Best be on your way before it gets dark."

"The key," I stated.

"Oh, right," he said after taking a long drag. He blew the smoke in my face. "Here it is. There's a gate right in front of the house. The whole place is very sturdy. It'll be a good getaway from a crowd."

I opened up the small leather bag I had hanging across my chest and put the key in a pocket next to a water bottle and extra ammo for my 9mm. "This way, right?" I confirmed with Jon by pointing in the direction Hannah had told me.

"Sounds about right." He smiled once more, making my skin crawl. "Alrighty then. I hope to see ya again."

"Oh, you will," I promised with just a little threat obvious in my voice. Jon turned and went back into the building, which I think was a long forgotten antique store.

Ivan put his hand on my shoulder. "Be safe, guys. If you don't come back, we will all kill you." He flashed his famous smile and winked.

"We got this," Brock said with a smile. We exchanged a quick goodbye with Ivan, Jason, and Wade and then began walking around the building. Hayden walked with me, staying by my side.

Hannah trailed behind him.

"Wait," Hayden said when we got to the edge of the tall, weedy lawn. "Riss," he started, looking contrite. "I can't let you go out there without me."

"Hayden," Brock started and put his hand on Hayden's shoulder. "I'll look after her. I won't let anything happen." Hayden clenched his jaw and looked at me.

"It'll be fine," I assured him and took a step closer. Mixed with the sun, his body heat radiated off of me. I slowly drew my eyes up, taking in his muscular chest, strong jaw, and beautiful hazel eyes.

"No," Hayden said definitely. "The last time you said that and left my sight you were beaten within inches of your life. I can't let you go," he repeated.

Brock chuckled and stepped back. "I knew you couldn't let her go."

Hayden nodded. "I'm coming with."

"Hayden, no!" Hannah protested. "I haven't seen you in over a year! I'm your sister. Stay with me!"

"Hannah," he said slowly. "Orissa is…she's, uh…she's my…my girlfriend."

"Oh," she exclaimed and leaned back. She ran her eyes over me and wrinkled her nose. "Really?"

"Yes."

"Huh." She continued to look me over, her eyes settling on my chest. "And she's wearing your tags? Oh my gosh, is this serious?"

"We'll talk when I get back," he told her. "Brock. Take care of my sister."

Brock nodded. "I will do that." He smiled warmly at Hannah. "I think we'll keep ourselves busy by making this place safer. You won't even know he's gone."

Tears filled Hannah's eyes as she stared at her brother. Sniffling, she wrapped her arms around him. "Please come back alive," she whispered.

"I will. Promise." He pulled away and smiled. "Come on, I've made it this far."

"Ok," she whispered. "Bye."

Brock held out his hand for her to take and led her back around the front of the building. I handed Hayden his pistol that he had dropped and clicked the safety off of mine. We slipped into the trees.

"Ashamed of me?" I asked him, holding an arrow in my right hand. We were already quite a distance into our journey.

"What?" he asked and ducked under a low branch.

"You didn't seem to want to admit I was your girlfriend back there."

"Oh." He stopped walking and looked away.

"So you were," I accused.

"No," he said, still not looking at me. I walked a few steps ahead and turned around. "That's not it at all."

"Then what is it?"

For the first time ever, I saw Hayden's cheeks redden. He began walking again. "I know you're my girlfriend. But..." He made a point to not look at me. "You feel like more to me than that."

I smiled and felt my heart do a stupid skip-a-beat thing. "I feel the same way."

"Really?" he asked, sounding genuinely surprised.

"Yeah. After all we've been through—" I cut off when Hayden grabbed my wrist. He held a finger to his lips and pointed to our left. A tree limb was pushed forward and snapped back, sending leaves fluttering to the ground. I strung the arrow and pulled back, waiting for the zombie to come into view. She stumbled across the uneven ground, groaning and gargling to herself. Her death-stained eyes looked blindly around, only able to descry what was a few feet ahead of her.

The point of the arrow split open her forehead. She fell instantly, her rotting body limp. I stepped up on a mossy fallen tree and jumped down close to the zombie. She was so far into the gummy stage that the arrow easily pulled out of her broken skull. I flicked a flap of molding skin off the point and knelt down to wipe the arrow as clean as I could.

Gagging from the pungent odor, I turned my head. Her horrible scent was so ripe it made my eyes water.

"Riss, get up," Hayden quietly ordered. "There's more."

I sprang to my feet and looked ahead of us. "Shoot?" I asked.

"Not if we can help it," he told me and unsheathed a buck knife from his belt. "Get the fast ones. I'll clean up the rest."

I nodded and swallowed my pounding heart. My breath quickened as adrenaline did its job, prepping my body for a fight. Three zombies plodded through the forest, reaching for us with dirty, blood crusted, outstretched hands. Their snarling death-groans surrounded us. By the time I had taken them down and grabbed the arrows, more were in their place.

Dragging his feet, the S2 lumbered at us, several yards ahead of his undead friends. Hayden took off, sinking his knife into the zombie's ear. He yanked his knife back and kicked the zombie away as it fell, only to take on another.

I couldn't keep up. Every time I fired an arrow and took down a zombie, two more were in its place by the time I yanked my arrows free. Frantically, I shot two more arrows and made no attempt to retrieve them. Jumping over the fallen log, I madly looked for Hayden. He pushed a zombie up against a tree and stabbed it in the eye.

Something pulled at my hair. I whirled around and used the end of my bow to hit a female zombie in the face. She snarled at me, thrashing her hands against my arm. Feeling like daggers, her once nicely manicured, acrylic nails were now jagged and sharp and tore open my skin. I brought the bow up and cracked her in the side of the head before scrambling away and yanking an arrow from the quiver.

Just as I was about to shove the point into her face, I tripped and fell, dropping the arrow. As if I had pissed her off, the zombie roared and blundered to me, falling to her knees and grabbing my ankle. I drew my other foot in and kicked her in the face, breaking her nose. I bent my leg up again and shoved her away.

Another zombie joined the soon-to-be feast. I spun around and crawled forward, gripping a tree and yanking myself upright. Using the bow, I hit Fake Nails as hard as I could on the temple. Something cracked and she wilted to the ground. I reached behind me for another arrow and almost screamed when I grasped a rotting hand, the skin peeling off underneath my fingers.

The zombie grabbed onto me, trying to sink its teeth into my neck. Getting a flashback from my martial arts training, I shifted my weight, bent my body forward and flipped the thing over my head. I had practiced that move with my instructor over and over until I had it down perfectly. Though, in the many times I had performed that move, my instructors arm had never ripped off like the zombie's did.

Brown, putrid blood splattered down my back and across my face. The zombie landed on the ground with a heavy thud. Still holding his arm, I used it to whack him over the head. Trading it for the arrow I had dropped, I stabbed him in his open mouth.

"Riss!" Hayden yelled. "Run!"

I turned to see him struggling with two zombies at once. He kicked the feet out from under a female S2 and shoved his knife into the skull of the second. He pushed the limp, heavy body on top of the fallen zombie and sprang away to my side. Grabbing my hand, he pulled me forward.

"We have to get to that house," I panted as we ran. "There are too fucking many!" I stole a glance behind me. Feeling like someone had shaken the hive. Angry zombies swarmed out, seeking blood. We were gaining distance but it did little to stop the overwhelming fear of being ripped apart.

"Which way?" Hayden asked and dodged out of the way of a tree.

"I don't know!" I called. "I wasn't paying attention."

"Fuck. Me neither." We kept running in any direction that didn't have a shit ton of zombies. My lungs started burning and every breath hurt worse and worse. Exhausted, my legs didn't function as well as I wished and I tripped over a twisted root. "You ok?" Hayden asked as he skidded to a stop.

"Yes," I said and winced as I pushed myself up. "I guess I'm not in as good of shape as I thought."

"Here," Hayden said and gently took the bow from me. "Put your hands up to help you breathe," he calmly instructed. "Shit, you're bleeding."

I nodded. "It's just a scratch." I took a deep breath. "Literally. Fucking zombie had jagged fake nails."

Hayden laughed. "Sorry. It's not funny. But it is."

I smiled. "Yeah."

Footsteps crashed through the peaceful forest floor. Hayden took an arrow from my quiver and strung it on the bow. He pushed out his air and steadied his arm, waiting for the zombie. With one eye closed, he aimed and released the arrow.

"Nice shot," I complimented.

"Thanks," he said with a smile and walked over to pull the arrow out of the skull of the zombie. Just as he straightened up, another zombie rushed over. He didn't have time to pull back on the bow; the S2 was fast. With a quick flick of his arm, Hayden used the arrow to kill him. "Ugh," he muttered when he yanked the arrow back. The zombie's eye came with it, nerve endings, tendons, and all. He carefully bent his arm back before flinging it forward, sending the eyeball flying. It landed at the feet of another zombie, a deteriorating teenage girl wearing a faded flannel shirt and ripped jeans.

I was too busy watching Hayden crack open her skull to notice that the zombies weren't only following us. They were in front of us too. I snapped my head around at the last second and dodged out of the way. My hand flew up on instinct, as if I was still holding my bow. That few seconds' hesitation cost me.

Their groaning growls grew louder as they approached and they appeared like rotting mist from the trees. I bent down and grabbed the knife that was strapped around my leather boot. I sprang up and sank the blade into the nearest zombie brain. I pushed him away, spun around and hit another.

"Hayden!" I called. "There's too fucking many!"

"I know!" he answered as he punched a zombie in the face. He hooked the bow under his arm and pulled out his own knife, slicing through the back of the zombie's neck and severing his brainstem. "Go!"

"Not without you!" I slashed the blade through the air. Grubby zombie hands closed around my shoulders. Her lips were brown and flaking apart, as if she had spent too much time under the hot, Texas sun. I kneed her in the stomach, but instead of slowing her down it only caused my jeans to soak up warm zombie fluids.

I put one hand on her chest and pushed away. Turning my head, I nearly screamed when I saw another S2 just feet from me. Torn flesh hung from his face, swinging with each jarring step. With missing teeth, he chomped at the air, letting me know what was to come. I twisted my shoulder, leaned back, and extended my leg, kicking the female away. She stumbled and landed on her back, rolling like an overturned turtle.

I ducked out of the way of the S2's grasp and swung, planting the knife into his cheek. The tip lodged in the roof of his mouth and didn't kill him. I yanked the knife back but he came with it. The female on the ground growled and flipped herself over. She dragged her deteriorating body closer and wrapped her hands around my ankle.

She couldn't bite through the thick leather of my boots, but she could easily cause me to fall.

"Get off me, bitch!" I shouted and jerked my foot up, only to bring it down on her head. I gave the knife one more tug before it came free. I shoved it through the zombie's ear before turning my attention to the ankle-biter.

"Hayden!" I yelled again. "Hayden!" I screamed frantically when he didn't answer.

"Riss, go!" his voice came from behind me. Holding an arrow

like a spear, he pushed it through a zombie's gaping mouth. I stumbled over the corpses that surrounded us and leapt up a hill to join Hayden. He handed me the bow. "You're better at this than I am."

I nodded and took it, noticing that he was holding his pistol in the other hand. We sprinted a few yards before hitting a wall of the undead. Hayden raised his arm, aimed, and rapidly fired, taking the closest down. He spun around, running backwards, shooting at anything that moved.

"Get the key!" he shouted. I brought my attention upward and peered through the trees; a tall, light colored stone fence was looming closer. Without taking my eyes off the nearing zombies, I dug my hand into my bag and felt around for the key.

"Here," I shouted to Hayden when he ran out of ammo. "Take mine!"

He looked at my hip and pulled the M9 from the holster and fired away. My heart threatened to beat out of my chest. I scanned along the fence, looking for the gate. Finally, I spotted it. A surge of adrenaline pulsed through me and I sprinted forward.

The gate was a six foot work of art made out of cast iron and aged wood. I skidded to a stop and dropped the bow, trying to will my trembling hands to be still. I gripped the key in between my thumb and index finger and shoved it into the lock. It made it halfway and stopped.

"Shit!" I muttered and pulled it out and quickly flipped it upside down. I pushed it back in, but it still didn't budge. I looked at the key and then the lock. "It's the wrong fucking key!" I cried.

"What?" Hayden panted, turning his back to me as he looked behind us.

"It won't fit!"

"Maybe you have it the wrong way," he suggested and pulled the trigger. My ears rang from the shot. I turned the key again.

"No, it doesn't fit! I've tried it both ways!"

"Are you sure?"

"Yes!" For good measure, I shoved it in once more. "It's fucking useless!" I threw the key to the ground.

Hayden spun and pulled a bobby pin from my hair, snapping several strands. "Pick it?"

"That'll take too long." I took the pin from him anyway and used my teeth to pull off the rubber ends. I bent it back and forth before sticking it into the lock.

"Hurry!" Hayden instructed and fired until the clip was empty.

- 167 -

He reloaded it and shot again. "Riss, now!"

"I'm trying," I yelled in frustration. I dropped to my knees and worked the pieces of the bobby pin inside the lock. The metal did nothing but bend. When it snapped and broke, I screamed out of anger and yanked my second—and last—bobby pin from my hair, causing my bangs to fall into my face. Ignoring them, I bent the second pin back and shoved it into the lock.

Hayden backed up until his legs pressed up against my body. "Riss, go!" he shouted. "I'll hold them off!"

"What? No!"

"We can't take them all—go!"

I turned my head. My stomach dropped in terror. An entire herd was upon us. Hayden fired two more times until he ran out of ammo. Something clicked inside the lock. I pressed on the cast iron handle hopefully, but the gate didn't swing open to freedom. I could feel Hayden twist as he grabbed another magazine from inside his pocket.

Then he let out a strangled shout of shock and pain. I looked behind me to see a tall S2 clamp his teeth down onto Hayden's shoulder.

CHAPTERFIFTEEN

I jumped up and shoved the zombie off of Hayden. It took a mouthful of his skin with it and I felt instantly sick when I watched his flesh stretch and snap. Blood poured from the wound. Hayden kicked the zombie in the knee, causing it to fall. As he stomped on its head, I worked with hysterical haste to pick the lock. I felt something click. I pushed part of the pin in just a tiny bit more.

The gate swung open. I grabbed the hem of Hayden's shirt and yanked him back. He stumbled but recovered and hurried through. We dropped to the ground, using our backs to push the door closed. Above us, zombies reached through the cast iron.

"Shit, Hayden!" I cried and turned to him. "What the hell?" I resisted the urge to hit him.

"What?" he wheezed.

"Stop doing that!"

"What?" he repeated, sounding just as confused as before.

"Using your body as a shield. Stop almost dying for me!"

"Not gonna happen," he said dryly. "What was I supposed to do? Let them bite you?"

I turned to face him, suddenly overwhelmed with emotion. I shook my head and let out a ragged breath. "I can't lose you."

He put his hand on mine and gave me a half smile. "You won't. Don't worry about it Riss," he promised. "Though, if we don't find a way to keep them from breaking through, we're dead anyway."

"I think we're dead." My voice broke as I spoke. I didn't see a way out of this. At least three dozen zombies were behind us; once they crashed through the gate there was nothing we could do to stop them. My eyes madly looked around the yard for anything useful. The grass was overgrown and the fact that we had no fucking idea what was inside the house only terrified me more.

"That," Hayden said and pointed.

"The gnome?" I asked incredulously, eyeing a lawn gnome with a red pointed hat.

"Yes. Get it!"

"Hayden—what?"

"Just go!" he urged. I scrambled to grab the gnome, cutting my hands on the lava rocks that surrounded the fence. I tossed it to Hayden. He shoved the pointed end of the hat under the gate, acting as a reversed door jam. "It's not enough," he said as if it wasn't obvious.

"That bench," I said. It was too heavy for me to drag over on my own. Hayden jumped up and helped me lift it. We set it against the gate.

"Now what?" Hayden huffed.

"You're bleeding. Bad. We need to get inside or...or something."

Hayden put his right hand over the wound and nodded. "Yeah. Inside. This isn't strong enough to keep them all out," he said and eyed the bench. And it wasn't, not at all, but a steady stream of blood dripped down Hayden's arm, pooling around his elbow and falling to the ground. I needed to stop the bleeding before working on a better barricade.

I picked up the bow and held an arrow at the ready. Hayden let go of his shoulder and wiped the blood on his jeans. He reached behind him and took a hold of the M16. Taking Hayden's lead, we circled the house. I let out a small breath of relief when the yard was secure. There was another gate in the back but, unlike the fancy front one, it was all wood and metal with no pretty cast iron bars for zombies to reach through. It was locked and sturdy; we decided it wasn't a threat.

"Ok," he said and let the machine gun hang around his shoulder. "Time to look inside."

"Right. I'll check the front window, see if anything alive—or *not* alive is in there." I put my hand on his shoulder. "How bad is it?" I asked and looked at the bite wound.

"I don't think it's deep." He looked at the glistening blood that was slowly dripping from his arm. "I'm kinda dizzy though," he confessed.

"It's hot, you've lost blood...you're dehydrated," I told him and let out a deep breath, blowing my bangs out of my face. I opened my bag and pulled out the water bottle. "Here, drink it. I'll go check inside the house."

"It should be safe in there. Hannah said they went inside."

I clenched my jaw and twisted the cap off of the water bottle and took a drink before handing it to Hayden. Though Hannah might have been innocent in this whole situation, I couldn't help but feel as if Jon had given us the wrong key on purpose. It wouldn't be so shocking if the house was full of zombies.

"Just let me look inside, ok?"

"Yeah, ok." We walked to the front of the house and stepped into the overgrown flower bed. I cupped my hands around my face and peered into the window. Seeing nothing, I knocked.

"I'll look around back," Hayden said.

"Ok," I replied without taking my eyes away from the window. I banged on the glass once more. I pressed my ear to it and listened but only heard Hayden knocking on another window. "All clear?" I asked when he returned.

"Looks like it," he said. He was holding his right hand over the wound again. The bleeding had stopped by this time and the threat of being eaten alive was wearing off, allowing the implications of Hayden's bite to sink in.

He led the way inside the house. With our guns raised, we slowly entered the grand foyer, our boots echoing on the shiny, pearl-white marble floor.

"I think your sister was right," I whispered. "It does look like royalty lived here."

Hayden shook his head. "In the middle of Texas? I'm going with the drug lord."

I rolled my eyes and smiled, turning around to close the front door without a sound. We slipped through the rest of the house, finding nothing. We explored the second level next and again, it was empty.

"Ok," I said and set my weapons on the island counter in the kitchen. "Sit."

Hayden pulled out a bar stool and heavily plopped down. I pushed up the sleeve on his left arm. The bite wasn't very deep—thankfully—but the edges were jagged and torn and a nasty bruise was already forming. I rummaged around through the cabinets until I found a clean towel. I also had to agree with Hannah on this place not being someone's main living quarters. Other than dishes, pots, pans, and dish towels, the cabinets were empty.

"Don't," Hayden protested when I picked up the water bottle. "That's the only thing we have to drink."

"This needs to be cleaned. The last time you got a bite you got sick, remember?"

"Yeah, but that was under different circumstances."

"And that's relevant because...?"

"I don't know. There's just no time to deal with this."

"Yes there is," I countered. "We're stuck here until that herd leaves. I'm not even going to think about going outside that fence anytime soon."

"You're right," he agreed and got up to open a few windows. The house was uncomfortably stuffy. "Hey," he called from another room. "There's a hot tub."

"Really?" I asked, knowing his excitement wasn't because he wanted to get in it. "Is it covered?"

"Yeah."

"Awesome. Let's have a look." Hayden opened a sliding glass door that led onto a large deck. There was a gas grill, a round, metal fire pit, a glass table with a broken umbrella and four folding chairs which were tipped over and covered in leaves. I cleared off rain soaked and rotten debris from the cover and peeled it off. The smell of chlorine wasn't strong, but the water was still pretty clear.

"You have a lighter, right?" I asked Hayden. He nodded and fished it out of his pocket. "Can you get a pot from the kitchen? And bring that towel." I took the lid off of the fire pit and dumped out the stagnant water. Dry, brittle leaves were stuck in the corners of the deck and would be perfect for burning. I scooped them up, flicked a spider off my wrist with more panic than I was proud of and dumped them in. Assuming there would be a pile of firewood nearby, I jumped down the steps of the deck to find it.

"What's wrong?" Hayden asked, returning with the pot and two towels.

"There's no fire wood," I complained.

"Hold that thought," he said and disappeared into the house. A moment later he emerged, carrying one of the wooden bar stools. He met my eyes and shrugged.

"It'll work," I approved and stepped back as Hayden smashed it. I picked up the smallest pieces and carefully stacked them around my pile. It took a minute to get the fire going. Hayden filled the pot with water set it on the mesh, metal lid.

"Oh, I found this too." Hayden extended a bottle of green

liquid to me.

"Dish soap?" I questioned.

"That's all I could find. It says it's antibacterial."

"I guess it's better than nothing. Grab a seat."

Hayden shook off two of the folding chairs and set them away from the heat of the fire. We sat in silence and waited for the water to boil. Carefully, I stuck the towels in the pot and used part of the bar stool to fish them out. After a minute of waving them around in the air, they were cool enough to touch. I blotted away the crusty blood on Hayden's shoulder until the fresh scab opened up. I folded the towel in half and wiped away as much dirt as I could.

I stuck the bloody towel back in the pot and put a tiny bit of soap on the clean towel. Trying to be as gentle as possible, I scrubbed the wound clean before rinsing off the suds. Finding a semi clean section on the towel, I wiped off the scratches on my arm.

"Better?" Hayden asked and stood.

"Not really," I replied. "We need a first aid kit. I bet you anything you need stitches. And some legit disinfection ointment." Hayden used the bloody towel to grab the pot from the fire. "And I need to find something to wrap around your shoulder; you're bleeding again."

"There are more towels," Hayden told me, ignoring the fact that he needed further medical treatment. I nodded and followed him in. After making a crappy make-shift bandage, we went upstairs to get a better view on the herd. There were a few stragglers but most had moved on. Where had they gone? I bit my lip. I hoped the guys had heard the gun shots and were expecting an attack. If they got everyone inside or on the roof, there was a chance the herd could have passed by without taking notice.

"What should we do now?" I asked Hayden as we walked down the stairs.

"We should go find that church before it gets dark. I don't think we have too many hours of sunlight left."

"Right. I'm down several arrows. Do you have much ammo left?"

Hayden patted his pockets and shook his head. "Maybe we should wait a little longer then."

"Yeah. Good idea." I walked to the back of the house and looked out at the back gate. "It looks like it's wide enough for a car, doesn't it?"

"It does. What are you thinking?"

"I'm thinking that's the driveway."

"It would make sense. But we have a problem. We have no way to lock the gates."

"Shit, you're right. We'll...we'll come up with something," I concluded and threw my hands in the air. "There's nothing helpful here. I don't get why this place is so empty."

"Oh, it hosts fancy corporate retreat getaways."

I raised an eyebrow. "Uh, ok."

"It does. There were brochures in the kitchen. I saw it when I was getting the towels."

"That explains the random location and lack of a garage."

"Hey," he said suddenly. "Did you ever tie bed sheets together and sneak out of your house?"

"I sneaked out a lot but never that way."

"Dammit. I have no idea if it will work then." He shook his head. "That was my plan for getting over the fence."

"No, it will work. If we cut the sheets into strips and braid them, it should be strong enough."

"Are you sure?"

I shrugged. "In theory."

* * *

Hayden tugged on our sheet-braided rope. He was on the opposite side of the fence than me, testing out how easy it would be to climb back to safety.

"Feels strong enough," he called. "It's holding my weight and not tearing. Come over."

I climbed up our ghetto ladder and grabbed the rough stone top of the fence. I tossed my bow down to Hayden and used the rope to ease my way to the ground. The tire tracks were hard to see; it was obvious no one had ventured to this retreat house long before the virus struck. The slight depressions in the land were discernible though, and the fact that there was a straight path cut through the forest was an obvious choice of what path to follow.

On high alert, we barely spoke as we made our way down the driveway. "I was thinking," I began, eyeing the trees. "I know you want to get Hannah back to the compound right away."

"You're right. I do," he said definitely.

"*But* we came all the way here to do something. Instead of driving all the way back home and then out here again, why don't we load up some supplies and have Hannah and her friends stay in the retreat house? The place is built like a fortress. I think it's pretty safe."

Hayden took a few long strides before looking at me. "That's...uh, logical," he finally admitted.

"It is. And it will only take a day or two to go on missions to get supplies. And as long as they stay put, they'll be safe here," I reiterated. "I'll ask the others what they thing to be sure."

Hayden shook his head. "No need. They'll go for it. It would be a good place for us to stay the night too."

I swatted a fly from my face and let out a breath of relief. "I just want this over with."

"Me too," he agreed. "I never thought I'd say this but I want to get back to normal, with normal being we go on missions and only worry about zombies."

I laughed. "Oh yeah. Those were the days. If we make it through this alive, we'll have some good stories to tell at least."

Hayden chuckled. "We'll get there someday. I promised you we would, remember?"

"I'm gonna hold you to it." I quickened my pace, eyes darting around the forest. It was nice yet unnerving to see not one remnant of the herd. "And I'm still counting on you to take me to a beach. I just want to sit in the sand, feel the ocean breeze, and sip a margarita."

"No ice," he reminded me and playfully elbowed my side.

"Damn. I'll just take the bottle of tequila, then."

Hayden began speaking but stopped abruptly. He stole a glance at me and nodded. Apprehensively, we walked out of the shade and onto a paved road. Hoping Hannah remembered correctly, we turned to the right and began moving again. Attracted to the dark pavement, the sun beat down on us almost unbearably. I'd kill for that ocean right about now.

"Fuck," Hayden muttered under his breath. We had found the church...and the herd. "There's no way we're getting in there."

"I think it'd be pointless," I whispered, my heart dropping, thinking that there was no way anyone inside would have made it. "We should double back before they sense us and come this way."

Hayden's shoulders sagged but he agreed. He put his hand on my back as we turned. Then someone screamed, their voice coming from inside the church. We looked at each other.

"They're still alive in there," Hayden exclaimed. "Riss, we have to—"

"I know," I interrupted. "I'm not going to leave anyone either, Hayden."

He nodded and stepped off the road. Half hidden by trees, we surveyed the damage. The stained glass window in the front of the church was broken; the sun reflected off of colorful shards of glass that lay scattered in the parking lot. At least two dozen zombies meandered about the parking lot, for the most part ignoring the open entry.

Someone screamed again, getting a few of the zombies' attention. I wanted to shout back a 'shut the fuck up' but bit my tongue. Following the sound of the yelling, two zombies broke away from their buddies to walk up the steps and bump into the closed front door. They took a step back and tried again, unable to figure out how to open it.

"It's a good thing the virus makes people into idiots," I huffed. "Well, after it makes them homicidal and crazy."

Hayden nodded. "The mind of a zombie isn't hard to understand. Well, their thought processes at least. Scientifically, that shit is confusing." He shook his head and looked at the church, his hazel eyes wide as he tried to come up with a plan of attack.

Another S2—a petite blonde boy who looked to be only about seven—wandered away from the parking lot and crossed the street. Limping, his foot caught on a bag of garbage and sent the contents scattering. Several pop cans rolled to a stop by the curb. The noise was enough to bring four more zombies out from behind the church. My eyes darted to the herd and then to the boy again. There was no way we could get past the herd and into the church. We knew there had to be over two dozen zombies out front, possibly just as many out back and God-only-knows how many were inside.

"We need to create a diversion," Hayden whispered. "Even if we did have the ammo, I don't know if we could get to them before they got to us."

"Yeah," I agreed, not taking my eyes off the child zombie. He entered the parking lot of a tiny strip mall, housing a Chinese take-out restaurant, a tanning and nail salon, a dog groomer, and a mattress store. Along with wishing I could order a bowl of chicken fried rice, I had an idea.

"Look." I pointed behind the strip mall to a park. "There's an ambulance."

"What do you want to do with it?"

"Use it to distract the zombies. The siren and flashing lights might be enough to make most of them leave."

Hayden tipped his head. "If you can get it started. If not...make another alarm go off."

"It worked before," I blurted and felt a twist of pain when I thought of Rider and my narrow escape in the zombie filled parking lot. Inadvertently, my face went blank and my eyes drifted to my feet. Hayden put his hand on my cheek and tipped my head up.

"I'm sorry, Riss," he spoke gently, knowing what memory was causing me pain. "I wish I could tell you it gets better, but it doesn't—obviously, since I still have nightmares about Ben's death."

"You suck at inspirational speeches, you know?"

Hayden laughed. "Yeah, I guess I do."

I inhaled and mentally shook myself. "Ok...it's ok. We should go back a little, cross the street, and sneak behind those buildings, down that hill, through the trees and into the park."

Hayden gave me a nod of approval and we took off, moving as quietly as possible. There was a pile of dead bodies behind the tanning salon. Gagging, I covered my nose and hurried around them.

"Nothing like the smell of death warmed over," Hayden grimaced. I no longer wanted fried rice. He raised his hand and motioned to a dumpster. "Get him?"

When I nodded, Hayden whistled, drawing the zombie out. As soon as he fell, Hayden jogged over to retrieve the arrow. He flicked off the blood and handed it to me. A few gummies shuffled in the back ally; none were enough of a threat to waste our time killing. We ran down the hill, hopped a fence, and entered the park.

Gravel crunched under my feet as we ran down the track that surrounded an overgrown lawn. Park benches were hidden behind tall weeds. Birds squawked and chirped like normal, oblivious to the never-ending human death.

A makeshift shelter had been set up—and taken down by bad weather—in a covered picnic area. The remains of cots, chairs, and coolers full of food were stained from rain and wind and covered with animal droppings. Behind that was the ambulance.

"Wait," Hayden called when I opened the door to the cab. He pointed to a police car several yards away. The door was ajar and the cop's corpse was sticking halfway out of the driver's seat. His hands, arms, and face had been reduced to nothing but bone. He looked around for zombies and sneaked to the car. Using his arm to shield his nose, he reached into the car and pulled the officer's body out.

Blinking hard, he looked away. I never before knew that the smell of rotting could be so strong that it burned your eyes. He took the gun from the cop's belt and then flipped the body over, removing his flashlight and handcuffs. I nervously looked around as Hayden leaned inside the car, stripping it of anything useful.

"This could come in handy," he said with a grin when he returned with two bullet proof vests, a shot gun, plus the small items he took off the body. Since it was too much to carry, we put on the vests and shoved the hand cuffs, pistol, and flashlight inside my bag.

"My turn to raid," I told Hayden. "You still need medical crap."

He looked at the bloody bandage on his shoulder, which had slipped down and was only covering half the wound. "Nah. I'm fine."

"It's not going to heal itself," I snapped.

"Uh, Riss. It actually will. That's kinda how wound healing works," he teased.

"Shut up. You know what I mean." I took a breath and felt constricted in the vest. "I don't like this," I complained and held the bow out for Hayden to take.

"You'll get used to it," he informed me. "I didn't like them at first either. Until it saved my life more than once." I met Hayden's eyes. He rarely brought up anything that had to do with his time overseas. He waved his hand. "Get your shit."

I opened the back door and leaned back in surprise. "Hayden," I whispered. "You gotta come see this."

He looked around once more before hurrying over. Whoever had been strapped into the gurney had died a long time ago; the only evidence of their body was the blood stained sheets and scrapes of hair and clothes. Only the larger bones were left; I thought I spotted a femur lying on the floor under another body. The second body was still dressed in a soiled paramedic uniform. They looked as if they had wasted away to nothing; skin was stretched over brittle bones reminding me of the horrific images we were forced to look at during my world history class.

Only that body wasn't dead. It was too weak to get up and move, let alone lift its head off the floor. A rattling wheeze was the closest it could come to growling and its fingers quivered as it tried to form a fist.

"So this is what happens when zombies don't eat," I noted.

"I guess so," Hayden said. "It's pathetic." He set the bow down inside the ambulance and stepped in, ending the poor creature's life. "I forget that they used to be just like us."

"Me too. I don't feel like they are human anymore." I stepped back and checked the park. Two zombies struggled to get over the fence. A few more aimlessly wandered through the tall grass. "Grab that bag," I told Hayden. "Stuff anything you can inside." I grabbed my bow and walked a few feet away. The gargling groans from the massive herd at the church were carried down to us with the wind. Despite the heat, I shivered.

"I grabbed a ton of stuff," Hayden told me and jumped out. "That bag is kinda heavy."

"I can handle it," I said shortly and took it from him.

"I know, but you said your ribs hurt."

"That was over an hour ago. I'm fine."

"You're more that fine, Riss, I know. But it's a known fact that I'm stronger than you."

I whipped around, ready to be mad. Then I saw the smirk on Hayden's face. "Do you want me to kick your ass?"

"You couldn't if you tried," he joked.

"After this is over, we're going to spar. And you will lose."

"Don't get your hopes up." Laughing, he gathered up his weapons. "Alright," he said seriously. "They will come from that direction. Are you planning on running or should we try our luck with one of these cars?"

"It's worth a shot," I agreed. We split up and tried the half dozen cars. Every single one was locked. "Running it is." I resituated the quiver and the paramedic bag on my back, twisting my leather bag to rest at my side. Hayden offered once more to take something. Annoyed with how bunchy I was feeling, I gave in and tossed him the bag full of first aid supplies.

We went over our escape route twice before opening the cab. A rotten body fell onto me, almost knocking me over. I shoved it away and stepped inside. The keys were in the ignition. I swallowed the lump of fear that had quickly formed and twisted. The engine sputtered. I fired it up again, afraid that if I held the key too long the engine would flood.

"One more time," I muttered to myself. Three tries later, the ambulance roared to a start. The low fuel light blinked and I laughed. *Just our luck*, I thought. It would be enough to cause a diversion. I looked around the dash, confused by all the buttons. Finally, I figured out how to turn on the siren and lights. The high pitched screaming rang in my ears. I backed out of the cab, stepped on the body, and stumbled.

Hayden caught me just in time and we took off, running away from the park as fast as possible. We darted across the street and turned, going in the opposite direction from the church. Zombies came from every direction. They filtered out of the church parking lot, moving toward the source of the siren. I rounded a corner, going behind a gas station, and skidded to a stop. A tall zombie, wearing a torn winter jacket, rushed at me. A hatchet was sticking out of his neck. Someone obviously hadn't aimed for the head.

I reached for it, kicked him back and yanked it free before swinging my hand down. Thick, brown blood sprayed in the air. Hayden pushed past us and shoved his knife into the ear of another. The stomping and dragging of feet echoed off the brick building. More zombies than the two of us could handle emerged from an alley and headed straight for us. If we turned and ran, we would be running into the street filled with the undead.

Hayden picked up the zombie he had just killed, slit open her stomach and hooked his arms under hers. We backed up against the wall. I held my breath as the zombies slipped past us. I watched Hayden close his eyes and remain perfectly steady as he held up our smelly zombie shield.

"Holy shit," Hayden mouthed when the last zombie passed us. "Let's get the hell out of here." He slowly put down the body and tip-toed over it. We crossed the alley and raced across another parking lot. I slowed to whack a straggler in the head with the hatchet.

Hayden slowed when he stepped onto the church parking lot. He held up his hand and looked around the building. "They're not all gone," he panted. "Hit and run."

I nodded in understanding and followed his lead, finding that I rather liked using the hatchet to bash in zombie brains. Together, we hacked and stabbed our way through the parking lot and to the front of the church.

Breathing hard, we slowed and stepped in through the broken window. The sounds of a struggle echoed off the barren walls. I looked around the large church, unsure of where to go. Ahead of us were closed, tall wooden doors surrounded by glass. I could see benches and an altar behind them. To our right was a narrow staircase; to the left was a hallway. Then she screamed again, her voice coming from above. Without a second thought, I raced up the stairs.

Three zombies clawed and grabbed at a group of terrified people. The screaming was coming from a little girl, who had herself wedged between an overturned table and a bench. Several others were hidden behind it as well, trapped between the zombies and a wall. A tall man and a dark haired woman were in front of the group, using metal candle holders to beat at the zombies.

The woman hit the closest zombie hard enough on the head to cause the bone to break, but not hard enough to damage the brain. She raised her arm to strike again but was pushed back and fell, landing hard on the wooden bench.

"Mommy!" the little girl screamed. She made a move for her mother but was stopped by one of the people backed up to the wall. I reached behind me for an arrow and paused at the top of the stairs to aim and release. The zombie fell forward, landing on top of the woman. Hayden moved past me and yanked the decaying body off of her. Another zombie, with foul smelling mud caked all over his ripped flannel jacket, grabbed Hayden's arm. With ease he twisted and threw it to the ground. He raised his leg and stomped on its head until it stopped moving. Using my bow and arrows, I hit another, causing blood to splatter across the face of the tall man with the candle stick.

"Thank you, Jesus!" the man gasped.

I shrugged. "Call me Orissa."

Hayden stepped forward. "Are you guys alright?"

"Y-yeah," the man stuttered, looking at us in awe. He turned around and inspected his friends. "We are, thanks to you."

The sirens still echoed, their wailing muffled by distance and the church walls. I wondered how long it would take before the zombies realized there was nothing to eat inside the ambulance. Would they wander back this way? I turned, planning on running down the stairs to check on their status.

"Wait." The women who had fallen spoke. "Don't leave."

"We won't," Hayden assured her. "We came here to find you, actually. Hannah sent us."

"Hannah?" the man asked. He set the candle stick down.

"You know Hannah?"

Hayden laughed. "Funny story. I'm her brother."

"Hayden?" an older man questioned. He pushed off the wall and stepped forward. "No, you can't be. She told us her brother Hayden was overseas fighting in the war."

"Yes," Hayden said calmly. "I was. But I'm back...obviously."

"Why should we believe him?" another woman whispered. "What if he did something to Hannah? Where is she?"

"Here," I tried and removed the dog tags. "Hayden Underwood, in the flesh." I motioned to Hayden.

The tall man apprehensively let the tags fall into his hand. "And you are?" he asked me once he had validated Hayden's identity. His eyes were still studying the blood flecked metal.

"Orissa," I introduced and slipped the chain back over my head. I tucked the tags into my shirt, where they fell in between my breasts. "His girlfriend. Hence the dog tags."

"Oh, yes," the man mumbled, his eyes flashing from Hayden to me. "Is Hannah alright?"

"Yes," Hayden answered right away. "She and her group ran into a little trouble with the herd." He skipped over the part where people had died. The two of us being here was enough to take in; plus it would be better to hear it from the people who actually knew the names of the deceased. "That's how we found them, actually. The rest of our crew is with them. We know of a nearby safe location we'd like to take you to."

"Is everyone else there?"

"Not yet. They, uh, needed some time to rest." Hayden smiled. "We can take you to them."

The woman stepped forward and I noticed that her daughter was hiding behind her back. "Why should we trust you?" Her voice shook.

"You shouldn't," I said honestly. "But what other choice do you have? That siren won't keep that herd away forever."

"Will they come back?" a frail, old woman asked. Her hands were twisted from rheumatoid arthritis. I wanted to ask how the hell she had made it this far.

"More than likely," Hayden said gently. "We should get out while we can."

I could tell he was on edge, and he had good reason to be. The herd outside was massive, and I knew he wanted to get back to his sister as well as our friends. The worry was growing inside me as well. What if part of the herd turned around and shambled down to that crappy, gray building? What would we find when we went back?

The tall man nodded. He turned around and got a nod from the old lady. "I'm Jim, by the way. And this is Lori and her daughter Amanda." He waved his hand at the dark haired woman and the little girl. Then he introduced the rest of his people. Agatha and Roger were the two older people, Janet was a mousy middle aged woman, and Ryan was a teenage boy who seemed to be around the same height and build as Jason. I was curious to know why he was stuck with the 'unfit' group.

Hayden straightened up. "Do you have a car?"

Jim nodded. "We have three that run."

"Two," Lori corrected. "Jon took the SUV."

"Right. We can all cram in, I suppose."

Glass crunched, the ominous echo sending waves of terror over the group. With deliberate calmness, I removed an arrow from the quiver and turned. The labored breathing and scuffling of feet became louder.

"Perfect headshot," Jim said quietly when the zombie's legs folded. "Were you in the Marines too?"

"No," I said honestly. "But I've known how to hunt since I was old enough to hold a bow."

Jim nodded and scanned his eyes over me. He wasn't checking me out but taking me in. The fact that I was heavily armed and covered in blood had to be somewhat startling. "So," he began. "How far away is the rest of our group? Will it take long to get back to them?"

"It shouldn't take too long," Hayden informed him.

"Well then," Jim started with a slight smile. "What are we waiting for? Let's go."

"Pastor Jim," Lori whispered. "I don't think we should go."

Jim looked at us for another few seconds before turning to Lori. He put his hand on her arm and turned away. Hayden moved to the top of the stairs, keeping watch for stragglers.

"They're strangers," I heard Lori argue. "I'm not going anywhere with them and we're *not* giving them the keys to our only cars! Look at them; do you want to get into a car with those two? They are dangerous."

"But they know Hannah," the teenage boy pointed out. "I don't think they will hurt us."

"That doesn't mean we should trust them. How do we know where Hannah really is? And why wouldn't she come with them?

Something bad had to have happened to her. It just doesn't make sense," Lori spat, shaking her head. "I'm not going. We've been here long enough and have been able to hold the zombies off. That herd will wander away like the rest do."

"Our doors have been broken," Jim reminded her. "They've never come into our church before."

"She wouldn't have sent them here if they were dangerous," Agatha put her two cents in. "And they are capable of defending themselves." She smiled, causing deep wrinkles to form around her mouth. "Plus that Marine is quite the looker."

Lori threw her hands in the air. "Fine. Go with them. Amanda and I are staying here until Jon comes back."

"You know," I piped up. "If we wanted to hurt you, kill you, take your supplies...you know, anything of the sort, we would have just let those zombies do the dirty work. Why save you only to kill you later? *That* doesn't make sense." I moved forward to get my arrows. "Look," I said and straightened up, flicking goo from the arrow tip. "We won't force you to go, but we won't wait here forever either." I gathered the rest of my arrows and returned to Hayden's side.

"They have every right not to trust us," he said quietly.

"Oh, I fully agree. I'm glad they don't trust us, really."

Hayden exhaled and nodded. "It will be dark soon," he commented after a few moments of silence.

"Yeah," I agreed and crossed my arms. I looked back at the little group. "Hayden," I began slowly. "I know you want to do this for Hannah, but if they don't make up their minds soon, we *have* to go. I don't want to make our own friends risk a night in that tuna can of a shelter."

"You're right." He turned and walked over to Jim and explained our own problem. "We will come back—with Hannah—in the morning," he concluded. "I just hope you're still here." He spun back around and met my eyes, knowing his dramatic speech would settle in soon.

I put my hand on the railing and descended half way down the stairwell before someone shouted, "Wait!"

Slowly, Hayden and I turned around. Lori rushed over. "We will come with."

I let out a sigh of relief. I was about to lead the way outside when Hayden asked if they had any personal items to get. And of course, they did. Hayden and the teenage boy, whose name I had already forgotten, went outside to keep an eye on the herd and to start the cars.

I followed Lori and her daughter down the stairs and into a big room with a vaulted ceiling. We went through a door next to a huge wooden cross and entered into another room, though this one seemed more like a large storage closet with only one tiny window. Cots and air mattresses were lined up against the wall, all with blankets neatly laid across them. Clothing and books were crammed onto a tall bookshelf and religious items had been respectfully stacked on a small table near the door. I picked my pony tail up off my neck; there was no circulation in here. With the added bullet proof vest, I was sweating my ass off.

I stood in the doorway while the others packed their stuff, keeping watch. I couldn't remember the last time I had attended a church service. I was forced to go as a child; my mother and stepfather went every Sunday, then again on Tuesday for Bible Study, Wednesday for some kind of youth group night, Thursday for meetings about missions and the occasional Friday and Saturday for reasons I didn't always know. Thinking back now, it was stupid of me to resent them for it, but as a child I felt neglected and unwanted, not to mention the fun feelings of being replaced.

My mom and I used to be close, we used to spend time together just doing silly, random things...until my real dad left her. She had sunk into a drunken depression that I was unable to pull her from. But everything changed when she met Ted.

A brass cup clattered to the floor, pulling me back to reality. Agatha huffed as she bent over to pick it up and set it back on the table. Everyone grew still, afraid that the noise was enough to catch the attention of a zombie or two. I turned my head and listened.

"Fuck," I said aloud. "The sirens stopped. Grab your crap. We need to go."

"We don't have everything!" Janet cried.

"It doesn't matter," I muttered and pushed the door all the way open. "It's not worth your life. Or mine. Let's go."

Jim nodded and zipped his bag. He breezed past me and knelt before the giant cross, silently saying a prayer. Being respectful, I stayed put until he was done. Once he stood, I pulled the hatchet from my bag and handed it to him.

"Just in case," I said quietly. "I'll lead them out, ok?"

Jim nodded and tightened his fingers around the wooden handle. I slipped down the aisle and pushed open the heavy door.

A lone S3 dragged a broken foot along the hall, smearing a trail of thick brown blood on the floor. I held up my hand, signaling the others to wait. I shot her with an arrow and dashed out into the hall to retrieve my ammo.

Heavy footfalls echoed a few yards away. I pulled back the arrow and waited. Whoever it was moved fast. Shit, had the zombies found something fresh to eat? I edged my way around the corner. Hayden put his hand up.

"It's me."

"No shit," I responded and lowered the arrow. "Ready?"

"Yeah. This way." He looked behind me. "Where is everyone?"

"In that room with the benches and the stage."

"The chapel?" he said with amusement.

"Shut up. Yes." I ducked back and waved to Lori. Tightly holding her daughter's hand, she took the lead and rushed into the hall. The gargling moan of a zombie loomed ahead. She staggered out of a bathroom; Hayden grabbed a fistful of her hair and smacked her head against the wall until her body went limp.

I stepped over the body, waving everyone on. Agatha, Roger, and Janet got into a blue SUV. The teenage boy was in the driver's seat, looking like he might have a panic attack at any second. Once Lori, Amanda, and Jim piled into the backseat of an Impala, Hayden and I scrambled into the front. Hayden stomped on the gas, tires squealing on the church parking lot.

The bulk of the herd was still gathered in the park. I let out a breath of relief and reached for the air conditioner, turning it up as high as it would go. Hot air blasted out, making me cough.

"It's kinda sad to see it go," Lori muttered softly.

"It is," Jim agreed. "It has served us well."

"Were you there long?" Hayden asked.

"Probably three months," Jim answered.

"Where were you before?" Hayden spoke casually, as if he was trying to make conversation.

"Most of us were in a quarantine shelter a few miles north. It was a nice set up for until the undead broke through the fences. A large group of us were able to get out unscathed. We spent the winter in a courthouse not too far from here."

"And then what happened?"

"Our camp got looted. There used to be forty of us."

"I'm sorry," Hayden said gently. "This world doesn't bring out the best in people, does it?"

"It is unfortunate that you are right," Jim agreed. "Though we have met a few gracious souls—such as you—along the way."

"Why did you stay in a church?" I asked, twisting around slightly in my seat.

"I was the pastor there," Jim replied. "It seemed only natural to go back. It had always been my calling; I thought the Lord would protect us."

"Yeah, well he needs to start doing a better job," I huffed, earning a 'be polite' glare from Hayden.

"Maybe he is," Amanda spoke. Her voice was soft and childlike, reminding me of Zoe and all her innocence. "He led you here."

I didn't know how to respond to her simple yet profound statement. Instead, I faced forward and enjoyed the cold air. Hayden turned onto the dirt road; the uneven and overgrown ground made for an extremely bumpy ride down the long driveway. We had to get out and move fallen tree limbs along the way, but with a little work the driveway wasn't impassable as Hannah originally thought.

Hayden stopped in front of the double doors and raced out of the car. He climbed up the make-shift rope with ease. I scooted over to the driver's seat, waiting for Hayden to open the doors. Everything was a shade darker under the trees, which caused my stomach to nervously churn. As soon as the blue SUV pulled through the doors, Hayden slammed them shut.

"Home sweet home," Janet said under her breath, looking at the house in awe. "How did you guys find this place?"

"Hannah found it," Hayden informed her. "Go inside, light whatever candles you have; it might be dark by the time we get back."

Jim nodded and extended the hatchet to me.

"Keep it," I told him. "I don't think you'll need it, but keep it."

"Thank you," he said with a small smile.

"The house is unlocked," Hayden continued. "Someone will need to shut and lock those doors behind us. Keep that rope up and I'll be able to get in."

"Thank you," Agatha said slowly. "Be safe."

Hayden nodded and opened the door to the Impala for me. Jim opened the other doors and we sped through. We turned left onto the road. Hayden accelerated quickly and we both hoped to find an intersection soon.

I watched the minutes tick by, knowing it would have been

faster to make a straight run through the woods, though it was much, much safer being in a car. Finally, we turned down the correct road and parked the car next to Hayden's truck.

"Hello beautiful," Hayden soothed and put his hand on the truck's hood. "I missed you." He shook his head. "Sorry you are so dirty, baby."

"You are pathetic," I jeered.

"Don't be jealous."

I rolled my eyes and smiled.

Hayden took the keys from his pocket and unlocked the truck. He grabbed a flashlight and jumped into the bed. "Nothing's been touched," he let me know.

"Thank God," I sighed.

"Tell me about it," he agreed and jumped down. "Let's hope it stays that way." He clicked the flashlight off. Together, we walked into the dim forest, nerves on edge. Eventually, the sun sank too deep and we had to turn the flashlight back on. I hated it; the bobbing beam of bright yellow was all too obvious.

"Underwood?" Ivan's voice called from ahead.

"Yeah, it's us," Hayden replied.

"About time. Penwell with you?"

"Of course. I can't get rid of her," he joked.

Ivan turned on his flashlight to let us know his location. "How did everything go?"

"Easy enough," I told him. "You guys ready?"

Ivan nodded. "I'll go get the others," he said and disappeared into the old building. Hannah raced out and threw her arms around Hayden. He hugged her tightly back and smiled. I waited by the door so I could scowl at Jon. It was too dark to tell if he was surprised to see Hayden and me alive. When he brushed past me with his eyes on the ground, my blood boiled. I was certain he'd given us the wrong key on purpose.

Anxious to get back to the safe house and take care of Hayden's shoulder, I let my anger go...for now and led everyone to the cars. It was hopeless to expect everyone to move quietly through the forest. I clenched my hands into fists in annoyance and calmed myself by thinking that if zombies did attack, there were other people for them to eat first.

"What happened?" Hannah asked Hayden when she opened the truck door.

"I got shot," Hayden said matter of factly as his sister looked at the blood stained passenger seat in horror. "And that's from

Riss," He pointed to the back, "almost bleeding to death—again."

"Looks like it," Hannah replied, her voice devoid of emotion. She moved into the back, allowing me to sit shotgun. She earned a few points for that. We took off, Hayden leading our caravan. "Who shot you?" Hannah asked quietly.

Hayden hesitated. "We ran into a group of not-so-nice people."

"And?" Hannah pressed, leaning forward.

"They shot me."

"Obviously," she sassed. "Why?"

"They wanted our weapons," he summed up.

"Where did you get shot?"

"Right shoulder."

"How did you survive?" she fired away another question. "Did it hurt? What happened to guy who shot you?"

"Orissa saved me, yes, and they're dead."

"You saved him?" she asked me. "How?"

I shook my head. "Luck, I think. And a lot of Grand Theft Auto style driving."

"Oh." She leaned back. "How did you almost bleed to death?"

"We'll talk about it later, ok?" Hayden spoke.

"Fine," she agreed and fell silent for a minute. "Do they know that Flint, Keirra, and Tyrell are dead?"

"No," Hayden said gently. "You guys need to tell them."

Hannah nodded. "You're right." She exhaled heavily. "I hate having to do this. It sucks."

Sadness pulled on Hayden's face. "I know. I'm sorry, Hannah."

"Thanks, Hay. Flint hadn't been with us long. But Tyrell and I met back in December. He knew Mom."

Hayden let off the gas involuntarily. "Right," he finally said, his voice tight. He cleared his throat and punched the gas. I reached over and put my hand on this thigh. He took one hand off the wheel and curled his fingers through mine.

* * *

As soon as we had unpacked everything and lit a shit ton of candles in the kitchen, I plopped the EMT's bag onto the counter and dug around until I found what I needed to clean Hayden's bite wound. Only my friends and Hannah sat in the kitchen with us. Jon was breaking the news about their losses, so I figured it was as good of a time as any to take care of Hayden.

Hannah, rightfully so, freaked out just a little when she learned that her brother had been bitten. Tears filled her eyes and she was worried he would die. Hayden had to show her his other two bite scars to convince her it was all right.

"You're infected?" she questioned.

"Technically," Hayden answered, tensing as I rubbed an alcohol swab around the edges of the wound. Washing it with soap had definitely cleaned out the dirt, but I wasn't sure how effective it was against preventing an infection. Jason, who didn't know of Hayden's unique condition sat on a bar stool with wide eyes, listening to Hayden quietly explain everything to Hannah.

"What do you mean?" she asked.

"I mean that the virus is in me. It just doesn't affect me."

"Are you serious?" Hannah asked.

Hayden nodded. "Matilda Burns was the first one to bite me."

"Mrs. Burns?" Hannah exclaimed. "From the bank?"

Hayden smiled and nodded. "That'd be the one."

"Holy crap," she whispered. "What did you do?"

I smeared bacitracin over the wound, careful not to press too hard. The bruise around it was a deep purple now. Something thumped against the front gate, making us all jump.

"I'll check it out," Brock said and pushed off of the counter. Ivan and Wade followed. I let out a breath, a little annoyed that I had let my guard down.

"I shoved her away and ran," Hayden admitted. "I didn't know what was going on and I didn't know I would have to kill anyone until a few hours later when I saw Mr. Miller eating his wife's intestines."

Hannah shivered in disgust. "I'm glad we left when we did. There was a warning on the news about a new flu strain," she explained. "We were told it was so strong that not even the flu shots could protect against it. A bus came through and took us down to Fargo. We stayed at NDSU for a while."

Hayden opened his mouth but was at a loss for words. Contrition clouded his eyes.

"He looked for you," I voiced for him. "That's why he went to your home town as soon as he got back in the States."

"Hayden," Hannah said softly. "Don't blame yourself."

"You guys were *right there*," he said through gritted teeth. Hannah put her hand on Hayden's right shoulder. "I could have saved you all."

Sensing the family tension, Jason excused himself from the room. I placed a thick piece of gauze and put it over the bite and taped it down.

"No," Hannah whispered. "I told you that Heather…Heather is gone, but I didn't tell you that she was one of the first to go."

"What?" Hayden breathed.

"She said she had a headache and then…" Tears pooled in Hannah's eyes. She blinked and they ran down her face. "That's the only reason we left. As soon as the doctors figured out she had that 'flu virus' she was transferred to a bigger hospital." She cast her eyes down. "We never would have gotten to the quarantine at the hospital if she hadn't gotten sick, though."

Hayden stood and hugged his sister. "I'm so sorry."

"I miss her," Hannah cried. I turned away, giving them space. I began packing up the medical bag when someone walked into the kitchen. I spun around; Jon stood a few feet from us, his narrow eyes taking in the scene of Hannah's tears and Hayden comforting her. Then he noticed the fresh bandage on Hayden's arm.

"What's going on in here?" he demanded. Hannah pulled away from her brother.

"It's ok, Jon," she whimpered and wiped her eyes.

He strode forward. "Hannah, what's wrong with your brother?"

"Nothing. We were just talking about—"

Jon pushed her out of the way, causing her to trip over the bar stool and fall to the ground. Hayden moved to catch her but Jon's fingers closed around the bandage. He ripped it off, his pointed face set in a scowl.

As if it was a reflex, Hayden shoved him back and stepped forward, ready for a fight. Jon stumbled and hit a wall.

"He's been bitten!" he wailed. "Look!" he pointed to Hayden's arm. "He's been bitten!" he repeated. "And you knew!" he accused Hannah.

I dropped the bag and rushed over, putting myself in between Hayden and Jon. Hayden reached down and helped Hannah to her feet.

"He's been bitten! He's infected!" Jon continued to cause a fuss. Lupe, Madison, Jim, and Lori cautiously walked up behind him, horror plastered on their faces. "Look! That's a bite wound!" Jon yelled. "He's infected."

"I'm not infected," Hayden said calmly and held his hands up. Hannah linked her arm though his, looking terrified. "Yes, that is a bite, but I'm immune to the virus."

"He's lying!" Jon quaked. "He's going to go crazy and slit our throats while we sleep. We have to kill him!" His hands trembled, but he still moved fast as he reached for the knife that hung from his belt. I raised my wrist in time to block his attempt at slashing it through the air. I clamped my hand on the base of his neck, pressing my fingers onto a pressure point, stunning him for a few seconds. I shoved him against the wall and kneed him in the gut. I took a quick step back, causing him to slide down to his butt. I pulled my pistol from my waist and pointed it at Jon's face.

"Listen here, you little prick," I threatened. "Hayden is not infected. And if you try that little stunt one more time, *I* will slit your throat in your sleep and use your blood for zombie bait!"

Jason, who had smartly gone around and entered the kitchen from the other side, had his gun aimed and raised as well. Jon put his hands up, eyes flicking from me to Jason.

"We're not here to kill each other," I stated slowly. "Got that?"

The front door clicked open. Brock entered first and was able to see us from the foyer. Immediately he had our backs, running to my side with his gun already drawn. Ivan and Wade were there only seconds later.

"What's going on?" Brock asked, not sure where to aim his gun.

"He's infected," Jon stammered, his hands in the air. "And she's crazy."

"Who's infected?" Brock clarified.

"Hayden."

"He can't be." Brock lowered his gun and took a step forward. "What are you trying to do?" he asked Jon.

"Nothing!"

"I don't believe that," he continued, his voice level. "This doesn't come of nothing." He waved his hand at Jason and me.

"She's crazy!"

"Yeah, so crazy," I started, "that shooting you wouldn't be my fault." I let out a breath and allowed my arms to rest at my sides. "He shoved Hannah to the ground and came after Hayden with a knife. Oh, *and* that's not to mention that he gave us the wrong fucking key! Hayden wouldn't have even gotten bitten if we didn't have to stop to pick the lock."

"You did?" Hannah squeaked and shot a hurt look at Jon. "Oh purpose?"

"Jon," Jim spoke, his voice tight. "Hayden is showing no signs of being infected. We don't want to act prematurely."

"Thank you," I expressed. "And not everyone who gets bitten gets sick, genius," I directed to Jon.

"That can't be true," Lupe mused.

"Yes, it is," Ivan took over. His body was relaxed and his voice was calm. There was something about him that begged you to trust him, from his charming smile to the professionalism in the way he spoke. "Hayden has been bitten before." He chuckled. "In fact, I'm starting to think he likes it, it's happened so many times. And he isn't the only person that we know of who has shown resistance to the virus." Ivan stepped in front of me and offered Jon a hand. "Now," he continued. "If you'd like to hear my completely non-medical expert explanation on this, follow me into the living room where we can sit comfortably."

I watched as the others reluctantly shuffled out of the kitchen, impressed with Ivan's ability to defuse the situation. Brock, Wade, and Jason stayed with us, just in case things went south again. I made Hayden sit once more so I could—again—patch up his arm. Ivan's voice carried through the house; I listened to his speech while I pulled out another piece of gauze from the bag.

"He's really not that bad," Hannah promised. "Things have been stressful lately. Well, more stressful than normal." She rested her elbows on the counter and yawned.

"I don't like him," I stated, securing another bandage around Hayden's muscular shoulder. "Or trust him."

"You don't know him," she countered.

"He pulled out a knife and went after Hayden. With no hesitation." I flicked my eyes to her. "And you're defending him?"

"He shoved you to the ground," Hayden said angrily. "I would love to pummel that guy."

"Hay," Hannah begged. "You should know that one of us got bitten a while ago. No one had it in them to kill her. We thought we could catch it in time but we were too late. Two people died that day. And we still had to kill Jenny. He thought he was protecting me."

"But I don't seem remotely crazy," Hayden pursued the argument. "I'm with Riss. I don't like him."

"I feel like he wants us gone," Wade noted.

"No!" Hannah urged. "Never. You guys don't know how

grateful we are! You have a *real* safe house. It's what we've been wanting for months!" She ran her hands through her hair and sighed heavily. "Can we talk about it in the morning? Today has been too much."

"Fine," Hayden huffed. His eyes met mine, letting me know this was far from over. "Get something to eat and rest. We all should," he added.

"You're right," I agreed but was feeling very unwilling to share our food supply with anyone at the moment.

* * *

It took almost an hour for the tension to dissolve. Jon still looked sideways at Hayden. Much to my chagrin, Jason reminded us that if the roles were reversed, we'd be just as suspicious of Jon. It was true, and I knew I wouldn't hesitate to stick a knife in his brain. I'd at least have the decency to wait until he *actually* turned before I did it, though.

After everyone had something to eat, Hannah's group settled in, lighting candles in almost every room and claiming their own space in the rooms upstairs. The sun was long gone and the night time air drifting into the house was almost pleasant. Ivan and I sat with Hayden and Hannah in the living room for a while, but when they started reminiscing about their family, we decided to give them some time alone and check out the front gate.

The wood was solid and able to withstand the pressure of being slammed against, though the thought of the lock breaking made us both nervous. I went back inside and grabbed the keys to the Impala and drove it around the front. Ivan moved the bench, allowing me to put the car in its spot. It would take a crap ton of zombies to get in now.

Bored, we joined Brock, Wade, and Jason on the back deck.

"No," Wade said with irritation. "You're wrong!"

"No I'm not!" Brock spat back. "He even agrees with me," he spoke and pointed to Jason.

Jason raised his hands in defense. "Not entirely. Batman is way more badass than Spiderman."

I smiled and walked up the steps. "What's going on?"

"Riss, you'll settle this. The Hulk. He would be the best choice against zombies, am I right?"

I shrugged. "What are my other choices?"

"Batman and Spiderman."

I shook my head. "I'd go with Ironman."

Ivan chuckled. "Not bad. He does have a lot of fire power."

"So does Batman," Jason brought up.

"But The Hulk is the smartest, well, when he isn't in Hulk form," Wade argued. "He'd come up with a cure. Plus bullets don't faze him. Zombies couldn't bite through his skin."

"You guys have way too much time on your hands," Ivan laughed. He leaned against the deck railing. "Let me hear all the debates," he said with fake professionalism. Some of the built up tension eased out of me as we talked and laughed, arguing over which superhero would be of greatest help to us.

With the sun gone for the night, the air was fresh. When the wind blew, it was almost chilly. Since we didn't feel safe enough from zombies—or Jon— to sleep as a group, we decided it would be best to sleep in shifts. Hannah had moved upstairs to crash for the night; Hayden came onto the deck just as we were going back in. Ivan, Brock, and Wade passed out on the couches in the living room, leaving Jason, Hayden, and me to patrol.

We sat on the deck for a few hours and split a bag of cheesy popcorn. Bored, we got up and walked around the house.

"You smell like death," Hayden told me.

"Thanks," I replied sarcastically. "So do you."

"You're worse." He playfully nudged me. "You always are. I think you like being covered in zombie blood."

"It's so good for your skin." I absent mindedly ran a hand over my hair and grimaced. There were chunks in it. "Hey," I said and stopped walking. "The hot tub has clean enough water."

"Good idea," Hayden agreed. The three of us walked back to our cars so Hayden and I could grab clean shirts. Hayden stripped out of his and splashed water over his face and arms, washing the blood from his body. That would have been easiest for me as well, but I hesitated since Jason was with us.

"We'll check out the front," Hayden stated and pulled his clean shirt on.

"Thanks," I said quietly. It wasn't like I was eager to take my clothes in front of Jason, but I never fully understood the stigma of being seen in a bra. A bikini top was twice as revealing as the bra I had on. I balled up my tank top and used it to scrub away the dried crusts that covered my body. It was a bit of a struggle to yank the band from my horribly tangled hair.

Deciding it would be easier to plunge my head under the water and shake out the crap, I took a deep breath and stuck my head under water. I came up for air, still not satisfied that I was clean enough. I took another breath and went under again.

I could feel the deck vibrating as someone walked across. Assuming it was Hayden, I continued scrubbing my hair. His body pressed up against mine. I gathered my floating hair into my hands, ready to pop up and turn around.

Heavy hands landed on my shoulders, pushing me deeper under the water.

CHAPTER SIXTEEN

Immediately, I panicked, pushing up against whoever was holding me down. I planted my hands on the side of the hot tub and propelled my body up. My attacker leaned on me, using his body weight to pin me. My hand slid down the plastic sides of the tub. In my struggle, I used up all my air. My body went rigid, begging me to take a breath.

I knew I would drown if I didn't do something. I couldn't calm down to think of a plan. Instead, I plunged deeper under water, hoping I could break the connection between my body and the large hands that gripped me. And then I would...swim to the other side? I couldn't think that far ahead. I thrashed around, trying to loudly splash water onto the deck.

On its own accord, my chest heaved and water rushed into my lungs. My body reacted by coughing, which only caused me to inhale more water. My finger tips tingled and I felt like I was going to throw up. My vision was already nothing but black in the dark water. Little white spots swarmed around me. Shit. I was drowning.

No. I couldn't give up. I used my remaining strength to reach up. My fingers smacked the edge of the tub. If I could only get a grip and use it to pull myself—

Suddenly, the hands let go. My head was too heavy to lift. I wasn't able to pull myself up from the water. Then someone grabbed me again, though this time they held me close to their body and backed away from the water.

"Holy shit, Orissa," Jason panted as we tumbled to the ground. I gasped for air, unable to breath. Jason quickly laid me on my side. Water spewed from my mouth and I painfully inhaled. A few feet from us, Hayden stood in front of Jon. Jon's shirt was soaked and he had a gun pointed in Hayden's face. Hayden stepped forward and in a swift, graceful movement, swung his arm at Jon, grabbing his wrist and swinging him around.

In just seconds, the gun was in Hayden's hand and Jon was on the ground. Hayden pulled back the hammer and knelt down, shoving the gun under Jon's face.

"What the fuck is wrong with you?" Hayden growled. Jon cowered away, raising his hands up defenseless. "You are going to pay for that," he threatened and used the butt of the gun to hit Jon across the face.

I began coughing up more stale, chlorine tainted water. Jason eased me into a sitting position. I leaned forward, coughing with all the force I could muster. I began shivering; I wasn't sure if it was from the chilly night air or from the shock of almost drowning. Jason put his hand on my shoulder, unsure of how he could help.

I looked up again to see the blurry shape of Hayden kicking Jon in the side. His hazel eyes flashed with pure rage. Behind them, a shadowy silhouette came into focus.

"Hayden!" Jason shouted in warning. Hayden looked up just in time and turned the gun on Lupe, who had her own shotgun aimed at Hayden. Jon rolled over and coughed up blood before struggling to his feet.

My ears were ringing. Feeling like I was still stuck underwater, I continued to cough as I watched the nightmare unfold. With one more kick to Jon's abdomen, Hayden aimed the gun at Lupe and shouted something to her. Jason's fingers began to press into my skin. I tried to pull myself up but failed; my body was still convulsing and heaving up water.

Another shadow crept through the dark yard, moving quickly without making a sound. Heart pounding, I attempted to stand. Hayden was out there alone. I had to go to him. The shadow became the outline of a person.

Hayden dropped to the ground and the shadow jumped, tackling Lupe to the ground. She squeezed the trigger as she fell; Jason grabbed me and pulled me down, as if the thin deck railing would protect us from stray bullets. Then he let go of me and shot up, yanking his own pistol free from his holster.

Wade wrestled against Lupe and easily pulled the shotgun from her hands. He tossed it to Brock, who was standing only a few feet away and flipped Lupe over, checking her for more weapons.

"What the hell is going on?" Lori yelled, skidding to a stop in the dark yard. Behind her, Jim, Madison, and Hannah stood, all on edge and faces full of fear. She was holding a knife; she must have thought someone was firing at zombies.

"They're trying to kill me!" Jon yelled. "They want to kill all of us!"

"Shut the fuck up," Hayden warned. "He attacked Orissa." Hayden turned and waved his hand at the deck. "We got here just in time."

Lori and Jim stepped closer to the deck, squinting in the dark. Behind me, Ivan clicked on a LED lantern. The bright light was too much for my eyes and I had to look away.

"Oh my God," Lori mumbled. "What the hell did you do to her?"

Looking like a shirtless drowned rat, I was definitely the portrait of a victim. Ivan knelt down next to me, removed his black button up, and draped it over me. Trembling, I stuck my arms through the sleeves and pulled the front closed. My fingers shook too much to work the buttons. With Ivan's help, I up righted myself.

"He was trying to kill her," Jason filled in. He stood close next to me, as if he was afraid I might fall over. Ivan put his hand on my shoulder and tipped his head in question. Understanding that he was making sure I was ok, I nodded and took a shaky breath in. Ivan jumped down the stairs and hurried to Hayden's side.

Hayden was still seething with anger. He turned away from Jon and pressed the palms of his hands into his temples. Then he whipped around and pointed the gun at Jon.

"Why would you want to kill her? You owe her. You all owe her!" He dropped to his knees and grabbed the collar of Jon's shirt, jamming the gun into his chest.

"Hayden!" Hannah called and began to rush forward. Jim caught her by the wrist and pulled her back. Ivan was there seconds later. He calmly bent down to Hayden's level and said something, too quiet for me to hear. Hayden closed his eyes and quickly shook his head.

"No!" he protested. "He shoved her under water. She almost died—again!"

Ivan leaned forward, ignoring Jon, his face level with Hayden's. He spoke again, his voice so soft and low it was merely a deep whisper. Hayden's body tensed and he looked at Jon with disgust. He let go of Jon's shirt and threw him onto the ground. Springing up, he gave the gun to Ivan and ran over to me.

"Oh God, Riss," he mumbled and wrapped his arms around me. "Are you ok?" Keeping one arm around my waist, he cupped a hand under my chin and tipped my head up to him.

I nodded. "Yeah," I croaked.

He moved my wet hair out of my face and shook his head. "He's not going to get away with this," he promised and I nodded again. I put my hands on his chest and turned away, coughing. Behind us, Ivan, Brock, and Wade stood guard while chaos erupted.

Lupe and Lori were yelling at each other in Spanish; Amanda stood in the doorway crying, and Jim and Madison confronted Jon. Jason met Hannah at the base of the deck stairs and quietly recapped what he and Hayden walked in on.

"Hayden heard the water splashing," he explained. "We knew Riss wouldn't make that much noise unless something bad happened. I was expecting a zombie, not..." he let his voice fall. "I don't like that guy," he concluded.

"I don't understand," Hannah choked out, her voice shaking. "Why would he attack her? She had to have started it. You heard her before! Those threats! Maybe she—"

"—no way," Jason interrupted. "She might come off as a tough bitch but Orissa would never do anything stupid like that. Not now, not when we—" he stopped himself and turned away, watching the silent exchange happening between Ivan and Jon. Jim slowly approached and knelt down to Jon's level. Ivan stood up and backed away, letting the pastor question Jon.

"You're shivering," Hayden said quietly to me.

"Yeah. It's a nice trade from being hot," I tried to joke.

"Where are your clothes?"

"On the table. I only grabbed a shirt. My bra and pants are wet."

"I'll get your bag," he offered. "Go inside. Dry off."

"What are we gonna do about them?"

Hayden shook his head. "I don't know. Ivan's got it for now." He put both hands on my face and kissed my forehead. "He's not going to get away with it. I won't let him," he promised, his voice icy. "Not this time. He hurt you. Now I'll hurt him." Hayden let me go and turned to walk to the truck and bring my clothes.

I stepped forward, ready to go inside, when I saw Jim lean over Jon. "What is wrong with you?" he boomed, his face clouded with anger. Ivan tipped his head, taking in the pastor's anger. "Violence toward other—others who are *helping* us! This is not like you, Jon!"

"It was done to us!" Jon yelled. "They took everything. They...they," his voice faltered and he cut off.

"That doesn't mean—" Jim started but was interrupted by Jon.

"Don't waste your time with that biblical crap! They killed my wife, Jim. My *wife!*"

"And would she have wanted this?" Jim countered. "An eye for an eye makes the whole world blind," he quoted, but not from the Bible.

"The whole world is already dead!"

"This will not make it right, Jon. What they did to us was wrong, but we are not like them! We are not like them, not at all; we have morals, we have ethics. Do not forget who you are! Helen would never want that!"

Jon waved his hand at me. "They have enough weapons. We can take down those assholes at Eastmoore and get our revenge!"

Jim took a breath to refute the desire for revenge. I put one foot on a stair. "Eastmoore?" I quietly repeated. Hayden turned his head, questioning. He strode over and protectively wrapped one arm around my shoulders. "Did he say Eastmoore?" I asked and Hayden nodded.

"What about Eastmoore?" Hayden spoke.

Jon snapped his head up and snarled at Hayden. "What does it matter to you?"

"What about Eastmoore?" Hayden repeated, each word slow and deliberate.

"It's none of your damn business," Jon sneered.

Ivan moved forward. "You better believe it's our damn business. Now answer the Goddamn question. What about Eastmoore?"

Jim shook his head and answered for Jon. "It's a hospital."

"Eastmoore State Hospital?" Ivan's voice echoed in the darkness. The stunned silence caused goosebumps to break out over my skin. I involuntarily shivered, making Hayden tighten his arms around me.

"You've heard of it?" Jim finally asked.

"We've been to it," Ivan said carefully.

"Recently?"

"Yes."

Jim turned away, shaking his head. "And you lived?"

"Not all of us," Ivan answered slowly. "What do you know about the hospital?"

Jon pushed himself to his feet. Hayden's body tensed; he moved around so he was shielding me. "I'm not telling you anything," Jon spat.

"Do yourself a favor and start talking," Wade said. "Or else we'll go back to beating the shit out of you."

"It happened a few months ago," Jim began, earning a scowl from Jon. Jim cast his eyes upon his and shook his head helplessly. "They attacked us and took everything we had." My heart sped up. When Jim said their old camp had been taken over, I assumed he had meant by zombies.

"How do you know it was the guys from Eastmoore?" Brock asked.

"Jon used to work there," Jim spoke. "He was a guard."

"You worked there?" Ivan echoed, his voice taut with disbelief.

"Yes!" Jon snarled. His long face twisted with confusion. "What does this have to do with anything?"

"How long did you work there?" Ivan continued. Jon didn't answer. Ivan loomed over him and repeated his question, just not as nice as the first time.

"S-seven years!" Jon stuttered. "What's it to you?"

"It's more like what's it to *you*. Cooperate and answer the questions and you just might live. If not, I have no problem letting Underwood finish what *you* started. "Seven years," Ivan recapped. "Are you familiar with the layout?"

"Of course I am!" Jon retorted. "I wasted seven years of my life working at the goddamn place!"

Lori carefully stepped away from the house. "What are you getting at?" she asked, her voice curious and gentle.

Ivan rocked back on his heels and crossed his arms. Jaw clenched, he looked at Hayden, who gave him a tiny nod. "You're not the only ones who want revenge on the residents of Eastmoore," Ivan's deep voice spoke. "And now it seems our plans have changed." His statement hung heavy in the air, full of unanswered questions.

"What is he talking about, Hayden?" Hannah asked. "What's going on?"

Hayden shook his head.

"Hayden!" Hannah repeated, her shrill voice adding to the

tension.

I turned to face Hayden, mind racing. If Jon had worked in the state hospital for the last seven years, then he would know the ins and outs and everything about it. And if he shared that knowledge with us—which he would, one way or another—our chances of not only surviving the attack but also winning would increase dramatically.

"What did they do to you?" Lori inquired, edging closer. "It has to be bad or else you wouldn't have driven so far from your safe house."

"And what did they do to you?" Wade countered. "That was bad enough to warrant killing us?"

"They attacked us," Jim repeated, his voice hollow. "Opened fired and took everything. There used to be more than double this number in our group, and that was before Hannah and her friends found us."

"Shut up!" Jon yelled, shoulders stiffening.

Ivan stepped forward, ready to break up a fight.

"They are strangers!" he shouted and waved his hand in my direction. "They do not need to know our business!"

"It seems," Jim said, struggling to keep his voice level. "That we have a common enemy. They have done nothing to cause distrust. I think it's time we trust somebody, Jon."

"He's right!" Lupe shouted to Jim. "How do we know they're not from Eastmoore, eh? Maybe their plan is to take us back in the morning."

"We're not from Eastmoore, you idiot," I couldn't help but shout back. "I think Hannah would know if her brother had been committed, don't ya think?"

She yelled back at me in Spanish; the only word I recognized was *punta*. I rolled my eyes and turned away, concealing a shiver.

"Ok," Brock said loudly, before the chaos could continue. "We need to hash this out, obviously. Everyone inside."

No one moved. Realizing that someone had to take the lead, I slipped my hand into Hayden's and walked inside, not concerned with changing my clothes anymore. I grabbed the LED lantern and went into the large dining room. Hannah and Jason filed in next, and then Lori, Jim, Jon, and Lupe, followed by the rest of my friends, who closely watched Lupe and Jon. Daniel, Ryan, Gage, and Madison stood nervously in the living room, having watched our exchange from the window. We all took a seat and stared at each other. Hayden kept his icy glare glued on Jon, making sure his loaded pistol was in clear view.

Trying to play the role of peacemaker, Brock stood. "You want revenge against the people in the hospital?" he directed to Jon.

"More than anything," Jon replied. His eyes flicked over me and I caught a glimpse of something I couldn't place. Remorse, maybe?

"So do we," Brock shared.

"Why?" Jon leaned forward. Hayden tensed.

"We'll get to that later," Brock informed him.

"No, you need to tell us now," Jon argued. "Why should I tell you anything when you won't tell us what happened?"

"Look," Brock pointed out. "You were caught red handed trying to drown Orissa. That is not something that is going to be forgiven, ok?" He didn't give Jon a chance to answer. "*But* if you can work with us, you just might be lucky enough to live to see another day."

Jon turned his eyes on me. "Is she worth killing over?" He crossed his arms and leaned back, shifting his attention to Hayden. "You wouldn't really take a life just for her, would you?"

"I already have," Hayden replied, his voice cold. "And I'll do it again." He glared at Jon. "You should know more than anyone the lengths you're willing to go when it comes to avenging someone you love. That is exactly what you were going to do, isn't it?" He balled his fists and took a step closer to Jon.

"Hayden!" Hannah exclaimed. She put her hands on the table and frantically looked back and forth between Jon and her brother. "Please, guys, no! Can we just—just stop this! No one is killing anyone, ok?"

"He gave us the wrong key, tried to stab me, shoved you to the ground, *and* he tried to drown Orissa! He is unstable," Hayden said in a voice so calm it was chilling. "And we do not tolerate threats."

As much as I wanted to force Jon outside the security of the tall, stone fence, we needed him right now. He had information we desperately wanted. Revenge was one thing, but taking out the real threat of Eastmoore was another. The safety of our home, of the rest of our friends, was on the line.

"Guys," I said. "As much as I'd love to string Jon up by his ankles and make him be a piñata for the undead, we need to put this behind us—at least for now—and work together."

"Are you fucking kidding me?" Hayden asked incredulously. "I would think you, out of all of us, would see how dangerous he is! Orissa, he tried to kill you! You can't just forgive him like that!"

I shook my head, flattered but frustrated with Hayden's blind loyalty to me. "I'm not forgiving, and I promise you I'm not coming close to forgetting. But if he can help get us in...we have to, Hayden."

Knowing I was right, Hayden huffed and looked away.

"She has a point, Underwood," Ivan said calmly.

"Fine," Hayden begrudgingly agreed. "But he makes one wrong move and I'm putting a bullet in his head. He stays tied up and away from us until we need him. And he's *not* staying at the compound when it's over. We get what we need from him and send him on his way."

"Fair enough," Ivan agreed.

"Ok," Brock said, regaining control over the conversation. "You need to tell us why you have a vendetta against the mentally insane."

Jon pressed his lips into a straight line, not wanting to answer. Once again, Jim spoke on his behalf. "There was a shelter set up in the high school. It was near Eastmoore, but not close. Trucks came with emergency food and supplies. It wasn't enough to last, but we hoped someone, some sort of organization would come through and save us. When it became clear that wasn't happening, most of the people left."

He stopped and shook his head. "The majority of the people who stayed weren't in any shape to travel, let alone face the monsters that roamed the earth. A few kind people, like Jon and his wife, stayed behind because they couldn't face leaving us to die. With fewer people, we didn't require as much room. We moved into a safer part of the school and established rules and routines. Life was far from easy, but it was possible. We stuck to our system and always had just enough to get by. And then a simple run to town for food went wrong, horribly wrong." He stopped and looked at Jon, encouraging him to take over.

"Our house was in the city of Eastmoore," Jon began. His rough voice emotional. "Helen, my wife, wanted to go back and see what was left. We hadn't been back since we left to take shelter at the school. I knew it was a bad idea from the moment she suggested it. But she had so much hope in her eyes I...I just couldn't say no. I knew we had food in our pantry; I was sure it would still be there."

Jon put his face in his hands and took a deep breath. He

looked up and continued. "There were weird symbols spraypainted on every house on our street. Helen thought it had meant a government-run rescue group had come through, marking the neighborhoods they checked. Helen was in the bedroom looking at old photos when I heard the car. I told her to stay put while I checked it out."

A disgusted smile twisted his face. "Imagine my surprise when Remy Davis gets out." Jon balled his hands into fists. "Fucking Remy Davis. You know, we worked together at Eastmoore for four years. He stayed with us when he went through his divorce. He was our friend." Jon laughed and hit his fist on the table. "He told me that he and a 'few' others were holed up in some cabin on the edge of town. He asked where we were staying. I told him. I told him *everything* and said they should join us. He said he was going to go back to his camp, get his friends and meet us at the school. And—" he cut off, his voice breaking.

"They met us, alright," Lupe picked up. "Met us with machine guns and tear gas. It was madness. Most of our group got gunned down. The rest...the rest weren't as lucky."

"They defiled her!" Jon said in a burst of anger. "Remy betrayed me—betrayed her! They came in and took her and touched her and—" he choked back a sob. "He put a gun to my head. Backed me up against a wall and made me watch as they took Helen's clothes off."

Hannah linked her arm though Lori's; I had a feeling this was the first time they had heard the full details of Jon's story. Jim had his head bowed and looked as if he was praying. Jon flattened his hands on the table and stood up, sending his chair flying.

"Don't you get it? They have to pay! They have to!" he yelled before whirling around and looking straight at me. "And if avenging my wife's death meant killing you then I would do whatever it takes!"

I couldn't help but feel a tiny amount of pity for the man. He was broken, so broken he was desperate. Still, it was hard to feel too much empathy for the person who just tried to kill me.

"Did they follow you?" Wade asked. "After you left the school?"

Jim shook his head. "I don't think so. The few of us who were left...we got in a car and drove without even looking back. Four hours later we ran out of gas. I grew up in this town, used to preach at a nearby church until the town ghosted out. We figured it was as safe of a place as any; why would Remy and the guys at Eastmoore waste their time in an empty town?"

"And then we found them," Hannah took over. "They had only been in that church for a few days. They had nothing to eat either. We didn't have much, but we traded a few cans of soup for a place to stay for the night. But we didn't stay for just a night, obviously."

"So that's our story," Lupe concluded. Tense silence fell over the table. Jon's tale was tragic and a lot to take in. He had a personal connection to Eastmoore and everyone inside. It made me nervous to think about the lengths the residents would go to take Jon and the rest of his group down.

"Hayden," Hannah pressed. "What did they do to you?"

Hayden's jaw was set and he stared ahead, though his eyes weren't focused on anything. I knew from the little line of worry in between his eyes that he was thinking how thing could have ended differently for me.

I cleared my throat. "They shot Hayden, kidnapped and tortured me, and killed one of our friends," I quickly summed up. "The first time we ran into them, we weren't far from home. We thought we took care of the issue but it was bigger than we ever imagined. When we came across them again, they remembered us and desperately want to find our compound. It's too risky. It's only a matter of time before we run into them again or they find us."

"So we really are on the same team," Jon spoke with bemusement. He blinked and shook his head. "Ok. We are. We really are." He put his hands on the back of the chair and leaned forward. "Orissa, I'm...I'm sorry."

I turned my chin up. "It's too soon to ask forgiveness; I still have water in my ear." I narrowed my eyes and pressed a smile.

Jason sharply inhaled. "What were you going to do?" he asked with curiosity. "After you killed her, I mean. What were you going to do with the rest of us?"

Jon frowned, ashamed that he had thought so far ahead. "I wanted to kill you and take your weapons from the moment I met you," he admitted.

Jim recoiled and looked like he might get physically ill.

"I was going to say he...Hayden went crazy after all and was the one who drowned her. I had to shoot him on the spot. And you," he directed toward Jason. "You got in the way. And then the others...I don't know."

"And her?" Jason nodded his head at Lupe. "What was she doing?"

"Back up," Lupe answered. The tension rose once more; it was awkward to be sitting at a dinner table with two people who openly confessed to having a plan to murder us all.

"This isn't happening," Hayden said definitely.

Ivan looked at Brock, who nodded at his unspoken request. "Hayden," he said gently. "Talk to me." He got up and walked around the table. "You too, Penwell."

The three of us regrouped in the kitchen. Hayden immediately objected. "You cannot seriously want to work with them!"

"Hayden," Ivan said. "Think about it! Jon can get us in. He can map out the hospital; tell us where the lights are. The information is invaluable!"

"He was going to kill us!" Hayden reminded Ivan, as if he wasn't aware.

I stepped forward and put my hand on Hayden's arm. "I don't want to work with them either. I agree that we need that info, but I don't think I can trust him. He's fifty shades of shadiness."

"All right," Ivan agreed. "But you heard him. He wants those motherfuckers dead just as much as we do. I can honestly say I don't think he would blow this." He paced around the kitchen as he thought. "How about this? We go back to the compound, discuss it all with Fuller. We get Jon to share his insight, draw us a map. But when it comes time for battle, he isn't ranked as an A1 so he can't go."

"No," Hayden and I objected at the same time.

"How is that better than having Delmont and Beau?" I questioned. "He's dangerous. He tried to kill me!"

"We get info then kill him?" Hayden suggested.

"Agreed," I quickly stated.

"Guys," Ivan interrupted.

"I'm not working with the enemy," I protested.

"Who is the bigger enemy?" Ivan countered. He shook his head. "We'll keep Jon under watch. Hell, we can handcuff him for the night. Give him no weapons. *After* we get our info, we can decide what to do."

I bit my lip as I mulled it over. "Ok," I agreed. "That I can work with."

Hayden nodded. "We should take the others back sooner than later. That old couple, the kid, my sister...this world wasn't built for them."

"Right," Ivan said. "Plus a few others have pretty bad injuries. We should wait until first light tomorrow. And you get some rest," he added. "You sure you're alright?" he asked me.

"I've been worse," I said wryly. "But I am so sick of coughing."

Ivan flashed a smile. "Wade, Brock, and I will keep watch. For zombies and on them. Go get your clothes. That shirt looks better on me."

I returned his smile and nodded. Hayden followed Ivan back into the dining room, wanting to make sure that Jon knew he was still walking on very thin ice. Once I was outside, I slowly walked to the truck, listening for anything that lurked outside the tall fence. Insects and frogs were like nature's white noise; it reminded me of all the summers spent in Kentucky. Leaves softly rustled when the breeze swept through the forest and raccoons hissed and screeched in the distance. Other than that, the night was quiet and still.

I pulled Ivan's shirt over my head and laid it out in the bed of the truck; my soaked hair and bra had gotten it wet. I unzipped my bag and searched for dry underwear, a bra, pants and a shirt. I haphazardly threw my own clothes in the bed as well and quickly got dressed. I flipped my head upside down and raked my fingers through my hair before attempting to brush it. I pulled it over my left shoulder and braided it as I walked back to the house.

The dining room was empty; Wade told me that the others had gone upstairs to sleep for the rest of the night. Jon was stuck in a bedroom; the guys had rigged up something to keep him locked in and out of trouble. Hannah was talking to Hayden, her excitement about leaving in the morning was obvious.

"You should sleep too," he told her and blew out a candle.

"I'm not tired," she assured him.

"Well I am," Hayden tried to convince her. "And I'm sure Riss is too."

"I don't want to go to bed," she pouted.

"You can stay up and bug Ivan then. But let us sleep, ok?"

"Ok," she easily agreed. I grabbed a water bottle and twisted it open. Hayden looked up and smiled when he saw me.

"Tired?" he asked and crossed the threshold into the kitchen.

"Mentally, no," I told him. "Physically, I'm exhausted."

"Me too. Want to lie down?"

I nodded and followed Hayden into the living room. Jason was curled up on the loveseat, already sleeping. I grabbed a soft, brown blanket that was folded on the back of the couch and shook it out. Hayden flopped down onto the couch and started unlacing his boots. Since I hadn't zipped my leather boots back up after changing, I kicked them off and sank down next to Hayden. He stretched out, and I lay down next to him. Hayden put his arms around me and pulled me on top of him. I draped the blanket over our bodies.

"Are you comfy?" I asked, thinking that supporting all of my weight couldn't feel good.

"Yeah, you?"

"Mh-hm," I replied. The couch was surprisingly comfortable.

"Now are you tired?" he asked with a laugh.

"Mh-hm," I replied again and ran my hand through his hair.

Hayden closed his eyes. "Me too." He pulled a blanket tighter around us and kissed me. "Love you," he whispered.

"Love you, too." I closed my eyes and listened to his heart beating, continuing to run my fingers through his hair. His body relaxed and his breathing slowed as he fell asleep. Taking comfort from the fact that Ivan and Brock were on guard in the next room, I heavily exhaled and fell asleep too.

The sound of people talking woke me up. The sun had barely risen; I had only been sleeping for a few hours at best. Still wrapped in Hayden's embrace, I rolled over, pinning myself between him and the back of the couch. The voice stopped when I moved, as if they were afraid of waking me up. Still half asleep, I listened to the conversation.

"Yeah," he spoke softly. "I do."

"How much?" Hannah asked.

"I don't know," Hayden sleepily replied. "As much as I can." My body begged me to go back to sleep but my mind was too curious. Unmoving—and refusing to open my eyes again—I listened.

"Enough to marry her?"

"Yes," he said with no hesitation. My heart jumped and I had to remind myself to keep a steady breathing pattern.

Hannah excitedly inhaled. "She'd be my sister! Well, maybe. I suppose she'd have to say yes first. Do you think she will?"

"Yes. Well, maybe not now," he sighed.

"What's wrong with now?"

"We don't have the luxury to think about weddings," he said

dryly. "People are dying. People we care about."

"Shouldn't that make you want to tie the knot sooner? Because any day might be your last?"

"Sure," he replied and let his head fall to the side. His arms around me loosened.

"Then why don't you get married right now? Jim's a pastor. He can do it."

"Can we talk about this later? I'm really tired, Hannah."

"Oh, right. I forgot. Sure. It's not like we don't have a lot to catch up on or anything."

"We have plenty of time," Hayden muttered. "The drive home," he reminded her. "We can talk then, ok?"

"Fine," she reluctantly agreed. "Night, Hayden. I love you."

He mumbled an incoherent response and exhaled. I opened my eyes, too close to the couch to see anything, and replayed the conversation over in my head. What *would* I say if Hayden proposed? Being Mrs. Hayden Underwood was a scary thought...and it was also something I wanted.

CHAPTER SEVENTEEN

"Rise and shine," Brock spoke, his words most unwelcome. I turned, burying my head against Hayden, groaning in protest. Hayden stretched and yawned. My throat was raw. *Great, just fucking great.* I lazily rolled over Hayden and grabbed my water bottle from the floor, hoping the soreness was only caused by being thirsty. "Get up," Brock told us. "Or else you'll miss our delicious breakfast."

"Ok," I mumbled and took a drink. Voices floated down the hall from the kitchen. Hayden and I were the only ones left in the living room. I pushed myself up and finished the rest of the water. I stretched; my back was tight. Whether it was from our crammed half a night's sleep on the couch or from the attempted drowning, I wasn't sure.

I put my palms together and reached up over my head and then slowly bent forward until I was touching my toes.

"That's a nice view to wake up to," Hayden teased. I looked between my legs and smiled. "But I like it better when you're wearing those tight yoga pants."

I turned around when he stood. "Hmm, I thought you'd prefer that with no pants." I smiled and put my hands on his shoulders. Hayden wiggled his eyebrows and pulled me in for a hug. "Did you sleep ok?"

"Meh. I've had worse night's sleep. Having you with me makes it better."

He quickly pressed his lips to mine. "Hungry?"

I nodded and let my hands fall. Hayden slowly got up and walked into the kitchen with me.

Wade and Ivan sat in the breakfast nook with Jon. Ivan was nodding along to something Jon was saying while Wade took notes. Jason was with Hannah and a few others from her group in the dining room. Hayden and I took our share of oatmeal with raisins and took a spot at the breakfast table. Wade was working on a crude sketch of Eastmoore.

"Is it repairable?" Jon asked.

"No," Ivan said confidently. "The thing blew up."

Jon smiled. "Nice work." He flicked his eyes to mine and nodded a hello. The animosity between Jon, Hayden, and me steadily grew as each second passed. He was unpredictable and borderline psychotic in his desperation. He belonged in Eastmoore along with the other murderous asshats. I hated working with him. *It's for the greater good*, I reminded myself over and over.

"He says there is a way in here," Ivan explained to us and pointed at the map.

Jon nodded. "The whole hospital was rebuilt not that long ago," he told us and then shook his head. "Only they were lazy with the construction. I'm sure you know how mental hospitals used to be." He paused to make sure we were following. "The cells are still there," he said ominously. "And connect to the basement."

Hayden crossed his arms and studied the map. "And how do we get into these cells?"

"They are all underground," Jon continued. "Almost like a tunnel. There is an entrance right outside the hospital yard. We used to have problems with teenagers sneaking in at night. There were rumors the place was haunted," he explained. "If we can get into the cell hall and into the basement, I can probably get you in unnoticed. The basement door is in the boiler room. I don't see why anyone would be in there, especially if they're only running on backup generator power."

"That's assuming we can get to the entrance," I replied tartly. "They have guards everywhere."

Jon finished off his water. "How did you get in the first time?"

"We filled the bed of a truck with dead animals and drove it through the fence," Ivan stated. "And a herd of zombies followed."

Jon's eyes widened. "And you drove it?"

"No," Ivan continued. "We locked the steering wheel and put a rock on the gas pedal."

"Impressive," Jon praised. "It worked? Is that how you got out?" he asked.

Everyone looked at me. "Along with the lights being out, yes,"

I said. "It was mass chaos. Everyone running around shouting about being under attack; it left us completely unguarded."

"Us?" Jon questioned. "Who were they? I might have known them."

"I wasn't alone. Uh, a guy named Carlos who was there for depression and some girl who said she was visiting her cousin."

Jon's head tipped back. "I remember Carlos. He was a good kid; he was really trying. Why was he locked up with you?"

"He wanted out and they wouldn't let him leave. He said they were convinced he would bring others back and try to take their supplies."

"I need you to tell me everything you know," Jon said rather gently. "If I can get an understanding of who is running the place and how many are left, I might be able to help you come up with a better plan. I knew a lot of those guys. Hated most of them, but I still knew them."

I swallowed and poked at my oatmeal. Hayden put his hand on my thigh. "They called the guy in charge 'Dre'."

"Yeah," Jon confirmed. "He's a white supremacist. He was trouble since day one." He shook his head and laughed. "The idiot pled insanity. I don't think he realized serving time in prison would have been shorter. Once you get committed to state, it's really hard to get out. He's a bad, bad person, but not insane. He knew what he was doing. I think the judge only accepted the plea because he knew that Adrian would never leave Eastmoore. He became popular among the other residents real fast; he could get them to do things they normally wouldn't do."

"Lovely. And a guy called Cutter acted like his right hand man."

Jon shook his head. "I don't remember that name. What does he look like?"

"He wasn't very tall," I recalled. "Gray eyes, scraggly chin strip bread that was banded."

"No, I don't think he was a resident. He must have been one of Adrian's guys from the outside." He slowly exhaled, a line forming between his eyes. "That's what I was afraid of. I knew it had to be...I just didn't want to admit it to myself," he said quietly and looked up. "Adrian was part of a gang. He must have taken over somehow and brought in his buddies." He clenched his jaw. "The inmates took over the asylum. We were always outnumbered. I knew they could do it if they wanted to." He closed his eyes before asking, "any idea how many are in there?"

I shook my head. "I don't know for sure, maybe a hundred? Treasure would be better to talk to," I added with a shrug.

"Treasure?" Jon asked.

"Yeah, she was the chick that was visiting her cousin."

Jon laughed and shook his head. "You mean Margret?"

My heart skipped a beat. "You knew her?"

"Pretty well. She was in and out of acute for years before finally getting committed. I was surprised it took that long; she has a history of drug use and personality disorders."

My head swam in a rush of embarrassment and anger. How could I not have known? I brought her back with me...and she put everyone in danger. Her obsession with Dre at least made sense now.

"Do you know anything else?" Jon carefully pressed. "Anything that could be useful."

"They were running low on supplies. I'm guessing they've wasted ammo and are low on that too from their interest in our weapons. When I first got there, Dre and a few others were out on a run. They left me alone—for the most part—until he got back and questioned me."

"Questioned," Hayden said sarcastically and raised his eyebrows.

"What did they do?" Jon asked. I knew my answer wouldn't give him any information that could help him. The pencil had fallen from Wade's hand and Ivan's dark eyes were on me. It was obvious I was beaten, but I hadn't shared the fine details with anyone. My eyes flicked over Jon's face. I wasn't sharing the details today.

"Beat me for info. Repeatedly."

"Why didn't you just make something up?" Jon asked.

"I had something they wanted. I needed to hold onto that for as long as I could. They were going to kill me either way." My eyes went to Hayden. "And I knew I needed to buy time. I never doubted that my friends would get me out of there."

Jon leaned back in his chair, thinking. I replayed the escape in my mind, remembering all too vividly Carlos being torn apart and turning around to see Rider stumbling toward us. I stirred the oatmeal and forced myself to eat a few more spoonfuls.

"I think," Jon finally said, "that if I can see Treasure, she will talk to me. I worked on her unit a few times. She'll remember me." He put his hands on the table. "When they attacked us at the school, Remy was the only one I recognized. Besides, a few others were committed to the same unit as Dre. Most of the residents there weren't capable of living a normal life, let alone one filled with zombies. Dre must have gotten rid of them somehow."

"You think most of the people at Eastmoore *aren't* crazy?"

Jon nodded. "Without their meds, most are unmanageable. When someone is committed to state it's because someone else, be it family or society, gave up on them. Therapy and treatments didn't help. They went to state to be *maintained* for the remainder of the pathetic life. I'm confident I can find out more when I talk to Treasure," he assured us.

Hayden bit the inside of his cheek and looked out the window.

"What are you thinking?" I asked him.

"Going home and talking to Treasure is a good idea."

"We drove all the way out here," I whined.

"You just said Treasure is crazy," Wade said to Jon. "How much can she really help?"

Jon nodded. "She isn't *crazy*. If I remember correctly her diagnosis was bi-polar and cluster B personality disorder traits."

"She tried to come back and warn the others about our plan of attack," I informed him. "Why would she help you?"

Jon's eyes narrowed, reminding me of a snake in the grass. "She won't know she's helping." He smiled and my oatmeal churned in my stomach. "We will just be talking about Eastmoore."

Ivan nodded. "As long as it works." He scanned his eyes over mine. "We will go home," Ivan stated. "Get details from Treasure and make a concrete plan of attack."

Hayden nodded in agreement and looked through the kitchen doorway at his sister. "And it would be safer for everyone."

"And a good night's sleep would do us all some good," Wade added.

"I'd love a real shower," I mumbled under my breath, though I wasn't happy about our wasted trip. Considering we'd run into Hayden's sister, I supposed I shouldn't consider the trip *wasted*.

Ivan and Wade got up to find Brock, who was on watch outside, and fill him in on our decision. Hayden tipped his oatmeal bowl and scrapped up the last bits with his spoon. Alone with just Hayden and me, Jon grew uncomfortable and excused himself, muttering that he wanted to inform his own friends of our change in plans. Hayden put his bowl down and twisted in his seat to face me.

"You really want to do this?" he asked.

"Of course," I said and wiped my mouth. "Why wouldn't I?"

His eyebrows pushed together. "Killing people is different than killing zombies, Riss."

"I know, Hayden."

"You've never taken a life, have you?"

I shrugged. "Kinda. I've killed a lot of infected, crazy people."

"They were going to die anyway," he reminded me. "If anything, you did them a favor and stopped them from becoming something horrible."

"I know," I repeated.

"What I'm trying to say is, when it all comes down to it, we fight in a war because we believe we are right. But so do they. They have families, friends...they go home at night just like we do. You can't think about that, though, ok? I've killed people, Riss, people who probably didn't deserve to die, in the name of war. It takes part of you, turns it dark. I don't want you to go through that."

I pressed my hand over Hayden's heart. "There is nothing dark inside of you."

He put his hand over mine. "Thanks, but that's not true."

"Yes, it is," I said stubbornly and laced my fingers through his. Hayden nodded. He gently pulled my hands forward. I moved from my chair into his lap.

"Orissa, I can't lose you. Any part of you. Before I met you, I fought because I had to, not because I wanted to. Now I have a reason to get up and put myself out on the line. There's something about you that's so alive, passionate, and vibrant...and angry," he added with a smile. "And I don't want that to change."

"I won't change," I whispered. He put his hand on my cheek, pulled my face back and kissed me.

Someone loudly cleared their throat; Hayden and I quickly broke apart. Daniel and Lori shuffled into the kitchen and rustled around in our bag of food. I stood and picked up the empty oatmeal bowls. I set them in the sink and wondered if anyone would ever be back here. By the time they did, the sticky bowls would be covered in fuzzy mold.

I looked around the fancy kitchen and thought about how quickly our priorities changed. And then there were those, like the annoying ex-news reporter Scarlet Procter—a gossipy woman back at our compound—who desperately clung onto the things we used to work night and day to have. I used to think it made her seem dumb to care about normalcy and the trivial things that previously brought entertainment, but maybe she was onto something. Maybe hanging onto those simple material things helped her keep her identity. Maybe by holding onto the past, it would keep us from changing too much, changing into a group of desperate people who would do whatever it took to ensure our own survival.

"Are we really leaving?" Hannah asked from the doorway.

"Yeah," Hayden told her. "Is all your stuff packed?"

She nodded. "Can I ride with you?"

"Yeah, of course," Hayden told her with a smile.

"Good. I'm gonna help the others get ready. We need to leave soon, right?"

"That would be ideal; we can cover the most ground in daylight."

Hannah smiled and hurried out of the room. Hayden and I helped Daniel and Lori put away our dwindling supply of food and drinks. Gage, the bleeding boy that I had briefly met yesterday, was sweaty and pale. Even I could tell his cut was infected. My stomach churned a little when I remembered how awful it felt to be septic. I reminded him that we had first aid supplies and recommended someone clean and properly bandage his cut, though I had no idea if it would make a difference at this point. He needed antibiotics, like yesterday. The old woman, Agatha, wasted no time and made Gage sit down so she could try her hand at playing nurse.

Since Hannah's group was down one vehicle, they were forced to drive with us. Hannah and Janet sat in the back seat of Hayden's truck. Janet's eyes scanned the blood stained cushions and her mouth tightened. But she didn't say anything.

Ivan had ambiguously gone over the map with Jon since he was familiar with the area. We had planned on retracing our steps, but Jon suggested a different route that cut through a ghost town and would shave off some time from our journey home.

Not even two minutes into the drive, Hannah started firing off questions. It was annoying but it made the last hour go by fast, especially when she brought up stuff from her and Hayden's past. I watched her in the rearview mirror and realized she looked a lot like Hayden. They had the same eyes, exact same shade of brown hair, and similar bone structure in their faces, which was unfortunate for Hannah. Hayden was a very attractive man and the strong jaw worked well for him. But for Hannah...not so much.

"Where were you when the whole outbreak thing happened?" she asked me.

"Indy."

"Oh, scary to be in such a big city! I went there on a school trip once. It was really boring. Sorry if that offends you," she added.

I laughed. "No, it's ok. I could see how it could be boring. I tried to convince myself that I liked the energy of the city but deep down, I don't think I really did."

"I know what you mean," Janet said, speaking for the first time since we had left. "I got a job in Huston after college. I loved the nightlife. But it got old fast."

I nodded. "Yeah. I wasted way too much time in bars."

"We didn't have fun bars in our town," Hannah pouted. "My friends and I were planning a trip for spring break to go to—"

The back driver's side window shattered. Blood splattered through the air, sprinkling droplets on Hannah's face. Janet slumped forward, her body held in place by the seat belt. Hannah screamed. The truck swerved and Hayden fought to regain control. I picked up my gun and pointed it at the broken window. A blue Charger revved its engine and tore out from behind a dust-covered diner.

"Get down!" Hayden demanded as I pulled the trigger, randomly firing in their direction. "Hannah, get down!"

"Janet!" she cried.

"She's dead! Leave it and drop!"

Hannah slunk down in her seat. Another shot echoed and the truck was hit again. Then all hell broke loose.

PART TWO

CHAPTEREIGHTEEN

Hayden stomped on the gas and jerked the wheel. Tires squealing, the truck turned down an alley. All the while shots echoed in the air; instantly causing my ears to ring. I jumped out of the truck, staying close to the side.

"Get on the floor!" Hayden told Hannah again and killed the ignition before getting out. The Range Rover pulled in next to us, sliding to a stop on loose gravel. My heart pounded and my hands shook. I didn't know if I should waste time putting on the bullet proof vest of if I should grab a machine gun and run into the street, hoping to shoot those motherfuckers before I went down in a blaze of glory.

Ivan scrambled out of the SUV, speaking into the walkie-talkie. Brock raced around and joined Hayden along the side of the brick building that we were hiding behind. The rapid firing of a high-powered rifle abruptly stopped, only to be replaced by the definite sound of metal on metal, followed by a terrifying hiss.

Hayden and Brock moved to the side of the building with their rifles raised, already in formation. I grabbed my quiver and bow. I had only gotten as far as putting the strap over my head when the firing started again. Drawn to the noise, three zombies staggered out of the through streets, coming around corners.

The Charger revved its engine twice, teasing us. Hayden signaled something to Brock, who took off. He raced by the truck and skidded to a stop next to a steel door. His hand gripped the rusty knob and he slowly opened it. After a quick look inside he waved to us. Ivan got Agatha and Roger out of the SUV. I opened the truck door.

"Come on," I said to Hannah, my voice shaking.

She stared at me, in too much shock to move. I grabbed her arm and pulled. She stumbled out of the truck, tripped over her own feet. I pushed off the truck and grabbed Hannah's hand, directing her into the building. Hayden fired off a few more rounds and joined us.

"Holy shit," he panted as he slammed the door shut. He fumbled with the lock. There was a foot wide section of open air vents above the door. Sunlight streamed through and illuminated the specks of dust that we had stirred up.

"Do you have a copy?" Ivan asked over the walkie and got no answer. I looked around the building; we had entered into the kitchen of a small restaurant. There was only a half wall separating the kitchen from the dining area, which boasted several round tables with chairs stacked on top and floor to ceiling windows at the front of the diner.

"Over here," Brock whispered and motioned for us to follow him. "There," he told Agatha and Roger and opened an empty walk-in freezer.

"You too," Hayden said to Hannah. Sweat rolled down his forehead and his hazel eyes were wide with fear.

"No," she protested. "I'm not leaving—"

"Get in!" Hayden ordered.

Hannah opened her mouth to protest again but was cut off when the glass windows at the front of the diner shattered. I dropped to the floor, covering my head as a reflex, as if my hands could stop a bullet from penetrating my skull. Hannah whimpered and crawled into the freezer. Brock rolled his flashlight across the floor to her; Hannah snatched it up and pulled the door closed.

The dirt and dust on the floor had been obviously disturbed. If whoever was shooting at us came in through the back, it would be all too easy for them to find our unarmed residents. I looked at the door, my heart pounding so fast it hurt. We needed to shove something heavy in front of it.

I put my hand on the cool tile, ready to push myself up when the Charger flew past as if in a drive by, peppering the front of the building with bullets. More glass shattered, and a few rounds whizzed overhead. I sank back down, with my back against a stove. Hayden was across from me, taking cover behind a counter.

Tires screeched as the Charger spun around. Fear coursed through me, increasing as the engine grew louder. Brock jumped up and opened fire as the Charger raced past. I almost screamed when a metal pot got hit, which knocked it from its hanger and caused it to clatter onto the floor.

"What do we do?" Brock asked as he dropped down again. "They know we're in here."

"If they're after our supplies, they can get to them," Ivan stated. "You got your keys?"

Hayden nodded. "Yeah, but it won't stop them. We need to get out there."

"Wade?" Brock asked Ivan.

Ivan shook his head; he still hadn't heard from them.

"Fuck," Brock said quietly. I was absolutely terrified. Whoever was out there was even more deadly than the zombies; they had weapons and were able to scheme and plan our demise.

The engine faded until we couldn't hear it anymore. Hayden crawled over to me.

"You ok?" he asked and I nodded. "Good." He looked at Brock and Ivan. "We need eyes. I'll go around and—"

He cut off when another vehicle rolled to a stop just outside the back door. A car door slammed.

"I think they went inside," a loud voice spoke. It was muffled but sounded familiar.

"You sure?" another man asked.

"Dunno. Where else would they be?"

"Fucking anywhere!" the second voice shouted. "They could be behind that Dumpster ready to shoot us for all we know!"

"Then let's grab the stuff and get outta here!" The distinct sound of the truck's tailgate being dropped made Hayden stiffen. "Hurry, load it!" the man shouted.

"It's locked! See if the keys are in the cab. And you were right; this truck is sweet! Look at that beauty in the bed!"

I swallowed and looked at the door. Should we burst through and hit them with the element of surprise? I turned my head to Hayden. His face was serious and his movements were deliberate and calm. I pressed my back to the oven.

Brock motioned to Hayden and looked at the door. Ivan crouched and nodded, signaling something to Brock. Hayden moved so he could shoot around the counter, holding himself up with his elbows.

"Riss," he whispered. "Be ready."

I nodded and scrambled to his side, taking cover behind a refrigerator. I aimed the M16 at the door. Brock crawled away from the half-wall, swiftly moving without making a sound. He and Ivan went to the door; Ivan pressed himself against the wall and Brock moved to the other side, putting his hand on the knob and slowly unlocking the door. Just as he was about to open it, shots rang out from behind us.

Ivan was in the line of fire.

* * *

He pulled the trigger and dropped, immediately pushing himself back. Brock dodged away, moving behind a wooden shelf. It did nothing to stop the bullets but it at least put him out of the sight. Hayden bent around the counter and began firing at the shooters. I whirled around and pointed the gun over the counter and blindly shot over the half-wall.

Someone screamed and the shooting ceased. Ivan sprang up and relocked the door before shuffling back.

"Brock!" I quietly called.

"I'm ok," he answered immediately. "You?"

"Yeah," I whispered, knowing that if we could hear the guys outside, they could hear us. I looked around. Ivan slid up next to me, using the fridge to hide his body. "We all are."

"I think you got one," Ivan said quietly to Hayden.

Hayden nodded and peered around the counter. "I can't see anyone; I have no idea how many are left."

"We'll get 'em," Ivan spat venomously. He put his hand to the walkie-talkie, attempting to reach Wade and Jason again. Just then, the guys in the back began shooting at the door. The metal was strong enough to stop the bullets — for now. At the sound of gunfire, the other half of that group began shooting again.

Ivan and I cowered to the ground. I locked eyes with Hayden, wishing I was next to him, though it wasn't as if I could defend him. I looked over the counter and through the broken windows. Bright sunlight streamed in, making the street appear white. I couldn't descry a single thing.

Jason's voice crackled through the walkie-talkie. "Do you have a copy?" he asked. "Hello? Guys? Do you copy?"

I couldn't help but internally smile to know that he was still alive. Ivan unclipped the walkie and held it to his lips.

"Yes, we copy," he said quietly. "What is your status?"

"We're in a grocery store," Jason explained. "I don't think we've been seen."

"Keep it that way," Ivan ordered. "Where is Wade?"

"He went to check things out."

Ivan pressed the walkie-talkie button and opened his mouth

to speak but cut off suddenly when someone kicked at the door. We all froze.

"I don't hear anything," one of the guys from the back parking lot shouted. "Maybe they're dead."

"Maybe not," the other yelled back. "Get your fat ass over here and help me load the rest of this shit!"

Brock slowly crawled toward the door. I watched his shadow move behind the shelf. One hand landed on the floor and he leaned his body forward. Then something caught my eye, and I thought it was a bug. My eyes flitted from Brock to the little red dot.

"Stop!" I shouted. Brock froze and flattened himself.

"What?" Brock exclaimed.

"There's a sight on you," I whispered.

"Fuck," Ivan muttered when his gazed fixed on the laser. "They can see us."

His words sent chills down my spine. I looked at the store front again. Where were the shooters hiding? Were they close?

"What's behind you?" Hayden asked Brock.

"A room with a table...a break room, maybe? And bathrooms," Brock explained.

"Any way out?" Hayden asked.

"There is a vent," Brock said. A moment later something metal clattered to the floor. "I can't fit, dammit," he cursed. "It looks like it leads to the side of the building." He hit the wall in frustration. "I can't get my shoulders in." The sound of scuffling echoed through the small diner. "I'm coming back to your side."

"Not yet. Get back in there," Hayden told him. "They were aiming for you. And that piece of wood isn't going to protect you."

"No," Brock argued. "I'm not hiding while you fight."

"Brock," I pleaded. "I don't want you to die."

He picked his head up and looked in our direction. He made a face and pushed himself back, grumbling about how he was joining us the first chance he got.

Jason's voice over the radio stole my attention and I snapped my head around to stare at the device as if it would allow me to hear better.

"You guys ok?" he asked.

"Janet is dead. We have the others," Ivan said dryly. "What about you?"

"We got everyone except Jon, Lupe, and Daniel. I think

whoever was driving their car got hit; I saw them crash into a fire hydrant. No one got out."

"How did you get away?" Ivan asked as his eyes scanned the restaurant.

"Wade," Jason stated, "pulled into an alley. Madison followed. We got out and he led us down the street and into another alley. We went in the back of this store. You got any zombies in there with you?"

"No."

"There were a few here. Nothing we couldn't handle." A few seconds of silence passed before Jason told us that Wade was back.

"I can see three guys on the roof across from you," Wade told us. "One has a clear shot inside. There are two guys in the street. Both are wearing body armor. Face and neck are exposed."

"And at least two more in the lot behind us," Ivan informed him. "What's the zombie situation?"

"Streets are starting to fill. Most look like they are in the S3 stage and are moving slow. They don't pose a threat. It's the goddamn men out there that are armed to hell I'm worried about. They've got you surrounded."

"Can you take any down?"

"Yes," Wade said confidently. "Just not from here."

"Good," Ivan said softly. Watch yourself."

"This isn't my first rodeo," Wade reminded him. "A fifty cal was my best friend for a couple of years."

"Things are different now," Ivan slowly replied. His eyes met Hayden's in an unspoken question.

Hayden moved his head up and down curtly.

"But if you can get a clear shot, take it."

"Alright," Hayden began and leaned toward us. "If Wade makes just one shot, it will take the focus off of us." He turned around and inspected the kitchen. To the right were the back door and the walkway to the front of the restaurant. To our left was a swinging door that led into the dining area.

"Scratch that plan," Wade's frantic voice spoke, causing me to startle. "We got zombies."

"How many?" Ivan blurted, his eyes widening.

"Enough," Wade responded before falling silent.

"Wade?" Ivan spoke and got no response. I looked up and met Hayden's eyes. Though they mirrored my terror, he forced a smile and gave me an encouraging nod. Moving slowly, he edged toward the swinging door.

Suddenly, there was a loud pop followed by a car alarm going off. The blaring siren screeched throughout the still, empty town.

"Turn it off!" one of the guys yelled over the alarm.

"I don't know how!" the other screamed back. "I ain't got the keys!"

Hayden snapped his head up and stared at me; we both remembered how quickly the zombies fled to the ambulance. Brock slid his M16 across the floor and stuck his head out from behind the shelf.

"Go," Ivan instructed. "Now!"

Taking advantage of the distracting alarm, Brock sprinted back to the kitchen. Ten horribly slow seconds ticked by, each one marked by the Range Rover's blaring horn.

"Hayden?" Hannah cried, cracking open the freezer.

He waved his hand. "Get back," he whispered harshly. "Hannah, do not come out!"

She nodded and pulled her head back. The heavy freezer door clicked shut, sending a cloud of dust into the air. Ivan retrieved the keys from his pocket and put his finger over a button. The two men outside were still frantically trying to shut off the alarm.

"Do it," Brock whispered. "Before they pop the engine and cut something."

Ivan turned slightly so he could see me. I nodded, agreeing with Brock. He pressed the button, bringing silence to my ringing ears. My breath left me in a ragged huff and my heart continued to pound. A bead of sweat rolled down my neck, but I wasn't going to risk setting down my bow to wipe it away. Hayden scooted his body another few inches.

"We need a visual," he whispered to me, probably seeing the fear in my eyes as he moved farther away from me. On his hands and knees, he crouched along the counter until he reached the swinging door. Flattening himself on the ground so he wouldn't knock into the doors, he pulled forward.

Then glass crunched under someone's foot.

We all froze. Hayden gripped his weapon and moved another few feet forward. The glass crunched again, but was followed by the sound of something sharp being dragged over the diner's tile floor. It took another step forward. My eyes flitted to Hayden, who was edging his way closer to the enemy. I slowly set the bow on the floor and put my hand on my pistol.

The gargling groan was almost welcome. With lungs full of rotting bodily fluids, the zombie exhaled loudly when it spotted Hayden.

"Gummy," he said quietly and I couldn't help but smile when I heard him use the stupid nickname Raeya had coined for S3s. "Nothing to worry about," he assured us. He slid under the swinging doors and fired. As soon as the body hit the floor, we were shot at again.

"Seriously?" Brock said over the gunfire. "Maybe those idiots will use up all their ammo," he grumbled and hunched down on the floor. I kept my eyes focused on the swinging doors until the rapid shots ceased.

"Shit," Hayden said.

"What?" Ivan demanded.

"Zombies."

"Where?"

"Street."

"Coming in?" Ivan asked.

"Three are in," he said right before the broken glass gave away their location. "We need to get out of here."

"How?" Brock asked. "We are surrounded. And now we have zombies."

"I can fit," I said quietly.

"What?" Brock turned to me.

"You said you almost fit into the vent. I'm smaller than you; I can fit."

"Riss no," Hayden said immediately.

"What else are we going to do?" I countered.

Ivan nodded. "Underwood, both the exits are covered. And now we have zombies filtering in. We need an out."

Hayden pushed himself back under the swinging doors and crawled over to take cover behind the counter. "What is your plan?"

"There's only two in the parking lot. Take them out and we go through the back," I told him.

"They can see the door," Hayden told me and I nodded. "How are you going to get over there?" He looked at the wooden shelf.

"I have an idea," Brock said and looked behind Ivan.

"The fridge?" I asked.

"Yeah. It's empty, right?"

Ivan cracked the door. "Thank God, yes."

"Tip it," Brock told him. "And push it into the walkway. It's long enough for Riss to crawl behind."

"You're a genius," Ivan said with a smirk.

Hayden scooted away and peeked under the swinging doors.

"Do it on three," Hayden instructed. "And then get down." He waited until Ivan got situated. I yanked the plug from the wall. Hayden nodded and began counting. As soon as he said 'three', Ivan shoved the refrigerator over. Hayden took out the three zombies that had meandered into our little safe house. "Down!" Hayden yelled. The four of us pressed our bodies to the floor as the guys outside opened fire. "At least they're predictable," Hayden mused once they stopped.

With his machine gun pointed to the front of the store, Brock stole a glace outside. He nodded to Ivan, who pushed the fridge into position. I crawled over, stealing a quick look back at Hayden. Still half under the swinging doors, I couldn't see his face.

But it was now or never. I tightened the quiver around my back and grabbed the bow. I kept my elbows low and my back as straight as possible. It would only take a few seconds to crawl across the narrow hall. I looked at the back door, still able to hear the two men looting our supplies. A car door slammed shut and someone laughed.

My breath huffed out of me and I wiped my sweaty palms on my jeans. Then I silently made my way into the bathroom.

"I'm in," I called once I reached a safe point. I carefully placed my feet on the sides of the toilet and looked inside the vent that Brock had already torn off the wall. "And I can fit." I put the bow inside, sliding it far enough to give me room. I hoisted myself up, bracing for the metal tubing to give away.

The air was stale and hot, making it hard to breath. It was a tight fit in the vent and I felt slightly claustrophobic. I pushed the bow ahead of me, wincing when it caught on a screw. The echo was amplified inside the vent. I paused, waiting to see if the sound was enough to cause the guys across the street to think we were firing at them.

After a few seconds passed, I moved forward, already able to see bright sunlight shining through the slats of the outside heater duct. I closed my eyes when I pushed through a dusty cobweb, telling myself that the thing was so old there was *not* a spider stuck in my hair. I turned my head and stuck my ear to the vent. The two men's voices drifted across the lot.

"What makes you think they're coming out this way?" one of

them asked.

"It's the only door," the other responded. His voice was so familiar. I just couldn't place it. "They ain't stupid enough to try the front. And when they do come out, save the bitch for me."

His words made me shudder. I turned back to the vent. It was held in place by four screws. *Son of a bitch*, I thought to myself and got to work. I started with the top two and then moved to the bottom left screw. My fingers hurt by the time it was loosened enough. Holding it with one hand, I used my nails to keep the vent steady. I removed the third screw and carefully swung the vent down so that it hung by its only remaining screw.

I curled my fingers around the sharp edges of the vent and pulled myself forward. The dining area of the restaurant was bigger than the back; it offered about ten feet of solid brick protection from whoever was in the front. The vent was about six feet off the ground. It wasn't too high to jump from by any means, but I wasn't about to take a nose dive onto grass-covered gravel.

After a moment's consideration, I pushed myself backwards and stepped back onto the toilet. With much less grace than the first time, I re-entered the vent feet first and shimmied my way to the outside. I stopped when my feet stuck out of the building. The two guys in the back where making comments about Janet's dead body.

I held the bow in one hand, closed my eyes, and jumped. My hair caught on a rough edge, knocking me off and causing me to flail. My ankle twisted when I landed. Gravel dug into my elbow. I held my breath, praying that neither had heard the fall.

"...I wasn't aiming for her," one guy stated.

"You have a piss-poor shot," the one with the familiar voice retorted. It sounded as if he slapped the other upside the head. "Never mind that. Look for the keys."

I pushed myself up, gritting my teeth at the pain my twisted ankle caused, and slowly moved forward. There was a dumpster alongside the building. Flies buzzed around it, enjoying the residual smell of putrid food leftovers. Ignoring the retched odor of crusty garbage, I crouched down and peered between the sun-warmed metal and the side of the building.

Two figures moved between the Range Rover and the truck. The blue Charger was parked behind our vehicles.

"There aren't keys," one of them spat.

"Then climb in the goddamn window!" Familiar Voice ordered. He turned around and leaned over the bed of the truck, eyeing the machine gun.

My heart stopped beating and my eyes widened in scared shock. His voice wasn't the only thing that was familiar. I swallowed my pounding heart and stared into the cold gray eyes of Cutter.

* * *

Something shuffled behind me. I whirled around to see an S3 round the corner of the building.

"Dammit," I mouthed. One of her eyes dangled from the socket and her arms looked like they had been through a wood chipper. Her gait was unsteady and twigs and leaves clung to her long and tattered skirt.

I wasn't worried about her attacking me. I was fairly certain she couldn't even see me—or anything anymore for that matter. She dragged a worn platform shoe over the gravel drive. I shook my head. She was making too much noise.

Glaring at the gummy, I pulled an arrow from the quiver and crept over to her. I set the bow down, raised my hand and shoved the arrow into her forehead, which provided as much resistance as a rotten orange. I caught her as she fell, she was surprisingly heavy for being so deteriorated, and set her gently on the ground as to not call attention to myself.

Wiping my hands clean on my pants, I turned around and picked up the bow. I slowly yanked the arrow from her head and flicked the zombie goo to the ground. I slunk over to the dumpster and took another look at the men.

Cutter had stepped into the bed. He had his hands on the machine gun and was peering through the scope as if he was imagining firing it. The other guy was using his elbow to clear away the glass that was left on the truck's broken back window.

I strung the arrow and stepped around the dumpster, my feet not making a sound. I let out my breath to steady myself, aimed, and let go. The arrow hit him in the nap of his neck, paralyzing, but not instantly killing him. His hands slid down the side of the truck as he fell.

Cutter looked over his shoulder. Not seeing anything, he turned back to the machine gun before he did a double take.

"Maurice?" he asked. "Where'd ya go?" He jumped out of the truck, landing on the passenger side. I laced another arrow and moved around the dumpster again. I waited until he rounded the tailgate to move forward.

Cutter's eyes widened and his hand flew to the gun that was tucked into the back of his pants when he saw his friend's body crumpled on the ground.

"Hey asshole," I shouted. "Remember me?"

Cutter's face went blank with shock for a second before he smiled. "I knew you'd be—"

I didn't give him a chance to talk. I let the arrow go. It sank into his abdomen, in the exact same spot where he had shot Rider. The gun fell from his hand. I reached behind me and grabbed another arrow.

"That was for Rider. Remember him, too?" I strung the arrow on the bow. "And this, this is for Hayden." I released my hold and the arrow pierced his shoulder. Cutter cried out in pain and fell backwards onto the ground. I considered leaving him there, writhing around in pain, but he wasn't worth the risk of attracting more zombies.

I retrieved one last arrow. "And finally, this is for me." Cutter's body went limp. Three arrows stuck out of him, one in his chest, shoulder, and stomach. I hit him in the places where he had hit me, just a little more literally.

Something clunked into the dumpster. I grabbed an arrow and spun around. A zombie with a very dislocated shoulder worked its way to me, loose arm swinging madly. He was an easy kill; I walked over to pull the arrow from his head as soon as I shot him.

I dashed to the side of the building and grabbed my other arrow that was still in the head of the gummy. I stuck the arrows back in my quiver and moved to the back door. I balled my hand into a fist but hesitated before I knocked; the guys couldn't just open the door can waltz out. Whoever was across the street could see into the diner and would open fire in seconds. The guys might be able to shimmy along the floor and get out, but even I couldn't expect Agatha and Roger to follow suit.

"Hey guys," I said softly. "Can you hear me?"

"You ok, Riss?" Hayden asked immediately, his voice close to the door.

"Yeah, I'm fine." I looked behind me. "Hayden," I began. "One of these guys..." I trailed off, looking at Cutter's body. Even though it was lifeless and unmoving, I was still afraid of him. And I hated that. "They are from the hospital."

"*The* hospital?" Hayden asked incredulously. "Are you sure?"

"Yes. The guy that shot Rider and kidnapped me is here."

"Holy shit, Riss, I'm coming out there with you."

"No," I protested. "There's no need."

"Is he still out there?"

"Yes," I said. "He's a few feet from me. But with a few arrows in him."

"Oh," Hayden replied, sounding rather surprised. "Good."

"Yeah. I'm gonna get our supplies back. Can you both unlock the cars? And don't move out until I say so, ok?"

"And don't do anything stupid," Hayden added.

I nodded, knowing he couldn't see me, and moved away from the door. I hurried over to the blue Charger. The keys were in the ignition and the trunk was popped. I reached inside and retrieved two bags of our food. I grabbed them before opening the Range Rover's back hatch. With my arms too full to grab the handle, I was forced to set the bags down.

Annoyed with myself, I threw open the door and haphazardly plopped the food inside. I raced back to the Charger and grabbed another armload of supplies, repeating the process until I completely emptied the trunk, which included a few rifles and boxes of ammo that we didn't have before.

In the backseat of Cutter's car was a bag of my extra arrows, I slipped my fingers through the handle and hoisted the heavy duffle off the seat, feeling more and more angry. What had they planned to do to us? He knew who we were the second he saw the truck.

I had to restrain myself from slamming the door closed in anger. I quietly moved to the front, stealing glances every few seconds for zombies…or even humans. I found cigarettes—which I threw to the ground—and more bullets in the glove box. There were empty water bottles and candy bar wrappers scattered on the floor and shoved along the dash. I grabbed the keys; a tiny magic eight ball hung from the chain.

"Are we going to win?" I asked the stupid toy and shook it. I smiled at the simple one word response of YES. "Good," I said aloud.

Suddenly, the guys across the street started firing again. I dropped down, huddling against the car for protection. My friends fired back in response. My heart pounded and I stared with wide eyes at the back of the building, hating that I didn't know how things were going inside.

When they stopped, my ears were ringing and the silence that followed seemed painful. Nervous sweat dripped between my shoulder blades. I swallowed hard and pressed my hands against my thighs to keep them from trembling. Not yet daring to move, I picked at the rubber on the Charger's tires. The urge of wanting to slash them flitted through me, but it quickly dissolved and yielded to another idea.

In an awkward crouch, I moved to Cutter's body, set the bow down, and grabbed his ankles. Then I began pulling him backwards, leaving a blood trail. I put his feet and legs on the floor of the driver's side and tried to position his arm in a way that I could easily grab it. I raced around to the other side and climbed in, taking hold of Cutter's arm so I could pull him into the seat.

It was easier said than done. He was literal dead weight and the long arrows sticking out from his body weren't making things any easier. Finally, I got him into the seat. I was sure I had yanked his right arm out of the socket. His body flopped forward; I leaned over and grabbed the seatbelt, securing him in place. I stuck the keys in the ignition.

"Shit," I swore. I needed to be able to tell the guys my plan. If we couldn't communicate, the whole thing was worthless. I quickly got out of the Charger and wiped sweat from my face. I was halfway to the door when I skidded to a stop, whirling around to look at the truck.

Only Ivan and Brock had their walkies, which meant that there was another in the truck. Smiling, I flew to the truck and pulled open the door and snatched the walkie-talkie from the center console.

"Hey," I said quietly into the device.

"Riss," Hayden replied. "What's going on?"

"I have a distraction," I told him and opened the back door, grimacing at Janet's body. I shook my head, angry and saddened that someone innocent had to die. "I'll tell you when to come out, ok?"

"Ok," he said with no hesitation. "I will have the civilians ready. Be careful, Orissa," he added softly.

"You too." I clipped the walkie to my belt loop and stepped on the rail. I unbuckled Janet's seatbelt and carefully moved her to the ground, thankful she was so petite. I wasn't sure what to do with the body. If I left it here, she'd get eaten by zombies. But I couldn't leave it in the truck.

Though I felt like I was wasting time, I grabbed a blanket from the back and covered her with it and then dragged the one-eyed gummy over, hoping her deteriorating scent would mask the smell of fresh meat.

Panting, I ran back to the Charger. I gritted my teeth and turned the key. The engine roared to life, but it didn't cause another shoot out. I sat in the passenger seat, thinking that my well- thought out plan wasn't as well-thought as I assumed. I shifted the car into drive and let the natural momentum slowly move us forward.

It was rather difficult to steer from the opposite side, and even more so when I had to lean over a dead body with three arrows sticking out in my face. When we turned around, I stuck my foot down on the brakes and shifted the car into neutral. I closed my eyes when I leaned close to Cutter's body and opened the windows.

"Get ready," I said into the walkie. I flicked on the radio and was greeted with nothing but static. I turned on an MP3 player and cracked up the volume. Then I shifted the car back into drive and kept my hand on the wheel. When the nose of the car was almost to the front of the restaurant, I rolled back, jumping from the slow moving car.

The impact of my bones on pavement instantly hurt but I had no time to let the pain register. I sprang up and flattened myself against the side of the building, hoping that the air conditioning unit would provide just enough cover to keep me unseen as I slid along the brick and dodged behind the diner. Under the air vent where I had made my escape, I stopped and caught my breath.

Hands shaking, I moved the walkie to my mouth and waited. The Charger slowly rolled into the street. I edged to the side of the dining area and dropped to my knees. The few zombies that milled about in the street took immediate interest and staggered over.

The two guys that were dressed in black body armor emerged from a building across the street, holding up their hands to whoever was on the roof.

"Now!" I said into the walkie. I pushed myself up and sprinted to the back. The metal door burst open and Hannah raced out, pulling Agatha along with her. Brock and Roger exited next, followed by Ivan and Hayden, who slammed the door shut.

Everyone pressed against the exterior wall of the building. They guys had their guns raised, and their faces were set with determination. Hayden stepped forward and pressed the truck keys into my hand.

"Where are you going?" I asked him.

"To kill those guys," he said, as if it was obvious.

I shook my head. "No. You could get shot—again!"

He put his hand on my waist. "Riss, I've done this before. We've done this before."

"But..." I started and trailed off, at a loss for an agreement. I didn't know what else to do; it wasn't as if we could stay behind this diner forever. We needed out, and we needed to get to Jason and Wade. "I'm coming with you."

Hayden looked down and quickly shook his head. "They're going to come," he spoke. "We might be able to head them off. But if they don't," his eyes flicked to the opposite side of the building, "we need someone ready." My head moved up and down and my eyes locked with Hayden's. Though I knew it was true, I still felt like he was brushing me off and keeping me safely stashed behind the brick building. "Keep them safe," he said.

"I will," I promised. Hayden's eyebrows pushed together. He held my gaze for another second before stepping away and jogging over to Ivan and Wade, who had moved behind the dumpster. I shoved the truck keys into my pocket and pulled the pistol from the holster. "The safety's off," I told Hannah and extended the gun to her.

She took it and nodded. I whirled around; the guys had disappeared from view. I grabbed an arrow and hooked the end on the string. "Aim for the head," I told Hannah. "Pretend they are zombies."

"Okay," she said weakly. I stepped away, briskly walking to the other side of the diner. Then I abruptly stopped. Agatha and Roger stood out in the open, exposed to not only the shooters but the zombies. And they had no way to defend themselves. I took a hold of the arrow with the same hand that was holding the bow and dug the keys from my pocket.

"Get in and stay low," I told them and unlocked the truck. I hurried over and opened the door. Agatha scrambled inside but Roger needed help. His joints cracked as he hunched down in the back seat. I silently pushed the door closed, not daring to risk hitting the lock button. "You should get in too," I decided.

"No," Hannah told me. "If they come back here I want to be able to help."

"Okay." I didn't want to argue. "Get behind the truck at least."

I looked around as Hannah ran around the truck. To the left of the diner was a hair salon. There was a rust covered minivan with four flat tires parked behind it. It would make an ideal location to hide behind and shoot at anyone who ventured back here. But, running away from the protection of the building wasn't a good idea.

Before I could even make up my mind, the explosion of rapid fire rang in the air. My body tensed and my heart skipped a beat. I closed my eyes and exhaled; I needed to keep it together.

"...I repeat, do you have a copy?" Wade's voice came over the walkie. I hadn't heard him over the shooting.

"Yes," I said into the walkie and held it up to my ear.

"Riss," he gasped. "Doesn't sound good on your end."

"It's not. I can barely hear you. You guys ok?"

"For now. This place is filled with zombies. We're in a storage room. I just don't have enough ammo to take them all down."

"Stay there. We'll be there as soon as we can," I promised and clipped the walkie back onto a belt loop. "Shit," I muttered to myself. Not only did I have no idea where the storage room they were holed up in was, I had no way of getting there. Tension rose inside me and the idea of crumpling to the ground in frustration flicked through my brain. I took a steady breath and shook my head. We would get through this, I reminded myself. I had no fucking clue how, but we would. I took a step back and resituated the bow and arrow in my hand. From the street, someone cried out in pain. The gunfire slowed down. I held my breath and waited. I knew that it wasn't Hayden who had been hit, but I couldn't rule out Brock or Ivan.

Dry grass and gravel crunched under foot. I pulled back the arrow and steadied myself. It was one of the guys dressed in black body armor; he skidded to a stop and put his hands up when he saw us. Blood streamed down his face. He was close enough to be more than an easy kill. I decided to wait just a minute.

"How many of you—" I started. A gunshot echoed from behind me and the guy collapsed on the ground. I whipped around. "What the hell?" I yelled at Hannah.

"He was going to shoot you!" she shouted back.

"He doesn't have a gun!" I lowered the bow and glared at her.

"Orissa!" she screamed and pointed. The guy grabbed my ankle. I jerked my leg up and back, but not before he was able to throw me off balance. I threw myself forward as I fell, purposely putting all of my weight on his stomach. The breath whooshed out of him and I saw that Hannah's bullet had lodged in the thick

Kevlar covering his chest.

The armor had saved his life, but it hindered his ability to move quickly and freely. Since he was too close to use the bow, I released my grip on it and rolled off of him, jumping back onto my feet. He brought himself to his knees and dove for me. I dodged out of the way and kicked him in the chest, right over the spot where the bullet had hit. He yelped and dropped back down. I grabbed the bow and quickly backed up. The next time he pushed himself up would be his last; the arrow lodged itself into his skull and he fell face-forward onto the grassy gravel.

"Are you ok?" Hannah asked with a shaky voice.

"Yes," I replied without thinking. "You?"

"I'm not hurt," she answered.

"Good," I said with a nod. I turned back to the shooter and hastily removed his bulletproof vest. "Put this on," I called to Hannah and threw it close to the truck. "And stay here. I'm going to see what's going on out there." I stepped over the body and moved to the side of the building, staying close enough to the wall that my hair caught on the scratchy brick. A few zombies gathered around a dark mass in the street, desperately clawing at the thick body armor. My eyes swept up to the top of the building across from us; an arm lifelessly dangled from the roof.

Fast paced footfalls pounded on the street. I drew back another arrow only to quickly lower my arm and stick the arrow back in the quiver.

"I heard a shot," Hayden panted.

"Your sister is trigger happy," I said and embraced him.

"Ivan thought one of the guys ran back here."

"He did," I told Hayden. "I got him. The others?"

"Two are dead, two—well one now—got away. He was on the roof and ducked inside before we had a chance to take him out. He could be anywhere," Hayden said with sudden realization. He dropped his arms from around my waist and pulled me to the side of the building. I stepped in front of him, hoping Hannah would see me first and not shoot.

I held up my hand when we rounded the corner. As soon as Hannah saw her brother, she raced over and hugged him. Hayden patted her on the back before gently pushing her away.

"This isn't over yet," he warned. "One guy got away. You need to lay low until I give you the all clear, ok?"

Hannah pressed her lips together and nodded. "Where did he go?"

"We don't know."

"You didn't see him running?"

"No, Hannah. If we saw him running then he wouldn't have gotten away."

"Oh, right. What are you going to do?"

"Ivan and Brock are on it. We'll find him. But he's scared, and scared people get desperate. I really need you to stay unseen." She nodded once more and stepped back toward the truck. Hayden jumped in the bed. "Keys?" he asked me.

I fished them out of my pocket and tossed them to him. I turned around and moved my eyes back and forth from one side of the building to the other. Hayden quickly reloaded his weapons, pulled a bullet proof vest over his head, handed the other to me, and shoved extra ammo in his pockets.

"You didn't hear Wade's radio call, did you?" I asked over the sound of a clip sliding into his pistol. I set the bow down and pulled the thick black vest over my head. It uncomfortably crushed my breasts against my sweaty body. Hayden handed me a machine gun and I re-accessorized myself with weapons.

"No, why?"

"The store is full of undead."

"Shit," Hayden swore and jumped down. "Do they need us?"

"To get out, yes. Hang on." I grabbed the walkie. "Wade?" I asked and go no reply. "Ok, maybe they do regardless."

Hayden adjusted the strap of his M16 and exhaled. "Fuck," he sighed. His eyes fell to the ground. "We're going. Hannah, stay here and stay out of sight. You know those two can't run. Maybe you should get back in the freezer," he mused before shaking his head. "No. Here, take the keys. At least you can get away if needed."

"Where are you going?"

"We need to help the others."

"How will I know you're ok?"

"You won't," Hayden admitted. "Until we're back."

"Hayden," she protested.

"We don't have time, Hannah. You're friends are in there. Be safe, sis."

"You too," Hannah said. "Both of you."

Hayden and I moved to the side of the building. I quickly relayed the message of our plan over the walkie so Ivan and Brock knew what was going on. Hayden stepped away from the brick, looked at the street, and waved me onward. We ran across the drive and took shelter by the minivan.

"Any idea where the hell this store is?" he asked me.

I shook my head. "I wasn't paying any attention," I admitted guiltily.

"Neither was I," he agreed. "I don't think any of us were. We never expected this."

"They were last in line," I recalled. "So they have to be farther down."

"Your guess is as good as mine," he said. "Let's go." We moved into an alley that intersected with the road we had been driving on. Jon's car came into view. Every window was shattered and the scent of gasoline was heavy in the air. I cast a glance at Hayden and he nodded.

Creeping forward with his machine gun raised, Hayden assessed the area and waved me to follow. We hurried to the passenger side of the wrecked car. Daniel was slumped over in the back; parts of his head were splattered on the seat. A thick lump of vomit bubbled in my stomach. Lupe's body was riddled with bullet holes and blood. Lifeless, open eyes stared straight ahead.

Jon was leaning on the steering wheel, blood soaking the deflated airbag. Hayden carefully reached in and killed the ignition. Slippery with blood, the keys slipped through his fingers. Out of habit, he jerked forward as if to retrieve them but stopped; it wasn't as if we were going to drive this thing home.

Then Jon gasped.

Hayden and I both jumped back. Hayden opened the door and leaned over Lupe's body, gently pushing Jon's body into an upright position. Glass stuck out of his neck; a slow stream of crimson steadily leaked from the wounds. His eyes fluttered and his body trembled. The front of his shirt was soaked in blood; I had no idea how he was still alive.

"Jon," Hayden said calmly. "Hey, buddy. It's ok."

Jon attempted to raise his hand and failed. His body violently shuttered. He opened his mouth. "Ehh," he panted.

"Don't talk, it's ok," Hayden assured him.

Jon's eyes fluttered open and swept over me. "I'm sorry," he panted and let his eyes close again. He trembled again before going still.

"Is he dead?" I asked my voice hoarse.

"I think so," Hayden replied and moved out of the car. He looked over the bodies and shook his head. "They shot with no hesitation," he breathed. Hayden wiped his bloody hands on his pants and picked up his machine gun. He looked down the street.

"Do you see that red and blue sign?" I asked.

"Yeah, you think that's it?"

"I can't read what it says from here, but possibly."

"Alright, let's go." After inspecting our surroundings, we jogged across the street and darted down an alley. Relief washed through me when we saw the SUV that Madison had been driving parked haphazardly behind Wade's Jeep. We edged past it and raced out of the alley.

Hayden was right; the paint on the red and blue lettering was faded, but the giant plastic words definitely spelled out the right location. We slowed at the entrance. My mouth was dry and I was so hot; I wanted nothing more than to find a stream or lake to jump in. Carefully, we stepped out of the sun and into the dusty lobby. The glass store front windows had been broken and from the bits of brown blood and leathery scraps of zombie flesh, I could tell it had been intact until today. The shards of glass were slick underfoot. I held my arms out for balance and carefully crossed through the lobby.

About a half dozen zombies pushed and shoved their way to get a piece of a fresh meal. I shot two with arrows while Hayden picked off the rest using his pistol. Lying unmoving in the middle of the zombie pile was Gage. Blood clumped into his curly red hair where part of his scalp had been gnawed off. His body had been split open with his rib cage cracked and pulled to either side. All that was left was an empty cavity; his intestines and organs had been devoured.

The metallic scent of blood made my stomach churn. I looked at the kid's dead blue eyes and cringed. Hayden put his hand on my back, which I almost didn't feel through the body armor. We walked around the massacre, anger boiling with each step. The death toll was rising, all because of those idiot assholes at the asylum.

"Please tell me that was you guys," Jason's voice spoke over the walkie.

I shoved my bow under my arm and struggled to get the walkie. Since his hands weren't as full as mine, Hayden unclipped it from my belt loop.

"Yeah," he spoke. "We're in. Where are you?"

"Back of the store. We can't see outside but I'm pretty sure we got a herd outside the door. I don't think it will hold much longer."

"We're coming," Hayden assured him. "Get back and get down."

"Ok," Jason replied. Hayden attached the walkie to his belt. We were standing in the front and center of the store, with two cash registers on either side. Rows of shelves ran parallel to us; most were dust covered and empty with the occasional can or stale box of crackers left behind. Rodent droppings gave the stale air a sickening feel, almost as if it was suffocating. The echoing death moans of the undead echoed through the empty store. Nails scratched the wall and festering hands slapped and clawed at the door. *Fuck*, I thought. Jason was right. There were a lot of zombies in here.

I motioned for Hayden to check the right side of the store while I investigated the left. I moved slowly, looking up and down each aisle, not seeing anything more than a few dead zombies. Hayden whistled; I snapped my attention to him. He held his finger to his lips and waved me to join him. Once I was by his side, he pointed down the last aisle.

It was the first time I was on the outside looking in. The horde reminded me of drunken teenagers at a concert, all pushing and shoving their way to the front of the stage in hopes of getting close to their favorite band.

"What are you thinking?" I whispered to Hayden.

"Open fire and hope to eliminate a good chunk before they come after us. There are too fucking many." I nodded and hooked the bow over my arm. Hayden grabbed the walkie-talkie once more. "You all down?"

"On the ground," Jason replied.

"Get ready," Hayden warned and stashed the device away. We both held up our machine guns. On the count of three, we opened fire. I swept back and forth, keeping the M16 at head level. The back row of zombies dropped and the others continued to press closer. Hayden and I slowly crept forward, our accuracy increasing as we neared.

Another handful dropped. And then the others began to turn and stagger their way toward us. We held our ground, and kept firing, hitting the ones that chose to come down the same aisle we were in.

"They're going around us!" I shouted to Hayden. His eyes flicked to the left.

"Hold steady," he instructed me and lowered his gun. He

turned and ran a few paces back and out of my range of sight. I kept shooting, though I felt like it did little to decrease the number of the undead that moved in our direction.

There was a crash behind me and I involuntarily jerked my head around to see what had happened. Hayden jumped back as another shelf tipped over, landing on a few zombies and preventing a few more from sneaking around and attacking us from the back...well, in at least one aisle. He raced back over and resumed shooting.

The empty chinking sound was most unwelcome. I didn't have time to hesitate. I discarded the M16 and grabbed an arrow, shooting as quickly as I could and still having deadly aim. Only seconds later, Hayden ran out of ammo as well. Not taking the time to reload, he switched to his hand gun.

The storage room door cracked open and Wade emerged, brandishing a rifle. With his help, the number of moving zombies dwindled. The store was far from clear, but the undead had dispersed enough for us to make a fast get away.

"Come on!" Wade yelled into the storage room. "And hurry!"

Hayden led the way, using his M16 to bash in zombie heads if any got too close. Jason had the little girl in his arms; she was screaming and crying but held on for dear life. Madison, Lori, Ryan, and Jim followed close behind. Wade stopped, waving the people forward. He turned and fired another round into the face of a tall and bloated zombie.

I ran along with the group, stopping only once to jam an arrow into the eye socket of a rotting gummy. Gray mold grew around her mouth and ears. We raced out of the store and into the parking lot. Several zombies followed us but got confused in the open air. Their eye sight was already poor; going from the dimly lit store to the blinding Texas sun was disorienting.

We stopped inside an empty cart corral, panting and shaking from the close call. I looked around at the rag-tag group, all gasping and wide eyed with fear. Most were splattered with blood—human or zombie, I couldn't tell. Then I realized someone was missing. I whirled around, expecting to see him. When I didn't, my heart plummeted to the ground.

"Where is Wade?"

CHAPTERNINETEEN

Hayden and I exchanged terrified glances. He shoved a new clip into his gun and sprinted forward, ready to go back and rescue his friend. But he didn't have to; Wade emerged from the grocery store seconds later.

"Sorry," he panted. "Had to take a detour."

My heart was racing so fast I felt light headed. "Jerk," I spat. "I thought you were dead."

Wade slowed and stopped in front of me. "Me, nah. I'm just as tough as you," he said with a wink.

"You wish," I said back with a grin.

"We need to keep moving," Hayden said. "The herd will regroup."

"He can't run anymore," Jim told us. I turned my head to him and noticed that Ryan was doubled over, trying to catch his breath. At least I knew why he had stayed in the church with the others; he was a severe asthmatic. "Can't we get our cars?"

"Do you want to go back there?" Hayden asked with his eyebrows raised. "Once the herd disperses, we'll get them. Until then, we need to get somewhere safe. Fast."

"We can walk," I said. "But we need to move. Now." It annoyed me to walk away from the store when so many of my arrows were still inside. I had plenty more; when Hayden and I raided an outdoor sporting goods store a while back I had grabbed every single arrow possible. Jason and I brought up the rear while Hayden and Wade led the small group.

"Did you guys get them all?" Jason asked.

I shook my head. "One got away. Ivan and Brock went after him."

Jason smiled. "They'll get him."

"Hopefully," I said, thinking that they would as long as the bastard didn't get to a car and speed away.

"Want me to carry something?" Jason offered.

"Sure," I said and shrugged off the machine gun. "It's empty."

He put the strap over his head.

"Thanks."

"No problem. You've kinda got your hands full."

"I'm getting used to it," I said, remembering my first mission. I was impressed with the ease in which the guys moved when they were covered in backpacks and weapons. "You will too."

He nodded and wiped sweat from his face. "Isn't it crazy?"

"What's crazy?" I asked, looking behind us.

"This," he stated.

I nodded. "I think I'm getting used to it too." I faced forward and ran my eyes up and down the back of Hayden's body. "And it's getting harder to remember what life was like before all the shit hit the fan."

"That's not good," he said quietly. "I try and think about it every day. I don't want to forget."

I gave him a half smile. "You won't," I tried to assure him, though I knew with my previous statement it offered little comfort.

"Someday this will be over and we'll go back to how it was."

I shrugged. "Maybe."

"You don't think so?" he questioned.

A zombie limped its way in our direction. Hayden turned and looked into my eyes for a second; it was all the communication I needed. I grabbed an arrow and shot it in the head. Wade yanked it out of the zombie's skull and hung back while the others kept moving.

"Thanks," I said and stuck the arrow back in the quiver. "And no," I said to Jason. "Not back to how it was, not completely. There are just not enough of us left."

"Yeah, that is true," he said, his tone dejected.

We ducked off the main road and entered a narrow alley. I didn't like feeling closed in; with only two directions to go, we would be screwed in an attack. A pile of rain-ruined, faceless mannequins spilled out of an overturned trashcan. I precariously stepped around the tangled plastic body parts.

"I've always thought these things were creepy," Jason muttered. "Did you know that some stores put cameras in the eyes? That way they can keep tabs on customers and see what kind of people come into their stores."

"Mhh," I responded, not liking how loud his voice sounded in the narrow alley.

"Did you ever see that movie where the mannequins are really real people?"

"No, I haven't," I replied quietly, hoping he'd get the hint and shut up. Maybe Hannah should ride with Jason on the way home. Even I wouldn't want to do that to poor Wade. Hayden held up his hand when we came to a break in the alley. Heat radiated off the brick buildings, trapping us in a stagnant sauna of summer air. A swarm of dark mosquitoes circled above us; I swatted at them and wished I had a lighter. Raeya used to get upset when I'd do that. She said it was wrong to torch innocent bugs. They didn't seem so innocent when they were flying around my face and sticking their needle noses into my skin to steal my blood.

My hand froze mid swipe. Mosquitoes. Blood. I whirled around. Zombies. Was it possible? There were lots of diseases that were transferred from insect to human. There was still an issue with West Nile virus in the country. The number of deaths from it climbed each summer. Would the blood thirsty little bugs even be interested in the thick, foul blood that slowly flowed through the veins of the undead?

And mosquitoes weren't the only bugs that lived on blood. Deer flies, lice, fleas, and ticks all fed the same way. I shook my head. The virus had started in late fall. There weren't too many mosquitoes left by that time. For the first time ever, I wanted to have a conversation with Dr. Cara.

"You ok, Riss?" Jason asked. I spun back around.

"Yeah. I'm just checking."

"Right. You can never be too careful. Do you see anything?"

I shook my head and glanced at Hayden. He crossed the street and waved the group onward. It would have made the most sense to retrace our steps, so when Hayden ducked behind another building it took me a few seconds to figure out his logic.

We were avoiding the horrific sight of the crashed car and the bullet ridden bodies inside. Having walked most of our journey, Hayden picked up the pace to a slow jog, not stopping until we rounded the corner of the restaurant.

Having finished with the body in the street, a handful of zombies milled about the parking lot. My eyes flashed to the truck where Hannah and the older couple were supposed to be safely stashed. They were feasting on the remains of Cutter's partner, who had fallen next to the truck. Once that was gone the scent of Janet's blood would no doubt lure them into the truck. With no hesitation, Hayden rushed forward.

"Hannah," he called and began shooting. Out of ammo, Wade gripped the handle of the shotgun and used it as a bat, smashing in the nose of a short, fat zombie. Faces glinting with wet crimson, the zombies were full of human meat and energized. Our movement caused them to immediately perk up.

Snarling and hissing, they turned in tandem and stretched out their arms. I exhaled and steadied myself before quickly firing off arrows. The female zombie's dress used to be covered in yellow daisies and I couldn't tell if she had been pregnant when she died or if her abdomen was overstretched from shoveling down food. She ducked inside the truck.

Agatha screamed. The truck rocked as Hannah reached over the front seat, pulling the old woman away from the broken window. Hayden shot at the zombie; brown blood speckled the air but didn't faze the S2. My quiver was close to empty. I reached behind me and pulled out the last arrow; the tip snagged on my hair and yanked out a few strands. I shoved the bow into Madison's arms and raced forward. Gunshots rang in my ears. My hand smacked the tailgate in my haste. I tightened my fingers around the shaft of the arrow as I grabbed her shoulders. My fingernails punctured her skin; sun-warmed slime oozed out from under her paper thin flesh. I had no time to acknowledge how disgusting it was. I threw her back and rammed the arrow through her open mouth.

No sooner was her body on the ground when another zombie raced forward. Covered in slime, my hand flew off the arrow when I tried to pull it back. Hands grasped my arm. I yanked it and stepped back, right into another zombie.

"Riss!" Hayden shouted, his voice muffled by the hungry, throaty groans of zombies. I dropped to the ground, painfully landing on a large piece of gravel, and rolled under the truck. I could see his boots as he ran, stopping next to the broken window. One zombie fell; it had been stabbed in the eye socket and its eye ripped out when Hayden pulled back his knife. It dangled from frayed nerves and ligaments down his face.

My eyes swept the parking lot. I crawled to my right, scrambling out from under the truck. Jason had everyone backed up against the side of the building and held up the empty M16. Wade and Hayden were in the middle of the horde, swinging their knives through the air with deadly accuracy.

"Here!" Hannah shouted and opened the passenger door. I

took my handgun and ran around. I fired four rounds before the clip emptied. I kicked a zombie in the chest and brought the butt of the gun down on her temple.

"Get them in the truck!" Hayden shouted to Jason. "Hannah!"

"Got it!" she yelled back and fumbled with the keys. Still in the passenger seat, she started up the engine. I wildly motioned for her to back up. Finally getting it, she nodded and hopped into the driver's seat and backed the truck up to the side of the building where Jason helped everyone scramble into the bed.

I turned my attention back to the unending stream of walking death. A child zombie hurried forward and I used the gun like a hammer to crack open her skull. A dog collar with a broken chain hung around her neck. I didn't have time to fathom what that could have been about.

Hannah gave a quick beep on the horn. Hayden turned to me and nodded. Wade hit one more zombie in the nose before the three of us ran. Hannah had moved to the back and opened both front doors. Hayden jumped in the driver's seat and Wade and I squished into the passenger's side, with me on his lap. Hayden put the truck in reverse and spun it around, jolting everyone who was sitting in the bed.

We drove out of the parking lot, running over a slow moving gummy, and turned left. We sped past Jon's car and turned off on another road before Hayden let off the gas. Leaving the truck to idle, he opened the door and got out.

"You guys ok?" he asked. I climbed off of Wade and exited as well.

"I think so," Jason answered. Jim and Lori hung onto Amanda, who had silent tears streaming down her face. "Where the hell did they come from?"

"They had been gathering in the street," I explained. "The noise from the shooting and now the blood attracted them. We have to get out of here. This place is a death trap."

Wade nodded. "What the hell did they want?"

"Me," I said, my voice sullen.

"Huh?"

"They were from Eastmoore," Hayden finished. "The same ones that killed Rider and kidnapped Orissa." His words hung in the air, bringing a slight chill over me.

"H-how did they find us?" Jason stuttered.

I shook my head. "I don't think they were looking. I mean, they saw the truck and knew it was us, but it was luck. Really,

really bad luck."

"Are we close to the hospital?"

"A few hours," I told him.

Hannah wrapped her arms around herself, frightened. "Where is everyone else?" she asked.

Jim looked at Hayden, who slightly shook his head. "I think we're all that's left," he said.

"No," she cried. "No."

Madison turned to Ryan and began crying. I more than understood the hurt of losing a friend, and I felt bad for them all. Though, now wasn't the time to fall apart.

"And the two that were with you?" Jim asked.

"They went after the last shooter," Hayden told him. His voice was calm and level but I could see the fear behind his hazel eyes. "Do you have the keys to your vehicles?" he asked, abruptly changing the subject. He grabbed a water bottle, warm from the sun, and twisted off the cap. "Help yourself," he said to the others.

"I have the keys," Wade told him and looked at Madison.

"I left them in the ignition," she sniffled. "I don't even remember if I turned the car off," she admitted guiltily and winced when she moved her arm. I noticed that her wrist was starting to swell.

"You did," I told her. "We walked past them. I would have remembered if it was running."

Her head moved up and down and she forced a smile. I faced Hayden. "We should get them now."

He shook his head. "Let's just stay here for a while."

I knew he was only saying that for the sake of the others. I took the water from him and downed half of it. "All we need is two of us to get the cars," I reminded him.

He ground his teeth while he thought. "Wade and I will go."

"Hayden, no!" Hannah protested.

"I'll go," I interjected. "I have plenty of arrows in there," I said and motioned to the silver box.

"No," Hayden said definitely. "We're going to wait for Ivan and Brock. If they run into trouble, we need to be here. Which reminds me...shit," he cursed and grabbed the walkie. "Ivan?" he asked. "Do you copy?"

"What do you want, Underwood?" Ivan retorted. I imagined his cheeky grin as he spoke.

"A fucking status," Hayden spat back, laughing.

"We're on our way back," Ivan said. "Chased the bastard out of town. Literally. We found him holed up in a shed."

"And?"

"He shot himself when we busted the door."

"Shit," Hayden quietly swore.

"You're telling me. I wanted to question the little fucker. Make him bleed. Do to him what they did to Penwell."

"That makes two of us," Hayden said grimly. "Where are you? The streets are full of zombies."

"We went East."

"How much ammo do you have?"

"Not much left."

"Alright," Hayden said and paused to think.

"We need to get another car, man," Wade spoke. "Riss and I can do this."

Hayden nodded and told Ivan and Brock to hang back and out of the zombies' line of sight. I finished the water, restocked my quiver, loaded my pistol, and took the M16 from Hayden, who had already loaded it in the time it took me to gather the rest of my weapons. I unbuckled the vest.

"You should keep that on," Hayden said.

"Why?" I questioned and continued to shimmy out of it. "Zombies won't shoot me."

Hayden only frowned, but he at least dropped the topic. Lori and Amanda got in the back of the truck with Agatha and Roger and Ryan and Madison squished together in the front. We armed Hannah and Jim, who took a seat in the bed of the truck. Wade and I perched along the tailgate as Hayden slowly pulled out from behind the building.

"Far enough," I said and Jason slapped the back window. Wade and I hoped out; I turned to give Hayden a lingering look goodbye. Without worrying about getting shot, we jogged down the main road.

"You ok?" Wade asked.

"Yeah, why wouldn't I be?"

"I don't know," he panted and shook his head. "Seeing the guys who kidnapped and tortured you could be traumatic or something."

"Oh, I guess," I agreed.

Our boots pounded in sync as we ran down the road.

"But I knew I was going to see them again soon. I'll admit it was unexpected and as much as I don't want to admit it, I was scared of him." I grinned. "Until I shot him."

Wade slowed and turned toward me. "That was the first person you killed, right? Who wasn't infected, I mean."

"Yeah," I said in a huff, happy to decrease my speed. "It was."

"Killing people..." he began and looked out at the street. "It can wear on you. You did what you had to do. Don't question yourself or you'll drive yourself mad. Trust me on that one."

"He had to die. If I didn't kill him, he would have killed me and who knows who else."

"Good," Wade affirmed. "Just remember that."

"I will," I assured him. We passed the horrific scene of the death filled car.

"Shit, these people are brutal," Wade huffed. "This world is perfect for them."

"Scary," I agreed and focused on breathing normally in the heat. "That car is going to be a zombie magnet in just a matter of time."

"It is. We better hurry."

We quickened our pace. A few zombies meandered about the streets but posed little threat. It made my stomach pinch with fear and I wondered where the herd had gone.

"Hey," Wade panted and pointed at a pet store. "That's their car, right? It's the same Mustang those Imperial pricks drove, I think."

"Yeah," I said when the crowned skull came into view."

"Shame they fucked up a classic," Wade muttered and pressed forward. We finally slowed to a walk when we reached the parking lot of the grocery store. I held my hand over my eyes and squinted.

"I don't think too many are in there," I mused and looked sideways at Wade.

"What's that look for?" he asked.

I smiled innocently. "Would you hate me if I went in for my arrows? It's a waste to leave them."

Wade raised one eyebrow, shook his head, and smiled. "Let's get your damn arrows."

"Thanks. And really, the thought of someone else taking them is unsettling."

Wade laughed. "You have an interesting take on things, Riss."

I shrugged and pulled my pistol from the holster. With precariously placed steps, we eased into the store front, the broken glass cracking under our boots. Wade went to the left and I went to the right, yanking my arrows free. Several zombies were pinned under the shelves that Hayden had knocked over. Their brittle nails raked along the tile until they bent and broke off, leaving brown blood streaks on the once shiny, white floor.

"Got them all from over here," Wade called. I put two more into my quiver. Since I had restocked my arrow supply, the rest wouldn't fit. I would have to carry them, though it wasn't as if I had far to go.

"Thanks," I told him and walked to the center of the store. Wade's cheeks were bright red and his stance wasn't centered. "You ok?"

"Yeah," he answered right away. "I hate the heat."

"Me too," I said and took the arrows from him. I snapped three into the holder on my bow. "What do you think the chances are we find a river or lake to detour to?"

"We could," he said. "I saw a park on the map. It's not close, but it's not all that far either."

"After this failed deviation from our mapped out trip, I doubt it'll happen."

"I'd even be happy to get in that little creek we drove over."

"Creek?" I quickly shook my head. "Oh, if you can even consider it that." We had driven over a small bridge on the way into town. The creek couldn't have been very deep but the thought of stepping into any sort of moving water was wonderful.

Wade grimaced and stretched his arms out in front of him. "Fucking cramps," he muttered and massaged his biceps.

"You sure you're ok?" I repeated.

"Yeah," he snapped before shaking his head in an unspoken apology. "I'm fine."

"If you say so." I bundled the extra arrows under my arm and lead the way out of the store. Wade shot and killed about half a dozen more zombies that crowded the alley. They were stuck, unsure of what to do or where to go in such a tight space. "Ugh, they smell like death warmed over," I complained and took a wide stride over a bloated body.

"Mmh," Wade said in agreement. He looked damn exhausted and the redness was spreading from his cheeks to his neck and arms.

"Turn the air on," I suggested when he opened the door to the Jeep. I tossed my arrows on the backseat of the SUV. "I am," I added so I didn't sound so motherly.

"We're not supposed to, Riss," he reminded me. "It's a waste of gas."

"Oh, come on," I pressed. "It's a short drive and it's hotter than hell out here. I'm turning mine on."

"We were given direct orders not to use the heat or air unless—"

"—absolutely necessary," I interrupted. "And it is absolutely necessary today." I pressed my lips together and leaned into the vehicle, turning it on and cranking the air before getting in. I rolled down the windows and waited a minute. Wade's gait staggered but he pulled himself into the Jeep and drove forward.

We drove out of the alley, turned around in the back lot of the grocery store and went out of the alley to head back the way we came. Wade revved the engine and ran over the zombies that lay on the hot pavement; his tires squashed a skull and brown and yellow pus splashed out. I wrinkled my nose at the putrid smell that filtered in from the air conditioner.

Seeing the Range Rover was a welcome surprise. Ivan and Brock sat in the front with Agatha and Roger in the back. Hannah was in the back of the truck and everyone else was outside, waiting to jump into their cars. Since the count was down, Madison, Ryan, Jim, Lori and her daughter all were able to fit into the SUV. Jason saw that everyone was seated and hurried to get into the passenger seat of the Jeep. Hayden waved to Ivan and dove into the truck, taking a seat next to me. We wasted no time getting the hell out of the zombie filled ghost town.

"Where are we going?" I asked and tilted the air vent to blow on my face. I rolled up my shirt and downed a bottle of water.

Hayden shook his head. "Just away for right now."

I watched the ghost town fade from view in the side mirror. "I think they were alone," I said, voicing a combined fear. "Just the six of them."

"I'm banking on that," Hayden told me. He nervously glanced behind him. We sped past an old movie theater. Though it was missing letters, the headlining show was several years old. I remembered going to see it with Raeya when we were freshman in college.

"What is he doing?" Hayden asked himself and watched the Jeep slow down. It veered to the side of the road before the wheels jerked it back to the center. The brakes flashed and it rolled to a stop.

"Guys," Jason's frantic voice came from the walkie. "We have a problem."

CHAPTERTWENTY

The driver's side door opened and Wade stumbled out. He made it a few feet away before doubling over and throwing up. Hayden threw the truck in park and ran out, speaking into the walkie-talkie. I rushed to Wade's side.

"Yeah, you're fine," I said to him. I grabbed a loose strand of hair and nervously yanked on it; I didn't know what to do. Wade rocked back on his heels and slumped to the ground, eyes fluttering. I sank down to his level, my fingertips numb and shaking with anxiety. "Hey," I said softly. "Wade?"

"I'm okay," he said and shook his head. "Just got dizzy."

"I think you're overheated." I pressed my hand to his cheek and noticed he wasn't sweating anymore. I looked up at Hayden. "And dehydrated."

"Get water," he said to Jason, who scrambled out of the Jeep. Wade had on a thin long sleeve shirt, which was crusted in zombie blood. My fingertips felt numb with nerves and I fumbled as I unbuttoned it. Boots pounded on the street and I didn't have to look up to know that Ivan and Brock had run over. "Here," Hayden said as he took the water from Jason. He squatted down to our level. "Can you drink?" he asked Wade.

"Yeah," he muttered. He twisted off the cap and handed him the bottle. Keeping his eyes closed, he took it and pressed it to his lips.

"It's warm," he complained.

"I know. It's all we have."

His body convulsed and he threw up again, though this time he was too weak to lean forward. I took the water from him, grabbed the collar of his shirt and ripped the buttons off. Hayden helped me yank Wade's arms free. I used the shirt to wipe up the vomit that dripped down his face and threw it to the side. His white undershirt was sopping with sweat.

"Is your air on?" Brock asked Jason.

"Yeah," he answered, his voice shaking.

"Pour water on something and hold it to the vent to cool it down."

Jason nodded and scuttled away.

"We need to get him back into the air conditioning," I said.

I stood back and let Hayden and Brock pull Wade to his feet.

"I'm alright," he protested and tried to push Hayden away.

"No, buddy, you're not," Hayden said gently. "You have heat stroke."

There wasn't much room to work with us all crammed in the back seat. And with the doors open, the cool air escaped.

"Can I help?" Hannah's voice asked from outside the Jeep.

"Yeah," Hayden said. "Do what Jason is doing." She nodded and went back to the truck.

I shoved the passenger's seat as far up as it could go and crammed myself into the back. I took the cap off of the water. "I know it's nasty and warm but you need it." I put the bottle to Wade's lips and poured a tiny bit into his mouth. He swallowed it.

"It's cool," Jason said and handed me a water soaked t-shirt. "I'll start on another one."

I placed the shirt on Wade's forehead, tucking it around so the wet material touched his neck. Brock moved to the other side and began unlacing Wade's boots.

"What do we do?" I asked Hayden.

He shook his head. "I've seen plenty of guys suffer from heat stroke overseas," he started. "The medic had to take care of them." He clenched his jaw and ground his teeth. "There was IV equipment in that EMT bag, wasn't there?"

"Yeah," I answered. "But none of us know how to do that."

"We have to try," he told me. "Or else..."

Hayden pressed the back door closed to keep the cool air in and went around to the other side, standing next to Brock. Hannah brought over a towel, which Brock draped over Wade's feet.

"Is he going to be ok?" she asked, standing close to her brother.

"Yes," Hayden lied. "If we knew how to start an IV," he added ruefully.

I flipped the shirt over on Wade's face and gave him more water. I pressed my fingers to his neck. "His heart is racing," I stated, the anxiety growing in my heart. "We have to do something!"

"Bring me the IV stuff," Hayden told his sister. "I'll try."

"You have no idea what you're doing," I reminded him.

"I watched you get poked more than once. It can't hurt, can it?"

I shook my head; I didn't know. It would hurt Wade, of course, to have a needle jammed into his skin multiple times. I tipped the bottle but the water just ran out of his mouth. "Wade?" I asked. He responded with a deep sigh and tried to open his eyes.

"Riss," Jason said and extended his arm. He gave me another damp cloth; I switched it out with the one that was covering Wade's face. "And you can cause nerve damage," Jason said to Hayden. "If you don't do the IV right."

Hayden balled his fists with frustration. Brock shifted his weight and bit his lip. I could tell he was thinking and coming up with nothing.

I closed my eyes and shook my head. "We drove over a creek before we got into that town. If we can get there, maybe we can cool down his body temp before any internal damage is done."

"Let's go," Hayden said. "Now."

Jason clamored into the driver's side and I stayed crowded in the backseat with Wade. Hannah jumped in along with us, offering to hold one of the wet rags against the air vent to keep it cool. The others, who had gathered around the Jeep, got back into their vehicles in a mad dash. Ivan led the way, going as fast as he safely could.

When Wade's breathing became labored, I folded up his shirt and stuck the cool rag on his stomach. He groaned and tried to sit up.

"Don't move," I soothed. "It's gonna be ok."

He mumbled something incoherent and let his head flop back down. I ran my hand through his dark blonde hair, brushing it off of his face. Like Rider, Wade was young, maybe a few years older than Jason at the most.

"Riss," Jason said and twisted in his seat. "There are vents in the back. The control is in the middle."

"Thanks," I said and set it on low; I didn't know if too much cold air too soon would be a shock to Wade's overheated body. Several minutes later, goosebumps broke out over my arms. Hannah handed me another cool rag. I carefully lifted Wade's head and put it along his neck.

"Thanks," he mumbled.

"You feeling better?" I asked hopefully.

"My head is throbbing," he said. "And I think I'm gonna puke."

"Sit up," I urged and put my hands through his arms. "So you don't choke."

"No. Don't wanna move." His body jolted. I put my hand on his cheek; his skin wasn't cooling down. I held up the water and was able to get him to take another sip. He closed his eyes again and became still. I swallowed—my pounding heart. After what seemed like minutes, he took a breath.

I turned the air up to a medium setting and kept replacing the wet rags. After several minutes, the top of Wade's skin was cooling down, but his entire body was still warm from the heat that was trapped between him and the seat.

"We're almost there," Jason said. "There is a sandy bank along the creek we're going to." I looked up when the Jeep left the smooth pavement and bumped along a gravel road Trees zipped by and the road gave way to an overgrown field, forcing us to slow down. The sun skipped behind the forestry, flashing in and out of the window. The Jeep came to a halt and Jason jumped out. He opened the door and extended a hand.

My legs had fallen asleep and I stumbled my way out. Ivan and Brock got to us first; they carefully lifted Wade out of the backseat and carried him to the water.

"Is it cold?" Hayden asked, looping his arm through mine so I could steadily walk. When the water level was high, the creek had to be about thirty feet wide in this spot. A rope swing dangled above the water; sunlight reflected off of a dragonfly's iridescent wings.

"No," Ivan answered. "But it's cool enough."

The small area of sandy beach was obviously man-made, as was the widening of the creek. Tables and benches surrounded the area in a semi circle and a tall, green forest erupted behind them. Squirrels circled up a thick tree trunk, tails twitching in the chase. A woodpecker's blows echoed across the vast lake, and a soft breeze rustled the leaves.

Two bodies decayed in the sand, their remains nothing more than wrinkled skin stretched over bone. Hayden gave Hannah his pistol and told her to be on the lookout for zombies. Lori and Madison were also armed and stood along the line of cars, sweeping their eyes over the forest.

"I might be able to do it," Madison said. She had taken a few steps toward us.

"Do what?" I asked.

"The IV."

"Great," Hayden blurted. Then he shook his head in question. "Wait, *might*?"

"Yeah. I've never done it but I've seen it done. I was a nursing assistant. I planned on going to nursing school next year so I always watched the nurses do stuff. I can try."

"That's good enough," Hayden told her and let me go to rush back to the truck. He grabbed the entire EMT bag and carried it down to the water's edge.

"Wait," I called before Hayden dumped it onto the sand. I reached into the truck and yanked a sleeping bag from under the backseat. Part of it was saturated with Janet's blood. I unrolled it and flipped it over, spreading it out on the sand.

Madison knelt down and began shifting through the contents of the bag. She chewed on the inside of her lip as she lifted up a pack of needles.

"Clean his arm," she instructed. Hayden ripped open several alcohol wipes and began scrubbing at Wade's dirty arm. He had thrown up once more and was unconscious. Sand filtered into my boots through the holes for the laces. I felt completely helpless, and it pissed me off. My lips curved into a snarl when I thought about Dre and the rest of his cronies at the asylum.

"Hayden!" Hannah cried. "There's someone over there!"

"I'm on it," I said without hesitation. I grabbed my knife from inside the truck and raced behind the picnic tables. His dirty orange vest caught my attention right away. He was looking up at the sun, squinting and babbling to himself. Clumps of dirt and bits of dried leaves clung to the end of the trail of intestines he was carrying. I purposely stepped on a fallen branch; it snapped loudly under my foot.

He turned his focus on me. Blood crusted the side of his face, giving me the impression that he had been hit over his ear. A festering bite wound had scabbed over and was covered in green, fuzzy mold. I tipped my head and watched. He hadn't been recently infected and yet he was still in the crazy stage. His shoulder pulled together and he shoved part of the entrails into his mouth.

"Trust me, I'm not going to steal your lunch," I told him. His blue eyes met mine and looked almost ashamed. "Can you hear me?" I asked then shook my head. "Of course you can *hear* me. I meant can you understand me?"

He gathered up his meal and stashed it inside his vest. After nearly choking, he coughed and snarled, like a good crazy. I backed up and away from the tree limb. He ran at me; I dropped to the ground, used my legs to catch his legs and twisted, causing him to fall. I flipped myself onto my knees and stabbed the knife through his chest.

His snarls sputtered and blood dripped from his lips. I exhaled, took a tight hold of the knife's handle and stood. Curious, I looked him over. He wasn't underweight and didn't appear malnourished. One of his shoes had come untied and the laces torn off. His hands were covered in scratches and there were remains of human flesh under his fingernails. A filthy scrap of a blue bandana was tied around his wrist.

"Interesting," I said and turned away. Knowing that crazies acted as zombie calling cards, I ventured deeper into the forest. The air was considerably cooler under the heavy shade. Around me, everything had fallen silent. The distant sounds of wildlife gave me some assurance that a horde wasn't clamoring their way through the trees. Still, I pushed in a few more yards. "Nothing," I whispered to myself and whirled around. I made it a few paces back toward the lake before I stopped.

The feeling of eyes on me prickled the skin at the back of my neck. My fingers tightened on the knife. I slowly turned my head to the side, sweeping my eyes over the forest. I nearly jumped when I saw her. Blonde curls flowed over her shoulders and a white and blue sundress cascaded over her slender body. Blood crusted around her mouth, and the front of her dress was stained with red and brown streaks. The rest of the blue bandana was twisted around her skinny wrist.

Her fingers twitched but she stood still, rooted in the spot. Her face was angled down; she glared up at me and a low growl escaped her mouth. She looked to be only six or seven years old. The virus hadn't fared as well in her small body; unlike the man she was with, blue veins were unnaturally visible and her cheeks were sunken in.

She was infected, that was at least obvious. But she was still alive, and still a child. I didn't want to shove the knife through her sternum and into her small heart. I held it in front of me, right at throat level. I was hoping she would run at me and stab herself, ending her miserable existence without forcing me to be the one to take her life.

Her eyes darted from me to the body not too far from us. She licked her lips and took a tentative step forward, focused on the body. My heart skipped a beat when I thought that she was capable of feeling human emotions. She looked back at me and, realizing that I wasn't moving, sprinted to the body. She dropped to her knees and put her hands on the man's bleeding chest.

But instead of showing any signs of grief, she tore open his shirt and opened her mouth. Her small fingers found the knife wound. She stuck them inside and pulled, attempting to yank open his torso. Sounding almost like tearing Velcro, she peeled his skin back. She wasn't strong enough to crack open his ribcage so she gave up and brought her head down, gnawing on his skin and lapping up the blood.

Disgusted and shocked, I didn't move for a few seconds. Then I took a silent step to the right, bent my arm back, and flung the knife. The blade lodged itself into the base of her skull. Her body slumped forward. I shook my hands and turned around, not wanting to retrieve the knife.

I stepped out of the comfortable shade of the heavy greenery and into the sun; its ray wrapped around my body like a thick cloak. Our group was gathered along the shore, arms crossed and shoulders tensed. Ivan stood with his back to the water, scanning our surroundings. Jason was jamming the end of a large picnic table umbrella into the sand, providing shade over Wade. Too concerned to be quiet, I didn't pay attention to where I put my feet. Lori whirled around, gun in hand, and looked at me. She nodded and faced forward. It annoyed me that the others couldn't take it upon themselves to keep watch. My boots sank into the hot sand as I crossed the beach and squeezed in between Hannah and Jim.

Madison had gotten the IV started. Her gloved hands were bloody; it must have taken her a few tries. Hayden knelt in several inches of water, holding the bag of fluids a few feet up in the air.

"Everything ok out there?" Brock asked me.

I nodded. "Just a few crazies."

"We should probably patrol," he suggested and I nodded in agreement. "Lori, Hannah, come with us," he directed.

I knelt down in the water and ran my hand over Wade's forehead, pushing back his hair. "You need a haircut," I said with a smile.

Wade tried to open his eyes, revealing a sliver of blue. "Your mom needs a haircut."

I laughed. "How are you feeling?"

"Heavy," he panted. "If that makes sense."

"Kinda," I agreed. "Are you thirsty?"

"Not really," he told me.

"You should probably try to drink anyway," Hayden suggested. Wade nodded and let me help him sit up. "Do you remember what happened?"

"Yeah," he told Hayden. "Everything. I felt fine and then it hit me. I tried to ignore it." He cupped his hands in the water, ready to take a drink.

"Don't," I said suddenly. "That can make you sick."

"The water's infected?" Madison shrieked. "And we're in it?"

"Don't be so dramatic," I retorted. "As far as I know, you can't become a zombie from drinking water. But it can make you sick with from E. Coli or Shigella bacteria. Trust me, it's not fun."

"Oh." Madison said. "So we can't even drink this at all?"

I shrugged. "We could boil it or add five drops of iodine. Actually, If you find moss, you can safely drink the water from it."

"Come again?" Hayden asked.

"Moss has small amounts of iodine in it," I explained. "But moss water leaves a nasty after taste in your mouth." I wrinkled my nose. "Can you bring me a water from the truck?" I asked Madison. She took off the bloody gloves and stood.

"It would be a good idea for the rest of you to cool off," Hayden suggested. "In groups though, half of you keep watch, ok?"

"Good idea," Hannah agreed and took off her boots. She helped Amanda unlace her shoes, held her hand, and walked into the slow moving water. Finally able to get the umbrella deep enough into the sand to stand on its own, Jason removed his shoes and pulled off his socks. He knelt down in the water, splashing it onto his arms to wash away the sweat and grime. Amanda ventured farther out into the water; Hannah hurried to keep up with her.

"Here," Madison said upon returning and handed me the water bottle. "What is the plan?"

"Uh," Hayden began and looked at me. "We need to cool off and eat. Then...then we need to rest."

I nodded and looked up at the noon sky. "Yeah. Ideally, we should find somewhere safe for the rest of the day and head out again tomorrow. I don't think any of us are in shape for a long car ride."

"I'm not," Hayden agreed. "I say we go back to that house we stayed in last night. It's safe."

I hated the thought of back tracking, but I knew Hayden was right. It was the safest place I could think of without wasting time looking for another location to take shelter in.

"Do you think those guys were alone?" Madison asked.

"Yes," Hayden and I said together.

"They would have come after us," I explained. "I don't know them too well, but I can guess the type. They wouldn't have run away from the fight, even though it would have been the smart thing to do."

"Right," Hayden agreed. "They would have come in guns blazing, not even stopping to think about the danger they were coming into."

"Ok. That makes me feel better," Madison said with a smile. Her bottom lip quivered. She shook her head. "I can't believe..." she started and trailed off, fat tears rolling down her face.

"Hey," Hayden said gently. "Get in the water, cool off. You'll feel better."

"Ok," she repeated and wrapped her arms around herself. Hannah stood when Madison approached and put her arm around the girl, who broke down sobbing.

"They lost five people?" Wade asked with his eyes still closed.

"Yeah," I said. "All just within minutes. And that's not counting the three that got eaten the day before."

He shook his head. "Fuck."

"Yeah," I agreed. "Give that to me," I said to Hayden and extended my arm. "I'll hold it while you rinse off." He frowned but handed me the IV bag. "There is soap in the truck," I reminded him. "Not that creek water will get you very clean."

"Being cleaner will feel nice," he said with a half smile. He pushed himself up and walked away. He returned a minute later, carrying an armload of clean clothes. "I brought you some too," he told me and set them down a few yards away from the water. He unlaced his boots and pulled his shirt over his head. I let my eyes linger on his muscular body, sweat glistening on his skin, and watched him walk into the water.

"He's lucky to have you," Wade said softly.

"Nah, I wouldn't say lucky," I brushed off his compliment.

Wade opened his eyes. "You have no idea, do you?"

"No idea about what?"

He let his eyelids fall and smiled. "Never mind. You two are a good fit, that's all."

"I think we are too. I've always thought that, though. We make a good team even when we're not *together*."

"Mh-hm," he agreed. He took a deep breath and pushed himself up. "You didn't remember to pack any aspirin, did you?" He rubbed his temples.

"I didn't, but Raeya packed my supplies bag. So there is some in there." I smiled at the thought of my friend, and felt a little homesick. "You were really dehydrated," I told him and looked at the bag of fluids. "It's going in fast."

"You can hook it on the umbrella," Wade suggested. He slowly scooted forward and I carefully looped the plastic hanger onto the umbrella crank. I took off my soaked boots and dumped the water out of them. The leather was already damaged from the nastiness that comes with killing zombies; the dark water stains would at least cover up the discolored patches that were dyed red from blood. I threw them behind us and stretched out on the shore, swishing away little bits of dark green algae that floated along the surface.

"Feel free to take off the rest of your clothes," Wade joked.

"You'd like that," I teased.

"I wouldn't be the only one," he laughed and eyed Jason.

I narrowed my eyes. "No. The last I checked, he thought I was too much of a bitch and was crushing on Raeya."

Wade laughed before wincing. He leaned back on his elbows, precariously placing his left arm so it wouldn't yank the IV. "He told me you're hot but he likes Olivia."

"Really?" I asked, wrinkling my nose. "Isn't she kinda young for him?"

"He's two years older," Wade informed me. He sounded tired and worn.

"Oh, that's not bad. Hayden is three years older than me," I thought aloud. "And I guess the dating pool is kinda limited at the compound." Wade smiled in agreement. His eyes drooped and I could tell he was struggling to stay awake. I unbraided my hair and combed my fingers through it, yanking out a couple knots.

"I wish I had a cold beer," I muttered. Though today had perfect beach weather, I couldn't relax to save my life.

The little girl slurping blood from what I assumed was her father flashed through my mind. Wade was conscious and talking, but I was still worried about him. The ball of anxiety made my stomach grumble. I pushed it aside and focused on destroying Eastmoore, fantasizing about having bombs to hide alongside the perimeter.

I stayed with Wade until the IV bag was empty and then switched out with Ivan. We took turns soaking in the creek, cooling off our overheated bodies and scrubbing the filth from our skin. Once we were all cleaned and changed into dry clothes, we moved into the shaded forest for lunch. Wade stayed in the air conditioned Jeep and fell asleep almost immediately after he ate.

I helped Hayden scrub away as much blood from the back seat of the truck as possible. The whole time he angrily muttered about the broken window. We stopped before we got too hot; the seat was sickly stained but the heavy metallic scent of blood was minimized.

* * *

The sun was beginning to set. Hayden and I slowly walked along the tall, stone fence. I pulled my hair from the messy bun it was in, raked my fingers through, and started braiding.

"Tired?" he asked me.

"I should be, but no. I still feel like we could get attacked with no notice."

Hayden nodded. "I know the feeling. I felt like that for my first year in the war." His jaw tensed. "I think it gave me an ulcer." He put his hand on the small of my back. "I don't have anything to say to make it better, sorry."

I shrugged. "Don't be. Having you with me is good enough."

"Is it now?" he said with a grin. He slipped his fingers down the back of my pants.

"Meh, you'll do." I leaned into him. We circled around the house once more before stopping at the gates. I had lost count how many times we had checked and rechecked everything. Certain we hadn't been followed by anything alive, there was little to worry out here. Still, I felt as if my heart was racing and couldn't slow down. The sound of shots echoed in my mind and the stain of panic tightened around me. I closed my eyes and shook my head.

"Riss?" Hayden said gently. "Everything ok?" He stepped in close and put his hand on my shoulder.

"You know how people in movies say something lame like 'This world isn't big enough for the both of us?'" I blurted.

"Yeah. What does that have to do with anything?"

"I think I finally understand what it means."

"Come again?"

"This world. It isn't big enough for the both of us, and I mean us and the people at the asylum. But it should be. I mean, we have the whole freaking country to share. But we can't. We can't sleep soundly at night in our own home because we know that they are looking for us. We can't go out on missions without worrying because we know that they might attack us. We *know* that they have every intention of finding us and destroying everything we have. I used to think that the saying was talking about physical space, but it's not. It's almost like the less people there are, the less space there is."

"That makes no sense, Riss."

"Yes it does. Think about it. A year ago, if someone gave you my picture and told you to go to Indy and find me, it would have been nearly impossible. But if I was in Indy now and you went to find me..."

"There wouldn't be many others to filter through," Hayden concluded. "I guess that does make sense...maybe." He shook his head. "But any way you look at it, there isn't enough room for them. Or anyone like them. Not now, not ever. Fuck. Can you imagine if they took over?"

I sharply exhaled. "The country would be run by a dictator."

Hayden nodded and traced his fingers over my collar bone. "But, that's assuming they are organized and smart enough to not only stay in power but create their own sort of politics."

"Isn't threatening to kill people politic-ish enough?"

Hayden gave me a lopsided smile. "Unfortunately, it's worked before." He let his hand fall into mine. I laced my fingers through his and picked up a foot, taking a slow step forward. We circled the house three more times before moving to the bed of the truck, sitting on opposite sides of the machine gun and waited for Ivan, Brock, and Jason to join us. They had taken an early shift of rest, and we agreed to have an informal meeting once they woke. Wade was upstairs sleeping in a bed; though he probably wouldn't wake on his own until morning, we had already told him that he wasn't allowed to do anything but rest anyway.

The sliding screen door hissed open. Hayden and I whirled around to see Ivan's tall figure carrying the LED lantern. We hopped off the tailgate and joined the others on the deck. Yawning and stretching, Jason was the last to leave the house.

"How's Wade?" I asked. There weren't enough chairs for us

all, so I settled in Hayden's lap.

"Sleeping," Jason answered. "But I think ok."

"Good." I twisted around to face Ivan and Brock. "So, I've been thinking and we've been talking."

"And?" Brock pressed.

Hayden put his hand on my thigh, giving it a reassuring squeeze. "I think we should attack the hospital now."

Ivan slowly moved his head upside down. "Why do you think that?" he asked, his dark eyes examining me.

"Element of surprise," Hayden explained. "They're down six men, and I would bet those were six of their best fighters."

"We had a plan," Brock blurted.

"Yeah, a plan that involved Jon talking to Treasure. And he's dead," I said bitterly, confused about my conflicting emotions. The guy had tried to kill me twice and yet I felt sorry for him and was saddened by his death. I shook my head; I would have to sort it out later. "And this was my idea. I'm not really sure how to do it, but if we drive one of their cars, they won't suspect anything."

"Until we get out," Ivan said slowly, emphasizing the obviousness of his implication.

I shook my head. "We won't be in it." I sat up straighter as the plan unfolded in my mind.

"If we can swing it, it will work," Hayden promised. "It's a crazy idea, no offense, Riss, but I do think it's plausible."

"I want more than plausible," Brock told us.

"It will take some preparation. Maybe a day's worth. The others can all stay here while we execute my brilliant idea." I flashed a smile and widened my eyes before quickly shaking my head. "Look, they fucked us in the ass how many times now? We're better than them, smarter than them. I'm not going to sit here and let them take anything from us. How many more of our friends have to die because of those assholes? Enough is enough. We've come too far to back out now. I say we go in there—all or nothing—and raise a little hell."

"Alright," Brock immediately agreed. "What do we need to do?"

Ivan tipped his head in question at Brock's sudden change of mind. "That was an oddly inspiring speech," Brock admitted with a shrug.

"Yeah," Jason agreed. "I'm in."

"Just *how* crazy is this plan?" Ivan inquired.

Hayden laughed. "Crazy enough to get us inside a lockdown facility full of mentally insane criminals."

Ivan blinked. "Fine. I'm sold." He smiled. "Let's hear it."

CHAPTERTWENTY—ONE

Hayden pulled the blankets back and tossed them on the ground. Clouds had covered the starry sky bringing in a welcome chill and the refreshing scent of a promised rain. He fluffed the sheet, unbuttoned his jeans, and stepped out of them. The air in the house was still stagnant and stuffy; I stripped down to my underwear and bra. Facing the window, I unhooked the bra and picked up the shirt Hayden had just thrown on the floor. I pulled it over my head and crawled in bed. Hayden sank down next to me, stretching out and snaking an arm around me.

I closed my eyes and rolled over, resting my head on his chest. He pulled up the hem of my shirt and ran his fingertips over my back. I sighed and curled my fingers around his bicep. Slowly, he rolled over until he was on top of me, the weight of his body crushing against mine. I inhaled, causing my breasts to press against his chest. My hands found his face and I pulled it down, lifting my head up ever so slightly so I could kiss him.

His tongue slipped past my lips and I bent my knees up, curling my legs around his body. He moved one hand down my side until he found the bottom of the shirt. Making a fist, he pulled it up and moved his mouth to my breast. I arched my back and moaned when, in a trail of kisses, he moved his mouth down even lower. He lifted my legs up and removed my underwear, throwing them over his shoulder before diving back on top of me.

I hooked my arms through his and pulled him up and tugged at his boxers. He flipped to his side and took them off. I reached down and took a hold of him, working my hands and making his breathing quicken. Then he put his hands on my shoulders and forced me down onto the mattress. I smiled as I struggled against him, enjoying being dominated.

He kissed and bit his way down again, and I had to press my

hands over my mouth to keep from moaning too loud. My heart was pounding when he finished and I immediately wanted more. With frantic desire, he moved up, situating himself between my legs. I put my hands on his butt and pushed him into me.

I gasped in pleasure, my brain only focused on how good everything felt. Hayden groaned and thrust against me. I opened one eye and stopped moving.

"What?" he asked.

"Don't you think we should use a condom?" I asked.

Hayden let out a breath. "Yeah," he agreed. "But we haven't before and we've been fine."

"I really don't want to get pregnant," I told him. "Not now."

Huffing, he got off of me and dumped his duffle bag on the floor, madly sorting through it. What felt like an hour later, he got back on top of me. "I can enjoy it now," I only half joked.

He grabbed my wrists and held them above my head. I closed my eyes and surrendered to him and came in a matter of minutes. I quickly twisted my hands, breaking his hold on me. I brought my legs up, grabbed his sides, and flipped us over, taking control. Having no issue with it, Hayden put his hands on my hip bones and rocked me back and forth. He pulled me forward as he finished, kissing me right at the end.

Panting, we broke apart and resituated comfortably on the bed, our warm skin sticking together. My body suddenly felt extremely fatigued. The still-pounding beat of Hayden's heart was calming and lulled me into a state near sleep.

"Riss?" Hayden asked softly. "You awake?"

"Kinda," I mumbled.

"Oh, never mind then."

"No, it's ok." I pushed myself up. "I have to pee anyway. I'd rather go now than wake up in an hour." I leaned over Hayden and felt around for the flashlight. I clicked it on and shuffled through the tangle of blankets and clothing for my underwear. I lazily shoved my feet through and yanked them up. I pulled Hayden's shirt over my head, not caring that it was on backwards and that the tag was itching my throat. I hurriedly scuttled out of the room and found the bathroom.

Hayden was sprawled out on the bed, still naked, when I climbed over him. He wrapped the sheet around us and held me in a tight embrace. I was getting uncomfortably warm but didn't mind; being physically close to Hayden was worth a little suffering.

EMILYGOODWIN

His lips brushed my neck, causing a shiver to run down my spine. "Do you want to get married?" he asked.

"Yeah," I answered. "Someday. I've always wanted to."

Hayden's body tensed and he stiffly exhaled. "Orissa, I mean, do you want to marry me?"

I pushed myself up and stared into his eyes, though it was too dark to read his expression. "Of course I do."

He wrapped his arms around me and pulled me back onto him. "Good," he said quietly.

"Wait." I pushed myself up again. "Did you just propose?"

I could feel him shrug. "I guess. It was kinda crappy, wasn't it?"

"Yeah," I slowly agreed with a laugh.

"Fine," he said and sat up as well. He took both of my hands into his. "Orissa Lynn Penwell, you are one of the most amazing, brave, and stubborn people I have ever met. Sometimes I don't even know what to do with you. But I do know that I never want to live a single day of my life without you by my side. I love you, Orissa, more than I can say. Will you do me the honor of being my wife?"

I was thankful that the dark hid my gooney smile. I squeezed Hayden's hands. "Yes," I said simply. "And," I continued. "I love you too, more than I ever thought was possible. With you, everything is just better." I wasn't as poetic as Hayden; I fumbled over my words. Giving up, I pressed my lips to his and closed my teary eyes. We lay back down, holding on to each other as if it was the only thing that mattered.

"What did you mean by 'not now?'" Hayden asked me.

"Huh?"

"You said you don't want to get pregnant now, implying you do later."

"Oh," I traced a finger over the ridges of his abs. "I do want to have kids...someday. I always imagined I would, but that's assuming that I somehow get my act together and turn into a responsible adult. So yeah, *someday* in the very distant future."

Hayden laughed. "Ok, good."

"Let's not even talk about that," I suggested. "Being engaged is enough for tonight."

"Do you want a ring?" he asked suddenly.

"I don't need one," I said softly. "I have these." I reached up and pulled on the chain; the tags were stuck between Hayden and my body.

"And that's enough?" He tightened his arms around me.

"Well, yes. But a big fat diamond isn't something I'd turn down," I said with a small laugh.

Hayden sighed. "Now I wish I got you one and asked in a more conventional way."

"There's nothing conventional about our situation," I reminded him.

"No," he laughed. "Not at all." He pulled me onto him and ran his fingers through my hair until I fell asleep.

Hayden's elbow to my stomach woke me up. Annoyed, I was about to yank the covers off of him and push him over to the other side of the bed when I suddenly stopped. He twitched again, his breathing growing faster.

"Hayden," I said quietly, not wanting to startle him. "Hayden," I repeated and put my hand on his chest.

He grabbed my wrist, opened his eyes, and twisted my arm. I jerked my hand back and grabbed the flashlight. I pushed myself away from him and clicked it on, setting the flashlight on the pillow to create enough light to illuminate my face.

"Hey. Hayden, wake up. You're having a nightmare. It's me, Orissa. Your fiancée," I added and then immediately felt dumb for saying it. With surprising speed, he sat up and grabbed my shoulders.

"Riss," he breathed.

"Yeah, it's me."

"Oh. Fuck," he said and ran his hands over his face.

"Were you dreaming about Ben again?" I asked carefully.

"Yeah. It's always the same dream over and over. We're driving down the road. We stop and get out and then..." he shook his head. "But you were there too, standing right next to him. It plays in slow motion. First your hair flew around your face. Then I saw the fire burning your skin. The blast sends you flying and then there is nothing left."

I didn't know what to say. I had a hard time imagining something that horrible happening to Hayden. To see it in a dream would haunt me as well. He took a deep breath, put an arm around me and lay down as he exhaled.

"Thanks for waking me up."

"Of course, Hayden." I pressed my lips to his neck and ran my finger over the scar tissue on his left shoulder. "Love you," I whispered.

"Love you, too." He leaned over me to turn off the flashlight. I rolled onto my side, pulling him with me. He spooned his body around mine, holding me tight until he fell back asleep.

* * *

Gray clouds covered the summer sky and misty rain sprayed in through the open windows. I shoved my hand into my duffle bag and rooted around for a clean pair of underwear. I put on the same clothes I had on yesterday; they weren't dirty enough to warrant a wardrobe change. Besides I was sure they would soon be filthy when Hayden and I set out to find supplies.

Hayden had already left to check on his truck. He was still upset about the broken window and didn't think the duct tape and plastic were enough to keep last night's rain from damaging the interior…as if the blood hadn't already done enough. I packed up the contents of my bag and exited the room, pulling out my tight French braid as I walked.

Jim sat in the living room with Madison and Ryan. Now that the threat of immediate danger was gone, the grief from their recent tragic loss crashed down on them. I pressed a smile and politely nodded as I walked past, leaving them to deal privately.

"How are you feeling?" I asked Wade as soon as I saw him sitting at the breakfast table. I stopped at the island counter and eyed our minimal food choices, deciding to go with canned fruit and cold Pop Tarts for breakfast.

"Like I was hit by a train," he said with a frown. "But a hell of a lot better than yesterday."

"You're resting the whole day," I told him.

"Yes, mom," he teased. I made a face at him before turning to my breakfast. "I heard about your plan. I like it."

"Thanks. It's a little out there, I'll admit, but it's all I have."

"No, I like it," he assured me. "We made a few adjustments and now I find it perfect." He smiled. "But you do know that Molotov cocktails burn out quickly."

"Not if you add powdered laundry detergent. It turns into a gel and burns longer instead of spraying and spreading."

Wade raised an eyebrow. "And why do you know these things?"

I looked down and shrugged. I didn't feel like explaining that my crazy grandfather raised me like a warrior because his PTSD turned him into a paranoid doomsday prepper.

"The internet," I said with no hesitation. "And I really like action movies. You can pick up on a lot if you pay attention to the details."

"Nice," he said, buying my lie. I smiled on the inside and stirred the syrup coated fruit with a plastic spoon. "You know I know you're lying, right?" he said with a smirk.

I lifted my eyes and glared at him.

"I won't pry," he continued. "But I am curious. Is this something you learned in jail too?"

I shook my head. "I learned most of my illegal tricks in juvie, not jail. I only spent one night in jail," I said pointedly, still ashamed of my poor choices.

Wade tipped his head and laughed. "You're interesting. And the kind of girl my mother would have hated."

"I *tried* to be that girl," I admitted and ate a spoonful of fruit. "It was a waste of time and I regret it now."

"How come?"

I shrugged. "I was so busy being angry at everyone that I didn't see that hurting them meant hurting myself."

"Interesting," he repeated. "When I was fifteen, I convinced my older brother to play mailbox-baseball. He was four years older than me and all the blame was put on him when we got caught. I never fessed up and told the truth. It took him almost a year before he would talk to me again."

"Were you guys close?"

"Not at all." He pushed his eyebrows together. "He bought booze for a graduation party I was throwing. The cops showed up but that time I took the rap for it. *Then* we were even."

"Do you miss him?"

Wade nodded. "I have no idea what happened to him. Rider and I came back to the States together. We stayed the weekend in an overrated hotel neither of us could afford. It was the first time either of us could legally drink. We spent the first night at the bar, trying to pick up girls. The next day..." he inhaled deeply. "The roads were closed. We couldn't get out of town. And then shit hit the fan."

I opened my mouth to ask him what it was like; I spent the beginning days of the outbreak stashed safely away in a hospital basement thanks to Padraic's quick thinking and compassionate heart. Just then, Ivan, Brock, and Jason came into the house.

"Morning, sunshine," Ivan teased.

"Morning," I said back with a pressed smile.

"About time you got up."

"No one woke us up," I reminded him. It had surprised both Hayden and me that no one came in to wake us this morning. We slept until what had to be after 10:00 AM.

"No one wanted to," Ivan went on and pulled out a chair. He turned it around and sat, resting his arms on the back.

I finished off the fruit. "Why?"

Ivan pulled back with a laugh. "We didn't know what we would be walking into."

"What do you...? Oh." I bit my lip and felt just a little embarrassment. "We tried to be quiet."

Ivan sighed and shook his head. "You're never quiet."

"I don't like to be," I confessed.

"Too much information, Penwell," he said with a smirk.

"Oh so you don't want details?" I egged on.

"No. Yes, maybe. No. Definitely no. You're like a sister to me. Details would be too much."

I laughed. "I thought guys always told each other sex details."

Brock looked at Wade; they both shook their heads. "Not usually," he told me. "Maybe when I was in high school but not now."

"Huh," I said. "I always tell Ray details."

"You do?" Wade asked, interested.

"Yeah. And she tells me details. On pretty much everything."

"Why?" Jason asked, his cheeks slightly flushed.

I shrugged. "I don't know. We just do."

Jason shook his head. "I'll never understand women," he muttered. I broke the Pop Tart into bite sized pieces and began eating again while the guys dug through our measly pile of food. The soft sound of sobbing came from the living room. My gut twisted when I thought of the horrific loss the group so recently suffered. Guilt over feeling happy that the tragedy had struck their group and not ours weighed on my heart. I pushed those distracting feelings away. Besides, they would be safe from here on out. And when they finally got to the compound, things would be dramatically better.

Brock and Jason joined us at the table, snacking on nuts and raisins. A few minutes later, Hayden came inside, muttering about the sad condition of his truck. He took out his frustration on a can of peaches, slamming it onto the counter. I looked across the table at Wade and rolled my eyes. He flicked his eyes to Hayden and stifled a laugh.

Hayden yanked a chair from the table and sat down with a

huff. I watched him take a bite of food and stare out the window at his truck. His face was twisted with abhorrence and sadness.

"So," I said to break the tension. "Which one of you is gonna have the next medical emergency?" I waved my hand at Wade and Hayden. "The three of us are covered."

Brock chuckled. "If it does happen, let's keep them spaced out. Only one medical near death experience is allowed."

"We need to find a hot nurse who can handle a gun and kick some ass to bring with us," Wade suggested. "Ya know. For safety purposes."

"Yes," I agreed. "A hot *male* nurse dressed in scrubs and a lab coat with a stethoscope hanging around his neck." I flashed a toothy grin at Wade, who scowled at me and took a drink of water. The clouds crackled with low thunder and the misty rain began to fall harder. The ominous weather soaked the carefree atmosphere and our conversation quickly changed to our plan for the day.

"You have the list?" Hayden asked Brock.

"Right here," he replied and smoothed out a folded piece of paper. "I wrote down things you can use as substitutes if you can't find the right ingredients for some of our more sensitive items. As long as we can get whatever we throw together to ignite, it really won't be that hard to make a bomb, which is scary to think about." He shook his head and slid the paper in front of me. "This isn't going to be a huge explosion," he explained. "But it will cause some damage. And even though the flames aren't as grand as they are in movies, it's ok. Most of the damage is caused by the pressure waves anyway. Those fuckers will bleed."

He went on to further explain exactly what we'd need and why. I tried to follow along but got lost when he started talking about the difference between detonations and deflagrations and something about exothermic waves. He flipped the paper over and pointed to a list. "And I've marked a few areas on the map that should be the most promising."

I nodded, thinking that Brock would be a better match than Ivan for my obsessive compulsive planning best friend. "Awesome."

"When are you leaving?" Hannah's voice came from behind us.

Hayden finished chewing and told her, "Soon."

"Can I come?" she asked hopefully.

"No," he said definitely.

"Why not?" she threw back. "You can't tell me what to do."

"I just did," Hayden said and twisted around to face his sister. "It's safer here. You're staying."

"I've been out there before, Hayden," she retorted. "I've been on the road for months and I'm still standing. I can handle myself. *You* taught me how to fight and how to shoot. I can help."

"You know the basics, Hannah. And your friends need you. You're staying," he repeated.

Hannah balled her fists. "You haven't changed one bit!" she said through clenched teeth. "Ever since Dad left us you thought you could boss me around."

Hayden stood. "We're not getting into this," he said calmly. "Not now."

"Typical," she huffed. "You *never* want to get into it. I'm going with you, whether you like it or not."

"I said no," Hayden told her firmly and walked past her to the sink. He rinsed the dishes off in a pot of boiled hot tub water and set them on the counter.

Fuming, Hannah grunted and stomped out of the kitchen. Witnessing the small family feud was nothing abnormal, but it was still awkward. Ivan began talking about professional sports, asking the guys how long they thought it would take before the NFL became organized again.

"I'm going to get the car ready," Hayden told me and did his best not to storm out of the house. My jaw tightened as I forced a smile and stood as well, piling my dishes alongside Hayden's and went upstairs to retrieve my boots.

"I'm sorry," Hannah said to me as soon as my foot hit the top stair. "I shouldn't have thrown a fit like a baby. Hayden and I never got along before all this, and I don't know why I expected things to change."

I felt suddenly defensive of Hayden; he had told me the story of waking up to find that their father had left his family with nothing. He was only thirteen and took it upon himself to take care of his mother and sisters, including getting a job and filling in the man-of-the-house role. I considered telling Hannah to stop acting like a whiny little bitch but thankfully stopped myself. She was Hayden's younger sister; he cared about her which, in turn, made me care about her.

"He's protective over people he cares about," I assured her. "I don't know why you'd even want to go out there with us anyway."

"You want to go," she retorted. "Why?"

"I think I'm good at what I do," I said honestly. "Hayden and I work well together. We'll be able to get our shit and leave."

She nodded. "I'm good too. I'm fast and sneaky. I can get by unnoticed."

I moved down the hall, trying to avoid talking to her any longer; it was wasting time. "Well, it seems that Hayden already made up his mind."

"You let him tell you what to do?"

"Of course not," I snapped. "But I'm not his sister." I shrugged and whisked past her. I grabbed my boots and sat on the edge of the bed. I yanked one on and tucked my pants into it.

"Isn't it hot wearing jeans?" Hannah asked, appearing in the doorway.

"Yes."

"They why wear them?"

"I want to have my legs covered." I zipped up the boot and stuck my foot inside the other, only to pull it out and shake out more sand.

"Will you ask him to let me go?" she tried.

"Hannah, look. This is important, okay? Just drop it, and you and Hayden can argue over who gets to pick the music on the way home." I stood and walked to the door. Hannah made no attempt to move out of my way. We needed to leave. Every second spent on this pointless conversation was a second we didn't have to spare. "Maybe you could just be our driver," I threw out, thinking it would be so boring she'd reject the idea and insist on toting a gun and being our third wheel.

"Fine," she finally huffed and stepped aside to let me pass. As if I'd given a stray dog a scrap of meat, Hannah followed behind on my heels. "A getaway driver; it's a good idea!"

I wanted to slap the palm of my hand against my forehead. *Son of a bitch*! I thought. Hayden would put a stop it it...I could only hope.

* * *

Hayden and I looked over the map with Ivan, Wade, and Brock, talking strategy. Hayden pushed out a chair for me and I sat, listening to the guys rattle off ideas.

"We drove through a town," Hannah started and stared at the map. "I think around here." She tapped the paper with her nail. "There were a lot of stores still full of supplies." She shook her head, sending tendrils of messy brown hair cascading around her face. "But we couldn't stay. There were way too many zombies."

Hayden and Ivan exchanged nods. "That will work," Hayden said and folded the map. "It's about two or three hours north, which is where we wanted to go."

"Great," Hannah said with a broad smile. "What car are we taking? I'm driving."

"No, you're not," Hayden told her, his voice heavy with annoyance. "Why can't you listen for once in your life?"

"Stop being so controlling," she argued.

"Hannah," he countered, struggling to keep his voice calm. "*Half* of your group just died. I think you should stick with the others. You guys really need each other right now. And it's dangerous out there."

"Really? It's dangerous. I would have never guessed. And I know half of our group died. That's why I want to do whatever is necessary to get revenge."

I couldn't argue with her there; she had a point. But still, trying to hold onto the precious time we were wasting was like trying to keep water from slipping through my fingers. "Just let her be the fucking driver," I sighed. "So we can get this show on the road."

Hayden glowered at me for a second before standing up. "Fine. As long as she can promise to take orders."

"Yes, Captain. I mean sir—sergeant—whatever," she said seriously. "I'm a good driver."

Hayden snorted a laugh and rolled his eyes. "At least there is no one else out there for you to run into." He pulled the keys to the Yukon that Madison had been driving from his pocket and tossed them to Hannah. We had agreed that driving the truck was too risky; it could be easily identified by anyone from Eastmoore and we couldn't be sure we *wouldn't* run into them.

We packed a decent amount of weapons but left the bulk here, in case of possible retaliation. Though we were sure no one had followed us back to the stone house in the woods, it wasn't worth the risk. Ivan, Brock, and Jason were going to keep a constant watch on the surrounding area. I shoved three water bottles and a can of mixed nuts into my bag and tossed it in the back; it wasn't much but it would have to do. Taking on the extra group exhausted our food supply at a scary rate. Hayden took a gas can from the bed of the truck and filled up the SUV; gas was another item on our to-get list.

"You're going to have to drive faster than that," Hayden told

Hannah, "if you want to make it back before nightfall."

I fiddled with the rear air vents and leaned back in my seat, glad I was an only child. Hayden plugged in one of his iPods and skipped through the music until he found a song he liked.

"Oh! I haven't heard this in forever!" Hannah exclaimed and turned up the volume. At least there was one thing they could agree on, even if it was obnoxious country music. I stole a glance at Hayden and saw that he was intently looking out of his window. I turned my head to the left and kept a watchful eye as well. At least with Hannah driving, Hayden and I were able to stay more vigilant to our surroundings.

"Do you even wonder where they're from?" Hannah asked when we drove past a small herd of zombies.

"Nope," Hayden replied.

"Sometimes," I admitted, earning a glance from Hayden. I shrugged. "But I try not to think about it. They're dead; it doesn't matter."

"That one," Hannah said and pointed to a skinny zombie dressed in black. "He was at a wedding, as the groom maybe. Oh! His zombie bride bit him right after they cut the cake. And then they killed and ate the rest of the wedding party."

"Sounds likely," Hayden muttered.

Hannah pressed her lips together and lowered her head a tiny bit. "You never know," I added. "People were going about normal business when it happened."

"That is true," Hayden agreed.

Hannah pointed at another. "What about her?"

"Stripper," Hayden said automatically. "Look at the way she's dressed." We all laughed.

"I used to play this game with Amanda," Hannah explained. "The church was safe until recently—obviously," she added with a quick shake of her head. "Zombies would occasionally wander in the streets. We could see them from the chapel windows." She fell silent for maybe thirty seconds. "What's your compound like?"

"It's nice," Hayden and I said at the same time. I smiled and leaned back, allowing Hayden to explain it in great detail. The time passed quicker than I thought it would. We stuck to the predetermined path; it was the fastest route and we could be found if anything were to happen. We had to make one small detour to avoid a parking lot full of zombies. With the sun heating up the pavement they marched on, their stench was bad enough to filter through the air conditioning.

"All gummies," I noted.

"Easy kill," Hayden agreed, but we didn't stop. When we were only minutes away from the star marked in our map, Hannah slowed down. "Do you remember your way around at all?" he asked his sister.

"Kinda. We drove through. The streets were filled; we couldn't even stay long." She pressed on the gas. "There was a super store, you know, the ones that have everything under the sun, at the other end of town. The parking lot still had a lot of cars in it, so we assumed that if people hadn't had time to leave, it might have had a lot of stuff in it."

"That's kinda what we've been finding," I told her. "Hopefully no one else discovered it in the mean time."

"It's a cute town," she noted. "But if it hadn't been overrun we would have stayed and not found everyone in the church." She turned onto the main road that ran through the middle of the town. "That store is off of this street." She let off the gas for a few seconds as we looked for zombies. When she didn't see any, she pressed her foot down hard on the pedal.

"Stop!" Hayden yelled suddenly. Hannah slammed on the brakes. The seat belt cut into my chest as my body lurched forward. As soon as I straightened up, I saw what Hayden had.

"Good timing," I breathed and unbuckled my seatbelt.

"Stay in the car," Hayden told Hannah and got out. I clicked the safety off my M9 and followed him. He poised his finger over the trigger of his rifle and scanned the houses that lined the street. I bent down and wrapped my fingers around the hot strip of rubber. It stuck to the pavement; I had to holster the pistol and use both hands to yank it up. Rusty nails poked through and I was careful to avoid slicing my hand open.

"What is that?" Hannah asked from inside the SUV.

"It looks like a homemade spike roadblock," I said and tossed the thing aside. On second thought I grabbed an end and folded it in half. Hayden looked through the scope of his rifle before jogging over to help me get the heavy coil of rubber and nails into the back of the SUV.

"I don't see anything," he told me. "But that doesn't mean no one's here." He lowered his gun and waved his arms. My own heartbeat was loud in my ears. I slowly turned my head. A two story red brick house with pale yellow shutters was directly in front of me. A thin layer of dust and dirt coated the covered porch. No one had been in or out the front door at least. I inspected the two houses around it, finding them both to be in a similar state.

"Let's keep going," Hayden said quietly and got back into the Yukon. We rolled down the windows and slowly drove down the street. We kept our weapons close but out of sight, not wanting to appear threatening in case another group had already claimed residence of this town.

The row of houses eventually gave way to an overgrown park. Vines twisted up along a swing set and tall thistles sprouted alongside a slide. Across from it was a strip mall. Thick cobwebs, skeletons, and black, plastic bats were visible through the hazy store fronts. A sun faded sign inside a fancy shoe store boasted their hot new winter boot collection, as well as a thirty-percent off Halloween sale.

"What the...?" I mouthed when the court house came into view. Hayden held up his hand and Hannah slowed. "There's someone inside."

"You sure?" Hayden asked.

"Yes," I promised. "Well, something is inside. It went past the window."

"Keep the car running and do not get out," he warned Hannah.

Hannah turned toward her brother. "You're going in there?" she asked, incredulously.

"Possibly," Hayden said. "We will check it out first."

"It looks like a death trap!" she argued. I couldn't disagree. A twisted barbed wire fence, with posts made from broom handles, tree branches, and pieces of metal surrounded the court house. The end of each post was sharpened like a spear. Along with the fence, barbed wire had been snaked along the ground, concealed by the grass. If it hadn't been stretched along the concrete walkway I wouldn't have noticed it at all.

"We'll be fine," I told her.

"I'm coming with!" she protested.

"Hannah," Hayden said in a calm, fatherly tone. "You agreed to be the driver, remember? Stay here."

"What if they come after me?" she countered.

Hayden's face twitched.

"Then what do I do?"

"Drive away," he simply stated. He set his jaw and looked behind the SUV. I knew he didn't want to leave his sister vulnerable.

"Stay here and keep watch," I told him. "I can go look."

"Not an option," Hayden said back. "Hannah, lock the doors. We won't go in, so you will be in sight." He gave her a look that obviously said 'this is why I didn't want you to come.'

"Fine," she agreed and rolled up the windows. Hayden and I started toward the court house, stopping next to the fence. I used an arrow to push it up and allow Hayden to crawl through. Once on the other side he held the sharp wire for me. We carefully picked our way through the tangled browning grass.

Hayden kept one hand resting on his machine gun. I had the urge to place my right hand on my pistol but knew it wouldn't look as natural as Hayden's hold on his weapon. Thin, gray clouds still covered the sky and the air had a slight sticky feel to it. My eyes swept the ground in front of me and I took another tentative step forward.

Something moved inside the building, the noise resounding off the thick walls. I jerked my head up and saw that the panes of glass from one of the second story windows were gone. They had been removed, not broken. Apprehension growing, I lifted my foot over a coil of barbed wire and leaned forward.

"Did you hear that?" I asked Hayden, who nodded. "It sounded like something got knocked over."

"You are right; there is something inside." He stepped next to me and nodded at the front door. "It could just be zombies."

"Hopefully," I said then realized it was an odd thing to hope for. We picked our way to the large doors. I cupped my hands around my eyes and peered in through the tinted glass, unable to catch sigh of much of anything in the lobby. I stepped back and knocked.

I could feel Hayden's breath on my neck. The leather on his boots crunched as he leaned forward. I bit my lip and waited. Moving my eyes to the side, I looked at Hayden. He nodded and stepped back.

"Hello?" he called.

I let out my breath. "Nothing."

"It could have even been an animal," Hayden pointed out. Zombies would have moved toward the noise."

"Yeah, maybe." I looked at the SUV; Hannah gripped the steering wheel and was staring at us, not minding her own surroundings at all. I exhaled and turned, leading the way back to the Yukon. "We heard something inside but it didn't respond to us," I said as soon as I sank into the seat.

Hannah snapped her open mouth shut. "Oh, ok. Good. So...what's the plan?"

"Get our supplies," Hayden said and closed his door. "And get the hell out of here."

"I like that part," Hannah told us and pushed the gear into drive. "I used to be excited to come across new people. Now it scares me."

"I don't trust anyone anymore either," I affirmed and shook my head. "Actually, the first person I came across tried to shoot me."

Hayden turned around and grinned. "What did you do?"

I raised one eyebrow. "Nothing. He was newly infected and not crazy enough to rule out all logic. We had a conversation, an odd conversation, before I even realized he had been bitten." I thought back to that day when this was all new to me. It instantly brought the still painful memory of Zoe to my mind. The next group of living people we came across died before our eyes, as we were unable to get to them in time.

"We've come across our fair share of unfriendly folk," Hayden said. "But nothing came close to Eastmoore."

Hannah slowed at an intersection. "I'm not sure which way," she said apologetically.

"Guess," Hayden said. "We can always turn around."

She closed her eyes and muttered something to herself. "Right feels right." She nodded at her own statement and cranked the wheel. A handful of gummies trudged around the road. Looking as if they were literally melting, they weren't much of a threat. Hannah unsteadily pumped the gas, jerking the car, as we passed them. I closed my eyes; if she kept driving like this I thought I might puke.

Garbage tumbled in the wind, getting stuck against a sign for a doctor's office. I whipped my head around, inspecting both directions when we pulled off of the main road. The parking lot was still full of cars, like Hannah had seen before. Hannah drove along the curb and stopped next to the entrance of the store.

The automatic doors were intact and barred from the inside. I took it as a good sign. Maybe nobody new had been here since Hannah's group quickly passed through a few months ago.

"Now what?" Hannah asked.

"You stay here and keep the car running," Hayden reminded her. He turned on a walkie-talkie and extended his arm. "If you see *anything*, tell us. We will be right out."

"Ok. Be careful, Hayden."

"We'll be fine," he assured her and opened his door. I reached behind me and grabbed two bulletproof vests. I pushed my door open with my foot and handed one to him. He pulled it over his head and adjusted the straps before arming himself. "Ready?" he asked me.

I pulled my shoulders back, causing the vest to uncomfortably constrict against my chest. "These things were not made for women," I complained and slipped the quiver over my head.

Hayden smirked and walked up to the door. He looked inside and then lightly rapped his knuckles on the glass. I pressed my ear to the door while he watched and the seconds slowly ticked by.

"Hear anything?" Hannah called from the SUV. Hayden turned and slowly exhaled, narrowing his eyes at his sister. He tightly shook his head and motioned for her to shut up. He stepped to the middle of the sliding doors and wrapped his fingers around the lock and gave it a tug.

"Alright my criminal," he said endearingly, "you're up."

I shot him a pointed smile and took two bobby pins from my hair. "How do you know what to do?" he asked.

"Watch," I said and showed him how I precariously bent the ends of the pins. "This is a simple lock; it's easy. I would need more than bobby pins to get through something more complex. But, if there was power, an alarm would go off right away, making the simple job not so simple."

"Interesting."

I nodded and twisted my wrist until I felt something click. "Try it now," I told Hayden. He pushed the door open just enough for us to slip through. "Ugh," I muttered when the first blast of trapped hot air hit us, wafting the smell of sewage and death up my nose. I looked around the lobby; there were carts and dirty gumball machines, as well as a few out dated arcade games and a children's mini merry-go-round.

There were more automatic doors in front of us, but they were blocked by pull-down metal bars. Hayden strode over and stuck his hand through, unlatching something.

"It's not locked," he stated and went to the other side and flipped up the other lock. "Which makes me think this was only down to keep out zombies." I reached behind me and pulled out an arrow and strung it in the bow, bracing us for the possible attack the noise of lifting the bars could bring.

Dust showered down, causing Hayden to sneeze. He waved his hand in front of his face to clear the air. I pulled the arrow back slowly and waited. Something scuffled deep inside the store. Hayden flicked his eyes back at me and I nodded; it sounded like a zombie. He grabbed the strap of his machine gun and turned it until the weapon was resting on his back, freeing his hands to extract the knife that hung from his belt.

He used his shoulder to push open the door, holding it for me to go through. To our left was a sea of registers; to the right was a large grocery section. A brightly colored sign that spelled out FRESH PRODUCE hung a few feet above me and I shuddered at the scent of rotting fruits and vegetables. I couldn't help but look, and when I saw that most had been cleared away it caused me to step closer with curiosity.

Most the fruit had turned into mushy slime by the time someone made a sweep of the shelves. A large black garbage bag was stuffed full at the end of the aisle; it lay on its side leaking foul smelling juices on the white and blue tile.

"S3, eight o'clock," Hayden whispered. I took a step backwards and steadied my arm. Her legs wobbled when she walked as if the bones might break at any moment. Her wrinkled skin looked like it could rip apart at any moment. I aimed and let the arrow go; it passed through her skull and zoomed down an aisle.

"Dammit," I cursed. "Now I have to go find it."

Hayden smiled and looked around before pulling out the list. "What do you want to get first?"

"Food, I suppose. It's all right here," I said and waved my hand to our right."

Hayden nodded and ducked back into the lobby to grab a cart. Our plan was to go up and down the aisles and grab anything and everything we could. We bypassed the rows of spoiled frozen food and walked briskly through the baking section. When we turned the corner and shot down the aisle full of canned soup, we were surprised to see the shelves rather empty.

"It hasn't been looted," I said aloud and grabbed two cans of cream of chicken soup. "But it looks like we went shopping the day before Thanksgiving."

"Yeah," Hayden agreed and bent over the cart to quietly dump an armload of soup in. "Something looks...off."

I nodded. "Let's hurry." We rushed through the aisle, filling the cart with more soup and cans of fruit and vegetables before moving on and loading up with crackers, cookies, tuna, trail mix, electrolyte sports drinks and a few hygiene items. We pushed the very full cart back to the lobby. Hannah waved to us and Hayden gave her an update over the walkie.

"I still can't believe we ran into your sister," I said and pulled another cart out from the line. The wheel caught and rattled loudly. I traded it for another and began to venture to the other side of the store.

"I know," he agreed. "Sometimes it doesn't feel real."

"It is," I assured him. "Do you think the garden center is still open? It was late fall when the virus hit."

Hayden shrugged. "The weather stays warmer longer here. Maybe stuff was on clearance. If not we can always—"

He cut off abruptly and I skidded to a stop. "What the hell?" Hayden shook his head and gripped the knife.

"I think it's a camp." I looked at the section of women's apparel. The displays had been rearranged, forming a wall. Several tents and mattresses were in the middle, surrounded by lawn chairs, grills, and piles of books.

"There's the missing food," Hayden pointed out. Three carts, all mostly full, were lined up next to the tents. "At least it's easy for us." He took a step forward and suddenly stopped. I let go of the cart and reached behind me. "Something is in there." With his arms held out slightly at his sides, Hayden moved toward the tent. "Hello?"

Whoever was in the tent grumbled. Hayden relaxed just a bit and went to the side. He gripped the zipper with two fingers and met my eyes. "On three," he mouthed and began silently counting before yanking the zipper down.

A gray hand slapped the ground. Fingers curled as it pulled itself forward. The gummy grunted in its effort.

"This is pathetic," Hayden said.

"You're telling me," I agreed and walked over to the front of the tent. Red curls were matted to her rotting face and she could barely open her eyes. If zombies could be tired, then this one definitely looked like she needed a nap. I released my fingers and the arrow nestled into her soggy head. I grimaced when I leaned in to get the arrow. Coughing, I moved out and took a step back, almost tripping over my feet in my haste. "There's a dead cat in there," I informed Hayden.

He nodded but was too busy going through a duffle bag to fully acknowledge how gross it was. "This is full of first aid stuff," he said and hefted it into one of the carts. "Whoever set up this camp gathered up what they'd need...and then got infected."

"Works in our favor," I quipped.

Hayden gave me a lopsided smile. "Yeah. It does." He strode away from the indoor camp site. "Back to the explosives," he said and took hold of the cart loaded with food and first aid supplies. He pushed it into the aisle before we continued toward the back of the store.

"Jackpot," I said when a small display of garden supplies came into view. The outdoor section of the store had been cleared of most of its lawn and garden items, replaced with Halloween and even a few Christmas decorations. The shelves had either just been stocked or no one could afford to spend any extra money on decorations this last holiday season.

Hayden grabbed two bags of fertilizer and plopped it into the cart while I picked up an entire display of vegetable seeds. I dumped it into the cart and tossed the cardboard to the side. The air was even stuffier this deep into the store; we grabbed the rest of what we needed from this section and left, rushing to get the rest of what we could from our list.

"It's kind of a shame to think we're going to pour all this out," I said when I put the sixth wine bottle in the cart.

"It's a crime," Hayden affirmed and placed a six pack of glass bottled beer in. "If it wasn't warm, I'd drink at least one." He gave the beer a sorrowful look and shook his head. The bottles were to be used for Molotov cocktails. They were the second to last item on our list. Hayden pushed the now heavy cart forward. We were on the lookout for the automotive section; along with the containers we needed to harvest fuel for our bombs, Hayden wanted to grab a few things for his truck. They were completely necessary, he assured me more than once.

"That way." I pointed to the blue, overhanging sign. "What are you going to do about—"

I cut off when something flew through the air. I grabbed Hayden's arm and yanked him out of the way, our backs slamming into an end cap filled with Barbie dolls. A yellow golf ball pinged off the floor in front of us. Hayden drew his weapon and my hand flew to the M9.

Another ricocheted off a shelf and bounced passed my shoulder. Hayden pulled me into him, trying to safely pin me between his body and the shelf behind us. Protesting against being protected, I ducked out from behind him and raised my gun.

"Hey!" I shouted. "Who's doing that?" The only response we got was a cascade of colorful golf balls raining down on us. One hit the back of my hand, bringing an instant sting to the bones. I jumped around the shelf and moved into the aisle. Hayden was a step behind and pointed at the direction the balls were coming from. Silently, we raced down the aisle to confront our annoying attacker.

All we saw was a trail of brown hair whipping behind a display of blue glass vases. Without hesitation, I fired, intentionally missing the potential target. Blood rushed through my body, pulsating from my pounding heart. Sweat dripped down my forehead as I ran. Hayden jumped over a square display of discounted movies to head her off; he disappeared from my sight and ducked down another aisle.

I ran after the person, boots slipping on the broken glass. I zigzagged across the walkway, dodging around a knocked over and broken flat screen TV. I rounded a corner and found Hayden face to face with the ball thrower.

He held his gun out, with the barrel buried in the young girl's chest. She pushed against it, snarling, as she clawed the air trying to get to him. Her fingernails were browned from dried blood. The despondent look on Hayden's face made a sick feeling form in my stomach. I stood to the side and he pulled the trigger.

The girl fell, fresh crimson staining her pale pink sweater. I walked around the body, noting the crusted blood outlining her mouth. Infected or not, killing someone so young was hard.

"I wonder how long she's been in here," Hayden said aloud and stepped away. We exited the aisle. "She's not dressed for summer."

"It's odd," I said quietly. I suppressed a shudder and looped my arm through Hayden's. "Let's get our shit and leave."

He nodded and led the way, retracing our steps. When we got to the spot where we had left the cart, Hayden and I exchanged looks.

"This is where we left it, right?" Hayden asked me and looked down the aisle for our missing cart.

"Yes. I'm positive." My eyes flicked to the pink boxes of inappropriately proportioned women.

"Then where...?"

I shook my head. "No idea." I swallowed hard and instantly felt paranoid.

"Hannah?" Hayden said over the walkie. A painful few seconds ticked by before she answered. "How are things out there?"

"Boring," she said. "I haven't seen anything out of the ordinary except one of those zombies Orissa calls sticky or something."

"Gummy," Hayden corrected. "Lay low and keep the doors locked."

"Ok. Did you shoot at zombies? I thought I heard shots."

"You did and yes," he told her. "We'll be out soon."

"Maybe," I spat and shook my head. "What the fuck is going on?"

Hayden's eyes filled with guilty terror. "She was infected right?"

"Most definitely," I assured him. "She attacked you. Plus she was covered in blood."

"But then who...?" he trailed off, shaking his head. "Maybe someone else is in here. They could have been in here."

I nodded and pressed my fingers into the cool metal of my gun. "Let's find them."

Hayden bent over and picked up a golf ball. "I have an idea," he stated and threw the ball as far as he could. We heard it bounce off the floor and clang into something. He picked up another and chucked it in the opposite direction. Taking his lead I scooped up three balls and threw them down different aisle. I held by breath and waited as the golf balls bounced and crashed off different items before slowly rolling to a stop.

Something scurried to our left. We took off, running toward the source of the noise. We raced through an aisle of silk and plastic flowers, the perfumed stems still fragrant, and rounded a corner before skidding to a stop. The bags of fertilizer, which had been on the bottom of the cart, were neatly stacked on the Craft Center's counter.

I swallowed hard and my finger hovered over the trigger. Hayden reached into his pocket and grabbed another golf ball; he pulled his arm back and gently rolled it down the center aisle. Its pocked surface rattled on the hard floor as it moved before abruptly coming to a stop.

"Hello?" Hayden shouted. "Anyone there?" He turned and

extended his arm to grab the heavy bags when the ball came rolling back. Quietly, we edged away from the counter and moved down another few aisles, where we found our cart. Only it was upside down and everything was lined up in a circle around it.

"Why do I feel like we're in a lame paranormal movie?" I asked out loud and stopped the ball with my foot. I let out a deep breath and lifted my head up. "Hey!" I shouted. "I don't have time for your crap. Come attack us like good crazies and get it over with. I'm really tasty, I promise!"

Hayden raised an eyebrow. "Classy."

"They're creeping me out," I said with a shrug. "And their wasting our time. It's hot in here and we have more shit to do." Hayden grinned and twisted the strap on his machine gun to free his hands. I stood a few feet back and kept my eyes peeled, growing annoyed of the cat and mouse game when suddenly a body came hurtling down the aisle.

I got a flash of his boyish face and blue eyes. He looked familiar, though with brown chunks stuck to his cheeks, it was hard to place him. I leapt over Hayden and threw out my leg, hitting the guy and knocking him to the ground. He popped right back up and I punched him in the throat. While the pain didn't register, he recoiled, unable to breathe.

"Hey," I said and looked him over. "It's Eric Sutton!"

"No fucking way," Hayden said and stood up. "I love that guy!" He took in the sight of the infected celebrity, famous for his raunchy comedies. "I never got to see his latest movie," he said ruefully.

I hit Eric in the throat again. "It came out like five years ago," I said incredulously. "Hollywood ran out of money, remember? There hasn't been anything new for a while."

"Sorry we don't get new releases shipped overseas," he replied sarcastically. Eric took in a screeching gasp of air and floundered at me; I hit him once more. His hands flew to his neck, clawing at his skin as if he'd be able to breathe if he tore it away. "Uh, Riss?" Hayden began. "Are you going to shoot him or use him as a punching bag?"

I scrunched up my face and kicked his legs, knocking him off his feet. Once he was on the ground I pulled the trigger. I heavily sighed. "That was something I never thought I'd do," I mused. Hayden's eyes met mine and I frowned. Shaking my head, I bent down and helped reload our cart.

We made it halfway through the store when Hayden said, "I

think we're being followed."

"You do?" I asked and resisted the urge to whip around and look behind me. Both of my hands were occupied pushing and pulling a cart. I didn't like not having a weapon in my grasp.

"Yeah. See those mirrors?" He flicked his eyes to the large, round mirror wedged at the top of the wall. "I swear I saw movement."

"Since when do S1s stalk the uninfected in such a smart way?" I rhetorically asked.

"Since they started living peacefully together," Hayden said under his breath. "Let's get the hell out of here."

On edge, we hurried to the front of the store. I pushed open the glass doors and swept my eyes back and forth over the registers while Hayden hurriedly moved the carts outside. Once our supplies were on the sidewalk, I yanked the metal bars down and scurried outside. Hannah jumped out of the driver's side to help us load everything.

"You should have gotten bags," she suggested. "It would make it easier to transfer everything. Can you go back and get some?"

"No," Hayden and I said together. Neither one of us wanted to go back inside. "This is good enough. We can organize it all when we get back to the camp."

"Ok," she agreed. "Did you get everything?"

"Pretty much," he told her. "We need fuel. It won't be hard to find a semi truck to take some from. There might even be a few behind the store."

"I thought you got flammable stuff already?"

"We did," he said. "We need more."

"Ah, I see." She nodded. "The explosions are going to look awesome."

Hayden's face went slack and his hand froze in midair, holding a can of soup. I knew Hayden would never put the words 'explosion' and 'awesome' in the same sentence. I watched Hannah twist away from the back of the SUV and grab a case of water bottles with a smile on her face. Did she not know the hell Hayden had gone through overseas?

"You know you won't see it, right?" I asked.

"Yeah," she replied. "And really, I don't want to. Blowing things up, fighting others…it scares me."

Hayden mumbled an incoherent reply and picked up the pace. I took a few steps back and glanced around the parking lot.

A gummy had spotted us but was moving so slow there was no way it would make it over here before we were done. I narrowed my eyes and watched him; it looked as if his legs were stuck together and he moved one baby step at a time.

Shaking my head, I loaded my arms with items from the cart and dumped them in the Yukon. Ten minutes later, we shoved the carts aside and got back into the SUV. Hannah drove us around back; a few more gummies wandered about and were quickly shot down by Hayden.

"Stay here," he told me and grabbed the gas cans and the piece of hose used to siphon. "And have my back."

I slipped the quiver over my head and nodded. "Stay in my line of sight then," I bargained. He nodded and hurried off toward a blue and white semi parked by the store's loading dock. I rummaged through my leather bag until I found my sunglasses. I put them on and leaned against the front of the SUV, careful to keep my skin off of the hot metal.

Hannah left the engine running and got out; she shaded her eyes and watched her brother get to work filling one of the gas cans. I cast her a sideways glance and exhaled.

"Why were you surprised that I was Hayden's girlfriend?" I asked.

Her body twitched with surprised and her cheeks grew red. "I wasn't."

"You cast your eyes down when you said that, so I know you're lying," I told her. "And I remember you being surprised."

"Oh, right." She grabbed the hem of her button up pink shirt. "You're just not the type of girl I'm used to seeing him with, that's all."

I wasn't expecting that; it was my turn to be surprised. "What kind of girl did he used to be with?" I asked, careful to keep the judgment out of my voice.

"He usually dated blondes, and they were…well, I guess you could say stereotypical. You know, kinda dumb and really girly. And you're just so self assured and confident and kinda badass. It wasn't what I was expecting."

"Oh," was all I could say.

"But it's not bad," she said quickly to assure me. "Heather and I always *hated* the girls he brought home, even though there weren't that many since he wasn't home that much with the war and all. She thought it stemmed from low self esteem or something. Like he purposely dated girls like that because he didn't think he was capable to doing better." She shook her head. "Heather was into that psychological stuff. She was good at it," she added quietly. I watched Hayden twist the cap on the gas can and move to another vehicle. "Anyway, that's why I was surprised. You come off a little...uh, intimidating."

I laughed. "Hayden said the same thing. He intimidated me a bit too," I blurted. I hadn't wanted to even admit it to myself, but he had. And it had little to do with his physical attributes. He was so liked and respected for being a good person by everyone at the compound. He was a good soldier and was good at what he did. Part of me was worried I couldn't measure up.

"I'm happy you're together," she told me with a smile.

I rolled my eyes and laughed. "Please. You don't even know me."

"No," she agreed. "But I know my brother. And I can tell he really cares about you."

I smiled and looked away, scanning the area for something to kill. I pushed off the SUV and turned around; Baby Steps had shuffled his way behind the store. Though he was still too far to strike any sort of fear in me, I grabbed an arrow and shot him in the head.

"How long have you been doing archery?" Hannah asked.

I sighed in relief that she had changed the subject. "Close to twenty years," I said. "My grandpa was into hunting and learning survival skills so he started me young."

"That's neat," she said. "You shoot so fast. It doesn't even look like you aim but you hit what you want to."

I shrugged. "I do aim. Especially when I'm trying to hit something small. I can just do it quickly, I suppose."

"Oh. Can you give me some tips?"

I nodded and spent the rest of the time waiting for Hayden chatting about archery with Hannah. After securing the gas cans in the back, we left the parking lot and stopped alongside an empty and overgrown field for lunch. The thin, gray clouds were dissipating, allowing the sun's heat to radiate upon the earth.

Turning off the car, Hannah got out and followed Hayden and me to the back. I pulled out the bag of food we had already prepared and dished out the contents. I stomped down a patch of clovers and sat, using them as cushions while I ate. Hayden took a close spot next to me and Hannah sat across from us, flinching away from the tall grass that tickled her arms.

"You'll never guess who we ran into," Hayden spoke and

tossed a handful of nuts into his mouth.

"Who?" Hannah asked with her mouthful.

"Eric Sutton," he replied. "And Riss killed him."

Hannah's jaw dropped as she gaped at me. "What? Why on earth would you kill him? He's freaking hilarious!"

"His jokes are lame," I said causally.

"He was a zombie, right?" she assumed.

Hayden shook his head, furthering Hannah's shock. Laughing, he finally said, "He was infected and insane."

"Oh. Dangit. That's really disappointing. He would have been fun to have around."

Hayden chuckled. "Next time there is an apocalypse, I'll be sure to find a comedian to bring with us."

We all laughed.

"Really!" Hannah pressed with a smile on her face. "It would be a good idea! They could boost morale."

"They are people too," I reminded her. "Maybe he would be sad. And there's nothing worse than a depressed comedian. Well, except a crazy one."

Hayden began quoting one of his favorite Eric Sutton movie lines when the smell hit me. I shoved the rest of my trail mix in my mouth and stood.

"What?" Hayden asked and sprang up.

I shook my head. "Not sure. The wind blew and I got a whiff of death." I swallowed my food and sighed. "It doesn't mean much. Dead things are everywhere."

"No," Hayden disagreed. "You are right." He was looking through the scope of his rifle. "There is a herd."

"Where?" Hannah cried and jumped up, spilling the can of mixed nuts on the ground.

"Far enough away," Hayden assured her. "But we probably should pack it up." He let out a breath of annoyance and scooped up his water bottle. I picked up an unopened can of mandarin oranges and cast a bitter look at the distant herd. Without the enhanced vision the scope provided, the herd was nothing but a gray haze in the distance.

I climbed into the back and set my bow and arrows on the seat next to me. I clicked the seatbelt into place and impatiently waited for Hannah to start the ignition and turn on the air. Hayden double checked the map, making sure we wouldn't veer too far off of our path to avoid the herd.

Still wanting the oranges, I held the can away from my lap and removed the lid. I drained the water out of the window and picked out the fruit with my fingers. Finally, Hannah was situated and cranked up the air. Though it hindered the vehicle cooling off, I left my window partially open in case I needed to quickly shoot at something.

"Turn here and go over that bridge," Hayden instructed.

"I thought Texas had sand," Hannah informed us and slowed to make the turn.

"It does farther south," I speculated. The bridge was rickety and almost nerve wracking to drive over. I looked over the rails into the dry creek bed and thought I saw hoof prints.

"Have you ever been there?" she asked.

"No."

Hayden turned around. "Riss has traveled a lot, though. She's been to a lot of interesting places."

I nodded. "That is true, though most of my traveling was outside of the US on mission trips."

"You did missions? That's so cool!" Hannah exclaimed.

"Yeah, cool," I agreed, not bothering to tell her I was dragged along by my mom and step dad. I felt a sting of pain when I thought about my parents; I had no idea what had happened to them. There were away on another mission in a very remote location. As far as anyone could tell, the virus had struck worldwide and no one was safe. I bit my lip and pushed the thought away, focusing on the quickly passing landscape that was dotted with patchy trees.

"Are there any granola bars left?" Hayden asked me. "I'm hungry."

"I think so," I said and leaned over to reach across the seat and grab the bag of food. My fingertips had just grazed the fabric handle when Hannah screamed. I jerked up, only to be thrown forward against my seatbelt as she slammed on the brakes. Something white and brown flashed in front of us. I didn't have a chance to make out what it was.

The Yukon swerved, tires spinning on gravel, and jerked off the road. I closed my eyes when the view out the windshield was nothing but brown and green. We crashed into the tree, throwing the SUV off balance. Branches broke through the glass and the sound of Hayden's head whacking against the passenger window resonated with a sickly thud.

CHAPTER TWENTY-TWO

"Hayden?" I asked when the car stopped moving. "Hayden?"

"Mmhh," he groaned. "You guys ok?" He unbuckled his seat belt and pushed himself up, shoving the air bag to the side. "Riss? Hannah?"

Safe in the back, I was fine. "I'm ok," I answered. Hannah whimpered and frantically pawed at the air bag. Hayden scrambled over to help his sister. Blood dripped down the right side of his face. The SUV was at an angle; neither Hayden nor I were able to open our doors because of the trees. I clambered out the left side and threw open the driver's side door. I stuck a knife into the air bag and pressed it down. One of Hannah's arms had gotten caught in between her and the air bag.

"I think I'm ok," she panted, fighting back tears.

"I think your wrist might be broken," I bluntly stated. "It's swelling already." Hayden pressed the release on her seat belt and I helped her out. "Can you walk?"

She nodded. "Did I hit it?"

I was about to ask what she was talking about when I remembered the brief flash of color. I stood back and turned; standing in the road, breathing heavily, and staring at us like we might come after him like zombies, was a horse.

"Oh my God," I mumbled. He was dripping with sweat and had sores on his face where the leather bridle had repeatedly rubbed his fur. Dirt and grime covered the brown leather saddle and part of a human leg hung from the stirrup. The rider must have fallen and gotten dragged until their leg split apart at the knee. Yellow bone stuck out around melting flesh that dripped and glistened in the sunlight.

The horse raised his head up and flared his nostrils; he was obviously used to humans but hadn't been around any in a long time. The reins had no doubt tangled around the poor horse's legs as he ran. One dangled a few feet from the bit and another was simply gone. I slowly held up my hand. The brown and white Paint stretched out his neck and sniffed the air.

I quickly snapped my attention back to Hayden. I grabbed his arm and steadied him as he exited the Yukon. "Fuck," I swore when I took in the extent of his injury and raised my hand to inspect the wound. He ducked away and swatted my arm.

"I'm fine," he spat, his attitude giving away the fact that he was far from fine.

"You could have a concussion," I told him. "I got one almost the same way but I didn't bleed. You hit the window hard."

"I'm sorry," Hannah whimpered and cradled her hand to her chest. "I didn't know what to do." She rapidly shook her head back and forth. "I knew if I hit it, it could come through and kill us."

"It's ok," I soothed, not wanting to deal with her crying. We had enough on our plate already. "Come sit down," I instructed. I kept my arm through Hayden's as I led him around the Yukon and into the shade. He sank down in the tall grass. As soon as Hannah was seated next to him, I jogged over to the SUV and yanked the back hatch open. With the frame of the vehicle bent, it was a challenge to pull free. I shuffled around through the jumbled mess of supplies and pulled out the first aid supplies.

"Here," I said to Hannah and handed her a blue plastic bag. "Bend it and shake; it will get cold." She nodded and struggled to twist the cold pack one handed. Taking it back, I popped the lump inside and shook up the contents before giving it to her. She gingerly draped it over her wrist.

I knelt down next to Hayden and looked into his eyes. I remembered Padraic saying something about my pupils being dilated...or maybe not being dilated? I couldn't remember. I shook my head at my own thoughts and blotted up the blood. At eye level and in Hayden's hairline, it was hard to clean and even harder for me to assess, partially because I had no idea how to assess for a concussion.

"It's not that deep, is it?" he asked.

I shook my head.

"It doesn't feel deep. But it hurts," he admitted. "And really, Riss, I'm ok." I just nodded and continued taking care of him. "Did the fuel spill?"

"No. It was smart of you to tie it down."

"I'm a genius," he said with a smirk. "How are you doing, Hannah?"

"My wrist freaking kills," she cried. "I can barely move my fingers."

"Then don't," he told her. "I can stabilize it for now. We have a doctor at the compound; he will take care of it."

She wiped away a tear and nodded. "Ok."

"You're not doing anything," I told Hayden. "I'll take care of both of you. You two took the brunt of that crash."

"You're overreacting," Hayden scolded.

"Shut up," Hannah told her brother. "Can't you see she's worried because she cares about you?"

Hayden glared at her but didn't say anything more. I disinfected his wound and gave him a wad of gauze. Not needing direction from me, Hayden pressed it to his head and leaned back against the tree. I moved to Hannah and carefully lifted the cold pack. A lump was visible through the swelling.

"My chest hurts from where my arm got pinned," she told me.

"Can you breathe ok?" I asked as if I knew what I was talking about. Up close, I noticed she had tiny cuts on her cheeks. I leaned in closer. "There's glass stuck in your skin."

She closed her eyes and whimpered. "Get it out?"

"Maybe," I replied honestly. "I can try." I opened up the first aid kit and dug around for a pair of tweezers. Painstakingly, I dug at her skin, picking out small fractures of the windshield. She tightly pressed her eyes closed, spilling tears, but remained relatively still. I had to give her credit for that. When I was done, I went back to the Yukon and looked for anything to use to splint her wrist. My eyes darted around our jumbled supplies and I shook my head; we had nothing useful.

"Yes," I whispered aloud and ripped open the carton of water bottles. I dumped them out and tore off the plastic. Grabbing the cardboard bottom, I went back to Hannah's side and used my knife to saw off two strips.

"Ow," she said through clenched teeth when I took her wrist. "That hurts, that really, really hurts. Stop, please, stop!"

"Hannah," Hayden spoke slowly. "Here." He stretched out his hand for her to squeeze. I gently placed the cardboard under her arm and taped it to her skin. I did the same with another piece on top, finishing off the crappy splint by wrapping it with tape.

"It's better than nothing," I assured her. Hayden pushed himself up and blinked. He carefully rotated his neck and stretched out his back. "Are you ok?"

"He's looking at you," he said. I sprang up and drew my gun. "The horse, Riss, just the horse," Hayden informed me. "Chill."

"Oh." The sound of hoof beats on pavement drew my attention a few yards down the road. He huffed and lowered his head. "Poor thing," I said to myself. Hayden took a step and faltered as if he had been spinning in circles, catching my attention.

"You ok?"

"I have a headache," he said and shook himself before walking over to the Yukon. I gingerly wrapped an ACE bandage around the cardboard splint. "The radiator's punctured," Hayden called. "We can't drive this."

"What do we do?" Hannah asked her voice tight.

"We're gonna have to walk."

"All the way back?" she exclaimed.

"Just until we find another car," I filled in. Turning back to the horse, I took a slow step forward. The horse snapped his head up and backed away. I looked at the ground and held out my hand. The horse sniffed the air. "It's ok," I gently spoke. Hayden leaned against the SUV and watched our exchange. Very slowly I moved toward the horse. When I was only a few feet from him, he picked up his feet and curiously walked the rest of the way.

He blew hot breath in my face as he sniffed me. Deciding I wasn't a threat, he pressed his head against my torso.

"Hey, buddy," I soothed and rubbed his muzzle. "I bet you've been lonely, haven't you?" The sun reflected off of a dirty brass plate on his bridle. I ran my fingers over the engraving. "Sundance," I spoke the horse's name. "I had a horse named Sundance a long time ago," I told him.

"I think he likes you," Hayden said quietly and carefully picked his way over. Sundance pushed his face into me and quickly brought it up. Recognizing the gesture, I turned around and allowed him to rub his head on my back.

"He has to be terrified and lonely," I said and struggled to keep my balance Sundance scratched his face on my back. "I don't know what to do with him other than take off his tack and set him free."

"I bet he'd like that," Hayden agreed and moved next to me. After Sundance sniffed him, Hayden pulled the mangled half leg out of the stirrup and tossed it aside. "He's huge."

I smiled. "He is."

"He doesn't look too bad. How long would it take a horse to starve out here?"

"I have no idea," I said honestly. "There is plenty of grass." I ran my hand along his neck and stepped down, inspecting the gear that hung from the saddle. A black and silver lead rope was coiled around the saddle horn, the neat coils kept in place by strips of bailing twine. A water bottle full of brown water was clipped to the back of the saddle. A machete in a leather sheath hung on the other side. "As long as he found water I suppose he could do alright. That is, until he got eaten by something."

Hayden closed his eyes and took a deep breath. I took my hand off of Sundance's neck and put it on Hayden's arm. I didn't have to ask what was wrong; Hayden acknowledged my concern by putting his hand over mine.

"I'm feeling a little dizzy," he admitted. He closed his eyes, took a breath, and smiled. "I'll eat, sit for a few minutes, and then be good to go, ok?"

I nodded my approval and tipped my head toward him. "Sit. I'll bring you food."

"That's right, woman," Hayden joked. I raised an eyebrow and scowled at him. He flashed a cheeky grin and gave me a quick peck on the lips before turning away. When I walked over to the Yukon, Sundance followed.

"You miss your people, huh?" I asked.

Hayden and I walked to the back of the Yukon. He sat in the open back and sorted through the food for something to snack on. I ripped open a box of sugary cereal and offered a handful to the horse, who eagerly ate it. I gave him a few more handfuls before setting the box down. Sundance nosed his way into the back of the Yukon, sticking his head in through the tail gate and nibbling on the box. I laughed and pushed him back. "Your owners must have taken you lots of places," I said and petted his head. "You're used to cars."

"When was the last time you rode?" Hayden asked.

"Shit," I swore as I thought. "It's been a while. I didn't have a chance to get down to my grandparent's farm much the last year I was in school. Until I got 'let go' from my job, I worked almost every weekend."

"And that's when you dropped out of school?"

I nodded. "It was still early enough to get my money back. I tried to get another job but couldn't. I felt lucky to even have had one in the first place. I really did intend to go back to school...eventually."

"You had to be close to graduating," he said and bit into a cookie.

I laughed. "Not as close as you'd think since I kept switching my major."

Hayden nodded and rested his head on my shoulder. Sundance nudged me for more cereal. "Are you concussed?" I asked Hayden.

"I feel kinda sick," he admitted. "I've had concussions before and I've never felt sick from them this fast. It's probably from the heat."

I wanted to believe that was true. I shoved my horse slobber-covered hand back into the box and pulled out a fistful of colorful circles. Sundance gobbled them up.

"I didn't know horses like cereal," Hayden stated.

"They like sweet things. Or basically anything you're eating. Kinda like dogs." I laughed. "I used to show my horse at the county fair every summer. One year he stole my hot dog right from my hands and ate it."

Hayden laughed.

"Hayden?" Hannah called and got to her feet. "Are you ok?"

"Fine," he groaned.

I twisted around and grabbed him a water bottle. I rolled my eyes. "How's the arm?"

"It's just my wrist," she said and nervously danced around the horse to get to her brother. "But it really, really hurts. You don't look too good."

"I'm good enough," he stubbornly spat. "Ready?"

"Ready for what?" she asked, her brown eyes latched onto Sundance.

"To walk," he said with annoyance. I could tell he was feeling worse as the minutes passed. "Which we wouldn't have to do if you knew how to freaking drive!"

"What was I supposed to do?" she argued back. "That stupid thing ran right out in front of me!"

"Guys," I said and put my hand on Sundance's muzzle. "We are kind of fucked right now and squabbling isn't going to do anything but annoy me."

"She could have swerved the other way," Hayden mumbled. I resisted the urge to glower at him even though I agreed.

"You're both hurt," I stated. "Hannah, get something to eat before we leave. Hayden, drink this," I said and handed him an electrolyte drink. "Rest for ten minutes, but don't close your eyes. Hayden, you can't sleep yet. Hannah, get your crap from the front once you're done eating. Then we need to get moving."

"You're bossy," Hannah said, matter of factly.

I dismissed her comment and set the box of cereal down. I turned around and reached under the back seat, pulling out the cans of food that had rolled underneath it. Sundance nosed at the cereal until he knocked the box over and spilled the brightly colored contents onto the ground.

Suddenly, his head snapped up. I whirled around; the white of his eyes were showing and his nostrils flared. The wind blew against us, whisking away the scent of decay. But not from Sundance's more advanced senses.

Hayden grabbed his bridle, softly talking to the frightened horse. I moved out of the SUV and gazed upon the horizon.

"Holy shit," I mouthed. The herd that we had avoided moved in an undead procession across the field.

* * *

I frantically looked at Hayden; on a good day we could outrun the slow moving herd. Right now he was in no condition to jog down the road, let alone run for his life.

"What?" Hannah asked me, seeing the fear in my eyes. And then, of course, there was her. I assumed she was in decent shape since she had made it this far. But her injury slowed her down too. "Oh my God," she cried when she saw the massive wall of death moving toward us.

Hayden used the horse to up right himself. He swallowed hard but remained stoic as he took in what was headed our way. "We need to go," he said calmly.

They would never make it. It could be miles before we found another car, and the pressure was on with dozens of zombies behind us. And what if we came across more zombies? Being surrounded wasn't something we could risk.

"Get the weapons," he said and stepped away from the tailgate. He faltered in his gait and caught himself, throwing out a hand at the last minute. My heart sped up and my breath got caught in my throat. Hayden was hurt—badly, and I knew he wouldn't admit it. He would do whatever it took to keep me safe, even if it meant endangering himself.

Without thinking it through, I yanked the lead rope free. I

clipped one end to the bit and threw the other end over Sundance's head, tying it to the other side of his bridle. I stuck my foot in the stirrup and began to hoist myself up, the saddle slipped; I jumped off and tightened the girth before getting on again.

"What are you doing?" Hayden asked, turning around too fast.

"Distracting them." I gently pressed my legs against the horse's side. He nervously danced in place; I yanked on the lead rope and kept him from bolting. "Hide," I told him and turned Sundance around. He trotted through the tall grass, emerging onto the road. Hooves clicking on the pavement, he obediently moved forward a few yards before shying away from the nearing herd.

He sank his head down and rounded his back. "Not now," I said through gritted teeth, bracing myself for the horse to start bucking. I pulled on one rein and put pressure on his side with my leg. To my surprise, he listened. I urged him to run faster; we were going at an angle toward the zombies. I opened my mouth to yell at the zombies but stopped, not wanting to spook the already terrified horse I was riding.

We made it another twenty or so yards before Sundance slid to a stop and reared. I pitched my weight forward and grabbed a tangle of his mane. "Come on, boy," I urged and pressed my heels into his sides. He landed with a grunt, his breath heavily escaping his nostrils. When I pushed him forward, he pawed at the ground and reared again.

It was enough to get the zombies' attention. At first only a few caught sight of us and hobbled over. Then, in one chilling movement, they all turned in unison and started their death march. Sundance nervously danced in place. I struggled to hold him back, wanting the zombies to get closer before he bolted. But the closer they got the less control I had. Sundance took off, ignoring my attempts to pull him into a controlled run. He was stronger than me, after all, and he knew it. I stole a glance behind us and my heart skipped a beat. A handful of the zombies were running at us, and they were gaining speed at an alarming rate. I loosed my hold on the reins and leaned forward.

We ran away from the crashed Yukon. I could only hope that the entire herd would follow in the wake of their leader and not straggle away to prey on my injured Marine. Afraid we were going too fast for the zombies to keep up, I pulled Sundance into a

EMILYGOODWIN

circle. He tossed his head in protest. I pulled my arm back to my hip. Finally he obeyed and we arched around in a wide circle.

The relief that I felt when I saw that the herd was still nipping at our heels quickly vanished. Panic took over and I realized I had no idea where Sundance and I would end up...or if the poor horse could manage to keep running for very long. He tossed his head again and I pulled back. The end of the lead rope that I had tied came loose.

"Oh shit," I mumbled and clung onto the rope, staring at it as if it would magically reattach to the horse's bit. Clarity smacked me in the face and I quickly gobbled up the loose end, not wanting Sundance to trip. I could only pull him to the left now, and that wouldn't do any good. Knowing that he would stop eventually, I rested my hand on the saddle horn and let him run.

He took me across another road and made a bee line for a wooden fence. My heart lurched into my throat. I hadn't ridden in over a year and it had been even longer since I jumped. For a split second I knew I was going to fall; I couldn't remember what I was supposed to do. At the last second, my body acted on its own accord. I gripped the saddle horn and leaned forward, shifting my weight onto the balls of my feet.

Then we landed. I let out the breath I didn't realize I was holding and rocked back into the saddle. Sundance raced forward with a renewed sense of motivation. My eyes swept up and the sight of a small, blue house bobbed into view. The large barn in the back miniaturized it.

"That must be your home," I panted as he sprinted toward the barn. "Uh, whoa!" I shouted and pulled back on the lead rope. "Sundance, whoa!" I said again without success. Giving up, I leaned forward, hugging my body against his to avoid getting scraped off when he darted through the open barn doors. He came to an abrupt stop and I flew forward, almost getting unseated. With shaky legs I slid off, suddenly aware that the only weapon I had was the pistol on my hip.

Sundance's body shook with the force of his heavy breathing. I looked around the barn; the stall in front of us had moldy hay and a water bucket with about an inch of water left in it. The stall had been picked clean since the last time a horse had been in it. A dust covered brass name plate was nailed to the stall door.

"This is your home," I whispered and ran a finger over the engraving of Sundance's name. "And this is your stall." He took a step forward to go in but I stopped him. "You need to walk," I said and began to slowly lead him out of the barn. Though he wasn't as fierce as Argos, having the horse with me calmed my nerves in an odd way. He provided a fast getaway and could hear way better than I could.

Tentatively, I stepped out of the barn, inspecting our surroundings. We turned right and went around the front, giving me a clear view of the back of the house. The back door swung open and a window was shattered. Remnants of blood and skin hung from the sharp points of the broken glass. Zombies had no doubt forced their way inside. I swallowed my nerves and kept walking the horse. Behind the barn was an overgrown sand arena. Parked next to it, was a Chevy truck hooked up to a small horse trailer. I stared at it hopefully, knowing there was no way I would get that lucky.

I didn't feel safe just yet. With Sundance by my side, I explored the rest of the property, finding nothing but tall grass and forgotten farm equipment. I went back into the barn. Sundance pulled forward; I let the lead rope slip from my hand and allowed him to dart into his stall. I ground my teeth and looked around once more before following him in. I quickly removed the saddle and bridle. My grandpa would throw a fit if he had to leave a horse hot and sweaty like this, but I didn't know what to do.

I stepped out of the stall and heaved the heavy leather saddle onto the cement floor. I pulled the machete from the sheath and left Sundance in his stall to search for anything useful. A few stalls down and across the aisle was what I guessed to be a tack room. Gripping the machete tight, I put one hand on the door knob and turned my head, listening. When I didn't hear anything, I twisted the knob and waited a few seconds before I pushed the door open.

I stood back, waiting for something to scurry out. But nothing did. Sunlight streamed through an exterior window, illuminating the room enough for me to investigate. Right away I could tell that Sundance had been an expensive show horse once upon a time. The most recent picture of him being ridden by a very proud teenage girl was dated five years ago, around the time the economy went from bad to worse. The tack room was fairly empty; I assumed Sundance's owners had sold his fancy and expensive show gear when times got hard.

I pocketed a small knife and opened a cabinet just out of curiosity. It was full of supplements and old prescriptions that I was sure could be useful with our own animals at the compound. I left the tack room and nervously looked outside; the herd was visible in the distance. I knew the fence would slow them down but it was only a matter of time before they caught up...or turned around.

I needed to find a car—now. The truck was too new for me to hot wire. I bit my lip and looked at it, debating on whether or not it was worth it to run into the house and look for keys. Knowing that the "what if" would kill me when I left on foot I ran through the yard and emerged through the smashed in back door, which led into the kitchen.

Blood and strands of long, black hair were smeared and dried on the white and yellow laminate flooring. Bits of torn up fabric decorated the scene, but there were no traces of the victim left. I briskly walked past it, holding the machete in front of me. There was a narrow hallway off the kitchen that led into the garage. Deciding it was my best bet for finding keys or hell, even a car, I quietly edged my way into the darkness.

"Jackpot," I whispered when my eyes adjusted. Hanging behind the garage door was a key rack and three sets of keys hung from it. I took them all and opened the garage door. While there were no zombies, I was still disappointed. A shiny Harley sat parked in the center. "Your loud-ass engine is the last thing I need," I said and rolled my eyes, though it wasn't as if I even knew how to drive a motorcycle. I left the house and, in the sunlight, took a better look at the keys in my hand. I let the motorcycle keys fall to the grass and jogged to the truck.

"Thank you," I panted when I pressed the unlock button and heard the locks shift in the Chevy. I pocked the other set of keys, which I assumed were for the horse trailer, and opened the truck's door. With trembling hands I stuck the keys in the ignition and turned. I wanted to hug the steering wheel when the engine came to life. I looked over the dash and past the barn; a number of zombies had tumbled over the fence and were quickly closing the distance.

Sundance trotted out of the barn and stared at the truck. I jumped out and raced to the back of the trailer. "If you load quickly, I'll take you. If not," I cut off and shook my head. "I can't stay here." As if he understood, the horse stepped out of the barn. I flew around to the side of the trailer and opened a metal door that led into a closet-sized storage room. I yanked a red halter from a hook and slipped it over Sundance's head. I tugged him forward and he obediently listened, stepping into the trailer like he had no doubt done many times before.

I swung the back door closed and ran to the truck. I put one foot in before I backed out, realizing that the herd would see me and try to follow. I could out run them in a vehicle, but I needed to make sure we had enough time to transfer our goods from the damaged Yukon into the truck.

A pack of cigarettes and a lighter had been tossed onto the passenger seat. I closed my fingers around the lighter and ran back into the barn. A spry S2 greeted me, growling and snarling and blowing horrid smelling breath into my face. It only took one clean sweep of the machete to take his head off.

"Nice," I said to myself and watched the head thump on the ground. I leapt over it and threw open the tack room, looking for anything to use for an advantage. I looked over the supplies so fast that I didn't see it at first. My chest began to ach from the fast pace of my heart. I was about to give up and just make a run for it when the plastic jug of mink oil caught my eye. "Yes," I whispered and took it. I pulled a dusty horse sheet off of a hanging rack and ran out of the barn.

Stopping behind the house, I tossed the sheet on the ground and opened the jug of oil, pouring it over the material. I knelt down and looked away as I ignited the sheet. I sprang away just in time to avoid getting licked by the flames. I sprinted to the truck, hitting one more zombie as I made a mad dash for the driver's seat.

Three zombies clawed at the metal trailer, trying to get a piece of fresh horse meat. I stomped on the gas a little too hard and felt Sundance shift his weight to regain his balance. I could gain speed going straight, but I couldn't barrel around turns with a live animal in the back.

My cheeks burned and I thought that taking him with me was a bad idea. But it was too late to change my mind. The truck and trailer bumped along the pasture and onto the driveway. I slowed only to turn onto the street then pushed the pedal down.

The fire shot up into the air, acting like the perfect beacon for the zombies. One had been dumb enough to get in it, turning himself into a flaming death torch. Yellow and orange flames spilled off of his melting skin, leaving little patches of the tall grass smoldering. He wandered a few feet toward the house before collapsing, his burned legs no longer able to support his weight.

His body kept burning, billowing thick black smoke into the air. The zombies that were still stuck at the fence watched the fire with transfixed, dead eyes, keeping about half of them too distracted to know that I had driven by.

Though Sundance and I hadn't ventured all that far, it felt like an hour passed before I let my foot off the gas when the Yukon came into view. I pulled over on the road, parallel to the crashed SUV. Hayden opened the back driver's side door and raced over to me.

"Holy shit, Riss," he said and took me in his arms. I pressed my face against his shoulder and hugged him tightly back. "I hate when you leave me."

"That makes two of us," I said, my voice muffled.

"Don't do that again," he said. "I'm serious. Stop leaving on your own."

I leaned back and looked into his eyes. He seemed more like his regular self; beautiful hazel eyes clouded with worry and fear and his strong jaw set with determination. "The herd isn't far; we have to hurry."

He let me go and nodded, turning to call to Hannah. I went to the storage room inside the trailer and returned with two buckets to use to transfer our items into the truck. The three of us feverishly worked together, all the while keeping an eye out for stragglers. When we were almost done loading the supplies, Hayden left Hannah and me to finish while he transferred the gas from the SUV into the truck.

"I already rerouted us," Hayden said and tossed an empty gas can into the bed of the truck. "I'll drive."

"Are you sure you're ok?" I asked and bent down to look under the seats of the Yukon to double check for renegade supplies.

"I'm fine," he assured me. "Got everything?"

"I do now," I said and grabbed his iPod. We jogged to the truck and got in.

"Are we ready?" Hannah asked impatiently. She carefully held her arm to her chest.

"Yeah," Hayden said. "We're leaving."

Not even Hannah spoke for the first part of our journey back to the fenced in house. Eventually, she asked how I got the trailer and why I decided to bring Sundance back with me.

"It seemed wrong to leave him," I simplified, not wanting to bring up the fact that the very first horse my grandpa bought me was named Sundance. And that his horses had run back to the farm the day before Zoe died, which had attracted the attention of a massive herd. But I didn't have time to secure them or bring them with us as we fled to safety. Not our entire group made it out of there alive; the seven of us who did were lucky. "And it would have taken longer to unhitch the trailer than it did to load him."

"Oh," she said and then launched into a story about how she was scared of horses after falling from one her senior year of high school. I longingly thought of the compound and the nice, sleep-inducing pain medications that Padraic could give her.

When we were about a mile away from our setup, Hayden radioed to the guys to let them know that we would be coming back in a different vehicle than we had left in. Brock and Jason greeted us at the gate, pulling them open just enough for the truck and trailer to get through.

As soon as the truck was in park, we got out. I went around to the back and opened the trailer.

"You brought a horse?" Brock asked, his eyes wide with shock.

"He kinda brought himself," I said. "Long story." I shook my head and waited until Sundance exited the trailer.

"What the hell are we going to do with it?"

"I have no idea," I said honestly. There was grass for him to eat in the fenced in yard, but we had no water or shelter to provide him with. "But I did think that we should go back and get that car today instead of tomorrow and maybe stop at the creek to get a bucket or two of water."

Jason shrugged and then laughed in bewilderment. "Why the hell not?"

Hayden walked around the trailer and joined us.

"Holy shit!" Jason exclaimed. "What happened?"

Hayden tightly smiled and eyed Sundance, who stepped out of the trailer. "This guy ran out in front of us and caused an accident. It's worse than it looks," he said and touched the drying blood on his head. "Hannah is worse than me."

"Go inside and get cleaned up," Brock instructed. "We'll unload everything."

"Alright," Hayden agreed. I watched Sundance sniff the air and cautiously take in his surroundings. When he walked away and lowered his head to begin grazing, I followed behind Hayden and Hannah into the house.

Everyone in Hannah's group made a big deal over the injuries and accident. And then they had to go outside to see Sundance, as if a brown and white spotted horse was some sort of rare mythical creature. The poor thing had to be just as stressed and exhausted as we were. I wished they would have just left him alone.

Ivan made a studier brace for Hannah's wrist while I took a look at Hayden's head wound. I re-cleaned the bite on his shoulder while the first aid kit was out. We joined Wade in the living room, plopping down on the couch. Though Wade insisted he was feeling much better, I knew it would be a wise idea to let him—and now Hayden—rest for one more day before we raged a battle with the people at Eastmoore.

Hayden closed his eyes and leaned against the arm of the couch. I got up and told him to stretch out and relax, but warned him I would wake him up frequently, just like Padraic had done to me when I was concussed. I ventured back outside and cleaned the cuts on Sundance's face.

"We're going to get that Mustang now," Brock told me. I kept a hand on Sundance's neck and turned around.

"Ok," I said calmly and gave him a fake smile. I hated the guys going back into that death trap of a ghost town without me. "I'll come with," I offered.

Brock shook his head. "Stay with Hayden. He seems pretty banged up; leaving him would cause unnecessary stress."

"Not if he's asleep," I countered. "I won't know what's going on with you and I will worry," I confessed.

Brock chuckled. "Tell me about it." He took the buckets out of the back of the truck. "When we get back I want to hear the whole story about the horse."

I nodded. "Deal. Be safe."

"We'll try," he said honestly. I walked with him to the Range Rover, and hugged him and Ivan goodbye. When the gate was locked behind them, I went back into the house and kept myself busy organizing our supplies and lining everything up that we would need to pack our explosives. I woke Hayden up after I assumed an hour went by. He stirred from his sleep with ease and got up to go to the bathroom and get something to drink. I took it as a good sign.

He went back to resting on the couch; I went back outside to keep watch and pace around impatiently until my friends returned. I fully investigated the storage room in the trailer and found a box of brushes. Lori and Amanda were sitting on the deck watching the horse eat; I waved them over and assisted the little girl in helping me brush the crusty dried sweat off of Sundance's fur. He was far from clean when I set the brush down and went inside to check on Hayden. I was happy to find him not only awake, but alert and deep in conversation with Wade. The two of them were discussing the best way to build our bombs and had begun putting different ingredients together.

Surrounded by trees, the light in the house faded quickly as dusk approached. Madison, Agatha, and Ryan prepared dinner for everyone, putting tuna salad, crackers, trail mix and a cup of canned fruit on plates and setting it properly at the large dining room table. We had just sat down to eat when the loud, rumbling motor of the 1970s Mustang drew near.

Jason rushed outside to open the gate and I followed behind, eager to see my friends and to give the poor horse some water. Along with the two buckets, the guys had found a relatively clean plastic garbage can that they had filled with water. Ivan helped me heave the heavy water filled can to the ground and drag it near the trailer. I clipped a lead rope around it, securing the garbage can to the trailer so Sundance couldn't accidentally knock it over.

We then finished our dinner and prepared for the night, lighting candles and clicking on flashlights. Jim insisted that the six of us sleep the entire night while he, Madison, and Agatha took the first watch, followed by Lori, Hannah, Ryan, and Roger. I wasn't particularly fond of the idea, but I was so exhausted after the eventful day that I didn't protest and agreed to a full night's rest.

Hayden and I crashed in the same bed that we had the night before. Since the sun had dodged behind clouds most of the day, the night air cooled off to a comfortable temperature. I lay on my back with an arm over my head; Hayden snaked his arms around my waist and nuzzled his face against my breasts. I curled my other arm up and stroked his hair until I drifted to sleep.

* * *

Bright sunlight greeted us the next morning. I started the day with a quick yoga routine and then went downstairs to get things started. After breakfast, everyone found a way to help get supplies ready for the attack on Eastmoore. Madison, Agatha,

Ryan, and even Amanda formed a Molotov cocktail assembly line; Amanda dumped out the alcohol and passed the bottle to Agatha, who filled it with carefully mixed, combustible juice, and Madison stuffed the kerosene soaked rags into the bottles. Ryan then gently wrapped the mini explosives in washcloths and dish towel and loaded them into a white, plastic laundry basket.

I worked with Wade and Hayden on preparing our bigger bombs while Jason and Jim patrolled and Brock and Ivan went over our crazy, yet detailed, plan of attack. By the late afternoon, everything was packed, loaded, and put together. We ran through two mock trials, pinpointing ways things could go wrong, and went over and over the rough sketch of the hospital that Jon and drawn.

Apprehension blossomed in my stomach when the sun set and we settled in for the night. The entire household was anxiously aware that when the day broke tomorrow, six of us would set out on a mission, and that mission would end in bloodshed. Tomorrow could very well be our last. Tomorrow, we were starting a war.

CHAPTER TWENTY–THREE

I snapped the band at the end of my braid and swallowed hard. The hot sun beat down on us, reflecting dizzying rays off the black street. I killed the ignition of the black Mustang, got out, and carefully shut the door.

"Ready?" Hayden asked quietly over the walkie.

"Yes," Ivan answered. "We are in position."

I looked at the white picture of a crowned skull painted on the Mustang's hood, tempted to find something to scratch it off with.

"So are we," Wade spoke. "There are two guys in the yard, armed."

Hayden peered through the scope of his rifle. "Nothing up front. There is plywood over the glass doors. And the windows are boarded up with something too, though that doesn't mean they're not watching."

"You sure the angle is good?" Ivan asked.

Hayden looked at me.

I eyed the front drive and the large sign that said "Eastmoore State Hospital" once more and nodded.

"She's sure," Hayden said.

"Alright. We'll be waiting. Get down fast."

"We know," Hayden assured him. He clipped the walkie-talkie to his belt. Still hidden in the safety of a garden shed and several overgrown, untrimmed bushes, Hayden and I suited up, slipping the bullet proof vests over our heads. "Is it ok?" he asked, voicing my worry that the vest would constrict my movements.

I stretched my arms up. "It's fine. Uncomfortable more than anything."

"Good," he said and adjusted the strap of his M16. He was covered head to toe in weapons and his pockets were weighted down with extra ammo. I buckled the quiver around my torso so that it would stay snug in place as we ran. Along with the bow and arrows, I had an M9 strapped to my thigh, a knife attached to my boot, and a pouch of ammo sitting close to my body under the quiver.

I extracted a specific arrow and carefully laid it on the ground next to our collection of Molotov cocktails. I took the lighter from my pocket and clicked it, testing the flame. I tipped my head up and squinted at the sun. I closed my eyes and took a deep breath. As I slowly exhaled, I attempted to relax my muscles. It didn't work. Nevertheless, I straightened up, looked at Hayden, and said, "Let's do this."

He nodded and opened the door to the Mustang. He plugged an iPod into the modernized stereo system and got into the car. We had spent hours searching through Hayden's collection of MP3 players until we found one that had the perfect sequence of songs. He turned the volume all the way up; the soft and gentle sound of rain falling into a lake floated peacefully from the bomb-ridden car. Meant to be played on a loop, after just two minutes the relaxing meditation tract would cut to some loud and obnoxious rap song with tons of base.

Hayden drove the car out from behind the security of the shed, pointing it directly at the main entrance of the hospital. He attached a crude device we had rigged up to the steering wheel, essentially locking it in place. He backed out of the car, careful to use the door as a shield as he shoved a small rock under the gas pedal. We didn't want the thing to barrel into the building; it had taken just a few trials to find a properly-sized rock that would keep the pedal from literally hitting the metal.

Next, he put half of a brick on top of it and ducked out. That brick was tied to another brick that would act as an anchor. Hayden rushed over to where I was standing and watched as the black classic car quickly accelerated.

The anchor brick jerked forward when the rope attaching reached its limit. As expected, it jumped and skipped along the uneven ground for several yards before catching on a clump of weeds. The half brick inside the car was yanked off the pedal and loudly clanked against the door. Going too fast to automatically slow down, the rope snapped and the Mustang continued forward, its tires rolling along the drive.

When it began to lose speed, Hayden and I raced through the lawn and dodged behind the large, brick and cement sign. The switch from the inaudible gentle rain to the ear popping rattle of the base startled me even though I knew it was coming.

I peered around the sign. A window cut in the plywood put up around the front doors flew open. There was an indiscernible flash of movement from inside the hospital. The car bumped into the cement stairs that led into the lobby.

Only a second later the doors burst open and four guys ran out, guns in hand. I heard someone yell the name "Cutter" and lower his gun. He stopped beside the car and tipped his head in confusion. He shouted something and two more guys joined him. They crowded around the car, no doubt trying to frantically figure out why there was a dead body in the passenger seat of their friend's car. It annoyed me that no one was smart enough to immediately reach in and cut the zombie-calling music.

It would be off soon enough. I shuffled around in the grass, trying to keep my head out of sight until I was completely ready. I strung the arrow and closed my eyes, feeling the way the breeze blew my hair around my face. When I opened them, Hayden was looking at me, his face reassuring. He held his lighter in one hand and put the other against the sign, ready to spring up.

I backed away from the small square of cement and pulled back the arrow, turning so Hayden could light it on fire. Hayden unfolded the fire blanket and draped it over his shoulders like a cape. We weren't right next to the hospital, but since we had no idea of how big the blast would be, better safe than sorry seemed to be the only choice in the matter.

I sprang up and blew out my breath to steady myself. My eyes focused on the back of the Mustang; the rear windshield had been removed to allow my arrow to serve as the detonator. I heard the shouts when someone caught sight of me. But they were too late. I released the arrow and stood transfixed, watching it soar through the air in a perfect arc. My heart pounded in fear that it might miss. I reached behind me for another arrow just in case when Hayden pulled me down. He pressed his body over mine, covering us both with the fire proof material just as the arrow landed in its targeted destination.

My ears instantly rung and the shock of the explosion resonated across the lawn. If I had still been standing, I would have gotten knocked off of my feet. Hayden bent his head down; his face pressed into my neck. I squeezed my eyes shut when a wave of heat passed over us and was too scared to breathe. Hayden tightened his hold on me. Even though the initial blast was over, things were far from finished.

EMILY GOODWIN

Brick crumbled from the building as part of the lobby collapsed. Hayden let out a deep breath and rolled off of me. He sprang to his feet and pulled me up. With only one quick glance at the ruined front of Eastmoore, he took off across the lawn, heading back to the shelter of the shed. I got to my feet just as quickly but felt hypnotized as I gaped at the destroyed building. Unlike Hayden, the only real life explosions I had seen had been small and controlled. Awe, sickness, and terror pulsed through my body.

There was nothing left of the Mustang. There were no people standing around it. The entire main entrance was reduced to nothing but a smoldering pile of twisted metal and crumbled brick, exposing the interior of the hospital. I had no idea there would be so much black, billowing smoke and that the smell of the explosion would choke me as much as it did.

"Riss!" Hayden shouted. I snapped my attention to him and darted across the lawn. He pulled me to him at the same time that he spoke into the walkie-talkie. "Phase One complete," he said.

"Kinda obvious," Wade said back. "The guys back here took off when they heard the explosion. They left the door open."

"Coming your way," Hayden spoke and stuck the walkie back onto his belt. "Ivan," he said and then paused for a second. "Status?"

"We're in the basement," he whispered. "We can hear them running around shouting. It sounds like pure panic."

"Good," I said quietly to myself. I turned my head and watched the black smoke continue to rise into the air. Forcing myself to look away, I grabbed a gas can and splashed gasoline onto the shed. Hayden grabbed the rest of our supplies and we took off. When we were a safe enough distance away, Hayden lit a Molotov cocktail and threw it, causing a small explosion that was followed by the shed catching fire. We used the flames and smoke to mask our escape. We had several yards to run in the open lawn. We stayed side by side and not even I dared to steal a look behind me.

The rapid fire of machine guns ripped through the air. I didn't think they were aiming directly at us, but my heart leapt out of my chest. Adrenaline rushed through me and we picked up the pace, not stopping until we were in the drainage ditch that ran alongside the state hospital's property line. I stumbled down the steep edge, ungracefully moving over the uneven ground. We crouched down in the tall weeds, panting.

"You alright?" Hayden asked.

"Yeah. You?"

"I'm fine." He turned around and grinned. "That was kinda awesome."

"Yeah it was," I agreed. "I hope Dre was one of the guys who got blown up."

"Dre's the guy that beat you, right?" he asked and I nodded. "I don't. That was too quick of a death for him. He needs to pay for what he did." His face turned serious. "I mean it, Riss. No one hurts you and gets away with it."

I smiled at Hayden. "And to think, some girls prefer chocolates and flowers. I'll take swearing vengeance on my enemies any day."

He returned the smile and pushed himself onto his hands and knees and began to crawl forward. We were still quite a distance from the greenhouses that we sought shelter in during our last go around with the residents of Eastmoore, and even farther from Wade and Jason.

Flames crackled behind us and the voices of angry men floated through the air. Someone pulled back on the trigger of a high powered rifle; bullets sprayed into the breeze. One hit the ground a few feet in front of us, causing a small cloud of dirt and dust to burst into the chaos. My muscles tensed and I momentarily froze before flattening myself to the ground. My arms covered my head as more bullets rained down around us.

I clenched my jaw and watched in spellbound horror as each bullet narrowly missed us. If we stayed flat in the center of the ditch, we wouldn't get hit. Well, that was considering that the shooters stayed a good distance away from us. But maybe they had seen us and were coming closer. I pressed my face into the dirt and tangled my fingers around a clump of grass, closing my hand into a fist so tight it ripped the roots out of the ground. I let go of my bow and moved my right arm back, my fingers closing around my pistol.

And then it stopped. The bang of shots being fired still echoed around us. But the shooter swept his weapon back across the lawn, not aiming at anything in particular. Hayden brought his body up and moved forward. I hooked my arm through my bow and pushed myself up onto my elbows. Painstakingly, we moved inch by inch. The grass and weeds were taller and drier than the last time I'd crashed through them; the fronts of my arms were scraped already.

"All set," Wade's voice came over the walkie. "Take cover if you're close." I stopped behind Hayden and began counting down in my head. I tipped my head up as much as I deemed safe and waited for the explosion.

Wade and Jason were hidden somewhere behind the hospital, working on the second phase of our plan. While everyone was distracted by the bomb in the front of the building, it had allowed them to sneak into the parking lot where the guys kept their cars.

Jason used bolt cutters to snip and weaken the chain link fence the people of Eastmoore had added to protect their vehicles, as well as the employee entrance to the facility from zombies. He clipped a straight line every few feet; it wouldn't take much for even a small herd to push through and claw at the door to the hospital.

While Jason was busy with that, Wade carefully inserted gasoline soaked ropes and rags into the fuel tanks of almost every car parked there. He had run the ropes to the back of the lot and poured a line of gas along the fence. The plan was then to place a second rope in that line of gasoline and drag it away from the fence and into the lawn. The entire thing was a giant spider web of highly flammable webbing.

Once their task was done, Wade was going to light the rope and watch it burn, taking shelter before the fire struck the vehicles. I kept my eyes on the sky and waited. A fly landed on the back of my neck, its legs itching and tickling, but I didn't dare move.

"There's a car down the road!" someone shouted not too far behind us. I couldn't help the evil grin that took over my face. There were three zombies and a propane tank inside the silver Mazda we had intentionally left within sight. When they shot at the zombies, the tank would most likely get hit and explode. "Let's get 'em!" a different voice yelled.

"Go right ahead, fuckers," I said under my breath. Hayden laughed and turned his head, flashing me a wicked smile. I thought of what those guys did to me, to Rider, to Hayden, to Jon and his wife, and the countless other innocent people they had, no doubt, preyed upon. And that *wasn't* mentioning all of Dre's victims before the virus hit. This lawless world was his playground, and it made me sick.

The first of the car bombs went off. Instinctively, Hayden and I ducked our heads. Another went off just seconds later, followed by a series of loud booms. We crept forward, taking advantage the distraction it was to have things exploding all around us. The people behind us screamed in panic and fear. It was hard to make out what they were specifically saying, but I was sure I heard several threaten to rip us apart when they caught us.

"I see it," Hayden whispered after we had covered more ground through the ditch. "Just a few more yards." I let out a breath of relief when the black box came into view. Wade and Jason had left it there to be our visual clue of when to climb out of the ditch. Hayden propped himself up and looked around. "Come on," he encouraged and held his hand out behind him. Since I was holding my bow, Hayden wrapped his fingers around my wrist and helped me to my feet. We stayed low as we hiked up the short yet steep incline.

"Heads up," Hayden spoke into the walkie.

"We can see you," Wade responded. Hayden and I darted through tumbles of weeds and grass. I jumped over a decaying zombie body and my heart suddenly felt like it was splashed in cold water at the same time the heat of fear burned my cheeks.

Rider's body had been left out here. Left for the elements to toy with. Would there be anything left? Would we even recognize the pile of soggy material and bones—all that was left of him? I shook the horrible thought away and focused on the present. We crashed through the trees; little branches snagged at my hair and face. We came to an abrupt stop when Jason and Wade appeared before us.

"Nice job with the explosion," Jason told me with a grin.

"Same to you," I panted and returned his smile. "Ready?"

The corners of his lips pulled up once again but I could tell he was scared shitless. And I couldn't blame him; despite my rage and desire for vengeance, I was scared too.

"I couldn't get a count but I'd guess half a dozen people ran out to the parking lot after the explosion," Wade informed us.

"Just as many, if not more, are out front," I said and adjusted my quiver around my back. "They bought the car decoy."

"Excellent." Wade turned away and held a pair of binoculars to his eyes. "Looks as clear as it will get. It's go time."

I took a second to look each of my friends in the eyes, knowing all too well that this could easily go south for us, as we could be walking into a trap. Hayden led the way out of the trees. We crossed through the bramble of the untended wild life until we got to the hospital yard. Jason had already clipped us a way in; he held back the chain link so we could sneak through.

The four of us sprinted under a swing set; the chains from the swings had been removed and the yellow, flexible plastic seats were tossed to the side. There were several picnic tables and benches set up around what once had been a well-kept garden. A creepy statue of an angel with a broken wing stood in the center, with her head turned up and her arms spread open.

My eyes latched onto the open door in front of us. The hallway was dark inside the hospital. The thought of the unknown terrified as much as it excited me. I swallowed hard and tightened my grip on the bow, my fingers ready to pull back an arrow and fire it into the heart of our enemy. Two glass panels sat on either side of the door. It was the kind of glass that had wire in between the panes; I was sure it would be hard to physically break, but I doubted its ability to stop a bullet.

We paused outside the door for a brief moment. When no one came screaming and shooting at us, we entered the hospital. Hayden and Wade held their rifles up to their eyes and moved with trained grace. I looped the bow over my shoulder and held out my pistol, face set and muscles steady. Jason's jaw was clenched and his fingers wrapped around the bottom of his machine gun so hard his knuckles were losing circulation.

A cheerful rainbow colored mural was painted on the wall to our left. A closed door labeled 'day room' was on the opposite side. There was another hall joining the one we were in, forming a 'T'. We silently eased our way into the building. I reached the end of the wall first and paused at the corner.

A dome mirror was stuck to the wall. I squinted as I tried to make out the dark shapes. One was tan and blue and looked slightly human. We waited and watched, but it didn't move. I stepped away from the wall, prepared to turn and continue when someone jumped in front of us.

He was brandishing a high powered rifle and opened his mouth to call out a final warning before he killed us all when his eyes met mine. He swept his gaze up and down my body, lingering two seconds too long on my breasts, which were uncomfortably squished together by the bulletproof vest.

His name was Joe, and he had been one of the few people I was lucky enough to have interacted with during my short stay at Eastmoore. His mouth fell open and his hold on the gun sagged.

"Hayden," he spat out, too dumbstruck by my reappearance

to notice the three, highly armed men behind me.

I tipped my head and flashed him a flirty smile before I bent my body back and hit him. My fist smashed into his face and I used my shoulder to knock the rifle from his hands. A shot rang out when it clattered to the floor.

As if the loud noise snapped him out of his daze, Joe brought his fist through the air. I ducked out of the way and his fingers cracked against the cement wall behind me. Hayden caught him and threw him into the wall, delivering two hard blows to his stomach. He brought his knee up in between Joe's legs and punched him in the face.

Joe reached behind him and brought his arm up, pointing a small hand gun in Hayden's face. The movement was fast and desperate, but Hayden was faster. My ears rang from the shot and I watched Joe slide down the wall, leaving a smear of blood trailing down behind him.

I bent over to pick up the rifle that Joe had been holding. It was an M4 Carbine and I admired the custom quad rail system. I put my pistol in my holster and claimed the rifle as my own.

"How the hell do they know Hayden?" Jason asked his brown eyes wide.

"They don't," I answered. "They think my name is Hayden."

"Why?"

"My tags," Hayden answered for me and I nodded.

Joe pounded frantically on the door.

"Let's go," Hayden continued. He grabbed the walkie-talkie from his belt and pressed the button. "We're in. We entered through a south door; we're not deep into the building yet."

"We've been waiting for you, Underwood," Ivan's smooth voice came over the device. "We are at the top of the stairs ready for some action."

"We're coming your way."

"It got quiet in here," Ivan told us. "Pure chaos for a while. Now there is almost nothing."

"I'll take it as a good sign," Hayden said and put the walkie away. "Do you recognize anything, Riss?"

I shook my head and walked down the hall. "No. I know I was on a lower level because I had to go up stairs to get to the main level. I was *questioned* in a room there. And we had to go up the same stairs to get out. I know we left through the yard but we didn't come in that same door."

"This place is fucking big," Wade swore. "We might not get to where you were."

"That's fine with me," I told them. "It was a seclusion room anyway. There was nothing useful in that hall."

"There should be a map," Jason started. "Places like this have to have them. You know, an evacuation map."

"He's right," I said and felt slightly dumb for not thinking about it before. I closed my eyes in a long blink as I thought. "They are in hallways, I think. Or anywhere near an exit that gets a lot of traffic."

"Then we need to keep going," Hayden instructed. We moved down the hall, the light thinning, the farther we went. Wade stopped and flipped a light switch on and off several times.

"They didn't restore that generator," he guessed. "The power must still be off on this side of the building."

"Good," I said. "The magnetic locks stopped working when the power went out. It must be a fire safety thing or something," I guessed. "When the backup power cut out, even the seclusion door opened."

"What would they do if it stormed?" Jason wondered out loud.

"That's what the generators were for," Hayden reminded him. "They are running this place on an energy system that was only meant to be used for emergencies. And it's completely working in our favor."

He slowly pushed open a thick, wooden door.

There were no windows in this hall. Hayden clicked on the light attached to his rifle and shone the yellow beam in front of us. Garbage surrounded a chair that was pushed up against a wall. The air stank of stale coffee and urine. Closed wooden doors with small windows centered in them lined either side of the hall. Wade put his flashlight up to one and peered inside.

"Bedrooms," he told us. "Well, if you can even consider it that."

We continued down the hall of rooms and stopped behind another closed door, though this one locked with a key instead of a magnet. I already had my lock picking equipment ready. I fished it out of my small bag; it had of course fallen down to the very bottom and was buried by ammo. Hayden pointed the light on the lock. I set my bow down and got to work.

Moments later we emerged into a nurses' station. It had been swept clean of all medical supplies and the small closet marked 'med room' had been raided. There was another door on the other side; we crossed through it and exited, ending up in another hall.

"This place is a fucking maze," I complained and pushed away the anxiety it was causing.

"I think we're in a closed unit," Hayden assured me. "Once we get out it will be easier to figure out where we are. Or at least I'm banking on it."

"It makes sense," Wade said and held up the flashlight, illuminating fingerpainted pictures done by residents. Held in place only by tape, the edges were peeling off the walls and rolling inward. Gunfire echoed from outside. We all froze, taking on a defensive stance.

"You guys alright?" Ivan's voice came over the walkie.

"Yes," Wade answered. "Still making our way in."

"Copy that."

There was another large door not far in front of us. It seemed as promising as any to be the door that exited the unit. Next to that door was a large silver frame with a Plexiglas front holding back a map. Hayden put his finger on the small red dot that gave us our current location. He was right; we were in the "south unit" of Eastmoore.

"We're on the first floor," Hayden spoke. "It looks like the center of the building has a cafeteria, activities room, therapists' offices, and a visitation room." He traced his finger around the cluster of black lines. "Administration is up front."

"And there are more units upstairs. This unmarked section," I said and leaned close to Hayden to point at a long rectangle that jutted out from the first floor. "Must be the ward for the criminals."

Hayden moved his hand to the left. "And there is a basement, though it looks like only half of it is used. This empty area has to be for the boilers and laundry rooms."

I looked at the map and tried to remember my walk from the seclusion room upstairs. It was dark and I hadn't been paying attention to where I was going. My attention was focused more on not dying. But I did recall the smell of musk and the clammy air. The seclusion rooms must be in the basement. I turned around to voice all that to Hayden when a very loud bang made us all jump.

"What the hell was that?" I asked. My heart felt like it could beat right out of my chest. Nervous sweat dripped down my back and my calves ached from resisting the urge to bolt into the hospital and open fire on everyone, ending this once and for all.

No one breathed as we waited. Hayden slowly let out his breath and shook his head. He turned back to the map and studied it for a minute longer before putting his hand on the metal handle. The door creaked open and the light from the flashlight weakly illuminated the base of a staircase. The door clicked shut after we stepped through. Sunlight filtered through a small, dirty window.

Suddenly, gunfire rang out. A bullet whizzed past me. Jason grabbed the handle and pulled; the door didn't budge. It was locked from the inside. Hayden and Wade acted on instinct and fired back. I jumped back and hit the wall, my eyes darting wildly around. Another shot fired. Four guys popped up from the stairwell their bodies kept safe by the cinderblock half wall, triggers pulled back. And there we were, standing in the open like walking targets. Hayden, Wade, and I dove to the ground. I extended my arms and fired the M4, knowing that my aim was nowhere near accurate.

The guys stormed down the stairs. Hayden grabbed my arms and pulled me behind a red, leather couch. Wade bumped into me as he scrambled to safety. I flipped an oak coffee table up and Wade helped me shove it up to the couch, creating a better barrier for us. My eyes widened in terror when I realized that Jason had stayed rooted in his spot out of fear.

"Jason!" I shouted and pulled back the trigger. His head jerked to the right and his body jerked toward us. He took a running step away, but not before shots from a machine gun peppered the wall behind him. A single cry of pain escaped from his lips and he collapsed onto the floor.

CHAPTERTWENTY—FOUR

"Jason!" I shouted again and scrambled up, fingers gripping the overstuffed leather. My nails dug into the cushion. Hayden pushed me down and popped up, firing at the stairs. Bullets ricocheted off the metal railing in a haze of smoke and sparks.

With my face twisted in terror, I stared at Jason's body, lying perfectly still on the ground. A pang of grief and guilt rushed through me, but it was quickly replaced by rage. Wade turned around and crawled away from the couch. Using a bit more caution, I rested the M4 against the couch and shot through the back. Bits of leather and stuffing flew into the air.

The door across from the stairs burst open and three more people ran in. My stomach lurched in horror. Jason lay on the floor, bleeding, while the three of us cowered behind a couch. We were surrounded. I felt like we were sitting ducks in the diner all over again.

"Get your lighter!" Hayden shouted to me and reached into one of the pockets of the camo military issued pants he was wearing. He madly unscrewed a lid on a glass bottle and shoved a piece of torn cloth inside, leaving only a few inches hanging out.

My eyes met his in a fleeting moment and I clicked my lighter. Hayden held the bottle up and the rag instantly caught on fire. He bent his arm back, careful not to spill the explosive liquid, and threw the cocktail. As soon as I heard the glass break I darted up, aimed and fired. Someone on the stairs let out a high pitched scream before tumbling down.

It all happened at once; the bottle exploded upon impact and the powdered laundry detergent splattered out into globby fireballs. The woman I had shot came tumbling down the stairs, her body crashing into another and knocking him off balance. The splotches of fire sizzled and popped. It had missed hitting our enemies but gave Wade the chance to duck out from behind the couch and grab Jason's arm. He heaved him back to us. I turned my head and almost shrieked in shock when Jason's eyes flew open. My initial thought was that he had turned and was waking up dead and we had to kill him. Blood dripped down his face. He blinked it away and gave us a weak smile.

"It's just grazed," Wade mumbled and ran his finger over Jason's head. "Holy fuck it just missed you," he said to Jason. He yanked him closer to the base of the couch. Screams of panic and anger came from the guys shooting at us as they dodged around the fire. Hayden and I broke apart and rose up in unison, shooting at the guys across from us.

They fired back and the bullet ridden couch collapsed. Someone scrambled from the door, quickly moving to where we huddled on the floor. Hayden twisted and fired, clipping the guy on the shoulder. He cried out in pain and fell back, his weapon flying from his hand. Hayden whipped around and fired off a couple more rounds.

Suddenly, the gunfire increased. Hayden ducked down to avoid getting hit. Wade leaned over Jason and picked up his gun, shoving a new clip in place. Then someone else screamed. With wide eyes and a hammering heart, I stole a glance over the couch. A body fell to the base of the stairs and someone fled out the open door. They didn't get too far before a bullet lodged in the base of their neck, causing their body to go rigid before face planting into the ground. My eyes swept to the other side of the room. Ivan and Brock stood in the threshold.

"You guys alright?" Brock asked and rushed forward.

"Jason's hit," Wade answered as he looked around. The air smelled like burned flesh, gun powder, and blood. "It grazed him."

Hayden moved around and grasped Ivan's shoulder. "Good timing," he panted.

"When we heard the shots and you didn't respond over the walkie, we knew you were in trouble," Ivan said casually and flashed a magnificent smile.

"Let's go," I said and looked through the door. "Before more come."

"Let them," Ivan said with a cocky grin.

"She's right," Brock agreed. "Any idea where to go?"

"Just out?" Jason suggested. He grunted as Wade helped him to his feet. "We've done enough damage, haven't we?"

"They can still kill us on our way out," Hayden said. "It's not over yet."

"And he's right," Brock agreed again.

"Then this way," Ivan said and motioned toward the door that the shooters came from. I picked up my bow that I had dropped and awkwardly shoved it over my shoulders. The M4 was empty but I didn't want to discard a weapon with so much detailing. Wade took it from me, saying I had enough crap strapped to my body already.

We left the stairwell and passed through a set of double doors. The rooms in this hall had to be offices; some still bore the signs with the therapists' names on the door. Not taking any chances, we looked in every one. Ivan and Brock stayed in formation as they inspected each room ahead of us on the right. Wade hung back with Jason and Hayden and I took the left side.

Something small and metal dropped to the ground and rolled to a stop. We froze. I inclined my head to the room in front of us. Hayden's eyes met mine and he gave me a slight nod. My index finger hovered over the trigger. I swallowed hard and let out a breath of adrenaline-fueled excitement. I tucked my elbows into my sides and hid behind the doorframe.

On a mental count of three, I spun around, arms out and gun raised. The office had been transformed into bedroom, complete with a canopy bed and a tall, wooden armoire adorned with jewelry. The décor looked as if it had been puked out of a pink, sparkly monster that was notorious for his bad, over-the-top taste.

I could only think of one person who would have an overly ostentatious and girly room like this during the fucking zombie apocalypse. My lips pulled back into a snarl when I looked at her. Kisha looked up from the bag she was packing and screamed. She automatically raised a gun and fired at me. I ducked back behind the wall, but not before I caught the horror of recognition on her face. I stuck my arm out and blindly shot into the room. I heard her heels click on the smooth tile. I flipped back around and fired again. She ran into what I thought was a closet. With no hesitation I took off after her, knowing Hayden was right behind me. The closet turned out to be a back door that led into a narrow hall. I sprinted down it, following the snap of her shoes on the hard floor.

I fired three more times as she ran around a corner. I pulled the trigger again and realized I was out of ammo. I shoved the gun back into the holster as I sprinted after her, sliding as I slowed. My hands slapped the wall and I pushed off, shooting myself around the corner. I reached behind me and wrapped my fingers around the slick shaft of an arrow, yanking it out in one swift motion. Kisha dove into a room marked 'exams'. I was only a step behind her. I flew in, pulling my bow off my shoulder and getting ready to shoot.

"Well I'll be damned," a male voice spoke. I didn't have to see the snaggled, yellow teeth or his overly tattooed skin to know that Dre stood just feet in front of me. "Long time no see, Hayden," he jeered.

Kisha laughed and smiled triumphantly, thinking they had me cornered. "How *dumb*," she giggled. "Come back for another go 'round, bitch? We ain't scared of you!"

Hayden stepped in behind me. "What about me?"

Dre made a move for his gun. I let the arrow go; it pierced his bicep. Kisha screamed and jumped away. Her hands flew to her hair, which was braided along her scalp and gathered into a high pony tail. Different colored clip-in extensions mixed into her spiral curls. Dre dropped his weapon and fell to the ground.

"Fucking bitch!" he shouted as he writhed in pain. "I will kill you!"

"Are these the guys?" Hayden asked me. I nodded and slowly pulled out another arrow. I strung it along my bow and pointed it at Kisha. Hayden stepped closer to Dre, angling the gun to point in his face.

"Wait!" Kisha cried. "Wait! I-I'll give you anything. We'll give you anything!"

"Can you bring back my friend you killed?" I said through gritted teeth. "Or give me back the time it took me to heal after you beat me?" My eyes flicked to Hayden. "Can you take back the bullet that almost killed him?" I shook my head and glared at her. "I didn't think so." I edged closer. "How many other people have you killed? You both are so pathetic. You're not smart enough to survive. If you didn't murder your way through life, you wouldn't be here."

Her eyes flashed with fear when the rest of my friends showed up in the doorway. Dre scrambled to snatch his gun; Hayden kicked it out of the way and stepped on his fingers.

"Please," she pleaded. "I'll give you anything!"

"You have nothing we want!" I shouted.

"Just you wait," Dre threatened and tugged at the arrow.

Hayden kicked him in the ribs. "My boys will be here any second."

"No they won't," Hayden said calmly. "I killed them," he said each word slowly.

Ivan stepped into the room. His dark eyes were set and his large frame had an air of intimidation. "Why the hell would your boys come rescue your pussy asses? You're up here hiding. You don't give a shit about them and they don't give a shit about you. And that's where we got you. You mess with one of us, you mess with all of us." He shoved a new clip into his gun and stopped behind me.

The sadistic smile on my face broke out of its own accord. I stared down Kisha, feeling like a hungry cat that had cornered a fat mouse. She fell to her knees and threw her hands up, begging for her life. And then I suddenly realized that I was sick of this. Sick of death, sick of dying. Sick of the bloodshed, the fear, the violence of what our lives had become. I didn't want to kill her as much as I didn't want her to live.

"Uh, guys," Brock said, his voice wavering. "His boys are here." I was only vaguely aware of what Brock was saying. My heartbeat pounded in my ears and I could feel my pulse pound through my fingertips as they precariously held back the arrow. Without taking my eyes off Kisha, I was able to sense Ivan turn around. He surreptitiously nudged me with his elbow. I was so focused on what was going on in front of me that I almost didn't hear the distant sounds of the undead shuffling. We had known that the explosions would serve as zombie attractions. I just hadn't expected them to get here so fast.

And I couldn't have been happier about it.

"Hayden," I spoke. "He's right. His boys are here."

"I don't give a fuck," Hayden spat, his anger directed toward Dre. He shook his head and kicked him again.

"We better go before they *eat* us alive," I stressed. Finally getting it, Hayden put his foot on Dre's gun and kicked it back. It skidded to a stop in front of me; Ivan bent over and picked it up. He pressed the release and caught the magazine as it slid out and stuffed it in his pants pocket. Then, in a matter of seconds, he disassembled it and threw the pieces on the ground. Hayden reached down, took and handful of Dre's shirt and punched him in the face before spinning around and linking his arm through mine.

Brock led the way, taking us in the opposite direction from the way we had come. The zombies had entered the hospital from the open back door. We had no idea how many had gotten in, let alone where they were in the hospital.

Dre and Keisha's screams answered that. We picked up the pace, running through another lounge. A sign that read 'Main Lobby' hung ahead of us like a mirage. We were almost there when an S2 staggered out from behind a desk. Her hands wrapped around Jason's arm.

He jerked back and stumbled, falling over and pulling her with him. I got to them first and yanked the undead bitch off of Jason. My fists closed around hair so grimy it felt like I was grasping seaweed. I pulled her back and threw her down. I grabbed the knife from my boot and shoved it into her forehead.

The six of us pressed forward, only stopping when we got to the front entrance. I looked around in awe of the damage. Parts of the building still smoldered. The glass in the windows was gone, reduced to nothing more than small shards. Even the metal frames that once held it in place were warped and twisted. The doors had been blown off the hinges and part of the exterior wall was missing.

Something crashed behind us. I whirled around only to face an encroaching herd. Their pace quickened when they caught sight of us. My hand flew up but stopped at my shoulder. There were too fucking many. We needed out; we would be cornered in the lobby fighting a losing battle.

"Riss!" Hayden shouted and frantically waved me forward. The other guys had already begun their trek over the uneven ground. Hayden took my hand to help me over the rubble. I wrinkled my nose in disgust at the scent of charred flesh. A piece of blackened metal caught on my boot; I hopped over it and landed on something extra crispy that crunched under my foot.

The steps leading to the front lawn had been destroyed. We picked our way around, knowing that simply jumping would promise a twisted ankle at the minimum. I tossed my bow onto the soot covered grass and grasped a ragged piece of brick, using it to steady myself as I crossed a jumbled pile of rubble. A blackened part of the Mustang's chrome bumper sat a few feet in front of me.

I pushed off the building and ungracefully waded through the remaining few feet of sharp and hot particles of brick. I let out a breath when my feet finally touched level ground. Once Hayden was next to me, I picked up the bow and jogged several yards away from Eastmoore before stopping.

Our entire group turned around and surveyed the state hospital. Smoke billowed from the back and the bricks still smoldered in the front. I could see the flicker of movement from the zombies as they struggled to cross over the rubble. They toppled over each other and the ones in the front became pinned to the ground as the others attempted to push themselves up. A young female S2 dragged her body to the ledge and tumbled off. One of her feet caught and she dangled from the ruined porch, snarling and reaching for us.

"Holy shit," I breathed. Hayden put his arm around me. "We did it." I turned my head from side to side, having to look at each of my friends' faces twice to be sure that we had all made it out alive. Jason wiped away the blood from his temple; the bullet had missed his brain by only tenths of an inch. All he had to show for it was a small tear in his skin. The edges were red and raw from the heat. It was no doubt painful, but it wasn't anything life threatening. "Let's get the fuck out of here."

Hayden tightened his arm around my waist. "Yes," he agreed. "Let's go home."

CHAPTER TWENTY—FIVE

Hannah was waiting at the gate for us, which she pulled open as soon as we came into view. Hayden and I got out of the backseat of the Range Rover. I looked around and subconsciously smiled when I saw the horse grazing near the house.

"How did it go? Did you kill them? Are we safe?" Hannah bombarded Hayden with questions as she threw her arms around her brother. Hayden hugged her back before gently pushing her away.

"It went as well as we could have hoped, yes, and yes," he answered. "Everything good here?"

"Yeah," she replied and rested her broken wrist against her chest. "And we packed everything except food for tonight. Are we still leaving in the morning?"

Hayden sighed and looked at me. Though the six of us were worn out and tired, we decided that we wanted to leave tonight and get this whole situation over with—for good. "We're leaving in an hour."

"An hour?" she exclaimed.

Hayden nodded. "We want to eat and then go home. This mission has gone on long enough."

Hannah moved her head up and down. I stepped around the SUV and stood next to Hayden. Jim, Agatha, and Lori emerged from the house, grinning when they saw us. Jim came over to Hayden and held out his hand.

"I asked and He answered," Jim said as he shook Hayden's hand. "Is it done?"

"Done and over with," Hayden replied, smiling back at the pastor.

"We're leaving soon," Hannah blurted. "Instead of tomorrow

morning."

Jim released Hayden's hand and looked at Hannah. "Good. I am anxious to get to safety—real safety."

"So are we," I said softly. I wanted to go home, talk to Raeya and do absolutely nothing for the next twenty four hours. It was the first time I was looking forward to being in the quarantine room.

"Well," Jim said. "I will let the others know. Thank you," he added after he stepped away. "For everything."

Hayden shrugged off the compliment. "It's what we do." He smiled and nodded before turning to me.

"Hannah," Jim called. "Why don't you come in and help me take things out to the car."

"Ok," she agreed and followed him into the house. I knew Hannah couldn't be much help with her broken wrist; Jim only asked her to come inside so she would leave us alone.

"Go inside and have someone clean your cut," Ivan told Jason as he opened the back of the Range Rover. Jason nodded and slowly walked inside, looking slightly bewildered that we had made it out alive. Wade chuckled and shook his head.

"I don't know if he's gonna want to go back out with us after this," he said.

I smiled. "I hope not."

"He did a good job, though," Wade reminded me. "You were a little rusty on your first mission," he teased.

Acting offended, I scoffed at him. "Me? I'm never anything but awesome!" I laughed.

"Oh yeah," Brock joked and made a deal of rolling his eyes. I smiled again before turning to the SUV. We quickly reorganized our weapons and carefully stashed away the extra Molotov cocktails for the journey home. Hayden and I unhitched the horse trailer from the old truck and hooked it to his truck. I spent a few minutes getting the trailer ready for Sundance's journey home while Hayden took the gas from the old truck.

Madison and Ryan carried bags of their belongings outside. Since we were down the Yukon, everyone was going to have to cram together for the drive home. I opened the door to the trailer's tack room and tossed out anything that wasn't necessary, creating space for their stuff.

Once everything was loaded, everyone sat outside in the shade and ate. We distributed the food and water and got into our cars. Sundance watched with curiosity and nervously edged closer, as if he was afraid of being left behind. I picked up his halter and lead rope and walked over to him. He lowered his head for me as I slipped the red halter over his ears.

"You'll be happy at your new home," I told him. "You're the only horse so you will get lots of attention." I gave him a handful of cereal before walking him into the trailer. "See ya soon, Big Guy," I said to him when I closed the trailer door and jogged to the gate. I opened both doors and waited as the cars drove through. We had decided to close the doors and keep this place free of zombies. It had served us well; maybe it would do the same for somebody else.

I climbed up the rope ladder and hopped into the passenger seat of Hayden's truck. I leaned back in the seat and sighed. I turned my head to look at Hayden. He met my eyes and smiled. At the same time, we reached over the middle and took each other's hands. I tipped my face toward the window and enjoyed the wind that blew through.

Part of me relaxed when the truck slowly turned off the dirt road and started the drive home. But the other part held onto fear that the closer we got to the finish line, the less likely we were to finish the race. I kept my fingers laced through Hayden's and my attention focused on the passing land, scouting for any signs of trouble. Eventually, the hyper-vigilance wore on me and I drifted into a light sleep.

* * *

I never thought the sight of Alex's face would ever be welcome. But when he emerged from the large, white doors of the brick estate, relief washed over me. We were home. We had done what we needed to do. It was over.

I stepped out of the truck and let out a huge sigh. I wanted to go inside, shower, sleep throughout the entire twenty-four hours that we had to spend in the quarantine room and then find Raeya and Padraic and sit in the overly crowded theatre room and watch a movie.

Two A3s walked over to us as well, directing the new residents were to go. Jones was among them. He gave me a bleak smile and avoided my eyes.

"We have a horse," I said, in case he hadn't gotten the radioed message.

He nodded. "I'll take care of it for you," he replied, still not looking at me. I raised an eyebrow at the oddity of his sudden lack of social skills but let it go, too tired to give a damn. I turned back to the truck and saw Hannah give Hayden a one-armed hug. The entire way home Hayden had debated on whether or not he should ask Fuller to give his sister a pass and let her stay in the quarantine room with us.

Hannah surprised me, and earned a few points in my book by saying it wasn't fair that she got special treatment over the others in her group just because of her brother. She said that as long as a doctor came out and took care of her broken wrist, she would be fine in the quarantine barn.

"I'll make sure Dr. Sheehan comes out to take care of you," Hayden promised her.

"Thanks," she said and released him from her embrace. "Love you, Hayden."

"You too," he said and walked with her into the barn. I knew he wanted to tell the others just how important she was to him. And even though she requested no special treatment, I knew she would get it whether she liked it or not.

"Penwell," Ivan called, his voice serious. I walked around the truck to find him, Brock, Jason, and Wade were gathered around Alex.

"What's going on?" I asked when I took in the sullen look on Alex's usually smug face.

"How was the mission," Alex asked, dismissing my question.

"Carried out, though not quite as planned," Brock stated. Concern was apparent on his face. Alex only nodded and the fact that he didn't ask for details made nerves bubble in my stomach. Jason stepped closer to me and crossed his arms. His dark eyes met mine in a questioning look and I shook my head, as if I would know anything more than him.

Alex kept his gaze focused on the barn, waiting for Hayden to return. Tension-filled minutes ticked by before he finally did. Automatically sensing the seriousness that had settled over the seven of us, Hayden rested his hand on my waist, too concerned to realize that Alex had yet to be informed of our couple status.

"I'm glad you guys came home in one piece," Alex said formally. His eyes flicked over our apparent injuries. "Though it looks like you've seen better days."

"We have," Wade said impatiently.

Alex nodded again. "I bet you're tired."

"We are," Brock and I said at the same time.

Alex nodded again and took a step toward the house. "Well, uh, I guess get yourselves settled into the quarantine room." He ran his hand over the back of his head and disappeared inside. The six of us quietly shuffled after him and went up to our rooms to grab clean clothes to wear for the next twenty-four hours.

We all knew something was up. My mind raced as I thought of what it could be. Had zombies attacked while we were gone? Did they get our livestock or even worse, any residents? Despite the late hour, I was tempted to go to Raeya's room and make sure she was ok. I paused in the hall before darting down the stairs. I hurried to her room and carefully grasped the door knob. I gave it a small twist. Discovering it was unlocked, I cracked it open. The dim light from the hall spilled in, illuminating the room just enough for me to see that Raeya was tucked in her bed. I bit my lip but resisted calling out to her, deciding it wasn't necessary to wake her up.

I stopped by the kitchen only to find Brock, Jason, and Wade already in there, loading up their arms with snacks to get us through the night. The air conditioning kicked on and I shivered. I looked at my arms and smiled at the goosebumps that broke out across my skin. After the almost unbearable heat in Texas, I welcomed the chill.

We bickered like siblings on the way down to the underground quarantine room about who got to take the first shower. I tried to persuade everyone that since Hayden and I could shower together and save time, it made sense for us to go first. Jason suggested we draw numbers out of a bowl, which seemed to be the fairest route to take.

Wade punched in the access code into the key pad and pushed open the door. Jason spent a few seconds looking around the room in awe before stepping all the way in. I set my pile of clean clothes on the arm of the couch and walked into the kitchenette to get a piece of paper. I had gotten so far as ripping it into six little sections when the door opened.

Hector, Gabby's father and Fuller's unofficial assistant, stepped into the room. He smiled at us, though it was obvious he was unhappy by the way his eyes showed no emotion.

"Hayden," he said gently. "Can we talk for a moment?"

"Sure," Hayden replied and exited the room. I watched Brock and Ivan exchange baffled looks. It wasn't odd for Hayden to report to Fuller while the rest of us stayed in the quarantine room. It made sense, really. We knew that Hayden wouldn't get infected and go mad and we knew that Fuller thought of Hayden like a son. It *was* odd for Hector to come and get Hayden. I mentally shrugged. Maybe Fuller was sleeping?

I scribbled numbers down on the paper and folded each square in half before piling them on the counter. I drew first and, of course, picked the number six. I was holding off hope that the last piece left that was reserved for Hayden would be one or two, but he got stuck with the fourth shower.

I sat on the couch next to Wade and Jason. Though I was more than tired, being dirty and worried made me stay alert and awake enough to impatiently watch the minutes tick by as I waited for Hayden to return. By the time it was my turn for a shower, he still wasn't back. I let Jason go ahead of me, hoping that by the time he was done, my Marine would be here.

But he wasn't. I showered and changed into my pajamas, settling onto one of the two twin beds at the back of the quarantine room. I picked at the knots in my sopping wet hair, leaning over the edge so the water droplets would fall on the floor. When it was finally free of tangles, I flipped my head upside down and rubbed the towel over my long locks. My hair hadn't been this long in years; I was way overdue for a trimming.

I heard the high pitch beeping as someone punched in the pass code to the door. I looked up, expecting to see Hayden. Hector stepped in once more and scanned the room. When his eyes settled on me, he tipped his head down.

"Orissa," he said. "Can you join Hayden in Fuller's office?"

"Uh, sure," I said and stood, dropping the towel onto the floor. "Why?"

"He'll tell you when you get there," Hector told me. I hurried out of the room wondering what Fuller would want. I couldn't possibly be in trouble. My stomach lurched when the thought of Delmont and Beau entered my mind. Maybe the herd *hadn't* gotten them. What if they retaliated against the compound somehow? What would that do to Olivia? My bare feet slapped against the cold tile hall as I pushed myself into a jog, only slowing when the closed door of Fuller's office came into view. Without knocking, I let myself in.

Hayden was alone. He sat in Fuller's desk, slumped over in the chair with his head in his hands. He didn't look up when I walked in. My blood turned cold and a wave of unease washed over me with a dizzying effect.

"Hayden?" I called. I quietly clicked the door shut. "What's going on?" There were several pieces of paper unfolded on the desk in front of him, covered in messy black penmanship. My eyes focused on them as I neared Hayden. When I saw his name written at the top, I instantly recognized it as a very long, hand written letter. I wondered who it was from and why the words had brought so much angst to my usually stoic boyfriend.

"Where's Fuller?" I asked and stopped next to Hayden.

He took a slow, deep breath and pushed himself up. His hazel eyes were glossy and red. His eyebrows pushed together and he swallowed hard. "Fuller is dead."

"What?" I asked, though I had clearly heard him.

Hayden nodded. "He died two days after we left. Heart attack."

I blinked and shook my head, not knowing what to say. "But he was healthy," I blurted.

Hayden shook his head and tapped the letter. "Not always. He started having issues a few years ago. With meds, he was fine."

"We could have gotten him meds," I stated, confused and scared.

"Well we didn't and now he's dead!" Hayden shouted. He put his head in his hands. I bit my lip and blinked back tears. Though I'd never seen eye-to-eye with the man, I never, ever wanted anything bad to happen to Fuller. His death saddened me and it also scared me. What would happen to the compound? Fuller made sure everything ran smoothly. And, with over three hundred people, that wasn't an easy thing to do.

"I'm sorry," I whispered and put my hand on Hayden's shoulder. He raised his hand so fast I thought he was going to push me away, but he wrapped his fingers around my wrist and pulled me into his lap. He buried his face in my chest and I put my arms around him, hugging him tightly. "I'm so sorry," I said again.

"He knew," Hayden spoke, his voice muffled. "He knew he was dying and he didn't say anything." I ran my fingers through Hayden's hair, sensing his anger. "He got everything ready but didn't bother to fucking tell me anything!"

"It'll be ok," I soothed. "Not today, not tomorrow, but it will be. We will get through this together."

His arms tightened around me. "Fuller wanted you to know that he's sorry for being so hard on you. He respected you, Riss. He said he was only hard on you because he wanted you to be ready."

I leaned away from Hayden so I could look him in the eyes. "Ready for what?"

Hayden swiveled the chair around and slammed his fist on the letter. "Ready to help me run the compound. He wants me to take over."

"What? You?" I shook my head. "But—you...why?" I stuttered. It wasn't that I didn't think Hayden would be a good leader, because I knew he would be. It just didn't make sense. Hector worked closely with Fuller and stayed at the compound. He knew how to run things. He didn't go on missions. He should be the new leader.

"And me? Uh, no," I spat. "That is a horrible idea." I had a hard enough time not getting myself killed. How the hell was I supposed to manage several hundred people?

Hayden's shoulders sagged and he rested his head against my neck. I clung to him, the seriousness of the situation pulling me down into a spiraling dark tunnel of trepidation. "That's not all," he said so quietly that I almost didn't hear him.

"What is it?" I asked gently.

Hayden moved the papers aside, revealing a small, black and silver flash drive. "He left me this. I already watched it. In it he..." Hayden stopped and shook his head. "Fuller knew a lot more than he let on. After watching this..." he cut off and shook his head.

"Hayden?" I gently pushed. Fear built up in me with each pounding heart beat.

He took a breath and looked into my eyes. "I know how the virus started."

TO BE CONTINUED...

OTHER BOOKS BY EMILY GOODWIN

ABOUT THE AUTHOR

Emily Goodwin is the international best-selling author of the stand-alone novel STAY, The Guardian Legacies Series: UNBOUND, REAPER, MOONLIGHT (releasing 2014), The Beyond the Sea Series: BEYOND THE SEA, RED SKIES AT NIGHT (releasing 2015) and the award winning Contagium Series: CONTAGIOUS, DEATHLY CONTAGIOUS, CONTAGIOUS CHAOS, THE TRUTH IS CONTAGIOUS (Permuted Press).

Emily lives with her husband, daughter, and German Shepherd named Vader. Along with writing, Emily enjoys riding her horse, designing and making costumes, and Cosplay.

www.emilygoodwinbooks.com
facebook.com/emilygoodwinbooks

14

BY PETER CLINES

Padlocked doors. Strange light fixtures. Mutant cockroaches. There are some odd things about Nate's new apartment. Every room in this old brownstone has a mystery. Mysteries that stretch back over a hundred years. Some of them are in plain sight. Some are behind locked doors. And all together these mysteries could mean the end of Nate and his friends. Or the end of everything...

"A riveting apocalyptic mystery in the style of LOST."
—Craig DiLouie, author of *The Infection*

PETER CLINES

PERMUTEDPRESS.COM

DAY BY DAY ARMAGEDDON
GREY FOX
BY J.L. BOURNE

Time is a very fluid thing, no one really has a grasp on it other than maybe how to measure it. As the maestro of the Day by Day Armageddon Universe, I have the latitude of being in control of that time. You have again stumbled upon a ticket with service through the apocalyptic wastes, but this time the train is a little bit older, a little more beat up, and maybe a little wiser.

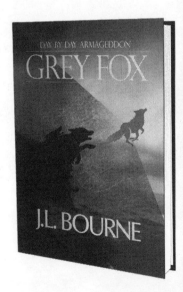

DAY BY DAY ARMAGEDDON
GREY FOX

J.L. BOURNE

DEAD TIDE
BY STEPHEN A. NORTH

THE WORLD IS ENDING. BUT THERE ARE SURVIVORS. Nick Talaski is a hard-bitten, angry cop. Graham is a newly divorced cab driver. Bronte is a Gulf War veteran hunting his brother's killer. Janicea is a woman consumed by unflinching hate. Trish is a gentleman's club dancer. Morgan is a morgue janitor. The dead have risen and the citizens of St. Petersburg and Pinellas Park are trapped. The survivors are scattered, and options are few. And not all monsters are created by a bite. Some still have a mind of their own...

—————— PERMUTEDPRESS.COM ——————

DEAD TIDE RISING
BY STEPHEN A. NORTH

The sequel to Dead Tide continues the carnage in Pinellas Park near St. Pete, Florida. Follow all of the characters from the first book, Dead Tide, as they fight for survival in a world destroyed by the zombie apocalypse.

BREW
BY BILL BRADDOCK

Ever been to a big college town on a football Saturday night? Loud drunks glut the streets, swaggering about in roaring, leering, laughing packs, like sailors on shore leave. These nights crackle with a dark energy born of incongruity; for beneath all that smiling and singing sprawls a bedrock of malice.

PERMUTEDPRESS.COM

TANKBREAD
BY PAUL MANNERING

Ten years ago humanity lost the war for survival. Now intelligent zombies rule the world. Feeding the undead of a steady diet of cloned people called Tankbread, the survivors live in a dangerous world on the brink of final extinction.

THE ROAD TO NOWHERE
BY BILL BRADDOCK

Welcome to the city of Las Vegas. Gone are the days of tourist filled streets. After waking up alone in a hospital bed, everyone seems to have fled, leaving me behind. Survival becomes my only driving force. Nothing was as it should have been. Things seemed to lurk in the buildings and darkest shadows. I didn't know what they were, but I could always feel their eyes on me.

PERMUTEDPRESS.COM

ZOMBIE ATTACK: RISE OF THE HORDE
BY DEVAN SAGLIANI

Voted best Zombie/ Horror E-books of 2012 on Goodreads. When 16 year old Xander's older brother Moto left him at Vandenberg Airforce Base he only had one request - don't leave no matter what. But there was no way he could have known that one day zombies would gather into groups big enough to knock down walls and take out entire buildings full of people. That was before the rise of the horde!

THE INFECTION
BY CRAIG DiLOUIE

The world is rocked as one in five people collapse screaming before falling into a coma. Three days later, the Infected awake with a single purpose: spread the Infection. A small group—a cop, teacher, student, reverend—team up with a military crew to survive. But at a refugee camp what's left of the government will ask them to accept a dangerous mission back into the very heart of Infection.

THE KILLING FLOOR
BY CRAIG DiLOUIE

The mystery virus struck down millions. Three days later, its victims awoke with a single violent purpose: spread the Infection. Ray Young, survivor of a fight to save a refugee camp from hordes of Infected, awakes from a coma to learn he has also survived Infection. Ray is not immune. Instead, he has been transformed into a superweapon that could end the world ... or save it.

THE INFECTION BOX SET
BY CRAIG DiLOUIE

Two full #1 bestselling apocalyptic thrillers for one low price! Includes the full novels THE INFECTION and THE KILLING FLOOR. A mysterious virus suddenly strikes down millions. Three days later, its victims awake with a single purpose: spread the Infection. As the world lurches toward the apocalypse, some of the Infected continue to change, transforming into horrific monsters.

THE BECOMING
BY JESSICA MEIGS

The Michaluk Virus has escaped the CDC, and its effects are widespread and devastating. Most of the population of the southeastern United States have become homicidal cannibals. As society rapidly crumbles under the hordes of infected, three people--Ethan, a Memphis police officer; Cade, his best friend; and Brandt, a lieutenant in the US Marines--band together against the oncoming crush of death.

—— PERMUTEDPRESS.COM ——

THE BECOMING:
GROUND ZERO (BOOK 2)
BY JESSICA MEIGS

After the Michaluk Virus decimated the southeast, Ethan and his companions became like family. But the arrival of a mysterious woman forces them to flee from the infected, and the cohesion the group cultivated is shattered. As members of the group succumb to the escalating dangers on their path, new alliances form, new loves develop, and old friendships crumble.

—— PERMUTEDPRESS.COM ——

THE BECOMING:
REVELATIONS (BOOK 3)
BY JESSICA MEIGS

In a world ruled by the dead, Brandt Evans is floundering. Leadership of their dysfunctional group wasn't something he asked for or wanted. Their problems are numerous: Remy Angellette is grief-stricken and suicidal, Gray Carter is distant and reclusive, and Cade Alton is near death. And things only get worse.

DOMAIN OF THE DEAD
BY IAIN MCKINNON

The world is dead, devoured by a plague of reanimated corpses. Barricaded inside a warehouse with dwindling food, a group of survivors faces two possible deaths: creeping starvation, or the undead outside. In their darkest hour hope appears in the form of a helicopter approaching the city... but is it the salvation the survivors have been waiting for?

—————— PERMUTEDPRESS.COM ——————

REMAINS OF THE DEAD
BY IAIN MCKINNON

The world is dead. Cahz and his squad of veteran soldiers are tasked with flying into abandoned cities and retrieving zombies for scientific study. Then the unbelievable happens. After years of encountering nothing but the undead, the team discovers a handful of survivors in a fortified warehouse with dwindling supplies.

—————— PERMUTEDPRESS.COM ——————

DEMISE OF THE LIVING
BY IAIN MCKINNON

The world is infected. The dead are reanimating and attacking the living. In a city being overrun with zombies a disparate group of strangers seek sanctuary in an office block. But for how long can the barricades hold back the undead? How long will the food last? How long before those who were bitten succumb turn? And how long before they realise the dead outside are the least of their fears?

ROADS LESS TRAVELED: THE PLAN
BY C. DULANEY

Ask yourself this: If the dead rise tomorrow, are you ready? Do you have a plan? Kasey, a strong-willed loner, has something she calls The Zombie Plan. But every plan has its weaknesses, and a freight train of tragedy is bearing down on Kasey and her friends. In the darkness that follows, Kasey's Plan slowly unravels: friends lost, family taken, their stronghold reduced to ashes.

PERMUTEDPRESS.COM

MURPHY'S LAW
(ROADS LESS TRAVELED BOOK 2)
BY C. DULANEY

Kasey and the gang were held together by a set of rules, their Zombie Plan. It kept them alive through the beginning of the End. But when the chaos faded, they became careless, and Murphy's Law decided to pay a long-overdue visit. Now the group is broken and scattered with no refuge in sight. Those remaining must make their way across West Virginia in search of those who were stolen from them.

PERMUTEDPRESS.COM

SHADES OF GRAY
(ROADS LESS TRAVELED BOOK 3)
BY C. DULANEY

Kasey and the gang have come full circle through the crumbling world. Working for the National Guard, they realize old friends and fellow survivors are disappearing. When the missing start to reappear as walking corpses, the group sets out on another journey to discover the truth. Their answers wait in the West Virginia Command Center.

PAVLOV'S DOGS
BY D.L. SNELL & THOM BRANNAN

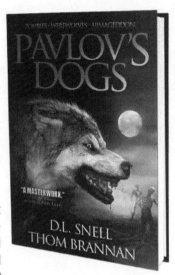

WEREWOLVES Dr. Crispin has engineered the saviors of mankind: soldiers capable of transforming into beasts. ZOMBIES Ken and Jorge get caught in a traffic jam on their way home from work. It's the first sign of a major outbreak. ARMAGEDDON Should Dr. Crisping send the Dogs out into the zombie apocalypse to rescue survivors? Or should they hoard their resources and post the Dogs as island guards?

PERMUTEDPRESS.COM

THE OMEGA DOG
BY D.L. SNELL & THOM BRANNAN

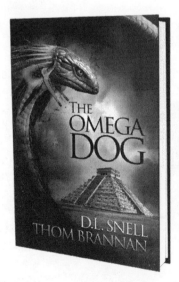

Twisting and turning through hordes of zombies, cartel territory, Mayan ruins, and the things that now inhabit them, a group of survivors must travel to save one man's family from a nightmarish third world gone to hell. But this time, even best friends have deadly secrets, and even allies can't be trusted - as a father's only hope of getting his kids out alive is the very thing that's hunting him down.

DEAD LIVING
BY GLENN BULLION

It didn't take long for the world to die. And it didn't take long, either, for the dead to rise. Aaron was born on the day the world ended. Kept in seclusion, his family teaches him the basics. How to read and write. How to survive. Then Aaron makes a shocking discovery. The undead, who desire nothing but flesh, ignore him. It's as if he's invisible to them.

— PERMUTEDPRESS.COM —

AUTOBIOGRAPHY of a WEREWOLF HUNTER
BY BRIAN P. EASTON

After his mother is butchered by a werewolf, Sylvester James is taken in by a Cheyenne mystic. The boy trains to be a werewolf hunter, learning to block out pain, stalk, fight, and kill. As Sylvester sacrifices himself to the hunt, his hatred has become a monster all its own. As he follows his vendetta into the outlands of the occult, he learns it takes more than silver bullets to kill a werewolf.

PALE GODS
BY KIM PAFFENROTH

In a world where the undead rule the continents and the few remaining survivors inhabit only island outposts, six men make the dangerous journey to the mainland to hunt for supplies amid the ruins. But on this trip, the dead act stranger and smarter than ever before and the living must adjust or die.

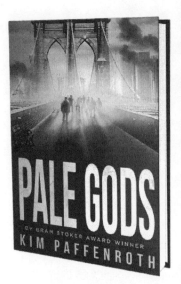

PERMUTEDPRESS.COM

THE JUNKIE QUATRAIN
BY PETER CLINES

Six months ago, the world ended. The Baugh Contagion swept across the planet. Its victims were left twitching, adrenalized cannibals that quickly became know as Junkies. THE JUNKIE QUATRAIN is four tales of survival, and four types of post-apocalypse story. Because the end of the world means different things for different people. Loss. Opportunity. Hope. Or maybe just another day on the job.

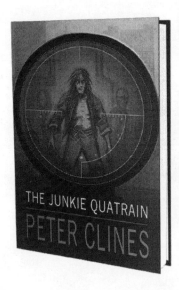

BLOOD SOAKED & CONTAGIOUS
BY JAMES CRAWFORD

I am not going to complain to you about my life.

We've got zombies. They are not the brainless, rotting creatures we'd been led to expect. Unfortunately for us, they're just as smart as they were before they died, very fast, much stronger than you or me, and possess no internal editor at all.

Claws. Did I mention claws?

BLOOD SOAKED & INVADED
BY JAMES CRAWFORD

Zombies were bad enough, but now we're being invaded from all sides. Up to our necks in blood, body parts, and unanswerable questions...

...As soon as the realization hit me, I lost my cool. I curled into the fetal position in a pile of blood, offal, and body parts, and froze there. What in the Hell was I becoming that killing was entertaining and satisfying?

THE KING OF CLAYFIELD
BY SHANE GREGORY

On a cold February day in the small town of Clayfield, Kentucky, an unsuspecting and unprepared museum director he finds himself in the middle of hell on Earth. A pandemic is spreading around the globe, and it's turning most of the residents of Clayfield into murderous zombies. Having no safe haven to which he can flee, the director decides to stick it out near his hornetown and wait for the government to send help.

PERMUTEDPRESS.COM

THE KING OF CLAYFIELD 2
ALL THAT I SEE
BY SHANE GREGORY

It has been more than a month since the Canton B virus turned the people of the world into hungry zombies. The survivors of Clayfield, Kentucky attempt to carve out new lives for themselves in this harsh new world. Those who remain have been hardened by their environment and their choices over the previous weeks, but their optimism has not been extinguished. There is hope that eventually Clayfield can be secured, but first, the undead must be eliminated and law and order must be restored. Unfortunately, the group might not ever get to implement their plan.

PERMUTEDPRESS.COM

THE KING OF CLAYFIELD 3
FIRE BIRDS
BY SHANE GREGORY

For weeks, he has fought the undead and believed that he was Clayfield's sole survivor. But when odd things begin to happen in the town, it becomes clear that other healthy people are around. A friend returns full of trouble and secrets, and they are not alone.

Something bad is coming to Clayfield, and there could be nowhere to hide.

INFECTION:
ALASKAN UNDEAD APOCALYPSE
BY SEAN SCHUBERT

Anchorage, Alaska: gateway to serene wilderness of The Last Frontier. No stranger to struggle, the city on the edge of the world is about to become even more isolated. When a plague strikes, Anchorage becomes a deadly trap for its citizens. The only two land routes out of the city are cut, forcing people to fight or die as the infection spreads.

—— PERMUTEDPRESS.COM ——

CONTAINMENT
(ALASKAN UNDEAD APOCALYPSE BOOK 2)
BY SEAN SCHUBERT

Running. Hiding. Surviving. Anchorage, once Alaska's largest city, has fallen. Now a threatening maze of death, the city is firmly in the cold grip of a growing zombie horde. Neil Jordan and Dr. Caldwell lead a small band of desperate survivors through the maelstrom. The group has one last hope: that this nightmare has been contained, and there still exists a sane world free of infection.

THE UNDEAD SITUATION
BY ELOISE J. KNAPP

The dead are rising. People are dying. Civilization is collapsing. But Cyrus V. Sinclair couldn't care less; he's a sociopath. Amidst the chaos, Cyrus sits with little more emotion than one of the walking corpses… until he meets up with other inconvenient survivors who cramp his style and force him to re-evaluate his outlook on life. It's Armageddon, and things will definitely get messy.

THE UNDEAD HAZE
(THE UNDEAD SITUATION BOOK 2)
BY ELOISE J. KNAPP

When remorse drives Cyrus to abandon his hidden compound he doesn't realize what new dangers lurk in the undead world. He knows he must wade through the vilest remains of humanity and hordes of zombies to settle scores and find the one person who might understand him. But this time, it won't be so easy. Zombies and unpleasant survivors aren't the only thing Cyrus has to worry about.

MAD SWINE: THE BEGINNING
BY STEVEN PAJAK

People refer to the infected as "zombies," but that's not what they really are. Zombie implies the infected have died and reanimated. The thing is, they didn't die. They're just not human anymore. As the infection spreads and crazed hordes--dubbed "Mad Swine"--take over the cities, the residents of Randall Oaks find themselves locked in a desperate struggle to survive in the new world.

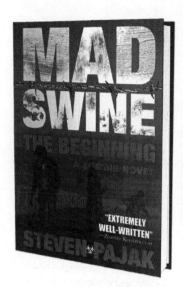

── PERMUTEDPRESS.COM ──

MAD SWINE: DEAD WINTER
BY STEVEN PAJAK

Three months after the beginning of the Mad Swine outbreak, the residents of Randall Oaks have reached their breaking point. After surviving the initial outbreak and a war waged with their neighboring community, Providence, their supplies are severely close to depletion. With hostile neighbors at their flanks and hordes of infected outside their walls, they have become prisoners within their own community.

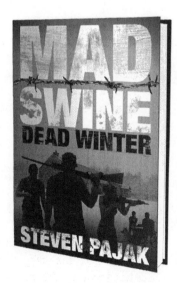

RISE
BY GARETH WOOD

Within hours of succumbing to a plague, millions of dead rise to attack the living. Brian Williams flees the city with his sister Sarah. Banded with other survivors, the group remains desperately outnumbered and under-armed. With no food and little fuel, they must fight their way to safety. RISE is the story of the extreme measures a family will take to survive a trek across a country gone mad.

PERMUTEDPRESS.COM

AGE OF THE DEAD
BY GARETH WOOD

A year has passed since the dead rose, and the citizens of Cold Lake are out of hope. Food and weapons are nearly impossible to find, and the dead are everywhere. In desperation Brian Williams leads a salvage team into the mountains. But outside the small safe zones the world is a foreign place. Williams and his team must use all of their skills to survive in the wilderness ruled by the dead.

DEAD MEAT
BY PATRICK & CHRIS WILLIAMS

The city of River's Edge has been quarantined due to a rodent borne rabies outbreak. But it quickly becomes clear to the citizens that the infection is something much, much worse than rabies... The townsfolk are attacked and fed upon by packs of the living dead. Gavin and Benny attempt to survive the chaos in River's Edge while making their way north in search of sanctuary.

PERMUTEDPRESS.COM

ROTTER WORLD
BY SCOTT M. BAKER

Eight months ago vampires released the Revenant Virus on humanity. Both species were nearly wiped out. The creator of the virus claims there is a vaccine that will make humans and vampires immune to the virus, but it's located in a secure underground facility five hundred miles away. To retrieve the vaccine, a raiding party of humans and vampires must travel down the devastated East Coast.

AMONG THE LIVING
BY TIMOTHY W. LONG

The dead walk. Now the real battle for Seattle has begun. Lester has a new clientele, the kind that requires him to deal lead instead of drugs. Mike suspects a conspiracy lies behind the chaos. Kate has a dark secret: she's a budding young serial killer. These survivors, along with others, are drawn together in their quest to find the truth behind the spreading apocalypse.

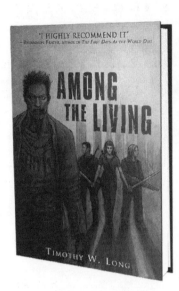

PERMUTEDPRESS.COM

AMONG THE DEAD
BY TIMOTHY W. LONG

Seattle is under siege by masses of living dead, and the military struggles to prevent the virus from spreading outside the city. Kate is tired of sitting around. When she learns that a rescue mission is heading back into the chaos, she jumps at the chance to tag along and put her unique skill set and, more importantly, swords to use.

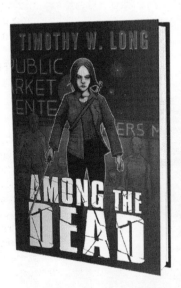

NOW AVAILABLE IN EBOOK!

LONG VOYAGE BACK
BY LUKE RHINEHART

When the bombs came, only the lucky escaped. In the horror that followed, only the strong would survive. The voyage of the trimaran Vagabond began as a pleasure cruise on the Chesapeake Bay. Then came the War Alert ... the unholy glow on the horizon ... the terrifying reports of nuclear destruction. In the days that followed, it became clear just how much chaos was still to come.

PERMUTEDPRESS.COM

QUARANTINED
BY JOE MCKINNEY

The citizens of San Antonio, Texas are threatened with extermination by a terrifying outbreak of the flu. Quarantined by the military to contain the virus, the city is in a desperate struggle to survive. Inside the quarantine walls, Detective Lily Harris finds herself caught up in a conspiracy intent on hiding the news from the world and fighting a population threatening to boil over into revolt.

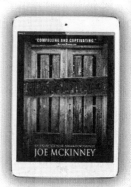

PERMUTEDPRESS.COM

THE DESERT
BY BRYON MORRIGAN

Give up trying to leave. There's no way out. Those are the final words in a journal left by the last apparent survivor of a platoon that disappear in Iraq. Years later, two soldiers realize that what happened to the "Lost Platoon" is now happening to them. Now they must confront the horrifying creatures responsible for their misfortune, or risk the same fate as that of the soldiers before them.

NOW AVAILABLE IN EBOOK!

41933647R00227

Made in the USA
Lexington, KY
02 June 2015